Let me tell you a l **about psych**

Everyone has these ideas about what you can actually do with it. There are a hundred dumb Reddit threads about how many magic tricks you could pull off, or how you could make amazing smoke rings. Whoop-de-fucking-do. Also, gambling. People online love to spitball about how it could help you win a ton of money, influencing roulette wheels or craps dice.

Plenty of people online claim they have psychokinesis, but you only have to do about five seconds' worth of digging to see that they were lying out their asses. If they really could move things with their minds, they'd either be dead, or in the same government program I'm in.

It's just me.

THE GIRL WHO COULD MOVE SH*T WITH HER MIND

JACKSON FORD

www.orbitbooks.net

Copyright © 2019 by Jackson Ford
Excerpt from *Velocity Weapon* copyright © 2019 by Megan E. O'Keefe
Excerpt from *A Big Ship at the Edge of the Universe* copyright © 2018 by Alex White

Cover design by Emily Courdelle and Steve Panton — LBBG
Cover photographs © Shutterstock
Cover copyright © 2019 by Hachette Book Group, Inc.

Orbit
Hachette Book Group
1290 Avenue of the Americas
New York, NY 10104
orbitbooks.net

Simultaneously published in Great Britain and in the U.S. by Orbit in 2019
First Edition: June 2019

Orbit is an imprint of Hachette Book Group.
The Orbit name and logo are trademarks of Little, Brown Book Group Limited.

The publisher is not responsible for websites (or their content) that are not owned by the publisher.

The Hachette Speakers Bureau provides a wide range of authors for speaking events. To find out more, go to www.hachettespeakersbureau.com or call (866) 376-6591.

Library of Congress Control Number: 2019930332

ISBNs: 978-0-316-51915-1 (trade paperback), 978-0-316-51916-8 (ebook)

Printed in the United States of America

LSC-C

10 9 8 7 6 5 4 3 2 1

*Dedicated to Dilated Peoples, Venice Beach,
and salted caramel ice cream*

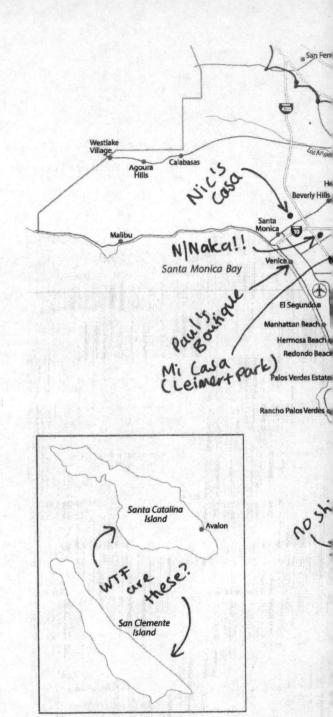

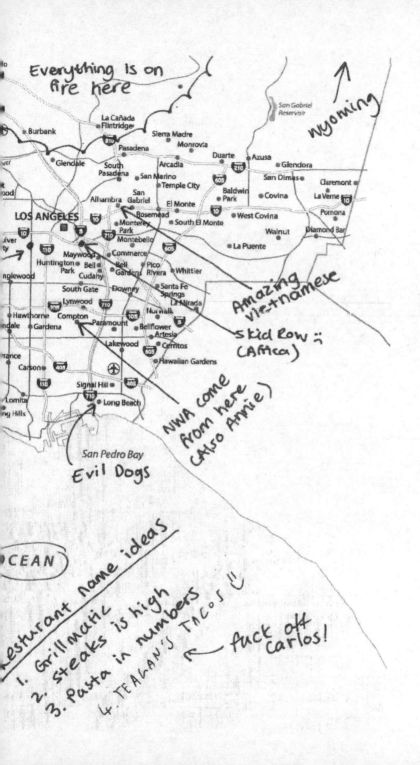

THE GIRL
WHO COULD
MOVE SH*T
WITH HER MIND

ONE

Teagan

On second thoughts, throwing myself out the window of a skyscraper may not have been the best idea.

Not because I'm going to die or anything. I've totally got that under control.

It wasn't smart because I had to bring Annie Cruz with me. And Annie, it turns out, is a screamer. Her fists hammer on my back, her voice piecing my eardrums, even over the rushing air.

I don't know what she's worried about. Pro tip: if you're going to take a high dive off the 82nd floor, make sure you do it with a psychokinetic holding your hand. Being able to move objects with your mind is useful in all sorts of situations.

I'll admit, this one is a little tricky. Plummeting at close to terminal velocity, surrounded by a hurricane of glass from the window we smashed through, the lights of Los Angeles whirling around us and Annie screaming and the rushing air blowing the stupid clip-on tie from my security guard disguise into my face: not ideal. Doesn't matter though—I've got this.

I can't actually apply any force to either Annie's body or mine. Organic matter like human tissue doesn't respond to me, which is something I don't really have time to get into right now. But I can manipulate anything inorganic. Bricks, glass, metal, the fridge door, a sixpack, the TV remote, the zipper on your pants.

And belt buckles.

I've had some practice at this whole moving-shit-with-your-mind thing. I've already reached out, grabbed hold of the big metal buckles on our belts. We're probably going to have some bruises tomorrow, but it's a hell of a lot better than getting gunned down in a penthouse or splatting all over Figueroa Street.

I solidify my mental grip around the two buckles, then force them upwards, using my energy to counteract our downward motion. We start to slow, my belt tightening, hips starting to ache as the buckles take the weight—

—and immediately snap.

OK, yeah. Definitely not the best idea.

TWO

Teagan

Rewind. Twenty minutes ago.

We're in the sub-basement of the giant Edmonds Building, our footsteps muffled by thick carpet. The lighting in the corridor is surprisingly low down here, almost cosy, which doesn't matter much because Annie is seriously fucking with my groove.

I like to listen to music on our ops, OK? It calms me down, helps me focus. A little late-90s rap—some Blackstar, some Jurassic 5, some Outkast. Nothing too aggressive or even all that loud. I'm just reaching the good part of "So Fresh, So Clean" when Annie taps me on the shoulder. "Yo, take that shit out. We working."

Ugh. I was sure I'd hidden my earbud, threading the cord up underneath the starchy blue rent-a-cop shirt and tucking it under my hair.

I hunt for the volume switch on my phone, still not looking at Annie. She responds by reaching back and jerking the earbud out.

"Hey!"

"I said, fucking quit it."

"What, not an OutKast fan? Or do you only like their early stuff?" I hold up an earbud. "I don't mind sharing. You want the left or the right?"

"Cute. Put it away."

We turn the corner, heading for a big set of double doors at the far end. My collar's too tight. I pull at it, wincing, but it barely moves. Annie and I are dressed identically: blue shirts, black clip-on ties, black pants and puffer jackets in a very cheap shade of navy. Huge belts, leather, with thick metal buckles.

Paul picked up the uniforms for us. I tried to tell him that while Annie might be able to pass as a security guard, nobody was going to believe that the Edmonds Building would employ a short, not-very-fit woman with spiky black hair and a face that *still* gets her ID'd at the liquor store. Even though I've been able to buy my own drinks like a big girl for a whole year now.

I couldn't be more different to Annie. You know how some club bouncers have huge muscles and a shit-ton of tattoos and piercings? You know how people still fuck with them, starting fights and smashing bottles? Annie is like that one bouncer with zero tattoos, standing in the corner with her arms folded and a scowl that could sour milk. The bouncer no one fucks with because the last person who did ended up scattered over a six-mile radius. We might not see eye to eye on music—or on anything, because she's taller than me—but I'm still very glad she's on my side.

My earpiece chirps—my *other* one, the black number in my right ear. "Annie, Teagan," says Paul. "Come in. Over."

"We're almost at the server room," Annie says. She sends another disgusted look at my dangling earbud.

Silence. No response.

"You there?" Annie says.

"Sorry, was waiting for you to say *over*. Thought you hadn't finished. Over."

"Seriously?" I say. "We're still using your radio slang?"

"It's not slang. It's protocol. Just wanted to give you a heads-up—Reggie's activated the alarm on the second floor. Basement should be clear of personnel." A pause. "Over."

"Yeah, copy." Annie says. She's a lot more patient with Paul than I am, which I genuinely don't understand.

The double doors are like the fire doors you see in apartment buildings. The one on the right has a big sign on it, white lettering on a black background: AUTHORISED PERSONNEL ONLY And on the wall next to it, a biometric lock.

Annie looks over at me. "You're up."

My tax form says that I work for a company called China Shop Movers. That's the name on the paperwork, anyway. What we actually do is work for the government—specifically, for a high-level spook named Tanner.

For some jobs, you need a black ops team and a fleet of Apache choppers with heat-seeking missiles. For others, you need a psychokinetic with a music-hating support team who can make a lot less noise and get things done in a fraction of the time. You need a completely deniable group of civilians who can do stuff that even a special forces soldier would struggle with. That's us. We are fast, quiet, effective and deadly.

Go ahead: make the fart joke. Tanner didn't laugh when I made it either.

The people we take down are threats to national security. Drug lords, terrorist cells, human traffickers. We don't bust in with guns blazing. We don't need to—not with my ability. I've planted a tracking device on a limo at LAX, waving hello to the thick-necked goon standing alongside the car while I zipped the tiny black box up behind his back and onto the chassis. I've kept the bad guys' safeties on at a hostage exchange—good thing too, because they tried to start shooting the second they had the money and got one hell of a surprise when their guns didn't work. And I've been on plenty of break-ins. Windows? Cars? Big old metal safes? Not a problem. When you can move things with your mind, there's not a lot the world can do to keep you out.

Take the lock on AUTHORISED PERSONNEL ONLY, for instance.

You're supposed to put your finger on the little reader, let it scan your fingerprint, and you're in. If you're breaking in, you either need to hack off a finger (messy), take someone hostage (messy, annoying), hack it locally (time-consuming and boring), or blow it off (fun, but kind of noisy).

My psychokinesia—PK—means I can feel every object around me: its texture, its weight, its relation to other objects. It's a constant flood of stimuli. When I was little, Mom and Dad made me run through exercises, getting me to really focus in on a single object at a time—a glass, a toy car, a pencil. They made me move them around, describe them in excruciating detail. It took a long time, but I managed to deal with it. Now I can sense the objects around me in the same way you sense the clothes you're wearing. You know they're there, you're aware of them, but you don't *think* about them.

If I focus on an object, like the lock—the wires, the latch assembly, the emergency battery, the individual screws on the latch and strike panels—it's as if I send out a part of myself to wrap around it, like you'd wrap your hand around a glass. And then, if I'm locked on, I can move it. I don't have to jerk my head or hold out my hand or screw up my face like in the movies, either. I tried it once, for fun, and felt like an idiot.

It takes me about three seconds to find the latch and slide it back. The mechanism won't move unless it receives the correct signal from the fingerprint reader—or unless someone reaches inside and moves it with her mind. It's actually a pretty solid security system. I've definitely seen worse. But whoever built it obviously didn't take into account the existence of a psychokinetic, so I guess he's totally fired now.

"And we're good." I hop to my feet, using my PK to pull the handle down. I haven't even touched the door.

"Hm." Annie tilts her head. "Nice work."

"Was that a compliment? Annie, are you dying? Has the cancer spread to your brain?"

"Let's just get this over with."

We're on this operation because of a clothing tycoon named Steven Chase. He runs a chain of high-end sportswear stores called Ultra, which just means they're Foot Locker stores without the referee jerseys. If that was all he was doing, he'd never have appeared on China Shop's radar, but it appears Mr. Chase has been a very naughty boy.

Tanner got a tip that he was embezzling money from his company. Again, not something we'd normally give a shit about, but he's not exactly using it to buy a third Ferrari. He's funnelling it to some very shady people in the Ukraine and Saudi Arabia, which is when government types like Tanner start to get mighty twitchy.

Now, the U.S. government *could* get a wiretap to confirm the tip. But even if you go through a secret court, there'll be some kind of paper trail. Better a discreet call gets made to the offices of a certain moving company in Los Angeles, who can look into the matter without anything being written down.

And before you start telling me I'm on the wrong side, that I'm doing the work of the government, who are the real bad guys here, and violating a dozen laws and generally

being a pawn of the state, just know that I've seen evidence of
what people like Chase do. I have no problem messing with
their shit.

We're not actually going anywhere near Steven Chase's
office. Reggie could hack his computer directly, but it would
require a brute-force attack or getting him to click on a link
in an email. People don't do that any more, unless you promise
fulfilment of their *very* specific sexual fantasies. The research
on that is more trouble than it's worth, and you'll have night-
mares for months.

Chase is in town tonight. He flew in for a dinner or an
awards show or whatever rich people do for fun, and it's his
habit to come back to the office afterwards. He should be there
now, up on the 30th floor. He'll work until two or three, catch
a couple hours of sleep, then grab a red-eye back to New York.
Which works just fine for us.

If you can access the fibre network itself—which you can
do in the server room, obviously—you can clamp a special
coupler right on to the cable and just siphon off the data as it
passes by. Of course, actually doing this is messy and complicated and requires a lot of elements to line up just right…
unless you have me.

The cables from every floor in the building run down to this
room. The plan is to identify Chase's cable, attach a coupler to
it, then read all the traffic while sipping mai tais on our back
porch. Or in my case scarfing Thai food and drinking many,
many beers in my tiny apartment, but whatever.

Chase might encrypt his email, of course, but encryption
targets the body of the email, not the sender or subject line. If
he emails anyone in the Ukraine or Saudi, we'll know about
it. It'll be enough for Tanner to send in the big guns.

The server room is even more dimly lit than the corridor.

The server banks stand like monoliths in an old tomb, giving off a subsonic hum that rumbles under the frigid air conditioning. Annie tilts her chin up even further, as if sniffing the air. She points to one side of the door. "Wait there."

"Yes, sir, O mighty boss lady."

She ignores me, eyes scanning the server stacks. I don't really know how she's going to find the correct one—that was the part of the planning session where they lost me. All I know is that when she does, she's going to trace it back to where it vanishes into the floor or wall. We'll open up a panel, and I'll use my PK to float the coupler inside, attaching it to the cable. It can siphon data, away from the eyes of the building's technicians, who would almost certainly recognise it on sight.

As Annie steps behind one of the servers, I slip my earbud back in. May as well listen to some music while—

"Shit," Annie says.

It's a quiet curse, but I catch it just fine. I make my way over to find her staring at a clusterfuck of tangled cables spilling out of one of the servers. The floor is a scattered mess of tools and loose connections. A half-eaten sandwich, dribbling a slice of tomato, sits propped on a closed laptop.

"Is it supposed to look like that?" I ask.

Annie ignores me. "Paul, we've got a problem. Over."

"What is it? Over."

"Techs have been in. It wasn't like this this morning; Jerian would have told me."

Jerian—one of Annie's Army. Her anonymous network of janitors, cleaners, cashiers, security guards, drug dealers, nail artists, Uber drivers, cooks, receptionists and IT guys. Annie Cruz may not appreciate good hip-hop, but she has a very deep network of connects stretching all the way across LA.

"Copy, Annie. Can you still attach the coupler? Over."

Annie frowns at the mess of cables. "Yeah. But it'll take a while. Over."

Joy.

"Understood," Paul says. "But we can only run interference for so long on our end. You'd better move. Over."

Annie scowls, crouching down to look at the cables. She takes one between thumb and forefinger, like it's something nasty she has to dispose of. Then she stands up, marching back towards the server-room doors.

"Um. Hi? Annie?" I jog after her, earbud bouncing against my shoulder. "Cables are back there."

"Change of plan." She keys her earpiece. "Paul? Tell Reggie to switch over the cameras on the 30th floor. Over"

"Say again? Over."

"We're going up."

I don't catch Paul's response. Instead, I sprint to catch up with Annie, getting to her just she pushes through the doors. "Are you gonna tell me why we've suddenly abandoned the plan, or—"

"We can't hide the coupler if they got people poking around the cables." She reaches the elevator, thumbing the up button. "We need to go to the source."

"I thought the whole point was *not* to go near this guy. Aren't we supposed to be super-secret and stealthy and shit?"

"We're not going to his office, genius. We're going to the fibre hub on his floor."

"The what now?"

"The fibre hub. Every floor has one. It's where the cables from each office go. We'll be able to find the right one a lot faster from there."

The interior of the elevator is clean and new, with a touch-screen interface to select your floor. A taped sign next to it says that floors 50–80 are currently off limits while refurbishment and additional construction is completed, thank you for your patience, management. I remember seeing that when we rolled up: a big chunk of the building covered in scaffolding, with temporary elevators attached to the outside, and a giant crane in a vacant lot across the street.

When the elevator opens on the 30th floor, there's someone standing in front of it. There's a horrible moment where I think it's Steven Chase himself. But I've seen pictures of Chase, who looks like an actor in an AD for haemorrhoid cream—running on the beach, tanned and glowing, stoked that his rectum is finally itch-free. This guy is...not that. He has lawyer written all over him: two-tone shirt, two-tone hair, one-tone orange skin. Tie knot as big as my fist. Probably a few haemorrhoid issues of his own.

He eyes us. "Going down?"

"We're stepping off here, sir," Annie says, doing just that.

He moves into the elevator, mouth twisted in a disapproving frown as his eyes pass over me. Probably not used to seeing someone my age working security in a building like this. I have to resist the urge to wink at him.

I haven't seen inside any of the offices yet, but whoever built this place obviously didn't have any budget leftover for the hallways. There's a foot-high strip of what looks like marble-textured plastic running along at chest height. There are buzzing fluorescent lights in the ceiling, and the floor is covered with that weird, flat, fuzzy carpet which always has little lint balls dotted over it.

"Jesus, who picked out the paint?" The wall above the plastic marble is a shade of purple that's probably called something like Executive Mojo.

"Who cares?" Annie says. "Damn building shouldn't even be here."

I sigh. This again.

She taps the fake marble. "You know they displaced a bunch of historical buildings for this? They just moved in and forced a purchase."

I sigh. Annie's always had a real hard-on for the city's history. "Yeah, I know. You told me before."

"And you saw that notice in the elevator. They just built this place. They already having to fix it up again. And the spots they bought out—mom-and-pop places. Historical buildings. City didn't give a fuck."

"Mm-hmm."

"I'm just saying. It's messed up, man."

"Can we get this done before the heat death of the universe? Please?"

It doesn't take us long to find the right office. Paul helps, using the blueprints he's pulled up to guide us along, occasionally telling Annie that this isn't a good idea and that she needs to hurry. I pop the lock, just like before—it's even easier this time—and we step inside.

There's no Executive Mojo here. It's a basic space, with a desk and terminal for a technician and a big, clearly marked access panel on the wall. By the desk, someone has left a toolbox full of computer paraphernalia, overflowing with wires and connectors. Maybe the same dickhead who left the half-eaten sandwich in the server room. I should leave a note telling him to clean up his shit.

The access panel is off to one side, slightly raised from the surface of the wall. Annie pops it, revealing a nest of thin cables. She attaches the coupler, which looks like a bulldog clip from the future, then checks her phone, reading the data that comes off it. With a grunt, she moves the coupler to the second cable. We have to get the correct one, and the only way to do that is to identify Chase from his traffic.

There are floor-to-ceiling windows on my left, and the view over the glittering city takes my breath away. We're only on the 30th floor, not even close to the top of the building, but I can still see a hell of long way. A police helicopter hovers in the distance, too far for us to hear, its blinking tail lights just visible. The view looks north, out towards Burbank and Glendale, and on the horizon, there's the telltale orange glow of wildfires.

The sight pulls up some bad memories. Of all the cities Tanner had to put me, it had to be the one where things burn.

It's bad this year. Usually, it's some kid with fireworks or a tourist dropping a cigarette that starts it up, but this time the grass was so dry that it caught on its own. Every TV in the last couple of days has had big breaking news alerts flashing on them. The ones tuned to Fox News—you get a few, even in California—have given it a nickname. HELLSTORM. Because of course they have.

This year's fire has been creeping towards Burbank and Glendale, chewing through Wildwood Canyon and the Verdugo Hills. The flames have made LA even smoggier than usual. A fire chief on one of the TVs—a guy who managed to look both calm and mightily pissed off at the same time—said that they didn't think the fires would reach the city.

"Teagan."

"Huh?"

"You got your voodoo, right?" She nods to the coupler. "Float it up into the wall."

"Oh. Yeah. Good idea."

The panel is wide enough for me to lean in, craning my head back. The space is dusty, a small shower of fine grit nearly making me sneeze. Annie shines a torch, but I don't need it. She's got the correct cable pinched between thumb and forefinger. It's the work of a few seconds for me to find it with my *voodoo* and pull it slightly outwards from its buddies, float the coupler across and clamp it on. Annie flicks the torch off, and the coupler is swallowed by the shadows.

What can I say? I'm handy.

"Aight," Annie says, snapping the panel shut. "Paul? We're good. Over."

"Copy that. We're getting traffic already. Skedaddle on out of there. Over."

Skedaddle? I mouth the word at Annie, who ignores me. She replaces the panel, slotting it back into place, then turns to go.

As we step out of the tech's office, a voice reaches us from the other end of the hallway: "Hey."

Two security guards. No, three. Real ones. Walking in close formation, heading right for us. The one in the centre is a big white guy with a huge chest-length beard, peak pulled down over his eyes. He's scary, but it's the other two I'm worried about. They're young, with wide eyes and hands already on their holsters, fingers twitching.

Ah, shit.

THREE

Teagan

Getting caught would be very, very bad.

Tanner would disavow all knowledge of our existence, like Tom Cruise in *Mission: Impossible*. Difference being, Tom is a movie star with a squillion dollars and a hot wife (I assume—I'm not big on celebrity gossip). He gets to go home afterwards. If our mission ends, Annie and the others go to jail, and Tanner stops protecting me from the people in the U.S. government who want to cut me open and take a look inside.

That was our deal. I work for her; she keeps me away from the people with scalpels and surgical masks.

But we *shouldn't* have been caught. It doesn't make sense. Building security isn't even supposed to know we're here. Reggie fixed the cameras in this part of the building, made it so they'd show empty corridors on a loop. How did this jack-off know we—

Ah. The lawyer. Probably something innocent too, an idle comment to the security chief as he passed him in the lobby. *Didn't know you hired out of kindergarten, Bob.* Bob, or whatever the hell is name his, going *Pardon me?* And the lawyer says *One of your crew, up on the 30th . . . looks like she's still in diapers.*

We don't carry guns. We're not that kind of outfit. Guns, Tanner once explained, complicate a situation. They remove options, instead of adding more of them. It's one of those things that sounds wise and profound until you think about it for more than two seconds and realise it makes absolutely zero sense whatsoever.

Bob's expression is thunderous. "You aren't on my detail. Who are you people?"

Annie doesn't hesitate. "Head office sent us over," she says. "They got some VIP coming in tomorrow, wanted us to make sure the place was clean." She flashes a knowing smile, as if she can't believe the higher-ups could be this dense. In my ear Paul says, "Annie, Teagan, what's happening? Over."

The chief's expression doesn't change. "Bullshit. Why wasn't I told?"

Annie shrugs, the same can-you-believe-this grin on her face. "Beats me. I just go where they say."

There's a moment where I think it's going to work. Then it's like a shutter comes down on the chief's face. "Stay right where you are," he says, gesturing to the two rookies alongside him. They both take a step forward, drawing their guns.

Or trying to, anyway. It's awfully hard to pull a gun when a psychokinetic force is holding it in the holster. Their matching expressions are ridiculous: identical confusion, followed by annoyance, followed by anger as they both try and yank their weapons out.

I'm not supposed to use my ability like this. Not in front of people who aren't on the team. It's part of the deal: never reveal what I can do, to anyone, ever. Then again, it's not like I'm being obvious about it. In my experience, the conclusion people jump to when something like this happens is usually not *OMG! That woman over there has astonishing psychokinetic powers!*

"What are you doing?" the chief says to the other two. He goes for his own gun, which also manages to miraculously catch on its holster.

Annie glances at me. "Are you—"

"Yup. *Run.*"

We take off in the opposite direction, sprinting down the corridor, the chief yelling at us to stop. As we turn the corner, I lose hold of the three guns, the men falling out of my range. I've only got about ten feet in every direction to play with, and behind us there's the rasp of leather on metal as all three of them finally manage to pull their pistols free.

Annie accelerates, charging ahead of me, long legs exploding out in front of her willowy body. She's built for speed. I, on the other hand, am built for lounging on the couch watching Netflix. I'm not very good in foot pursuits.

Annie ignores the elevator doors, shooting right past them. Smart. No point trapping us in a metal box that the guards in the main security room can control—assuming we'd even have time to navigate the touchscreen next to the doors and wait for the elevator to arrive. It's not like Bob will let us call a time-out.

Instead, Annie heads for another door, a little further down the corridor. One with a push-bar across it and big stencilled letters on its surface: fire door—keep closed. She slams through the door, and I tumble in after her. "Close it!" she yells.

I reach back with my PK, slamming the door shut. Then I reach deep into the push-bar mechanism, grabbing the latch, twisting it, jamming it in place. *Let's see them figure that out.*

A split-second later, one of them reaches the door, his body slamming into the metal. The push-bar doesn't move, the fucked-up latch refusing to give. Finally, a break. I sag back against the wall, panting, stitch burning a hole in my side.

Annie speaks rapidly into her earpiece. "Paul, we need an exit. And tell Carlos he might need to do some fast driving."

"Copy." This time Paul doesn't bother giving her shit about not saying *over*. "What's your location?"

"On the fire stairs."

The stairs are bare, dusty concrete, well lit by glowing fluorescents. Our footsteps thud loudly in the enclosed space as we move down, going so fast that our feet barely touch each step. I'm concentrating so hard on not falling over that I don't see that Annie has stopped until I almost crash into her.

"What the shit?" I say, only just keeping my balance.

"Listen."

Footsteps. A lot of them. Coming from below us, and coming fast. Annie turns and starts heading back the way we came, taking the stairs two at a time.

I take a second to ask God, really and truly, why he hates me so much. Then I start climbing.

The chief and his compadres are still banging at the door I jammed shut. Annie moves past with a glance, leaping up the stairs to the floor above.

"Paul," she says, pulling at the fire door. The footsteps from below are louder now, maybe twenty seconds away. "Thirty-first floor. Pull up the schematics. And get Reggie on the cameras."

It's easy to see what she's thinking. We can't go down using the stairs, and it's a sure bet they'll be watching the elevators, ready to lock us in the second they see one moving. That leaves hiding—holing up somewhere until the heat dies down.

It's a great idea, except for the tiny detail that it sucks. They'll just tear the place apart looking for us—assuming we even find a decent, non-obvious place to hide. It creates more problems than it solves.

There's another solution. A better one. Annie might be too dopey to realise it, but luckily for her someone else brought her A-game tonight.

I picture the outside of the building, the construction, the floors cordoned off. Yeah. Got it. We can do this. I never thought I'd go for an idea that involved *more* stairs, but you can't have everything.

"Paul," I croak. "Hold off on that."

"Say again? Over."

"What are you doing?" Annie hisses, half in and half out of the fire door.

In answer, I sprint past her, lurching onto the next flight of stairs. "Just follow me."

"Teagan, what the fuck?"

"*Follow me!*"

She makes a grab for me, misses. Just as well. I really don't have time to explain this to her, because the running footsteps from below are closing fast.

There's a moment when I think that's she going to ditch me, running off by herself to hide. Then she hits the stairs, swearing, shouting that she's going to kill me. Good thing I have a head start, or I'd be legitimately terrified.

I ignore her, concentrating on making it through my own personal hell. My legs feel like they're going to separate at the knees, like an overheated machine spinning itself apart.

Somehow, we manage not to lose ground to the security guards coming up from below. And finally, *finally*, we reach the 50th floor, where the construction starts. The fire door has a notice taped to it, a lot of fine print about not entering the site without a hard hat and all visitors reporting to the foreman. I yank open the door, and a gust of wind from the change in pressure nearly shoves me back down the stairs. I force myself through, wait for Annie to come charging past, then slam it shut. My mind scrunches the lock closed.

The floor is wide open to the outside world, a skeleton version of the ones below. It's an incomplete maze of bare ply-wood walls and bundles of dusty electrical cables, metal sheets stacked in neat piles. The only light is a bare bulb, a few feet away from us. A cement mixer sits off to one side, lurking in the half-darkness.

Annie puts her hands on her knees. "You. Stupid. Why."

"Not stupid." I can barely get the words out.

"We should have. Hidden. Waited for—"

"Yeah. No." I stagger away from the fire door, picturing the outside of the building in my head again. South-west side— that's where we need to go. And I'm pretty sure west is on my left, so that means...

Annie jogs after me. It really is disgusting just how quickly she gets her wind back. "Teagan, if you don't start talking in the next five seconds, I'm gonna—"

"Ha!" I spot what I'm looking for. "There."

The temporary elevator.

I spotted it, attached to the outside of the scaffolding, when we climbed out of the van. The builders use it to move between floors, so the tenants don't have to share their nice, clean elevators with guys in cement-stained boots.

"You're joking," Annie says. A gust of wind almost drowns out her words, a wind thick with smoke.

"Nope. We need to get down, right? And what's the one elevator they *won't* be monitoring from the security room? Or able to stop once it starts moving?"

She stares at me, slowly shaking her head.

"I think the words you're looking for are, *Thank you. Teagan, you're a genius, I'm sorry I was ever mean to you.*" I have a little bit of my own breath back now, and use it to skip over to the cargo lift. It reminds me of ones window cleaners use, with a metal gate you have to swing open to climb inside and a big, clunky control box. "Come on."

"Teagan." She still hasn't approached the elevator. From somewhere behind her, the guards are hammering at the fire door.

"What are you waiting for?" I hold the gate open for her. "Come on. Time to skedaddle."

"It doesn't go down."

"What?"

"The elevator." She sounds like she wants to murder me or collapse to the ground or possibly both at once. "It doesn't go to the ground. It only goes to other floors of the site."

"Oh, come on," I say, leaning over the side to look. "Of course it…"

Doesn't.

The elevator runs on two thick vertical metal tracks, neither of which extends below the floor we're on. Street lights blink up at me from fifty floors down, wind blowing my hair in a thousand directions. I tilt my head back—the tracks go all the way up the building, all the way to what must be the 80th floor.

"But that doesn't make sense." My voice sounds very small. "How do they get building materials up here?"

Annie points. I follow her finger to a crane on a vacant lot across the street, its scaffolding shrouded in shadow.

"Oh."

I didn't actually check to see if the construction elevator really did go the way down to ground level. I just assumed it did. I'd forgotten about the crane. And now that I think about it, it makes sense to use one for lifting heavy materials, and build a smaller elevator so the workers can get between floors. Definitely more sense than building eighty stories' worth of elevator strong enough to lift all the materials the construction company needs.

I give Annie my most winning smile. "So. Hide?"

She squeezes her eyes shut, mutters something dark, then shoves past me onto the lift. "Paul," she says, stabbing at the up button. "Tell Reggie to kill the cameras on the top floors."

"Uh, copy?"

"We could probably hide here," I say, pointing to the construction site. "There might be a—"

The look she gives me could shatter concrete.

"I'm going to take us to a floor they don't know we're on," she says sweetly. "If that's OK with you."

"Yup." I give her a thumbs up. "That sounds excellent. Let's do it."

FOUR

Teagan

It's a bumpy ride up. The wind buffets us from all directions, the metal clanking and creaking as the elevator ascends. The tiny engine sounds like it's going to blow a gasket at any moment. Annie stands by the control box, arms folded, eyes shut tight. I put my hands on the outer railing, looking out over the city—hey, if you can't admire the view in the middle of a chase, what's the point? Plus, from this side of the building, you can't see the fires on the horizon. Which is just fine by me.

"Annie, Teagan." Paul's voice is a focused monotone. "Reggie tells me the top-floor cameras are taken care of. What are you thinking? Over."

"Copy," Annie says. "We don't know yet. Over."

"OK? Are you coming out on the north or south side of the building? If it's the north side, there's an alley. We could—"

"We don't know, Paul. Teagan hasn't decided yet."

I ignore the barb, mostly because I don't want Annie to hurl me off the side.

The construction site on the 80th floor is even more bare-bones than the one on the 50th. Very few of the walls are up, and there's almost no machinery. Annie doesn't hesitate,

making for the fire stairs at the back of the site. "Paul." Her
voice is soft, as if she's worried someone might hear. "Can
you pull up the blueprints for the top floors and a list of tenants? Over."

"Got 'em both already. What do you need? Over."

"Give us an office to hide in."

"Hold on...OK...All right, looks like somebody just
moved out of Suite 8213. Should be clear. Over."

I'm a little worried we'll be met by guards, but they probably don't know exactly where we are yet. And the stairs
themselves are quiet, with nothing but the hum of the lights
and our feet slapping on the concrete.

The hallways on the 82nd floor are different from the ones
below. The marble looks real, and the carpet is thick and soft
under my black lace-ups. There's no one around. Even the
aircon sounds muted.

The door to 8213 is another identical one, on the north-
west side of the building. Same thick wooden surface. Same
completely useless biometric lock. I go to work, reaching into
the latch mechanism as Annie hovers nearby.

I must be getting tired. It takes almost six seconds to open
this lock. The one on the server room door didn't take more
than three.

"Done," I say, straightening up. "Let's—"

Which is when Annie sucks in a horrified breath, grabs me
by the shoulders and shoves me through the door.

"Stop! Now!" someone yells. As Annie pushes me, I get a
split-second glimpse of the rest of the corridor. Bob the security chief is there, along with three other guards—ones much
bigger than the two who chased us before. They're sprinting
right towards us, and they look *pissed*.

I stumble into Suite 8213, lose my footing, crash to a

tangled heap on the floor. "Close it!" Annie is shouting. "Close the door!"

I react instantly, reaching out and slamming the door closed, locking the mechanism. A second later someone is hammering on it, rattling the handle.

Guess Bob isn't as dumb as he looks. If I weren't completely freaked out right now, I might start clapping.

There's not much in the office—certainly nothing we can use. There's some furniture: a desk, an ergonomic chair, a disconnected computer tower. The windows are floor to ceiling, and the view is spectacular, even counting the fires on the horizon. Bob is leaning against the door now, the lock straining in the frame. I focus harder, willing both the lock and the door to stay shut.

"Annie?"

"I'm thinking."

"Annie?"

"I said, I'm thinking!"

The seconds tick by, and she doesn't move. It's like she's running through every possibility, pulling and discarding ideas, desperately trying to find one that works. How long is it going to be before one of them shoots the lock off or batters the door down?

In my earpiece Paul says, "Annie. Get out of there. Over."

"Uh…" The hammering gets louder. "Yeah, Paul, just a second."

Now she's scanning the ceiling. What is she thinking? That we can crawl through the vents? Squash into them alongside the cables? This isn't *Die Hard.*

Beyond Annie, through the windows, Los Angeles glitters. The fires paint the night sky.

My amazing cargo elevator stunt didn't work. Neither did

hiding. We are running out of options here, and if at least one of us doesn't come up with something good, we are well and truly fucked. We may as well just cut to the chase and throw ourselves out the—

My hand strays to my belt. To the giant metal buckle there. Annie's one is identical.

I reach back with my PK and grab the ergonomic chair behind the desk. The seat is mesh and foam, but it's supported by a metal frame. There's a single leg jutting down from below the seat. The base has five points, each with a roller ball, so its owner can scoot around the office when he's bored. It's easy to lift and heavy enough for what I have planned. I might have fucked up with the elevator, but not even I could get gravity wrong.

"What the hell are you doing?" Annie says. "That's not gonna stop them."

"Got that right."

I hurl the chair at the plate-glass window. Which doesn't break. With a deep *boing*, the chair bounces back into the room, nearly braining Annie in the process.

She stumbles back, hands raised. "Jesus!"

"Sorry."

Abruptly, whoever is hammering on the door stops. Someone shouts at the others to make room. Which means they're going to shoot the lock off.

"Frost," Annie says. She's using my last name, which must mean she's *really* pissed.

There's a muffled bang from behind the door. The lock judders, but holds.

Snarling, I lift the chair high, turning it so its underside is pointed right at the glass.

Annie shakes her head. "No."

"Yeah."

"No. *No!*"

I sprint towards her. And as I move, I hurl the chair at the window.

It punches right through. As a rush of roaring wind fills the room, I grab Annie around the waist and hurl us after it as a second gunshot blows the lock off the door.

Which just about brings us up to speed.

FIVE

Teagan

Let me tell you a little something about psychokinesis.

Everyone has these ideas about what you can actually do with it. Scalpel-less surgery, using air molecules as an infinitely sharp blade. Getting a job as an assassin, and pinching off blood vessels or ripping hearts open without even touching your victim.

Yeah. No.

There are a hundred dumb Reddit threads about how many magic tricks you could pull off, or how you could make amazing smoke rings. Whoop-de-fucking-do. Also, gambling. People online love to spitball about how PK could help you win a ton of money, influencing roulette wheels or craps dice. Tanner gave me a friendly warning about that once: *If I ever catch you in a casino, I will bury you in the deepest, darkest hole I can find.*

Plenty of people online *claim* they have PK, but you only have to do about five seconds' worth of digging to see that they're lying out of their asses. If they really could move things with their minds, they'd either be dead or in Tanner's programme.

It's just me.

Plus, my ability has limits. Anything over about three hundred pounds is a no go—I've been up to that line before, more times than I can count, and it's like a weightlifter reaching failure point. The harder I try, the bigger the headache is afterwards, and the more food I need to get my energy back.

And I can't lift organic matter—no carbon or hydrogen molecules. They don't listen to me, no matter how nicely I ask them to move. My parents were never able to figure out why, and neither could the government science geeks after Wyoming went to shit. I have an effective range of ten feet, no more.

And as for air molecules? I'm surgical, but I'm not *that* surgical.

It takes about ten seconds to fall from eighty-two floors up, and Annie and I have already spent about two. If I'd taken a moment to think, which is what Reggie is always telling me to do, I might have realised that while I was perfectly capable of lifting both myself and Annie—even together, we're well under the three-hundred-pound limit—the belt buckles weren't. I concentrated all of our weight onto two points, both of which decided this wasn't really their scene. Snap. Even if I'd applied force to them slowly, which I tried to do, they were just never going to cut it.

All the same, give me some credit: when the buckles snap, I don't panic. I go for the next best thing: our crappy uniforms, with all their synthetic fibres. But there's too much organic material there, too much cotton, so the weight ends up spread across too few points. It slows us for a second, then the clothing starts to tear, my jacket and shirt splitting across my back.

I let go. The only thing worse than splatting onto the sidewalk would be doing it naked.

Annie screams, arms flailing at my back, an expression of sheer, stunned horror on her face. My stupid tie flaps against my forehead, the freezing air howling in my ears. If I don't come up with a brilliant idea *right now*, there isn't going be enough left of us for Tanner to—

The chair.

The one I used to smash the window glass. It's tumbling just below us.

I don't think; I just do, throwing my PK as far out as it will go. I feel the chair almost immediately and rip it towards us, fighting with the buffeting air and the chair's kinetic energy. Almost there. Almost...

The plan is to flip the chair upright, then pull myself and Annie into the seat. Then we'll float down on our magic chair, make a smooth landing using the roller wheels on the metal legs, and high-five before making our escape into the night. What *actually* happens is that the chair hits me side on, wedging my body between the base and the seat.

I grab on tight, holding onto the mesh seat like it's a life raft. "Hang on!" I shout to Annie, my words ripped away by the rushing air.

We're too heavy for me to stop completely, not with our momentum and our combined weight. But I can slow us down. A lot.

It's a really weird sensation—like trying to hold a door closed when a thousand tons of water are pushing on the other side and you're also on a moving bus. An ache blooms at the base of my skull, my body fighting to deliver enough power. The Edmonds Building rushes past us, the windows strobe-lighting as we fall. We're perhaps three seconds from hitting the ground.

What I want to do is turn our fall into a sweet-ass glide, all the way to the ground. What *actually* happens is that we start to move sideways.

Really, really fast.

We zip past the buildings, maybe forty feet off the ground, lights from cars on the freeway just visible. We're heading right for the strip of tarmac on the building's north side: an alley filled with dumpsters and parked cars and giant potholes. The Edmonds Building is on our right, a multi-storey car park on our left.

If there's anyone in the alley, they're about to get one hell of a surprise.

The chair slides, threatening to slip away from me. At least Annie has stopped screaming. She's moved on to the panicked-hyperventilation section of tonight's programme.

"It's OK!" My voice is just audible over the rushing air. "I've got th—"

"*Frost, watch out!*"

We're heading straight for a sign, one advertising EASY DAY RATES! and EARLY BIRD PARKING! I swear loudly, throwing us sideways, only just managing not to splatter us across it. Unfortunately, the move tilts us, which means we start to slide off the chair's frame. We're ten feet off the deck, coming way too fast.

"Hang on!"

"Frost, I'm gonna fucking kill y—"

I throw every ounce of PK energy I have into the chair, pulling it back, pulling *us* back. We rear up like an attacking cobra, and then we're dumped onto the ground.

We've got plenty of momentum left. It sends me rolling, tarmac scraping my exposed hands. A shattered bit of glass slices through my jacket, scratching the arm beneath, right before I slam into the side of a dumpster.

Things go blurry. There's a ringing alarm going off right next to me. I stick my finger in my ear to block it out, only to discover that it's inside my head.

I sit there, head bowed, waiting it out. When it drops to a low ringing, it's replaced by a tidal wave of pain—one that starts at the base of my skull and goes all the way down to my toes.

"Fucking...*ow*." I squeeze my eyes shut. Somewhere ahead of me, Annie is groaning.

Very slowly I get to my feet. I'm banged up, the world fuzzy at the edges, the lights above us way too bright, but at least I can stand. Nothing broken, as far as I can tell. I touch the graze on my arm, finger pushing through my torn jacket. It's not as bad as it feels. I think I'm good.

The alley we're in is typical downtown LA: dumpsters, bags of reeking garbage, puddles of unidentifiable brown liquid, walls so graffitied that the original surface isn't even visible any more. The chair, its seat shredded to hell, lies nudged up against one of the dumpsters. Above us, light paints a fire escape's shadow onto the wall. It's hot—in the nineties, easy—and there's the definite stench of smoke in the air, a scent that's been hanging over the city for days as the fire chews at its northern edge.

A series of fire doors lines the Edmonds Building—new, but already starting to rust. There's nobody around. Although there *is* a siren, a real one this time, getting closer by the second. Who knows what the security guards would have told the cops when they called them? *Police? Someone impersonated one of us, then dived out a window on the 82nd floor. No, we don't see a body. No, we don't know why they did it. Please don't hang up.*

"Annie? You all right?"

Another groan answers me. She's up on all fours, head hanging, a puddle of puke underneath her.

Amazingly, I still have my earpiece. "Paul. We're in the alley. North side. Come get us."

I don't register his reply, because right then I get real woozy. I bend over, hands on my knees until it passes. The base of my skull throbs, like it has its own heartbeat.

I stay there for a minute until it subsides, then stumble over to Annie. "Any survivors?"

She lurches away from me, moving like she's drunk, almost slipping in a patch of puke and ending up collapsed against the wall. Her clip-on tie is gone, torn away, and there's a nasty scrape on her cheek.

"What," she says. "The fuck."

"Oh come—"

"*What the fuck?*" Suddenly she's just yelling, angrier than I've ever seen her. "*What? What?!*"

"You're welcome!" What is she freaking out about. We made it, didn't we?

Annie buries her face in her hands, then slides her arms up until they're cradling her head. "I'm done," she says after a long moment, letting her arms drop. "No more. No more jobs with you. I don't care *what* Tanner says. Fuck you, and fuck her. We just...That was...No. Never. I'm done."

"I didn't see *you* coming up with anything."

"I didn't get the chance!" she roars at me. She's shaking. Like, really shaking. Her dark skin has gone grey, and her eyes won't stay still. "We wouldn't even have *been* up there if it wasn't for you."

Maybe it's the look on her face, or just the adrenaline catching up with me, because it's then that I start to shake too.

A car horn. Loud and insistent. Carlos and Paul, parked across the alley entrance, the van sideways to us. Annie and I stumble over, still shaking, somehow managing to make it to the van without falling over. Carlos is behind the wheel, cap pulled down low over his eyes. A few yards down, on our side of the street, the garish open sign of an all-night convenience store blinks at us.

We reach the van as the side door slides open. Paul peers out, blinking behind wire-framed glasses. He's wearing his usual striped button-down, his bald head gleaming under the street lights.

"How on earth did you get down so fast?" he says.

Annie roars in his face, then hurls herself into the van.

"Annie? Jesus, are you all right?" Paul tries to follow her and gets another incoherent yell for his trouble.

"I'm fine too, by the way," I say.

He ignores me, crouching down in front of Annie, who ignores him. She's sitting on the low bench that runs along one side of the van's interior; the other is packed solid with radio equipment, tool racks, stacked duffel bags. A wire-covered bulb in the ceiling fills the inside with harsh white light.

"Think I'll sit up front," I mutter.

I swing round to the passenger side, and Carlos pops the door for me. Behind us, through the partition, Annie growls at Paul to leave her the fuck alone.

On the jobs we do Paul handles comms and logistics while Carlos does the driving. He's a big guy, with a blocky, angular face and stubble that never seems to vanish no matter how often he shaves. He's wearing a flannel shirt despite the heat, the sleeves rolled up to expose the intricate tattoos lining both arms. The tattoos mix a hodge-podge of images, classic American muscle cars nudging up against snarling tigers and leaping dolphins. The biggest piece is a grinning, colourful *día de los muertos* skull with flowers for eyes, wrapped around the inside of his forearm.

Carlos flashes me an evil grin as he puts the van in gear. "Yo, I got what you need." His Mexican accent gets stronger when he talks like this. "Get you real fucked up. First taste is free."

"Shut up and give me the goods."

He laughs. "Glove box."

I pop it, and the sight of the bag of beef jerky nearly makes me faint with joy.

"You're my hero," I say between mouthfuls of delicious salty meat.

"I'm everyone's hero." He's pulling slowly out of the alley, looking left and right for cops. "What's up with Annie?"

I tell him what happened, bracing myself for the freak-out. It doesn't come. Instead, he just says, "Huh."

"That's it?" I say.

"What?"

"I pull off an amazing last-second save, and all you can say is 'Huh'?"

"You know Annie's scared of heights, right?"

"Well, yeah, I mean, it was pretty scary and all, but I had it totally under—"

"No, like *really* scared of heights. Like one of her worst fears."

I open my mouth to reply, then close it again. Thinking back to the cargo elevator, how Annie stood with her eyes closed, not moving. And in the office where we placed the coupler, how she stayed away from the windows. Didn't even look at them.

"Huh," I say.

A siren splits the night behind us. Carlos guns the van, and we're gone.

SIX

Jake

The most effective way to destroy people is to deny and obliterate their history.

In all the books Jake had read—and he'd read many, stolen from libraries or shoplifted from second-hand stores or borrowed and never returned from shelter break rooms—that was the one phrase he'd never quite got out of his head. It would come to him in odd moments, drift across his mind as he tried to fall asleep, shivering under cold bridges or freeway overpasses, as he stepped out of gas stations and corner stores in towns that he and his mother might have lived in when he was a kid.

It always bothered him that no one knew who actually said it. Most people attributed it to George Orwell, to *1984*, but Jake thought most people had shit for brains. He'd read *1984* three times, and he'd never come across it. Everybody was going around parroting this bit of wisdom without knowing or caring that its own history had been obliterated.

Then again, he knows a thing or two about being denied a history.

The quote crosses his mind again as he rides down the

freeway, heading towards the glimmering skyscrapers of downtown LA. Beneath him, the Royal Enfield Bullet Classic growls and roars, its tailpipe spitting as he weaves his way through the late-night traffic. It's not a good sound, and it's got him worried: a thrown engine might be the one thing that could ruin tonight. But Jake and the bike have been together a long time, since the Detroit days, and it's always come through for him. Royal Enfield started making bikes over a century before, in 1901, and the Bullet Classic dates from 1933. His isn't that old, of course, even if it sometimes acts like it.

His helmet suddenly feels too tight. As he slows to pass between two honking pickup trucks, Jake reaches up and unclips the chin strap, pulling it off and wedging it in his lap.

He's tall, a little over six feet, with a lanky frame and a dirty crop of shoulder-length blond hair. It blows about his head as he accelerates, framing a face that could be that of any aspiring actor in LA—the kind of actor that populates every audition in town, clutching well-worn headshots and proudly talking about the Best Buy commercial they did, or the indie movie from six years ago that performed well at film festivals. It's the face of a barista, of the barman who pops your beer, of the guy across the hall in your apartment building with whom you're on nodding terms but never actually speak to. If anybody chose to look closer, they'd note the rips in the leather jacket, the ancient Timberland boots held together with straps of duct tape, the scabs on his hands. But they never look.

The Enfield's engine blats, its rusted green gas tank reflecting headlights from every direction. The air stinks of smoke from the fires, but Jake doesn't mind. Tonight is the night he finds out who he is. Chuy has promised him everything, all of it, the mother lode. Every detail of his past. As long as as he can do what he promised.

There's no way he's letting this opportunity slip. No way, no how.

A grin splits his face. He feels good. *Really* good. Even the old pain in his jaw, the familiar ache from endless clenching as he sleeps, is barely background noise. Fifteen years he spent in foster care. Fifteen years of bumping up against a federal system that either couldn't or just plain wouldn't help him. Documents that they wouldn't let him see. That they misplaced. That they didn't give enough of a shit to look for. Why would they? For a kid that would almost certainly be rehoused in a few months, a year at the most? They didn't care that his history had been obliterated. No matter how hard he begged and pleaded, they wouldn't help him. Even the good ones, and there were very few of those.

No one would tell him where he came from.

The road ahead of him curves, the traffic tightening. As he brings the bike to a gentle halt, Jake glances at the car next to him and sees a tiny face looking back at him through the rear window. A little boy, maybe three or four, strapped into a car seat and staring with undisguised wonder.

The sight rattles him a little—what's a kid like him doing up this late? Then he relaxes. Parents coming back from a party, maybe, the kid dozing in the back seat, waking up briefly and spying him through the window.

Jake grins at the boy, his own teeth reflected in the glass, and flips a cheerful, almost lazy salute. The boy laughs, delighted— Jake can't hear him, but he can imagine the laugh, crystalline and clear. One of the adults in the front seats turns around, saying something to the boy, who ignores her.

An idea blossoms—an absurd, risky idea, one that on any other night he would shy away from. All the drivers around Jake are looking forward, concentrating with herd stupidity on the clogged road ahead. And the drivers behind him won't be able to see what's happening. So why not? Why the hell not? If he's going to have any audience tonight, why shouldn't it be a child?

He makes an elaborate show of looking around. In reality, he really does check—simply because the night is going well doesn't mean he wants to tempt fate. But nobody is looking at him, the drivers all concentrating on how terrible it is to be stuck in a traffic jam.

He looks back at the boy, holding eye contact. The helmet in his lap rises until it's level with his chest. He winks at the goggling child, puts a raised finger underneath the floating helmet, and makes it spin like a basketball.

The kid's mouth falls open, his eyes huge in delighted disbelief. As he turns to tell his parents, Jake drops the helmet back down. The kid is going nuts in the car seat, pointing, bouncing up and down. The mother glances at Jake, her gaze dull, uninterested. He pities her. There is no one else with a Gift like his, no one, and she doesn't even realise it.

The traffic moves. With one last glance at the excited boy, Jake accelerates, gunning the throttle and speeding away, leaning into the highway as it curves.

He has come a long way. A thousand miles, a thousand different sleeping spots. In a way he's grateful for all of it because it led him here. To this great and glorious night, when he will finally find out where he came from. He has three tasks to complete, and the night wind is rushing through his hair, and the bike's engine is now steady, purring underneath him.

His history might have been denied, but it hasn't been obliterated yet. And if there's one thing he's discovered over the past fifteen-odd years, it's that he is very hard to destroy.

SEVEN

Teagan

It's nearly midnight by the time we get back to Paul's Boutique.

That's what I call the house we use as our office, even if nobody else does. Technically, Reggie's the one who runs the show, not Paul, but I'd been listening to some Beastie Boys a couple of weeks into our time there and the name was too good not to use.

Surprisingly, they didn't want me to put a sign on the door.

It's in Venice Beach, which itself is kind of a strange name. It makes the place sound a lot nicer than it is. It's got some OK spots—a few nifty restaurants and coffee shops—but mostly it's just bungalows, bad bars and bullshit tourist stores. And our office. Because they have to put us somewhere.

Reggie lives in the back room, and we work out of the front. It's on a street called Brooks Court that is only marginally nicer than the alley Annie and I crash-landed in earlier tonight. I would have preferred Carlos to drop me off in Leimert Park, where my little apartment is. It's on the way. But Reggie insists on a face-to-face debriefing after a job, and I've been dumped on for missing them in the past.

I've moved apartments a bunch of times since Tanner first

stuck me in LA, but I've always worked out of the Boutique. It might be kind of a shithole, but walking inside after a job, sitting on the ratty-ass couch and drinking a beer or a cup of coffee is like letting out a breath you've been holding for a long time. It's my way of transitioning back to being a normal person. One with a life that doesn't involve doing black-bag jobs for the U.S. government.

Besides, you can climb up on the roof if you know how. It's a great place to sit and drink a beer.

Annie is out the van the second Carlos pulls in, even before he cuts the engine, barging through the door leading to the living room like it personally offended her. Paul follows, stopping for a moment to fiddle with the garage door remote.

Carlos has been silent for most of the way back—he's like that when he's behind the wheel, preferring to concentrate on his driving. Now he puts a hand on my shoulder. Speaking very gently, he says, "How many organs would you sell right now for a cup of coffee? Be honest."

"For your coffee? None of them. You can have a toenail clipping."

"I think I snorted a toenail clipping once. It's not as bad as you would think."

"That's amazing."

"Yeah, I know. You would not believe what the coke has been cut with by the time it gets to Mexico."

"No, I mean it's amazing you're still able to speak, with all the horrible things you've done to your brain."

"You break my heart. You want coffee or not?"

Coffee. Jesus, yes. It'll help replace some of the energy I lost with my chair stunt, although it's going to take one monster of a takeout and a long nap before I get it all back.

There's a rap on my window. It's Paul, making the wind-down gesture with his hand. He does not look happy.

I hit the button, lowering the window. "You rang?"

"Annie told me about what you did."

Scratch that. He's not unhappy. He's furious. It's not explosive, like Annie; he's doing a very good job of holding it back. But the tightness of his shoulders, the narrowed eyes and thin-set lips give it away.

"Dude," I say. "Come on. Can I just—"

"It was reckless. It was irresponsible." He actually ticks these off on his fingers. "You put both your lives in danger. You acted without consulting me..."

"Next time I'm falling out a skyscraper, I'll be sure to call you up to discuss our options." I give him a thumbs up. "Go team."

"Now you just—"

"*Paul*," Carlos says. "Maybe we do this inside? Get some coffee and talk, huh?"

Paul exhales. Collects himself. After a long moment he gives a brisk a nod. "Yes. All right. Good idea." Then he turns on his heel and makes his way into the house.

"Why you gotta be such a dick to him?" Carlos says.

"*I'm* a dick to *him*?"

"Yeah. Paul can't help the fact that he has..." He snaps his fingers. "*Palo por el culo.* You know? Stick in his ass? That how you say it?"

I snort. "Yup."

"He's born that way," Carlos continues. "You should be more considerate, man."

My laugh tastes bitter. Didn't I just save us? Pull us out the fire? I admit, I screwed up with the construction elevator, but I couldn't see another way out of that room. It wasn't what you'd call safe, but it was also the only option that didn't get us arrested, or shot.

Carlos pops the door, then looks over his shoulder at me. "You OK? For real?"

I roll my neck, wincing. "Sure. What's a job without a little bit of whiplash?"

"You gotta be careful, man. You leave that shit too long without fixing it, it sticks around."

"I'm fine. Besides, tonight wasn't nearly as bad as Long Beach."

"You just fell like eighty floors. How was it not as bad as the Long Beach job?"

"They had dogs in Long Beach, Carlos."

He rolls his eyes. "Again with this. Just because you're not good with animals..."

"No, I'm perfectly fine with animals. I love animals. As long as they don't want to eat me."

"It was *one* dog, and it was like half a foot long."

"You didn't see it. It was *motivated*. Give me an eighty-floor drop over that any day."

"Not sure Annie would agree with you."

He grimaces, realising he's hit a soft spot. I don't mind too much. Carlos and I give each other shit, but he always makes me feel better. No matter how gnarly things get, talking to him always helps. Maybe it's because he knows what it's like to go through hell and come out on the other side OK. More or less.

He grew up poor in Tecomán, in Colima State. From what he tells me, it makes the worst block in LA look like paradise. His old man used to be a racing driver, and the one thing he made sure his son could do from like age ten was drive. Turns out, Carlos was pretty good at it—good enough to attract the attention of the local Zeta gang.

From age sixteen, he was the guy waiting outside while the Zetas knocked over businesses or held meetings with corrupt officials or swung machetes. He would probably still be doing that now if the cops hadn't decided to strike back at the gang and tried to get him to roll on them. Faced with either life in prison or a machete swing of his own, Carlos skipped across the border. He ended up on Tanner's radar, somehow, and now he's here.

He's probably the only person in China Shop who I'd actually choose to hang out with. He and I have spent many, many nights at bars around Venice Beach, knocking back beers and talking shit, him telling me endless stories about his rotating cast of boyfriends and hook-ups. He *really* doesn't want to go back to Mexico—not even if he had a new identity. Mexican laws are slowly swinging towards legalisation of gay marriage, but it's still the kind of thing that you have to keep quiet. At least in LA, he told me, he can date whoever the hell he wants.

"See you inside, Teags," he says.

"Yeah. Go make my coffee, bitch."

His eyes widen. "*Bitch?*" He puts a hand on his chest. "You call me bitch? I, who am descended from Aztec kings?"

"Only one sugar this time, sweetie. Thanks."

"I am a man." He makes his voice tremble. "Not some simple kitchen servant you can order around. You play with my emotions, señorita. I have *dignity...*"

"You have a job making coffee, that's what you have."

He leans in suddenly, conspirational, grinning. "If you still got that toenail, we could always—"

"*Ugh.* Get out."

He goes, laughing, closing the van door behind him. In the silence that follows I have to fight off the temptation to just close my eyes and go to sleep right there. I'm hurting a lot more than I'd expect, and it's not just the whiplash. I always feel it the day after I push my ability—a pain that ranges from aching muscles to full-on migraine—but I can't remember feeling this sore so soon after. I must have hit it a little harder than I thought.

Using my PK burns energy, but no one has managed to figure out how that energy makes it from my body across the room to whatever I'm lifting. I've been stuck inside particle chambers and hooked up to ECGs and dosed with low-level radiation, and the scientists doing it still couldn't get a decent working theory together. My parents might have known, once—after all, they were the ones who made me, fucking with my genetic code in ways that had never been done before. But they're gone, along with all their research.

God, I need that coffee.

It's always amazed me that Tanner, who has access to all sorts of bottomless black budgets and off-the-books accounts, couldn't give us a half-decent office to work in. The front part of the house is a spacious open-plan kitchen and living room, which has been converted into a workspace. Paul is the only one with an actual desk, a cheap Ikea number over by the window, covered in piles of drifting paper. A corkboard with faded invoices hangs on the wall next to it. Faded invoices and a photograph of a kid in a soccer uniform—Paul's son, Cole.

There's a whiteboard against the opposite wall, its surface smudged and dirty. The view from the window is breathtaking: a line of plastic garbage bins against the opposite wall of Brooks Court, next to a very rarely spotted power junction box covered with graffiti. There's a poster plastered on the wall, a mess of lurid orange and green advertising a club night from three months ago. I've often wondered who put it up there and why they chose that spot—if they were specifically trying to target us, or were just high and had to meet their poster quota.

I pull off the ridiculous tie, dumping it on the counter. The surface is always sticky, no matter how much we clean it. The kitchen is sparse: there's a microwave and a coffee machine perched on top of it, a tiny bar fridge underneath. Carlos is rummaging in the cupboards, the machine already set up for grinding.

At least the couches are decent. There are two of them, big and leathery and super-comfy, positioned in a broken L-shape in the middle of the room. Annie is sitting on one, head down, bent over her phone.

There's no sign of Reggie yet. Paul is over by the white-board, tapping at something on his Palm Pilot. Yes, an actual Palm Pilot. It has a black-and-white screen, a slide-down physical keyboard and a leather cover. He point-blank refuses to upgrade—even his cell is an old-school brick, which he keeps in a pouch on his belt. Ask that thing to go online, and it would probably melt in your hand. He refuses to own a smartphone, which he says is the worst possible name for something that can be hacked so easily. When I reminded him that Reggie had installed scramblers in *all* our phones as standard, he just told me I was being naive.

"Hey, everyone?" Paul says. "Just a reminder, after we're done *debriefing*—" he looks at me "—we need to talk about a couple of jobs tomorrow."

Behind me, Carlos mutters something ugly-sounding in Spanish. He's still rooting around in the cupboards.

I pick up the tie again, waving it at Paul, knowing I shouldn't piss him off more than I have already, and not caring. "I'm gonna strangle you with this. Seriously."

"And *I* am going to make sure that we're working as

we're supposed to. I don't know why you still have a problem with it."

Jobs. He's not talking about covert special ops stuff. He's
talking actual work.

China Shop isn't just a name on a tax form. If you're doing
black-bag jobs in a city, it's pretty helpful to have a way to
move around without getting noticed. And nobody notices
moving vans. They're part of the background: the traffic and
people and noise that most people in a big city don't think
twice about. When we're gathering intel for a job, Paul will
slap a special removable decal on the side of the van—a big,
snorting, grinning cartoon bull that looks derpy as hell—and
we'll case as much of the area as we can.

But somewhere along the line, Paul decided that the whole
moving-company thing shouldn't just be a front—that we
should do *actual* moving jobs, so we would appear more legit.
Somehow, he got Reggie on board with the idea. Plus Tanner's
approval. And now China Shop Movers has a website. And a
phone number. And every couple of weeks Paul will convince
some poor bastard that Annie and Carlos and I are the best
solution for moving their furniture around. We will actually
go and perform actual moving jobs.

Having PK makes it a little easier—as long as you don't
make it obvious that you're not exactly lifting a dresser with
purely physical strength—but I still don't enjoy getting up
at ass o'clock and hustling to the office, just so we can drive
to some godforsaken house in Downey or Torrance to move
furniture. Day one: assist in the capture of international drug
lord and/or terrorist mastermind. Day two: assist with moving
a refrigerator down a flight of stairs.

But that's just who Paul Marino is. He's a details guy. Along
with running comms on our jobs—ironic for someone with

phone tastes from around 1995—he's the one who gets all our gear for us. Uniforms, equipment, whatever. He takes the clothes we use to be laundered; he keeps itemised lists of everything in the house and the van, and if you even borrow so much as a single screw, he'll not only know about it, he'll make you write him a receipt. Yes, we may be a top-secret government operation going on cool missions, but *someone* has to be responsible for the details, and at least Paul seems to actually enjoy it.

What still blows my mind is how well he seems get on with Annie. She's like the anti-Paul. They should piss each other off just by being in the same room.

I don't know a ton about her life—you'll be stunned to hear that we don't usually hang out away from the office—but Carlos told me she she has a record. A bad one. The kind of record where they throw you in prison if you even apply for a job that isn't construction or fast food. She was born in LA—in Watts, to the south—and she's got a lot of history with multiple gangs. West Coast Bloods, MS-13, 38th Street, even some of the Sureños. Most of those names weren't familiar to me until about a year ago. Annie was a kind of freelancer-slash-fixer, doing whatever job needed to be done for whoever could pay her. Until Tanner found her.

That's another thing I don't understand about Annie. We might not get along, but she is *crazy* smart. Which kills me. She should have been running a corporation, not getting busted for felonies in South Central. I once asked Carlos about it, and he'd given me a strange look. "You don't know a lot about growing up in Watts, do you?" he'd said, taking a pull of his beer.

Not even I could argue with that one.

"Hey, does anyone know where the coffee is?" says Carlos.

"Top shelf, left cupboard," I reply.

"Looked there."

"Look again. It's . . . Fuck."

I finished the coffee this afternoon. And forgot to tell Paul we needed more.

"It's fuck?" Carlos says. "What does that even mean?"

"Never mind. It's fine. I'm actually OK."

"You finished it, didn't you? Yo, *I* wanted coffee too."

Paul shakes his head, reaching over and writing something down on the whiteboard. "This is why we have a requisitions list," he says.

"Why do we even need one? I use my PK, I need caffeine. I shouldn't have to write it down every time."

"And I shouldn't have to ask you to not use that abbreviation every time. What is it with you today?"

I brandish the tie at him. "You are this close, man. Death by clip-on. I'm not kidding."

Paul doesn't like it when I use the term PK. He spent a bunch of time in Asia when he was with the navy, and speaks passable Korean and Vietnamese. Also a little bit of Cantonese, from his shore leave in Hong Kong. In Cantonese, PK is an abbreviation of *pook kai*, which means literally, go die in the street. Not exactly a phrase you'll see in the guidebooks.

"Hey," Annie says. She's still on the couch, elbows resting on her knees, arms dangling. Like a boxer listening to an unworthy opponent talk trash at a weigh-in. "Are we just not gonna talk about what happened back at the Edmonds?"

"Oh, we're going to talk about it," says Paul, folding his arms.

I close my eyes. "Annie, I didn't know—"

"Cos that?" She points a finger at me. "That was some straight bullshit right there."

Carlos squeezes past me, his arms raised in a placating gesture. "Let's just take it easy."

"No." She says. "No, no, no, Carlos, you don't get to say shit. You were in the truck. You didn't see what she did."

It's all I can do not to start yelling. "I got us out of there."

"Fuck that. You just did the first thing that came into your head and hoped that it would work out OK."

"*It did!*"

She shakes her head. "You don't get it. We plan these jobs for a reason. We put in hours of prep for a reason. Everybody except you. You think you can just show up, do the one or two things you're supposed to do with your voodoo mind shit, and call it a day. Hell, maybe you can. But what that does *not* give you the right to do is make decisions when shit goes bad."

What is she even talking about? Prep? How the hell are we supposed to prep for a job going south like that? Isn't that when you're *supposed* to think outside the box?

"Annie, that's not—"

"Don't fucking interrupt me. I'm not done." She levels a finger at me. "You put us at risk because you couldn't stop and think for one goddamn second."

"Agreed," Paul says. He's doing the finger-ticking thing again. "It was reckless, it was irresponsible, and furthermore—"

"Oh *come on.*" I look between them. "This is not the first time we've been in trouble, and it definitely isn't the first time we've almost had our cover blown. What about... what about that job at the hotel?"

"What hotel?" Annie says.

Paul frowns. "You mean Bell Gardens? Wasn't that a casino?"

"Whatever. Yes, Bell Gardens. That cop wanted to arrest Carlos, and—"

"Yo, don't bring me into this," Carlos says.

"—we had to make a break for it. Imagine what would have happened if he really *had* managed to shoot our tyres out."

Paul removes his glasses, digs the heels of his hands into his eyes. "It's not the same thing."

"Got that right," Annie says. "See, what I think? I think you wanted to do it."

Silence falls on the room. Everyone is looking at me now. A hot flush creeps up from the collar of my uniform shirt.

"What are you talking about?" I say.

"I think you wanted to use your power. Your ability. Whatever the fuck it is. I think you were looking for an excuse. Tanner got you opening doors. Unlocking safes. I think you got bored, and you're acting out. You ever pull that shit again on a job, you ever deviate from the plan even a little bit, I will throw you out a fucking window mysel—"

"Sounds like things went smoothly, then," says a voice from the door.

Regina McCormick glides into the room, the motor in her wheelchair making an almost inaudible whine. The chair is a clunky black bulldozer with battery packs hanging off it and tyres that could take it off-road. She sits in it like it's a throne, her good arm resting lightly on the control stick.

Reggie is in her late forties, with very thin crow's feet radiating out from piercing brown eyes. As always, she's dressed in thick grey sweats. She must have been tying up loose ends from the job, or she'd have been in the room with us already.

Reggie wasn't the first black woman to fly an Apache helicopter, but she was one of them. She's never told us much about her past, but I do know that after the crash in Afghanistan that left her an incomplete quadriplegic, she became very close to

Tanner. Spent years retraining as a programmer too. When Tanner put me to work for her, Reggie was who she got to run point.

Behind her, just visible through the door to the back room, is what she calls her Rig. It's a giant multiscreen system that she controls with a combination of eye movement, voice commands and a pair of giant trackballs. When she's plugged in, she looks even smaller than usual, two huge water-cooled towers on either side of her chair, the screens towering above. But she is one monster of a hacker.

All the same, I've never quite been able to get a handle on Reggie. She doesn't speak a lot about her life before China Shop, which I guess is understandable. There's plenty online about her service record: her citations, the operations she's taken part in, a few old newspaper stories from when she was a track star at her high school in New Orleans. It all ends about ten years ago with a simple story on a local news site headed: PARALYSED PILOT RETURNS HOME. After that? Zip.

She's never told me much about her past, although God knows I've asked. She just smiles, then tries to talk about something else. The one time I pushed, she stopped me with a curt "I don't want to talk about it."

I don't know this for sure, but on the one occasion where everybody at China Shop actually hung out together, it came up. A job we were supposed to run got postponed, and we ended up sitting around in the backyard waiting to hear if it was happening or not. Reggie was inside, working her Rig, and the topic of how she got the job here came up.

Paul swore blind that he'd heard that it wasn't Reggie who owed Tanner for something, but the other way round. He wouldn't say where he got the info, so none of us knew how seriously to take him. Then again, Paul isn't a known bullshit artist, and I'm not sure he actually has a sense of humour. Even if it wasn't the whole truth, there was a grain of it there.

As far as I can tell, she's the only one of us who hasn't been manipulated or coerced into this job. The rest of us? We work for Tanner or we're fucked.

Maybe that's a little harsh. We're not slaves. We're technically government workers, which I think is hilarious—salaried employees of the nameless agency Tanner runs. We get health benefits and dental, for fuck's sake, run through the convenient cover of China Shop Movers. We can go anywhere we want throughout the greater Los Angeles area. But if Tanner decided one day that we weren't worth protecting, that would be it.

"Carlos," Reggie says. She grew up in Louisiana and has an accent thick enough to spread on toast. Her voice is slightly breathy and strained, thanks to a weakened diaphragm. "Why is every single cupboard in my kitchen open? Didn't your mother raise you right?"

"Looking for the coffee. Teagan finished it."

Reggie glances at me. "You should drink chamomile, dear. It's much better for you. Speaking of which, Carlos, would you kindly brew me a cup? It's been a long night."

Carlos nods, earning a smile from Reggie. "Annie," she says, manoeuvring her chair around the couch. "You seem upset."

"Got that right. Teagan nearly blew the whole thing to shit."

"I did not. That was—"

Reggie lifts a finger, silencing her. "That's why we have these debriefings," she says, looking in my direction as if she can sense that I wanted to head straight home. "So we can deal with problems to make sure they don't reoccur."

As Carlos makes her herbal tea—which of course there's plenty of because nobody but Reggie actually drinks the stuff—she gets the story out of first Annie, then me. By the time we're done, the tea is steaming by her left hand, and the room feels like it's holding its breath.

A year ago this kind of post-mortem would have scared the shit out of me. Reggie was Tanner's woman in LA, which meant that she was, in effect, Tanner herself. I didn't know if she was on our side or not. But over the past year or so she's put herself between us and Tanner, backing us up on the rare occasions when a job really has gone bad, like it did in Bell Gardens.

The debriefings we have tend to be pretty loose. Reggie and Paul might have a military background, but there are no acronyms here—no infil and exfil zones, no sitreps. Just us, Paul's whiteboard and chamomile tea.

"Teagan," she says when we've finished, turning to me with a faint engine whirr. "That wasn't very intelligent. You put both your lives in danger, and you risked revealing your abilities. We've talked about this."

I nod, reluctantly.

"The construction elevator would have been bad enough. It wasn't a half-bad idea, as ideas go, but you should have cleared it with Annie."

"We didn't have time. There were—"

Reggie silences me with a look. "I expect better from you in the future. More importantly, I expect you to think before you act, which is something else we've talked about before. And you, Annie. Part of your role is to solve problems quickly and efficiently. When you're on a job, Teagan is under your command. If she does something you do not agree with, that constitutes a problem, and you should have taken immediate control."

Annie's voice is brittle. "I didn't head for the 50th floor. Or throw us out a window."

"True." Reggie inclines her head. "But you did make the decision to leave the server room and go up to Chase's fibre hub. There were other options on the table for you too."

Annie mutters something, but after a few moments gives Reggie a tight nod.

The smile that breaks on Reggie's face makes her look twenty years younger. "That's done then. You're all safe, and we got what we needed, so let's say no more about it. Mm. Carlos, I've told you a dozen times, you have to let the water sit for a few seconds after it boils, or you'll scald the leaves."

EIGHT

Teagan

I finally change out of the rent-a-cop uniform, spending a few minutes in the Boutique's bathroom as I change into jeans and my favourite shirt, a bright purple T depicting a cartoon monster about to swallow a city, the words *Eat Local* below it. After the clunky security-guard boots, my Jordans feel like heaven.

I'm starting to stiffen up, and it's all I can do to keep my eyes open. I need to get some more food inside me before I sleep. Something more than jerky. And forget delivery—I can go five minutes out of my way and pick it up myself.

The downstairs bathroom, which we use as a kind of half-assed locker room, is just off the part of the house where Reggie has her Rig. She's there when I come out, working the trackballs, the only light coming from the six giant screens that surround her chair on all sides.

"You'll mess up your eyes," I say.

She scoffs. "Honey, I've had twenty-ten vision since I was a kid. I got better eyesight than you do."

"Twenty-ten? Is that even a thing?"

"Ah, the ignorance of youth."

"If you say so, Grandma."

She waves an arm at me. "Get out of here. See you bright and early tomorrow."

"Yeah, yeah. Night."

I head back into the living room/office, lost in thought. Annie and Paul are still there, leaning up against the kitchen counter on the far side, their backs to me, talking in low voices. "...can't fit it in there," Paul is saying. "You'd have to take the whole back off the van."

"But we can do it?" Annie replies. "Right?"

Paul shrugs. "I mean, sure, in theory, there're a bunch of ways to—"

At that instant both he and Annie look in my direction. Paul stops dead. It catches me off guard, and for a second the question of what they were talking about dances across my tongue.

You know what? I don't care. Whatever it is, it's between them, and I am way too tired right now.

"Night, folks," I say, squeezing past them.

Annie says nothing, but Paul gives me a tight nod. "Yeah, Teagan, see ya," Paul replies. His tone is frosty but still polite.

I'll give him this: he's annoying and anal-retentive, but he's a professional. He might have been angry with me, but now that the debriefing is over, he's keeping it to himself. He's a former navy quartermaster, and unlike Annie and Reggie he *loves* talking about his past. Blue-collar upbringing in Ohio, high-school football champion, his time in the navy.

Of course he usually skips over the parts from after that. For someone obsessed with details and logistics, Paul was an absolutely terrible businessman. He tried everything, from selling web ads to flipping houses, even tried to market an app where you tapped on the screen to make virtual grass grow faster.

He's got not one but two failed marriages, and child support to pay. And say what you like about Paul, he's a pretty good dad—or at least I assume so, given how often he talks about his son. But he is *drowning* in debt, and China Shop is a decent, secure, guaranteed income. He is forty-four, balding, with a swelling beer gut and just about zero chance of finding an alternative career.

And I'll say this: Tanner knows how to pick people. It would be easy to surround me with a group of special forces operatives—career soldiers with beards and ugly tattoos, who could run a tight ship and make sure that nothing went wrong, ever. The reason we have our current motley crew is that we all have a lot to lose. If China Shop ever disbanded, through a job failing or us getting caught or me revealing my powers, we would all be screwed in a number of interesting ways.

Carlos would almost certainly be deported, right back to the hands of the Zetas in Tecomán. Annie would never be able to hold a decent job again—not with her record. Paul would go bankrupt, and there's a very good chance that he'd never see his son again—not after a few missed child support payments. Reggie might be OK...but it's Tanner who paid for her Rig. Her life would get a lot harder if she wasn't with us.

And then there's me.

Here's what happens if I fuck up, or if Tanner decides I'm not worth the trouble. I don't get deported, or get a visit from the cops. No, I get a visit from some nice men with black ski masks, who whisk me off to a faceless building in North Dakota or Virginia or Missouri and give me to the security-cleared scientists who are desperate to cut me open and figure out how my parents made me. I work for Tanner as her own private psychokinetic operative (sounds cooler than it is, believe me), and she keeps those assholes off my back.

I step past Paul and Annie, out into the garage. Carlos has the van's hood open, tinkering with something inside. He doesn't realise I'm there until I slap him on the ass. "Night, sweetie."

"*Mierda*," he mumbles, almost bumping his head on the raised hood. "Aight. Later, bitch."

It sounds forced. Said on reflex. He must be tired too.

As I move along the side of the van, he straightens up. "Walk you to your car?"

I don't particularly want to people right now—even with Carlos. But there's something in his eyes, an unsettled look.

"Everything OK?" I ask.

"Yeah. Yeah, for sure. I could just do with a walk, is all."

The alley is quiet, baking hot, with just the faintest rumble of traffic. There's almost no light save for the faint glow from the lights on the main drag. The smoke isn't as bad in this part of town. I take a deep breath, savouring the scent of the air: a little smoke, a lot of ocean, the faintest hint of jasmine and surf wax. Someone, somewhere, is getting high.

Carlos and I walk in silence for a few moments. My Jeep is parked at the far end of Brooks Court, right after it spills out onto Main—technically, we're not supposed to park in the alley, and I have more than one ticket to prove it.

"Long night, huh," Carlos says, as we turn the corner. I'm already digging in my bag for my keys.

"What? Oh, um, yeah." I'm barely paying attention, already thinking about whether there'll be traffic on the 405 at this time of night, and whether I should get bulgogi, or splurge and go for some fried chicken.

"That was some pretty crazy shit back there." He pulls a cigarette from a pack. "You mind?"

I shake my head absently. He knows better than to offer me

one, of course—I don't smoke, don't want anything that hot anywhere near me. But I don't mind if others do it.

My Jeep, a rusty black '06 Wrangler, is a short distance away. Its name, in case you were wondering, is the Batmobile. I bought it with my first cheque from Tanner's Los Angeles Bureau of Insane Shit. The Batmobile is the bomb. It's crusty and messy and has an engine that Carlos regards as a personal challenge, and I love it to pieces.

"Well," I say. "This is me. I'll see you tomorrow."

He nods, not looking at me. He's lost in thought, eyes somewhere in the distance. I wait for him to respond, and when he doesn't, my heart sinks a little. Something's wrong, and he's not going to tell me what it is.

And no, before you point out the obvious, it's not what happened with Annie. Carlos would never give me shit about something I got into shit for already—not seriously, anyway.

"OK. What's up?" I say.

"Huh?" He jerks himself out of his thoughts. "Oh. Nothing. Have a good night, Teags."

He turns to go. I nearly let him too, even though it's not like him to be this straight up. Every atom in my body just wants food and bed, and really doesn't feel like dealing with someone else's problems right now. Except Carlos isn't just someone else, and I'm not going to leave whatever this is bottled up inside him. Friends don't do that to each other.

I drop my bag next to the Jeep's front tyre. There's a low concrete wall running along the sidewalk opposite my car. "Sit."

"I..."

I point to the wall. "Carlos Jesús López Morales," I say. "Sit your ass down."

He sits his ass down. I plop myself next to him. It's probably not a smart move, since getting up again is going to take some willpower, but fuck it.

I nudge him. "You can talk to me, *cabrón*. You know that right?"

"You really shouldn't say that. In Mexico that'd get you knocked out, you say it to the wrong person."

"Then why'd you teach it to me?"

He says nothing. Which is *really* odd. I practically served it to him on a silver platter.

"Dude, come on. Talk to me."

"I'm just..." He scratches his head. "Just missing home, that's all."

"Home? Like Mexico?"

"Yeah. Kind of."

"I don't get it. Don't you have, like, a price on your head there? Plus, the way you talk about Tecomán..."

"I know, but—"

"And the whole gay marriage thing...I mean, no offence, Carlos, but you haven't exactly made it sound like a barrel of..."

I stop when I see the set of his shoulders.

"I just...I don't know, man." Again, the hand scratching the head, running across his buzz cut. "I was just waiting for you guys tonight, in the van, and I was just thinking about it. We used to go down to this beach when I was little—Playa Cuyatlan. Not the most beautiful beach in the world or anything, but it was all right, you know? And I just..." He lets out a sigh, long and slow. His eyes have gone back to the middle distance. "You ever just get bored?"

"You're running around doing secret-agent shit, and you're bored?" I don't mean it to sound as dumb as it comes out. Maybe it's just because the question cuts a little too close to the bone. It's not that *I'm* bored—my life is way too weird for that. But what happens if that changes? What if I want to get out? Or if I get older, and can't do what I do now? Somehow, I don't see Tanner giving me a gold watch and wishing me well.

I can't change jobs or leave town, and so far I've done a pretty good job of ignoring these problems. Carlos's question makes that impossible.

"Maybe bored is the wrong word," he says. "It's just like... I didn't wanna be working on cars for the rest of my life, you know?"

"Thought you liked cars."

"I *do*. But..."

He trails off. I'm about to prompt him when his eyes light up. "Hey—you wanna get out of here?"

"What do you mean?"

"Take a road trip." He hops off the wall, spreads his arms. "Fuck it, let's get out of LA for a while. I was reading about this amazing place, up by Point Reyes, these really cool cabins. We stay there, we check out the area, we go try the bars or whatever. Just hang out."

"Carlos..."

"No, for real." He points in the direction of the China Shop offices. "*Vámonos*. In fact, fuck it, I'm sick of this shit. Let's just go tomorrow. We go back in there, tell Reggie we need some time off. We can head up there in the morning. Just hang out, drink some beer. Laugh at the other tourists."

"That's not..." I take a deep breath. Carlos is being genuine here—I love hanging out with him, and he'd be amazing to road trip with. But that's not why I'm hesitant. "I think it's a good idea," I tell him.

"Great! Let's—"

"But not tomorrow, OK?" Just taking off, as tempting as

it is, would not exactly earn me brownie points with Reggie and Annie. Or Tanner. As much as I'm not known for my forward planning, these are not people I can afford to piss off more than I have already. "Let's talk to the guys properly. Let's make sure they know *why* we want to take time off. Maybe we can convince the whole office to take a break—like, all of us, going to Tanner and just saying we need a vacation."

"But—"

I push myself off the wall, tilt my chin up to look him in the eye. "I know you're feeling it, dude. I get it too. And I *do* think it's a cool idea. But I need sleep, and I don't want to spend the night worrying about whether or not Reggie's nuclear explosion is gonna take out the whole of LA, or just Venice."

A smile flickers across his face. And in that instant I want to say, *Fuck it.* Take what I just told him and throw it in the trash. The idea of spending the weekend getting drunk in Point Reyes is almost too good to turn down.

I make the thoughts stop by gripping his hand tight. "We'll do it, man, for sure. Let's just do it right."

He won't meet my eyes. "I don't know if that's gonna happen, though. You know what the guys'll say. They won't let us."

I stand on tiptoes and give him a peck on the cheek. "Yeah, they fucking will."

Someone on a motorcycle shoots past, the sound way too loud, dopplering into the night. The tiredness comes rushing back, settling on me like a blanket.

"I gotta go," I tell Carlos. "*Hasta luego, cabrón.*"

He forces a smile onto his face. "*Sí. Hasta luego.*"

But as he turns away, the worry comes back. The uncertainty. The feeling that I've just let an opportunity go, and I might never be able to get it back.

NINE

Teagan

There's traffic on Slauson, because this is LA, and not even the fact that it's nearly 1 a.m. can change that. The Batmobile moves at a crawl, inching along behind a rumbling train of Priuses and Civics.

Maybe it's a good thing I'm not driving at sixty right now. I didn't get formal driving lessons until after I arrived in LA. Before that, it was just Dad's truck in our backyard, which meant I could drive, but knew dick-all about traffic signals and road laws. Driving takes concentration, and right now I can barely keep my eyes open. My stomach is *not* happy with me, and neither are my lungs. Even this far south, the smoke from the fires in the north worms its way down my throat, turning it scratchy.

Normally, I like to blast music while I'm driving—the Batmobile's speakers are ancient, but it's got decent volume. No Bluetooth or even a CD player—just a radio. Right now it's tuned to Power 106, which is playing a bunch of old-school rap. Volume down low. Every so often a bunch of ads will play: car commercials, shady loan offers, ads for Universal Studios. The kind where they squash the terms and conditions into about three seconds of voiceover at the end of the AD, making it sound like the guy reading it snorted an entire bag of coke right before he got in the booth. I let it wash over me, comfy as a security blanket.

I love Los Angeles.

Even now, when I'm exhausted and cranky. A lot of people hate it—even those who live here. Too smoggy, too expensive, too full of actors and writers and shitty movie people. They hate the fact that it hardly ever rains or gets cold, which is insane to me. But I fell in love with the place from the day I got here. I love the huge sky, the constant hum of traffic, the restaurants and bars it feels like only you know about. I even love the history, although there's no way I'd let Annie know that. I love how nobody here gives the tiniest shit where you come from.

And I fucking *adore* the music. I'll admit: there are a lot of gaps in my knowledge. Most of what I got growing up was what my parents listened to, and most of *that* was what happened to be on the radio. Country, bluegrass, 80s pop. Nothing that held my attention for more than a minute or two. But I knew what hip-hop was, and after I came to LA I got a huge dose of it, right into the mainline. It was everywhere, and hearing it was like having a light come on in a dark room.

At the same time I'm not here by choice. I'm here because of Tanner and the deal she offered me. What does that make LA? A prison? Is it still a prison if you never want to leave?

I don't know. I don't have any answers, and I'm too tired and hungry to think of any.

On the radio a commercial ends—car loans, cable rental, I don't know—and there's a split-second of silence before the station ident plays. It goes on for a little too long, as if the DJ was caught napping.

The traffic doesn't let up as I dogleg south, heading for the late-night Thai spot. At the point where Fairview meets La Tijera there's a house party going on, a bungalow blaring bass, dozens of people spilled out onto the sidewalk, swigging from red plastic cups. My gaze drifts to the other side of the street, where there's a vacant lot bordered by a chain-link fence and overgrown with weeds. The fence is decorated with several ancient curling notices, cable-tied to the links.

Is that a good spot? Maybe . . . if I did it right . . .

It's not a good spot. It's a crappy piece of land in a not-too-awesome neighbourhood that would probably drain what little savings I had. All the same, I can't help but see it there. See the building, the tables and chairs through the slightly frosted windows, the big wooden door with the discreet metal plaque.

My restaurant.

Before I know what I'm doing, I've popped the glove box and pulled out my little spiral notebook. I don't have the energy to actually add anything more than the location details tonight, but it's filled with notes on ingredients, scrawled ideas for specials, hastily scribbled phone numbers and website addresses for equipment auctions. The sketches I've done of the interior, wildly out of any possible budget I'd ever have, with a huge zinc bar and reclaimed wooden tables, a pinpoint-precise kitchen layout.

I haven't settled on a concept yet, but I will. Right now the front-runners are Italian or a classic steakhouse. I've toyed with the idea of Vietnamese, dreaming of the *pho* and *bahn mi* I'd cook, but I know I'd never do it better than the little mom-and-pop spots I've visited in countless strip malls across the city. It doesn't actually matter: I am still going to find a way to work in my own restaurant kitchen. Fuck knows how.

I haven't really got to that part yet. It hasn't stopped me saving, squirrelling money away in the hope that one day...

Tanner will never let you.

There's a break in the traffic, and I take it, the Batmobile's engine grumbling as it takes me down 64th.

LA doesn't do late-night eating. Unless, that is, you know where to look. I do. I barely register ordering the takeout, which is fine, because they barely register me. I've been coming there for a whole year, and I don't think the girl behind the counter has said more than three words to me. Not that I care right now. In minutes, I have steaming bag of plastic containers stuffed with pad thai and a side order of mango salad, the gem-like segments slick with juice. Most of it is gone before I leave the parking lot.

Twenty minutes later I'm in Leimert Park. Home.

Roxton Avenue is deserted as I pull the Jeep to the kerb. As the thump of the Batmobile's door echoes into the night, I stand for a second, my legs a little unsteady. The street lamps turn the gnarled jacaranda trees into fractal shadows on the pitted tarmac, and the Spanish-style bungalows with their tiled roofs are dark and silent. Somewhere, very distant, a dog barks, just audible over the hushed traffic.

There's another sound too—the clinking of bottles. I look down towards the end of the block to see Harry pushing his bulging shopping cart. His belongings are wrapped in black plastic bags, hanging off the side of the cart like pontoons.

Anand, my landlord, pointed him out after I moved here. Said he wasn't quite right in the head—that he went out of his way to avoid people even as he walked the streets and never asked anybody for food or change. I don't even know if his name is actually Harry, or if that's just what Anand decided to call him.

A lot of the neighbours don't like him because they're assholes. But he waters the jacarandas, and doesn't make too much noise, and picks up any litter he sees. He comes and goes at odd hours, a gaunt figure with a huge scraggly black beard over a surprisingly pale face that could be thirty or fifty, his blue raincoat a common site on the street.

I try to remember to leave any empty bottles I have out on the kerb for him, so he can get the deposit back, and they're always gone a few hours later. I kind of wish I could do more for him, but I don't really know how to start. It's one of those things I need to get better at.

My spot is actually a tiny construction at the back of the bungalow on my right, built by my landlord to rent out. As I turn towards it, my subconscious, which has been trying to get my attention for quite a while, grabs hold of me a little more forcefully.

There's a car cruising down the block towards me, head-lights splitting the night. One I'm pretty sure has been following me since I left the Thai place.

It's one of those things you're aware of but don't think much about: the same car always in your rear-view, making the same turns you do. Maybe it's because we spend so much time on freeways in this city, where cars can sit behind each other for an hour or two, or maybe it's because I'm so damn tired, but I just didn't spot it.

A drop of lead falls into my stomach. Yeah, it's definitely been tailing me. I recognise those headlights, even if only at the back of my mind. I stand frozen, takeout bag clutched in one hand. Shit. Is it because of the Edmonds? Some other job we pulled? A loose end we didn't tie up?

Unless it's Tanner's people.

Don't be stupid. There's no reason for Tanner to take me

out, and if there was, she'd be a little more forceful than this detective-novel bullshit. But if whoever is in that car does make a move, what the hell am I going to do? I don't dare use my ability in public. Not if I want to actually remain in public.

And at that moment, just behind me, there's the sound of very soft footsteps.

TEN

Teagan

At that point instinct grabs hold of my worry about not using my ability in public and knocks it the fuck out.

I spin round, the takeout bag swinging, already wrapping my mind around the first thing I see: an empty plant pot at the edge of a nearby driveway. And there *is* someone behind me, a figure looming out of the darkness.

I grab the pot, start to lift it—and stop cold.

"*Nic?*"

Nic Delacourt lifts both hands, a bemused expression on his face. "Whoa. Hey."

I blink at him, utterly stunned. There's the sound of an engine, and the approaching car accelerates past us. The driver is a thickset, bald, middle-aged dude. He doesn't look in our direction, just coasts off into the night.

"Didn't mean to scare you," Nic says. He's wearing a black button-down over dark jeans. His shaved head gleams under the street lights, as does the slim silver band on his left index finger.

"Wha..." I'm having trouble working my tongue. "Wh-what are you doing here? It's like one in the morning."

"I actually arrived at about nine?"

"Nine." I stare at him. "You've been waiting here since nine."

"Pretty much."

"Four hours."

"Uh-huh."

"Just sitting here."

He looks sheepish. "Yeah, I kind of fell asleep."

"Fell asleep?"

"On your doorstep."

"You didn't maybe think to call? Or text?"

"Uh, did you maybe think to check your phone once in a while?"

"There's nothing on my..." My phone. My *dead* phone. Which had a billion notifications and app alerts on it anyway, and which I haven't exactly been paying attention to tonight.

"I put it on silent," I say.

He raises an eyebrow. "Really."

"And I thought you were supposed to be in Vegas this weekend?"

"I was."

"So why—"

"Look." He holds out his hands. "You weren't answering, so I decided to come knock on your door. When you weren't here, I figured I'd sit and wait. But it was a long drive back today and I just drifted off. I know that's creepy, but I swear I didn't mean for it to happen like that."

"Dude..."

"Can I come in? Just got something I want to run by you."

I blink back at him. "Um, OK? That sounds kind of ominous."

"It's not. I promise."

The adrenaline is draining out of me now, leaving me

hollow and sore. I have to stifle a yawn. "Dude, it's good to see you, but is there any way we can do this tomorrow? I'm really tired."

"Five minutes. That's all I ask. And I promise you won't regret it."

"Nic…"

He spreads his arms wide, flashing a huge, winning smile. I know that smile well. It's one that has got him past countless park rangers who want to see his climbing permits. The same one he uses on surfers in the line-up, at far-flung spots up the coast where the unwritten rule is locals only. On hostesses who claim not to have any tables left. It doesn't hurt that he's easy on the eye. He looks like Chadwick Boseman from *Black Panther*, only with a shaved head and a sense of humour. I loved that movie, but T'Challa wasn't exactly Mr. Good Times.

I've known plenty of people with a smile like his. The difference with Nic is that it doesn't vanish when he's got what he wants. It's one he wears all the time, no matter who he's talking to. There's no deceit behind it. No slyness. It's as honest as a cup of coffee, and about as impossible to resist.

"Come on," he says. "I camp out on your doorstep the whole night, and you're not even a *little* bit curious?"

I close my eyes. Which is a mistake, because the temptation is to keep them closed and just pass out right there.

"Fine. But if you take too long, I'm gonna crash and burn on you."

The smile gets even bigger. "Yes! Thank you. I promise you won't regret this."

We head across to my place. It's through an archway on the side of the house. We have to be quiet, as the path goes right by my landlord's bedroom window. I'm in a little extension, accessed via a flagstone courtyard.

As we make our way through, I have to tell Nic to walk a little more quietly. He's a big dude, six four at least, and he has this way of walking where every footstep sounds like he's trying to kick holes in the ground.

I do have a few friends outside work. Shocking, I know. Nic is one of them. He's a local, born and raised in LA, the son of two schoolteachers from Pico Rivera. I'd grabbed a spot at the counter of a new bar in Little Tokyo and was busy slurping a pretty good bowl of ramen (with kimchi in it—unusual, but not a deal breaker) when Nic and his girlfriend Marissa sat down.

We got talking, and then we got drinking, and then we were exchanging numbers. Unlike a lot of people, they weren't too bummed out by the fact that I wasn't on Facebook or Instagram. And the one big thing we had in common was food. Both of them were *obsessed* with food.

Marissa—a sound designer for one of the big studios— has always been a little cool with me. Perfectly polite, just distant. Nic, though? We clicked. It was like we'd been friends for our entire lives. He is incapable of saying no to anything, ever. Whether it's eating something seriously out there like cricket stir fry—surprisingly OK, once you get past the wings—or taking a last-minute trip up to Joshua Tree to go bouldering, he wants in. Even though he probably twisted an ankle on the last climb. He's enthusiastic, but not very good.

When he's not climbing sheer rock faces and jumping out of aeroplanes and surfing massive winter swells, he works as a special assistant in the district attorney's office. A lot of my surprise at seeing him tonight is because I wasn't expecting to run into him until Monday or Tuesday. He was supposed to be at a law conference in Las Vegas this weekend with his boss.

"Why didn't you call out or something?" I say over my shoulder. "You scared the shit out of me." *And I almost brained you with a flowerpot.*

"I did. Said your name like three times. You didn't turn round."

"Sorry. Been kind of a long night."

"Out with the guys?"

"Yeah, um. Annie had us over for dinner." Jesus. The only way Annie would have me over for dinner is if I offered to renovate her kitchen for free.

"*Annie?* The psycho one from Watts?"

"Yeah. She's surprisingly OK when you get to know her." *Ugh.* "How come I didn't see your car?"

"Parked round the block. Didn't want to ruin the surprise."

"What surprise? I still don't get it."

"You'll see. Hey, if you went for dinner, what's with the food?"

I'm fumbling with my keys and don't quite catch his question. "Huh?"

"The takeout. Didn't you say you ate at Annie's?"

Dammit.

"Just feeling hungry on the way home." I put my key in the lock, glad that it's dark, and he can't see the flush creeping up my cheeks.

He sniffs the air. "Bangkok Central? 64th?"

"How did you—"

"You're predictable, Frost."

I crack the front door, reaching out to flick on the hallway light. Behind me, Nic scuffs his feet heavily on my doormat.

My government salary isn't huge, but it's OK. It lets me

afford a place slightly nicer than the LA average. When Nic asked about it, I just told him I got lucky with the rent. I could probably save more if I moved to San Pedro or the North Valley, but I like the neighbourhood, and I like my landlord. I put up with the tiny living room and the kitchen that's more like a broom closet and windows that need a major coat of paint.

There's a full clothes horse against one wall, and a whole stack of boxes I haven't unpacked from my move a year ago. Anand was cool with me painting the walls an amazing scarlet, but the paint pot is still in one corner, long since crusted over.

The couch is old but comfy, with a good-size coffee table in front of it—one which, I'm a little ashamed to say, still has a plate with the remains of the carbonara I cooked last night. There's no TV, mostly because I never got around to buying one. What I do have are boxes and boxes of records next to a vintage turntable on a battered dresser. I get them from thrift stores, and from the amazing Fat Beats. The speakers—a big black pair of Yamahas I got for nothing at a yard sale—are probably the thing I care most about in this place. They've got a particular sound that I love, which I'm sure is the result of years of dust and grime building up inside them.

Also cookbooks. Everywhere. Plus every restaurant memoir I can get my hands on. I read odd passages while I stir risotto, or while I'm waiting for my coffee to brew. Also while I eat, and while I'm walking around my apartment. There are even one or two I keep in the Batmobile, to read when I'm stuck in traffic. A dog-eared grease-spattered copy of Anthony Bourdain's *Kitchen Confidential* lies face down on the kitchen counter, spine broken.

There are a few books of poetry scattered here and there, too. I'm a sucker for old-school poets—Ezra Pound, T. S. Eliot.

That crowd. I still don't really know why their poems get to me, but they do, and I like to keep them around.

In one of her few moments of not being a bitch, Tanner said I could pick a new name for myself when I moved to Los Angeles, if I wanted. My first name took a lot longer than I thought it would. Eventually I picked an Irish name. Teagan means "little poet," which was silly—I don't have a drop of Irish in me—but I liked it. I chose Frost as my surname, after Robert Frost, who is at number-one position on my Top Five Dead or Alive list.

And as it turned out, the universe wanted me to pick that name. It was Carlos who told me about one of the pioneers of LA hip-hop, Kid Frost. After I heard that, the deal was done. No way I was picking any other name. Even if the big song that Kid Frost is known for, "La Raza," has *not* aged well. To enjoy it, you have to be really drunk and in the mood for stupid karaoke.

We crash on my couch, Nic with his legs stretched out, me cross-legged, digging at the plastic bowl of pad thai with a pair of chopsticks. "So you're done with the conference?"

"Kind of. It's only wrapping up on Sunday."

"I don't get it. Aren't you gonna have to go back to Vegas?" I pull out my phone, glance at the clock. "You need to have to leave in like four hours." Another thought, one that makes me frown. "Where's Marissa tonight?"

He shakes his head, not meeting my eyes. "They don't need me there."

It doesn't escape my notice how neatly he dodged the question about his girlfriend. "Really? I thought they told you—"

"Look, what are you doing tomorrow night?" Nic leans forward, elbows on his knees.

"Um...nothing, I don't think. What—"

"Cool. Listen, I'ma pick you up at like four-thirty. And we gotta dress smart."

"OK." I swallow a mouthful of food, trying to keep the confusion out of my voice. "What are we doing?"

"It's a surprise."

"What? Tell me."

I flick a tiny bit of sauce at him from the end of my chopsticks, and he ducks, laughing. "Tell *meeeee*."

"Fine. I'll give you a clue. Plum granita. And don't you dare google—"

"N/Naka." Thank God I've already swallowed my latest bite of pad thai, because my mouth drops open. "We're going to N/Naka?"

"What? How the fu—" He throws up his hands. "Of course. You've been perving the sample menu on the site. Should have known."

"*You got a table at N-fucking-Naka?*"

"It's an early reservation—like five-thirty. I did a favour for an attorney I know, one Niki Nakayama sometimes uses, and..."

I nearly upend the takeout as I start screaming, knowing I'll probably wake my landlord up and not caring. N/Naka. One of the best restaurants on the planet, with tables booked years out and an endlessly shifting Japanese *kaiseki* menu. It's the Los Angeles Holy Grail, the Great Mission that Nic and Marissa and I have talked about for months but never actually pulled the trigger on.

I'll have to figure out how to pay for it. N/Naka isn't cheap. Obviously. With drinks and tip, you're looking at five hundred bucks—not easy on my salary. But fuck it; I don't want to let a chance like this slip away. He was right: this was *totally* worth camping out on my doorstep for.

"Marissa must have flipped her goddamn lid." I collapse back against the couch, already tasting the plum granita and otoro tuna and wagyu beef.

He doesn't say anything. When I look over at him, his eyes are on the floor between his feet. The smile is gone.

"Wait. You *did* tell her before me, right?"

"She's not coming," he says.

"What? Dude, if you could only get a two-seater, it's totally cool. I don't mind if just you guys go." It is *not* totally cool, but I am also not a complete asshole.

"No, she's..." He sighs. "We're taking a break. Maybe a long one." He lets out a breath in a long, slow sigh. "We had a fight before I went to Vegas. She wants to move up to Vancouver—they do a bunch of filming up there, and you know she was born in Ontario, so...anyway, I don't think it's going to work."

Oh no.

"But I've been thinking. About you and me. Because I *love* hanging out with you, Teagan, and I think we work well together. So I figured, why the hell not? I was going to burn the favour with Jerry Hale at some point anyway, and I just thought, you know?" He's speaking quickly now. And he's got this look in his eyes: like he's eyeing the horizon, watching as a wave builds and builds, already planning how he's going to ride it. "I was kind of hoping I could ask you there, maybe see if you were up for it...and of course *you* spend all your time stalking sample menus online, so..."

Shit. Shit fuck ass goddammit.

This is why he showed up unexpectedly. I'm not exactly sad to see Marissa go, but I didn't think he'd...

Who am I kidding? Of course he'd do something like this. I just didn't want to see it coming, because now I'm going to have to tell him no, and I'm going to have to lie about the reason.

God. Fucking. *Argh*.

He's waiting for a response. Slowly I put the pad thai down on the coffee table.

"I don't think it's a good idea," I say.

"What? Why?"

"Because…because you shouldn't give up that easy. You and Marissa…you guys are good for each other." *Really, Teagan? Really?*

"Yeah, but…" Now he looks like the wave has dumped him and is busy dragging him across the seabed.

"I just feel like you need to give it a chance. She's angry, you're angry, everybody's angry." I'm flailing now, constructing an argument on the fly. "I know how you feel about her. Don't let one fight mess things up for you."

I grab his hand, grip tight. "I do appreciate you asking. Really, I do. But I…We're friends. I'm not really ready to take that step yet."

There's a silence. A very long, very awkward silence.

"So." Nic won't look at me. "Do you want me to cancel N/Naka, or…"

"What? No. Definitely not." I force a smile. Last thing I want is for him to burn this favour for good. "We'll go. Just… as friends. I'll be there."

"OK. Cool."

Another silence. Nic's face is impossible to read. Looking at him, I feel a little part of me wither and die. Because he's right. We do work well together. He would make an amazing boyfriend. God knows, I've thought about it before.

And I can never, ever have him. Or tell him why.

The worst thing is, he won't ask again. Or at least, not for a long time. I've seen how Nic treated Marissa, how much he respected her. He's not one of those douchebags who refuses to believe that no means no, who thinks having a woman is their *right*. Those fuckers can go die in the street. If I've said no, he'll respect that. But...

I shouldn't feel guilty. That way lies madness. At the same time, it's going to change how we relate to each other from here on out. What is it going to mean for our friendship? I have friends outside work, but we're not talking double digits here. I really, really want to keep the ones I have. Nic is a good dude, but he's also human, and he isn't immune from feeling rejected.

"So. Four-thirty?" He gets to his feet, straightening his shirt.

"Yeah," I say quietly. "I'll be here."

I walk him to the door, give him a hug. He smiles at me as he steps out, as if our entire conversation never happened. As if we were just two friends shooting the shit on a night off. He walks away without looking back, his body swallowed by the shadows.

I stand in the doorway for a moment, body sagging against the frame. In the distance Harry's cart is moving along the sidewalk, its load of bottles clinking.

I hate lying like this. Not telling him the truth sticks in my gut. But what else am I supposed to do? How am I supposed to date him, knowing at any point he could discover that China Shop isn't a moving company and I don't have what you'd call a regular job? How am I supposed to be with someone when I have to lie to them?

Superheroes in comics and in movies pull off that secret-identity shit all the time. But this isn't a movie, or a comic, and I am definitely not a superhero. Secret identity? I can barely pull off the identity I have. I won't do that to Nic. I won't put him in that situation.

Oh, who am I kidding? That's just surface level. If that was the only thing stopping me, I'd figure it out. I'd find a way to keep my secret-agent life under wraps. The real reason I can't date Nic is because of a quiet voice inside me. *You don't want another Travis. You don't want that to happen again.*

Travis.

A name I'd sooner forget, and one which I'll never be able to.

Oh, fuck this. I'm sorry, but fuck it. Right now I'm so tired I'm not sure I can make it to the bedroom, let alone get my clothes off. Solutions to life's problems can wait.

Somehow I find my way to the bed. Kick out of my pants, swap my shirt for an oversized Lakers T, brush my teeth. Put my phone on charge. I make sure all the windows are open in the hope that at least some cool air will sneak in, then I collapse on top of the bed.

The last thought before sleep takes me is that Nic smelled nice tonight.

ELEVEN

Jake

Jake's hands are shaking.

He did it.

He really did it.

His first task. Complete. One step closer to finding out who he is.

His bike is parked on the corner of 6th and Figueroa, nudging up against a street lamp. At this time of the morning there's hardly anybody around. The only sign of life is a homeless person limping across 6th, right where it starts to curve over the freeway. Jake crosses to his bike, and it's only when he tries to sling his leg over that he realises it isn't just his hands shaking. His entire body trembles, as if an earthquake is rumbling up through the Californian earth.

Nobody stopped him. Nobody saw him. They didn't even know he was there. He slipped in and out like a ghost. It shouldn't have been this easy, this fast. He rolls it around in his mind, trying to find a mistake. He can't. So far, on this glorious night he hasn't let Chuy down.

"I did it," he says. His hands are sweaty, so he blows on

them, barely aware that he's doing it. "I did it, Chuy. It's done. I handled it. I did."

Should he send Chuy a message? Call him? No—better to breeze through the other tasks and only then make the call. The conversation unfolds in his mind. *Yeah, it's done. For sure. Nah, no problems, we're good. Thank you, I appreciate that.*

Headlights. Bathing him and the bike in a yellow glow. An electric car moving silently through the night, creeping up Figueroa towards him. Jake tenses, his Gift feeling out everything nearby. The street lamp. A trash can. The loose rivets on a nearby metal railing. The cute knee-height metal fence in the tree planters that border the street. If this person stops, if they get out the car…

But of course they don't. Why would they? He huffs a breath, another, calming himself as the car slides past. A Chevrolet with both an Uber and a Lyft card in the front window. The driver, a young guy with a trim moustache, glances at Jake. He looks away, uninterested, eyes back on the road. The passenger in the rear is shrouded in shadow. The car hisses past, vanishing into the night.

"You're OK," Jake says. There's no one around, not even the homeless man. Just the distant rumble of traffic from the 110. *You're OK.*

He smiles at the memory of her voice. He can always count on her. Even now, even when it would be so, so easy to give in. She's the only other person—outside of Chuy of course—to ever know about what he can do. He can't risk failing tonight because doing that would mean failing her. It would mean never finding out who she was, where she came from, and that way he'd never find out those things about himself.

Her name was Lauren. She was young—still a teenager when she had him, that much is certain. When he first began to show signs of his Gift, she wasn't scared. They'd been staying in a tiny apartment in Iowa—Sioux City, maybe Duluth, he's never been entirely sure—and he'd started to move objects around. Just a little—picking up his toy fire engine with his mind, moving a coffee cup from the rickety kitchen table to the sink, letting it rotate in the soft winter sunlight through the window, not even realising he was any different until his mom stopped dead in the arched kitchen doorway, a soft moan escaping her as she stared, wide-eyed, at the spinning cup.

She'd hugged him. Held him close. Hadn't said a word.

Those are his earliest memories. The coffee cup. The fire engine. The sight of his mother in the doorway. He has so little of her now, and he held on to those memories with all his strength. They'd kept him going through some very dark nights.

She never shrank from his power. Was never scared of it. He remembers the comic books she bought him. *X-Men* and *Justice League* and old issues of *Spider-Man*. He remembers her pointing to Jean Gray, a blaze of red and green and yellow leaping off the page, and saying, *She's like you. Like the girl version of you.*

And he remembers the one thing she taught him above all else. *Keep it a secret.* Never use it, not ever, not even if there was no other choice.

Most of his other memories of that time are a blur. The apartments changed—sometimes better, sometimes worse. The towns changed. One of them was Cedar Rapids, Iowa, he knows that much. It's a town he walked flat a few years back, coming up with nothing, certainly nobody who remembered either of them. Ditto for Cumberland, Ohio. He remembered the red-brick church, remembered standing before it, holding her hand. Cold wind searing his skin. Nothing else. Certainly no one who recognised him, no one who went, *Oh, you're Lauren's boy, right? You've got her eyes. How's she doing these days?* They'd found their way to Nebraska. Omaha. Big skies and wide dust-swept streets. He hates how incomplete his memories from this period are—the ones he does have are separated from each other like monuments in a vast desert. Their house, with a door that was nearly falling off its hinges. His mom giving him a new comic book—a new *Spider-Man*, although even that is unclear—and telling him to read it in his room while she talked to a man he didn't know: a man in a dark suit with a sweat-stained shirt collar. His face is a blur in Jake's memories.

And then one day his mom didn't come home.

They wouldn't tell him where she was. They wouldn't answer his questions. They just took him to another house— one with other kids and two grim adults who looked him up and down like they would a prize steer. No matter how much he cried and begged, they wouldn't tell him anything.

His mother is dead, of course. She was probably dead before he ever arrived at that house, because there is no way—ever, not in a million years—that she'd just leave him. He accepted that she was gone a long time ago. What he couldn't accept— what wouldn't go away, like an itch that he could never scratch—was that he didn't know what happened to her. More than that: he didn't know a single thing about her or where he'd got his Gift from. If she didn't have it, then why did he? Who was Lauren? He didn't even know her last name.

And they wouldn't tell him.

He'd tried. He'd asked. He'd demanded. He'd thrown things. Not with his power (*never use it, not ever*), but he'd thrown things. He'd been labelled a problem child almost from the beginning.

He didn't last long at the first house. Or the second. Or the third. Eventually, they put him in a house in Lincoln run by a crotchety, overweight old lady called Denise. The three other boys in the house barely talked to him—it was if they were worn out, like toys where the batteries had been drained to almost nothing. Undaunted, he'd asked Denise the same question: *Do you know who my mom was?*

She went to Brazil, Denise had said, a smile twisting across his face. *Went to convert the Indians in the darkest jungle.*

Jake had stared at her, eyes huge. When Denise roared with laughter, he'd leaped a foot in the air, bolting for the stairs. He'd shut himself in his room, frantically scanning a comic he'd gone through a dozen times already. Again he had no idea what to feel. She hadn't abandoned him for Brazil, wherever that was—no way, not ever. But then why would Denise say that? Where was Brazil, and why were there Indians in the jungle?

It took him three days to pluck up the courage to ask, and when he had, Denise had looked at him like he'd gone crazy. *What the hell are you talking about, boy?*

My mommy. You said . . .

And that strange smile had come a second time. Like she'd found a five-dollar bill in his jacket lining. *She ain't in Brazil, kid. She went to rob a bank. They killed her partner, but she got away. I heard she's hiding out in Mexico somewhere.*

Jake had screamed. He'd cried. He'd rushed at Denise, beating tiny fists against her midsection, while Denise laughed and laughed.

After that it was like she'd discovered a new game. She'd go to work at a second-hand clothing store in town, and in the evenings she'd drink her cheap gin and mixer, and lie to him. She'd tell Jake that his mommy was in prison, that she was trying to swim across the Pacific, that she'd joined the French Foreign Legion, that he'd dreamed her all up.

Once she told Jake that his mom had been upstairs the whole time, trapped in the attic. Jake had called her a liar, a *liar*, but later, when he thought Denise was passed out downstairs, he'd tried to pull down the stairs leading to the attic, balanced on a chair, fingers reaching for the hanging rope. Of course Denise heard him. Of course she roared with laughter.

The other boys didn't care. They didn't even have enough energy left to bully him.

By then Jake had more control over his ability. He still didn't have a name for it, but he was just starting to realise that no one else could do it. He fantasised about using it on Denise, shoving his little red fire truck down the woman's throat as he laughed. He never would. His mom had told him to never use it front of other people, and there was no way he was going to let her down. It would be like losing a part of himself, and he held to it even as the crevasse between them began to mist up, even as her shape on the far edge began to fade.

Denise is dead now. Heart attack. Jake didn't even get to see it happen. There were more homes. More grey kids. More harried, brusque foster parents. And still they wouldn't tell him anything.

He'd grown beyond comic books then, was reading more widely, and found himself obsessed with history books. World War II, Egypt, the colonisation of Australia, the Civil War—all of it. History made sense to him in a way that made-up stories didn't. This happened. Then this. And then this. And that is how we came to be where we are today.

Even when he'd aged out, the system wouldn't help him. Nebraska was one of the few states that didn't have an open adoption records law, and every agency he contacted came up empty. He didn't have enough money for a private detective, so on the morning of his eighteenth birthday he'd left the house he was staying in—a tumbledown structure on the edge of Lincoln run by a thin, feeble man whose name he now forgets—and struck out on his own.

The deal he has with Chuy is simple: he helps Chuy with three specific tasks, and Chuy will give him all the information he needs on his mom. On where he came from. Chuy can do it; he's proved it already, thanks to the photo.

Jake dips his hand in his jacket. The photo is still there, in the inside pocket. A printout on flimsy white paper. He doesn't need to pull it out—it's seared in his memory. He was only a baby then, a grinning little goon in a red sweater, but you could already see the resemblance to the woman holding him. Blonde, smiling, no older than sixteen or seventeen. A photo he hadn't known existed until Chuy gave it to him.

Jake clambers onto his bike. The shakes aren't so bad now. He guns the engine, then takes off, U-turning on Figueroa. He heads west, towards Hollywood.

Above and to his right, the Edmonds Building blots out the sky.

One down, two to go.

TWELVE

Teagan

The flames crawl across the ceiling, spread across the walls in huge, rip-pling waves. The axe is heavy in my hand, wood grain rough against my skin. Sweat stains the handle.

Laughter. Behind me. I turn to look and...

Music.

The dream fractures, real life forcing its way in. My body is completely paralysed, frozen by sleep. When it kicks to life, I jerk up from the pillow, cricking my neck, my eyes rocketing open. Music. My phone. Has to be. Did I not put it on silent?

I grope for it, hand fumbling in the dark. It flops against a water glass on my bedside table, knocking it over, water gulp-ing over the edge. "Shit."

The music is my ringtone: Rakaa's "Mean Streak." Great song. Loud and aggressive and fun. Unless it wakes you up in the middle of the night.

The phone is still in its flip-open carry case, an old one with this shitty little 3D unicorn thing on the back—a cartoon char-acter smoking an enormous joint, familiar under my fingers.

Reggie is calling. Did I oversleep? Nope. It's still dark

outside. The phone's clock reads 3:52 a.m. I've been asleep for
a little under two hours.

I hit the answer button, collapsing back on the pillow.
"What? Fucking what?"

"Teagan." Reggie sounds breathless.

My head is *pounding*. "Reggie, wh—"

"Red light, Teagan. Repeat, red light."

That wakes me up.

Our little team doesn't have cute call signs. I wanted us to,
but nobody would let me, mostly because I insisted that Paul
be known as Agent Whiteboard. What we *do* have is a series
of what Reggie calls lights: shorthand for when something
goes wrong on a job, and we need to act fast. You don't ignore
lights. Ever.

A red light is a bug-out, mission aborted, drop whatever
you're doing and regroup at the office. The only thing more
serious than a red light is a black one, which is code for *Move
to Oklahoma and change your name and never talk to anybody
ever again.*

"On my way." I squirm out of bed and immediately regret
everything. And not just because my feet land right in the
puddle of water. I am *sore*. Like I've run twenty miles, then
turned round and run all the way back—payment for the PK
I used last night. My stomach is an empty roaring hollow, and
my head... It's like I'm drunk.

Clothes. Some jeans, worn two nights previously and left
crumpled on the floor. An old Jurassic 5 tank top. I throw
my leather jacket over it, jamming an arm into the sleeve,
realising it's inside out, flipping it the right way round with a
strangled curse.

I stumble out of my place into the baking-hot night, get
halfway to the sidewalk before I double back, swearing, to lock

the door. Phone, wallet, both in my jacket, which it's actually too hot for right now, but whatever. House and car keys in my hand. Red light. Why the hell would Reggie call a red light? It doesn't make sense. The job is *over*.

I'm so lost in my own head that I don't realise Harry is there until I smack right into him.

He's just crossing in front of the archway leading to the street, pushing his overladen cart. If I wasn't still half-asleep, I would have noticed him right away, but I am, and so I don't. I hit his cart hard enough to send the black bag on top crashing to the sidewalk.

His soda cans explode across the street, clanging and clattering. Harry yelps in surprise, jumping back like he put his hand in a wall socket.

I skip around the cart on one leg, torn between wanting to yell at him and wanting to apologise profusely and help him get his cans back. He looks terrified, panic-stricken, still taking stuttering steps backwards.

I have to go. You don't fuck around with a red light. "I'm really sorry!" I yell, sprinting for the Jeep, leaving Harry gawping at me. It takes me three tries to open the Batmobile, and then about thirty seconds to start him up. My hands are shaking too badly.

It's a miracle I don't crash. I'm barely aware of what I'm doing, operating on muscle memory, zig-zagging the Batmobile in and out of the traffic as I head for Venice Beach. More than once, a fire engine rockets past me, its siren drilling into my skull, heading for the orange glow on the northern horizon. The HELLSTORM.

Thirty minutes later, I swing the Batmobile into Brooks Court, nearly knocking over the trash cans opposite Paul's Boutique, screeching to a halt behind the open garage door.

The van is still there. Before I'm halfway out the car, Paul pokes his head out the front door.

"You," he says, pointing at me. "Inside, now."

Normally, talking to me that way would get something pointy thrown at your head. This time I just shove past him. The drunk feeling hasn't gone away, and every single muscle in my body is letting me know just how much of an asshole I am.

They're all there. Carlos, leaning against the kitchen counter, arms folded, still as stone. Reggie and Annie, standing by the couch. Annie is still wearing her security-guard uniform—Jesus, didn't they go home? Either way, it's impossible to miss the grim expressions on their faces.

I come to a wobbly stop by the end of the counter, gripping it to keep myself upright. "Hi. Sorry. I'm here."

Reggie gestures to the couch. Her face looks even more lined than normal. "Sit down, Teagan."

"Just tell me wh—"

Annie points to the couch. The look on her face is total poison. "Sit the fuck down."

Movement behind me. Paul and Carlos. And they're not just moving closer to the group. They've both taken up positions at my six o'clock, between me and the door.

What the hell is going on?

I move to the couch, lowering myself onto it, sure that at any second I'm going to wake up. I don't. Carlos refuses to look at me, which is something he's never done, ever.

"You have some explaining to do," Paul says.

That does it. I leap off the couch, causing Carlos to take a step forward and Paul to take one back.

"Listen, cock-womble," I growl at Paul. "I have had two hours of sleep. I just drove halfway across the damn city, and if you don't tell me what's going on—"

With a slap, Annie plants a piece of paper against my chest. The poisonous look is still on her face. "This, bitch."

"Don't you tou—"

Then I see what's on the paper, and my throat just closes off.

The seconds that tick by feel like minutes. Eventually, I manage to force out a few words. "What am I looking at?"

"It's from the Edmonds Building," Reggie says quietly. "Thirtieth floor."

The paper is a printout of a photo. It shows a man in his early thirties wearing a tight black T-shirt. The picture quality is pretty good. His earrings, tiny diamond studs, glint under bright office lights. He looks familiar.

He's lying on his back on the carpet, his body lit by a camera flash. Eyes open, staring in horror at the ceiling. And around his throat...

It's a piece of steel reinforcement bar—what house builders call rebar. It's tough to see because it's almost *buried*, twisted tight like it was nothing more than a length of wire. It wraps around his throat three times, dug in so deep that it's almost decapitated him. The carpet around his body is soaked with blood.

"That's Steven Chase," says Annie. "Like you don't know already."

The room contracts, the walls inching closer.

"Got that off a police contact," Annie continues. "After Reggie got an alert for the building on their systems." She glowers down at me. "You wanna tell us something, Teagan?"

How the hell do you strangle someone with a piece of rebar? You'd need *immense* strength. Or...

The final piece slides into place.

"You can't think I did this?"

I didn't kill anyone. Why would I? How can they not know

that? And when do they think I did it? I was with them, and then I was with Nic, and...

And in between I was driving home. Alone.

"It's a fake," I tell them. "It's gotta be. You can't do that to a piece of steel. It'd break, wouldn't it?"

The thoughts are like water falling through my fingers. I hate how desperate I sound, hate how dry my tongue is in my mouth.

Annie grunts. "First thing we checked."

"Steel with a low carbon content bends just fine," Paul says quietly. "It's ductile enough."

"Ductile?" I look at him. "The fuck is—"

"It can bend. You can wrap it around something as long as you don't bend it twice at the same spot. Of course, you need machines to do it, unless..."

"Unless what?" But I already know what.

This is impossible. Whoever did this was just strong, maybe super-strong. Surely someone with enough upper body strength would be able to...

But that wouldn't curve the steel. It would *bend* it. The rebar would be kinked along its length. The one in the photo isn't: it's coiled like a spring, the curves smooth. That isn't possible. Unless, of course, there was an even force acting on it, applying pressure from everywhere at once.

Like the kind of pressure a psychokinetic might exert.

"Teagan." Reggie wheels her chair forward an inch. "I'd like you to tell us exactly what you did when you left the office."

I can't look away from the rebar. From the ruin that is the man's throat.

"Uh-uh," Annie says. "Don't just shake your head. Start talking."

"Teagan." Carlos sounds desperate. "Please. Just tell us what happened."

"I couldn't do this," I say. "There's no way. I'm not even *close* to that strong…"

My phone goes off. And this time it's a different ringtone. A very distinctive one: Britney Spears, singing about being a slave for you.

Slowly I lift the phone out of my pocket. That ringtone is assigned to exactly one person, and from the look on Reggie's face, she knows just who it is.

Tanner.

THIRTEEN

Teagan

"Good morning, Ms. Jameson."

Moira Tanner might have let me pick my new name, but she still calls me by my old one. As always, she sounds like she's leaning back in her chair, feet propped up on a desk. And as always, I want to drop the phone and run like hell.

I swallow. "I didn't do this."

"I am aware of the situation in Los Angeles." Her accent is soft New England, breathy and genteel. "And I find myself somewhat . . . conflicted . . . as to how I should respond." A slight noise over the phone, a shifting of expensive fabric against chair leather. "Please explain to me how tonight's target died."

The lights in the room are too bright. "I was with the guys," I say. "Then I got some food on the way home, then I was with a friend. Go look at the traffic cams on Slauson, you'll see."

"Ms. Jameson."

"There's no way I could have done this. No way. I don't know who did, but—"

"*Emily.*"

Her tone changes only the tiniest bit, but it's enough to cut me off cold.

"I did not ask for your whereabouts," she says. "I asked for an explanation of how this man died. I dislike repeating myself."

Which is when the most obvious part of this—whatever this whole situation is—slides into place.

I'm not alone.

"Who's out there?" I say.

"I beg your pardon?"

"This had to have been done by someone like me, right?" The implications are popping in my head like fireworks. *I'm not alone.* "But it wasn't me, which means there're other people out there with abilities. You said—"

"You know as well as I do that you were the *only* survivor of what happened in Wyoming. I shouldn't have to explain this to you. There is no one else with your ability." The way she says the word makes it sound like it has a bad taste in her mouth. "And if there were, do you seriously think I wouldn't know about them?"

After they brought me in, the people from the government spent *months* questioning me about my parents, getting more and more frustrated when I couldn't tell them what, exactly, had been done to me. And they got nothing from my genetic samples—nothing that would help them recreate the abilities in another person.

Of course, maybe they did eventually have a breakthrough—in the past year, perhaps, while I've been in Los Angeles. My DNA is still on file, so who knows what they figured out? But then...if whoever did this is working for them, why is Tanner asking me what happened?

Maybe she wants me gone, sent down for a crime someone else committed. But there are much easier ways to do that than framing me for murder. She wouldn't need to set me up. She'd just make a phone call.

And even *if* I'd wanted this man dead, I couldn't have done this. Bending rebar in this way takes strength I simply don't have. Which means whoever killed this man is much, much stronger than I am.

"I swear to you, I have no idea what's happening here," I say. My imagination is in overdrive: China Shop, Nic, my restaurant, my city, all of it gone, vanishing as a needle goes into my neck and a black bag goes over my head. "Just…just give me some time, OK? Let me figure this out."

"No."

"I don't—"

"I asked for an explanation, and I haven't got one. I'm disappointed in you, Ms. Jameson. I thought you understood our arrangement."

"Listen. Just listen to me, OK?"

"I've given your team orders to detain you. You're to wait there until you're collected."

"What do you mean *detain*?"

Paul has a gun.

I feel it before I see it. I was too messed up to notice before, but I'm getting it now. A Glock, it looks like. Big and hefty and mean. He's holding it loosely, almost casually, by his side. He doesn't look like a balding forty-something dad any more. He looks like he's back in the navy, standing on the deck of a cruiser, watching the enemy fighter appear on the horizon.

He's the only one with a weapon, but both Annie and Reggie are stone-faced. Only Carlos looks uncomfortable.

"What are you doing, Paul?" I say. There's no power in the words. None at all.

"I've asked Mr. Marino to secure you," Tanner says in my ear. "I'm aware that you can probably disarm him, but that that will change how you're treated later. Drastically." A moment's pause. Then: "Come in quietly, Ms. Jameson. Don't make it hard."

Paul moves the gun to his front, wrapping his other hand around the grip.

I bare my teeth. "Paul," I say, "you'd better be real careful what you do next."

His expression doesn't change. "Everything's under control here, ma'am," he says. He's talking to Tanner, even though the phone isn't on speaker.

I am not very good at planning ahead. I may have mentioned that once or twice. It's even worse when I'm angry, and right now my mood has gone from scared to mightily pissed off. So I reach out with my PK, right across the room, and rip the gun out of Paul's hands.

He tries to hold on to it, is nearly jerked forward onto his face. Ironically, he's too well trained to fire. His finger is away from the trigger, on the outside of the guard, and he doesn't have time to get it in there before I take it away from him.

Reggie's eyes go wide. Annie snarls, taking a step forward.

I don't like guns. But I'm from Wyoming, so I know what to do with them. I release the clip with my mind, letting it drop to the floor. With the gun pointed away from anything important, I pull the slide back, ejecting the round and catching it with my PK. The phone is still pressed to my ear.

Nobody moves. Not even when I drop the gun behind the couch.

Carlos looks desperately worried. Paul is more furious than I've ever seen him, and Annie looks like she wants to tear my throat out with her teeth. Even Reggie looks dark, eyes narrowed.

And there's something else there too. Not just anger: hatred.

As if their worst suspicions have been confirmed. Reggie, less so, but Annie and Paul...

A year I've been on this team. A year I've been working with them. They've seen what I can do, and they've seen me when I'm not doing it. We don't hang out much, but at the very least they treated me like a human being. Except that wasn't true, was it? It was all an act. Here, right now, this is how they see me.

A freak. Something not human.

My face is flushed, heat creeping up from the base of my neck. The shame makes me even angrier. Who the fuck are these people to judge me?

"Ms. Jameson—" Tanner sounds almost satisfied "—that wasn't wise."

How could she know what happened? The phone isn't even on speaker. Which means she expected it, was waiting for me to disarm Paul.

I'm breathing too loudly, like I've run a marathon. "Listen to me. Just for one second. If I were... If I did this, then why would I come in when Reggie called? And if I really am the only person with PK, why would I use it to kill someone?"

The words give me a little bit of strength, because what I'm saying makes sense. "If I wanted to kill someone, I'd shoot them. I'd frame someone else. I wouldn't use my ability, then just go home and wait for you guys to find out. Right?"

Silence.

"Just let me find out what's going on," I say. "I didn't do this, but I can't prove it if I'm... if you take me in."

"Your alibi doesn't hold up," Tanner says. "There was a period this morning that you were unaccounted for."

"You haven't even given me a chance," I spit back. "There'll be traffic cameras, like I said. The people at the takeout place. My friend Nic. *There's no way I could have done this.*"

"Then who did, Ms. Jameson?"

"I don't know."

"You do see the predicament I'm in, don't you?" Not a hint of emotion in her voice. "Come in, Ms. Jameson. If you really are innocent, we can—"

"What? Get me a lawyer? Read me my rights? When's my court date set for? Am I gonna be allowed to plead, or am I gonna be too drugged to speak?"

"Due process will be followed."

"Due process? Are you fucking kidding me?"

All the old fears are coming back, the days from before reaching out to grab hold of me.

"You know exactly what happens if you bring me in," I say. "Even if it turns out I was right, your bosses will never let me back out. I know how this shit works."

More silence. No one in the room moves.

"I have done everything you asked for," I say to Tanner. "Everything. You didn't give me much of a choice, but I did it anyway. I've been working for you for a year. I have *earned* a little trust."

"Is that so."

"Yeah. It is. You owe me this. Let me figure this shit out."

Still nothing. For a good ten seconds.

"Put me on speaker," Tanner says.

I do. Her voice, tinny and distorted, loses none of its menace. "You've got twenty-two hours."

"Twenty-two? Not twenty-four?"

"No, Ms. Jameson." She's speaking very softly now, which is never a good sign. "Twenty-two hours' time will be 5 a.m. Eastern Standard tomorrow morning. Five a.m. is when the director gets his morning coffee. And with that coffee he will either be receiving a full and complete explanation or a report

that you are in custody. Those are the *only* two options. Do I
make myself clear?"

Five a.m. Eastern. That's 2 a.m. here. OK. I can work with
that. "Yeah. Clear."

"Mr. Marino? Ms. McCormick?"

"We're here," Reggie says.

"You will keep control of the situation. Understood?"

Paul's mouth is set in a tight line. It isn't hard to see why:
the meaning behind the words is clear. If they fuck up, or let
me run, then it'll be on them.

"We understand," says Reggie.

"Good."

Tanner hangs up.

Annie strides to the window, her back to me. "This is
bullshit."

"I didn't do this," I say.

"Yeah, OK. We just got the Incredible Hulk in town. Or
someone *else* who can just, like, magically do what you do.
That's much more believable than you going off on your
own mission."

"Annie," Reggie says, turning to face her. "Dial it back.
Right now."

I point at the picture. My finger is shaking. "I didn't do
this," I say again. In the back of my mind, there's a digital
clock, numbers ticking down: 21:59 ... 21:58.

"I'm not helping you." Annie. Paul glances at her. "*We* are
not helping you. Not any more."

"Whoa." Carlos gets between us, hands out, like he's stopping traffic. "Enough, OK? *Tranquilo.*"

Annie ignores him, pointing at the phone in my hand,
clicking her fingers once. "Call her back. Call her back, let me
talk to her. I didn't have anything to do with this. I'm out."

And then we're all yelling: me, Annie, Paul, just screaming at each other. Paul looks like he wants to rush the couch, try for his Glock again.

"*That's enough.*"

Reggie's face contorts as she says the words, muscles corded in her neck. She doesn't raise her voice often. It takes a lot of effort—her lungs aren't very good. But you can still hear the military in her.

"Teagan," she says, "I want you to look me in the eye and tell me you didn't kill this person."

"You hacked the cameras before, right? Why can't you just do it again? You'll see straight away it wasn't me!"

"First thing I did. They're down across the whole building. Have been from shortly after you arrived back here. Could be they rebooted after we were there tonight—it's what I'd do. Break the whole system down. Or it could be something else entirely."

"What about traffic cameras? I drove home. They would have spotted me all along Slauson."

"Did you run a red light?" Paul asks.

"I'm being framed for murder, and you wanna know if I *ran a red light?*" I throw up my hands. "You know what, Paul? Yes. I ran every red light between here and Leimert Park. I also didn't check my blind spot before changing lanes, and I never once used my turn signal. Happy?"

"If you didn't run a red light, you won't be on the cameras."

"I... Wait. What?"

"Cams in this city only get footage if you roll into an intersection when you're not supposed to. They don't just run all the time. You know how much footage that would be to store? There's no point."

"Shit. What about the restaurant?"

"Maybe," Reggie says. "But my guess is they won't be open for a while. And they almost certainly won't store their security footage on a network. So I'm going to ask you again: look me in the eye—no, *Teagan*. Look at me and tell me you didn't kill this person."

My eyes meet hers.

"I didn't," I say with a lot more strength in my voice than I feel. "I swear."

Reggie holds my gaze for a moment more, then nods. "All right then."

"You don't seriously believe her?" Paul says. "Because I can't tell you how many irregularities there are in her story."

He stops as Reggie turns to face him. She looks old then. Old and tired.

"I get that you don't like each other." She straightens in her chair, chest rising and falling with exertion. "But you're so quick to judge her, you're blind to what's in front of you."

"Oh, come on," Annie says.

"Nah. She's right," says Carlos. "If she was gonna kill someone, why do it with her..." He taps his forehead. "You know? Doesn't make sense."

"We don't have all the facts," Reggie says. "And I agree with Carlos. It wouldn't have made sense to kill Steven Chase this way if Teagan didn't wanna get caught. There are things we aren't seeing here. That makes me nervous."

"So, what, we just let her go?" Annie jabs a finger at me. "She'll run. Just take off."

"You can't keep me here," I snarl.

"Annie," Reggie says. "What do you think happens if China Shop as we know it ceases to exist?"

It's hard to miss the sudden uncertainty that passes across Annie's face. Because she and Paul and Carlos must all be thinking the same thing. Without Tanner's protection, without China Shop, what do they have?

Reggie glances at me. "If Teagan really did do this, then it doesn't matter. China Shop's done, and so are we. But what if she didn't? What if there are things here we aren't seeing? Are you going to let everything we've built come to an end because you weren't willing to fight for it?"

"She'll *run*." Annie speaks as if she's amazed she has to explain this.

Reggie gets there before I do. Which is good, because I wouldn't have been nearly as polite as she is. "Do you seriously believe there is a place Teagan can go where Moira Tanner can't find her?"

"So what do we do, then?"

"We work the problem." Reggie lifts her chin. "Teagan included."

Annie chews on her bottom lip for a long moment. Then her shoulders slump, and she says, "Aight. We'll do it your way."

Behind the counter Carlos exhales, long and low. I sit down, burying the heels of my hands in my eyes, rubbing so hard that little sparks dart across the darkness behind my lids.

Again, that thought, something I never believed would be possible: *I'm not alone.*

Reggie spins her chair, wheels whirring. "Annie, work your contacts. Find out why someone would want Chase dead. We're pressed for time here, so get Carlos to help you. Teagan, the restaurant you stopped at tonight..."

"Bangkok Central."

"Bangkok Central. They won't be open, but perhaps we can talk to them when they are. Paul, you can help me work the databases. We need to see if there's ever been any mention of a person with Teagan's abilities."

"What should I do until the restaurant opens?" I say. But they're already moving. Paul follows Reggie through to the other room, where she has her Rig. Annie strides past me to the garage.

Carlos pulls on his jacket, getting ready to head out to join Annie. I push myself off the couch, gritting my teeth as my muscles protest, then swing past the counter and wrap my arms around him.

"Thank you," I say, my voice muffled by his jacket.

He returns the hug. "'S'OK. I know you probably wanted to murder Paul a few times before, but I'm pretty sure you'd never kill someone for real. You know?"

"You scared me. When I came in you looked like...like you thought I..."

"It was too much, man. I had to think it through. But I got your back, Teags, don't worry about it."

I hold the hug for a moment longer, then pull apart. My face is wet. Have I been crying? I turn away from him, not wanting him to see, then wondering why I don't.

My brain is starting to work again. I know who I can talk to. And I know exactly where he's going to be. If anybody knows about what went down at the Edmonds Building, it'll be him.

"Want a cup of coffee before you go?" I slide past Carlos. "I'm making. Actually, I may just have to drink the whole jug, so—"

A smile flickers across his face. "No coffee, remember?"

I pause in the middle of filling the machine with water. "Right."

"Carlos!" Annie shouts from the garage. "Come on."

"What you gonna do?" he asks.

I can't just hang around until the restaurant opens. Those

are precious hours I could be using. And now that I think about it, there *is* someone I can talk to.

"Skid Row," I say. "Maybe someone saw something."

He frowns. "That a good idea?"

"You got a better one?"

A loud honk of a car horn. "*Carlos!*"

He gives my shoulder a brief squeeze. "*Hasta luego, cabrón.*" Then he's gone.

I stand for a minute in the kitchen, trying to gather my thoughts. According to my phone, it's 5:13. That should be more than enough time to—

More honking from the garage. "Teagan!" Annie yells. "Move your damn car!"

Shit. I forgot where I parked. I bolt out the kitchen, slamming the door behind me.

Twenty-one hours and fifty-three minutes to go.

FOURTEEN

Jake

When he'd prepped for tonight, Jake had gone above and beyond. There was too much at stake not to.

It was Sun Tzu he turned to, as he usually did. He didn't have his own copy of *The Art of War*, sadly, but there were plenty online. It was much a historical document as a set of rules. Business people loved it, a fact that filled Jake with scorn. Sun Tzu hadn't written his text so that stockbrokers could close a merger.

What he'd taken from it this time round was *Attack where your enemy least expects you.*

He had had no choice but to hit his first target at work. Steven Chase didn't come to LA all that often, and his office was where he was going to be, so Jake had made do. But for the second and third targets, he and Chuy had decided to hit them at home. All of them in one night, before they even realised it was happening.

He's on South Fairfax Avenue in Faircrest Heights, west of downtown. The streets are clean and fresh, there are more than a few BMWs parked in driveways and the neat houses are dark and silent. He's parked the bike a few blocks away, not wanting any of the neighbours to later identify the distinctive blat of its engine, especially since he'd done a pass-by of the house a day before.

He's etched the house in his mind: a simple anonymous bungalow, grey with an attached garage. It's set back a ways from the street, a coil of tangled hosepipe on the browning lawn.

A poor approach would be to sneak through the backyard. All he needed was one insomniac neighbour casually glancing out of his rear-facing window at the wrong moment. Better to walk right up to the front door like he belonged. Housebreakers didn't come from the front.

Not that he planned on breaking in. Why would he? The bungalow might have burglar bars, but it was a sure bet that in this heat the windows would be wide open. It didn't look like the kind of place where the owner could afford AC. All he needed to do was find the bedroom and send one of his rebars at the sleeping form in the bed.

He'd been careful to clean the rebars in hot water before the night started, and had yet to handle them. He couldn't be completely sure he wasn't leaving trace for the cops to find, but it'd be a lot easier to stay undetected if he didn't actually have to enter the killing room itself. They're slotted into an oversized hiking backpack, slung over his shoulders.

He saunters up the walk, hands in his pockets, helmet tucked under one arm. When he reaches the house, he stops for a moment, gazing around him idly as if getting his bearings. Then he heads up the driveway, footsteps muffled on the dirty concrete.

The door has an opaque window set into it at head height. He pretends to ring the doorbell for the benefit of any unseen watchers. Then he strolls around the side of the house as if intending to rap on a window at the back. He knows precisely where the bedroom is; this isn't his first visit to South Fairfax Avenue or the first time he'd been to the back of the property.

The bedroom is in the north-east corner. Jake slips down the narrow passage separating the garage from the next house along, sidestepping a mower that looks like it hasn't been used in years. Above the house the sky is faded very faintly orange from the fires. The street behind him is as still as a church.

The window is open, just as he'd thought it would be. Quietly, without using his hands, he opens the zipper on his backpack, one of the pieces of thick rebar hissing against the fabric as it slides out, hovering beside his head.

The bed is parallel to the window, next to a nightstand cluttered with pill bottles and half-full drinking glasses. He peers inside, eyes adjusting, trying to spot the body under the sheets, only...

Only there isn't one. The sheets are rucked and folded, recently used, but there's no one in the bed.

It throws him, but only for a moment. His timing was a little off, that was all. The man might have got up to go to the bathroom, pissing out some water from one of the innumerable glasses on the nightstand. All he has to do is wait.

Which is when the baseball bat nearly takes his head off.

If the rebar hadn't been hovering where it was, right by his head, it would have. Had it been even a few inches higher or lower, the bat would have split his skull like a rotten fruit. The rebar rebounds, crashing into his head, sending him stumbling. He loses his mental grip on it, the steel whirling down the path behind him.

The figure swings again, grunting, a dark silhouette against the glowing sky. Jake feels the bat pass inches from his face, the tip nearly grazing his nose. It *whangs* off the burglar bars, and it's the sound more than anything else that turns Jake's legs to water.

The target had seen him coming up the walk. Jake had been so focused on appearing casual for any neighbours who might be watching that he didn't think about the target himself or what he might be doing. He'd thought the first target would be the toughest to get to, but of course footsteps outside an office, even late at night, are no cause for alarm.

The figure lifts the bat high over his head like a man about to split a log. Jake reaches back with his mind, grabs the piece of fallen rebar, and sends it whirring towards the man's throat.

His aim is off. He's reacting too fast, or it's too dark to see, or the adrenaline is making him shaky. The piece of rebar catches the man's raised arm, bounces off, clanging against the wall of the house.

The man grunts again, and the bat comes whistling down. Jake scuttles backwards, and the wood cracks against the paving stones. This leaves the man's neck exposed, his arms out of the way.

This time Jake does not miss.

The rebar, still held by his mind, flips off the ground and wraps itself around the man's neck, metal creaking as it bends. He drops the bat, staggering, clawing at his throat. Somehow he screams. His grunts get faster, each one becoming a high-pitched bellow, too loud, way too loud in the night air.

Jake—furious, terrified—reaches for the bat. He grabs it with his mind, drives it end first into the man's body.

Solar plexus. The words blare in his mind as he stands, shaking, in the shadows at the edge of the house. A disabling hit, a strike into a bundle of nerves. The man falls to his knees, and Jake drives another piece of rebar into his open mouth and out the back.

The man's cries cut off, his whole body jerking like a sleeper suddenly woken. The rebar exits through his neck, tunnelling through flesh like a worm, driven by the full force of Jake's power. Blood falls to the paving stones in a soft rain.

With a thought, Jake pulls the rebar fully out, flips it, aims it and shoves it deep into the man's left eye socket.

This time the man makes no sound at all.

Jake stumbles away, back towards the street. For a long moment he stands at the end of the driveway, bent over with his hands on his knees. His long blond hair hides his face like a shroud. Distant voices reach him from the far edge of the block, and he instinctively sinks back into the shadows.

Son of a *bitch*.

Slowly he calms himself down. It doesn't matter that he messed up. The dude's dead, isn't he? Or if he isn't, he'd like to know his secret. *Hey, buddy, I'm impressed. What is it? You work out? Eat your vitamins?*

He snickers, then laughs, the sound bursting out of him. He puts a hand over his mouth, his body shaking. For a long moment he believes—really believes—that he's never going to be able to stop. He'll just laugh, and laugh, and laugh.

Eventually the laughter fades. The shaking doesn't. That was close. Way too close.

But it's all good. The neighbourhood around him is silent— no sirens, not even any lights on in the houses. This heat, the guy'll start to stink pretty quick, but by the time anyone notices, Jake'll be long gone.

He half turns, intending to retrieve the rebar, then thinks, *Fuck it.* What does he care? He left no prints, and if there are any traces—hair, sweat, whatever—it's not like he's in a system. He's been very, very careful about that.

Another quick look around. Then a walk back towards

where he parked his bike, sticking to the darkest, most shadowy parts of the sidewalk. Two down, one to go.

A thought crosses his mind, dark and poisonous: Chuy betraying him, vanishing, leaving him with nothing. Nothing to stop him. Hell, maybe he'd even call the cops himself, tell them to look into a drifter with a motorcycle, hangs around the Mission sometimes...

Chuy wouldn't do that. He didn't do it before, and he's not going to do it now.

Are you sure? How sure?

The thought grows like a cancer, a tumour nestled at the centre of his brain. He's being set up. Chuy's using him...

He stumbles to a halt. Takes a deep breath, smelling smoke, jasmine, the scent of rotting garbage somewhere. Smoke.

Chuy could have betrayed him a hundred times already. He hasn't. He's not going to do it tonight. "Relax, compadre," Jake mutters to himself.

But he's still shaking. To calm himself down, he recites his favourite quotes. Sun Tzu: *Know thyself, know thy enemy. A thousand battles, a thousand victories.* Churchill: *The farther backward you can look, the farther forward you are likely to see.* They are less quotes than mantras, the words as close and familiar as a favourite shirt. As always, he comes to the one mantra that calms him most of all: an ancient one, written on the Temple of Apollo on Mount Parnassus two and a half thousand years before Christ. *If you ignore the excellences of your own house, how do you pretend to find other excellences? Within you is hidden the treasure of treasures! Know thyself and you will know the Universe and the Gods.*

Chuy won't betray him. Hell, Chuy could have blown the whistle on the very first day they met.

He, Jake, had come in from Vegas, where he'd been working construction. A guy on the road team—a big tattooed dude named DeSoto ("Like the old cars," he'd said when he introduced himself, flashing a mouthful of tarnished silver) had said he had a cuz in LA, Eddie, a guy who could hook Jake up with some work.

Only the cuz wasn't there. Jake got to what was supposed to be his apartment in Inglewood, and the woman who'd answered the door looked at him like he was crazy. "Ain't no Eddie here," she'd said, a squalling baby bouncing on her arm.

Jake had looked around the festering building hallway, looked at the plaster already coming out of the wall in chunks, the silhouetted figure at the far end with a joint glowing like a dying star, heard the deep bass from a dozen competing sources rattling the flimsy doors in their frames and decided not to push the issue.

He had nothing against any of it—he'd spent plenty of time in spots just like it—but the only work he was likely to find here was the kind that might get him killed. Either that, or caught, and he had no desire to plunge back into the system.

Once he'd aged out of the last foster place, the one with the cats—or was it the one with the old stereo?—the people who ran the country's databases had conveniently forgotten he existed. You'd think they'd keep an eye out, purely on the basis of how long he'd been in their care. (*Fifteen years.* As if he needs reminding.)

He'd kept his power to himself. He was proud of that. Even when he was young, he had a sense that it was a secret, that the people who ran the homes—grey, blurred faces whose treatment ranged from indifferent to actually abusive—would use it against him. And really, back then, what good was it? The most he could do was levitate a book across a room, which was a neat trick likely to bring a world of shit down on him if anybody ever saw him doing it.

He hadn't worried about the kids in care with him. He was big enough, even early on, that nobody hassled him. They were ghosts, moving through darkened hallways, nodding to each other in passing. Some were OK, some weren't, but sooner or later they all faded back into nothingness.

So he acted normal, hid what he could do. He bided his time, and when he finally aged out, he'd taken off. First in a stolen Nova, then, when that died on him, a bike he'd taken from outside a sawmill in Minnesota. He'd thrown himself into trying to find out about who his mother was, and how she'd given him this strange, miraculous Gift. He'd started at the first home he could remember and worked his way back, cajoling and pleading and wheedling information out of reluctant foster parents who only vaguely remembered him.

The state hadn't helped. The state—states plural, actually—simply didn't care. He was bounced from office to office, and the trail ran cold within weeks. Frustrated, he'd started looking himself, hitting the road, running jobs here and there to keep food in his stomach.

Drugs and booze were never an issue—he'd tried both exactly once, making sure he was alone while he did it, and all they'd given him was a crushing hangover both times—but God, he could have used some once in a while. Because he got nothing.

It had been 987 days since he'd left Ohio, and the last nugget of information about his past—a possible relative of his mother in Bucktail, Nebraska—had gone nowhere. As useless as the missing Eddie. It left him in a deep depression, and he barely remembers the days that followed it. Lacking anything better to do, he rolled through Fort Collins, then Provo, heading out to Vegas as the weather got cooler. The winter with the road crew is a blank space in his mind, save for DeSoto's flashing teeth.

The books he stole were the only thing that kept him going. He buried himself in history: American, European, Chinese. Obscure stories about the gold rush in Australia and the Boxer Rebellion. Things that had happened, that had been witnessed and recorded and written about. He mined wisdom from them, tucked each quote away like a precious jewel.

He'd experienced a flicker of excitement when he first hit the LA traffic, felt the cars cosy in all sides of him. Wasn't LA supposed to be a city of second chances? He'd read that somewhere, he was sure of it. What LA *was*, as a matter of fact, was a big anonymous American city. Just like all the others.

He'd made it work. He always did. He'd slept under an overpass in Pomona for a while, leaning up against his bike, lying half-awake, sure someone would try and take it from him. He still had a little money left over from Vegas, but not much, and he began to worry that he wouldn't have enough for gas. That would be bad news. He'd have to leave the bike, and if someone took it while he was gone...

He was down to his last ten dollars when he got a job, washing dishes at a crappy restaurant in Monterey. The owner advanced him his pay cheque in exchange for Jake working a bunch of unpaid overtime. It was enough—just—to fill the bike with gas. None left for food or a place to sleep, but that was OK. He'd been through plenty of shelters and soup kitchens, and he knew the score.

The LA Mission was the closest. He'd head up there for the 12:30 p.m. service: soup, rolls, the occasional plate of greens swimming in fryer oil. He thought he might be hassled, his blond hair and sharp features marking him out—it had happened before—but nobody bothered him save the usual hey-man-got-a-smoke-want-some-crack-good-good-smoke. He let it all wash over him, utterly indifferent. Homeless people, after all, were only human.

It had been a long time since he'd used his power. He'd been very, very careful to keep it under wraps, knowing that it would get him on the radar of the authorities faster than any boosted purse or unpaid diner bill or siphoned gas. There were times he almost forgot about it, going days without even noticing his grip on the objects around him. But of course it was a part of him, this strange power that he knew so little about, that came from nowhere and nothing and which would likely remain that way for ever and ever, amen.

The food tables at the Mission were set up in a big cafeteria room, noisy and hot and tight with bodies. He'd got his soup, his roll, his little pat of butter. He'd been walking towards an empty plastic stool at the far end of the table, his mind a million miles away. Someone had left a battered paperback— *Fifty Shades of Grey*, he'll never forget—on one of the stools. As he'd passed by, he'd brushed the book, knocking it off the stool.

He'd been holding his tray in both hands, and he didn't even think about it. Just reached out with his mind, grabbed the book. It hovered in mid-air for a full second before he realised what he was doing and let it go like it had burned him.

Panic surged inside him, feeling like it was going to burn him alive. A room packed with people, and he'd just used his power. He was fucked. It was over.

He hardly dared raise his eyes to look. When he did, tearing them away from the sprawled paperback with its artfully knotted tie on the cover, he realised that no one had seen. No one. Not a single person had looked in his direction. The hundreds of other homeless in the room were intent on their meals, their conversations, their petty arguments. He'd escaped.

He breathed out a long shaky sigh, so relieved that he thought he was going to pass out. And when he looked up, a woman was staring right at him.

He didn't know her name. She was just a volunteer, sweeping up some broken glass at the far end of the room, a figure in a flannel shirt with the sleeves rolled up, dirty jeans with a rip in one knee. But she'd seen. Jake knew from the moment he looked at her. *She'd seen.* And in her eyes...she was about to start yelling, screaming, *Holy shit, did anyone else see that?*

Except she didn't. She'd blinked, shaken her head and gone back to sweeping. She hadn't seen anything. He could almost see her mind working overtime to justify it. *I'm tired, done too much overtime, need a drink. Seeing things.*

Jake had moved on, trying hard not to shake. By the time he sat down, he was feeling a little more calm. It had been stupid to lose control like that, but ultimately it wouldn't matter. If she was going to start shouting or approach him, she'd have done it already. He was reasonably sure she wouldn't tell anyone.

Except of course she did.

She told Chuy.

By the time Jake reaches his bike, his earlier panic has dissipated. He actually finds himself whistling as he straddles it, dislodging the kickstand. Tuneless notes are obliterated by the *blat-blat-blat* as he kicks the engine into life.

He has only one more stop to make. One stop before he gets everything he ever wanted. And he is OK. Shaken, sure, but OK.

Know thyself and you will know the Universe and the Gods.

As he heads west, the sky behind him is just starting to lighten.

FIFTEEN

Teagan

How do I even start to describe Skid Row?

Maybe one word'll be enough. And that word is *bullshit*.

It's bullshit that there's a seven-square-mile homeless camp in the middle of downtown LA less than two minutes from the Edmonds Building. It's bullshit that two thousand people have to share nine dirty, stinking public toilets. It's bullshit that they're forced to take down their tents every day because some Los Angeles County official decided that it looks bad to have them up. It is *total* bullshit that the city's attempts to fix things have nothing to do with actually rehousing these people or taking care of them, but just taking advantage of the low rents to move in people they deem more respectable. Start-ups and hipsters and hacker spaces.

Do I sound preachy? Am I making you uncomfortable? Deal with it.

I love this town, but I will never understand how everyone here is OK with Skid Row. Then again, I don't have the first clue what to do about it myself.

It's nearly 6 a.m. when I park the Batmobile on San Pedro Street at the edge of Skid Row. It's actually a miracle I managed to drive the whole way over here. I felt like I was going to fall asleep at the wheel, and when some idiot in a Prius with a USC bumper sticker nearly drove into me on the 10, it actually took me a couple of seconds to react.

I am officially a danger to myself and others.

It's probably a good thing that I plan to go on foot from here. Skid Row's streets are full of people moving in weird, unpredictable directions, and the last thing I want to do is knock someone over. I kill the engine, then sit for a few moments staring out the windshield at nothing. Thinking.

About Steven Chase. And whoever killed him.

Whoever did it is another me—however the hell that's possible—only they're different. There is no way I could bend a piece of thick steel like that. I just don't have the strength.

It wasn't just my parents who tested my ability. If anything they held back. The government, though? They didn't give a fuck. They put me through endless tests at a facility in Waco, Texas. A crappy series of prefab buildings in the middle of a windy-ass desert. They wanted to see how far I could push my PK—range, power, precision, all of it.

They made me use my ability in extreme heat and cold and noise, which was a barrel of laughs, as you can imagine. They also subjected me to a fake kidnapping, bursting into my cell at three in the morning dressed in black ski masks and yelling in Russian, waving flashlights and automatic weapons in my face.

I broke three noses and two arms with a flying chair, shattered a kneecap with a desk and knocked someone unconscious with the butt of their own gun. I also didn't lift more than my maximum weight while doing it, which they somehow managed to monitor. Probably a good thing—if I had, those idiots might be dead instead of sitting in the infirmary with a cool story. And no, I'm not sorry. You put a gun to my head? I don't care if it's loaded with blanks. I will ruin your day. It's possible they could have repeated the exercise, but it's kind of hard to recreate a stressful situation when the subject will probably just roll her eyes and go, "What? Again?"

Point is: I have limits. Tested, confirmed limits.

After four years in that shithole, four years of stress tests and range tests and blood tests and stress tests and range tests and blood tests, they'd finally had enough. I wasn't going to be a soldier for them, nor was I actually giving them anything useful. They'd exhausted all their testing options, and at that point they were fairly evenly split about whether to cut me open and dig around inside me, or just put me in a very deep hole and forget about me.

Which is when Tanner stepped in. She had what she described as an alternative scenario. Perfect situation for her: if I ever step out of line, she steps out of the way of the people who want to cut me open and/or bury me.

Whoever killed Steven Chase did something that shouldn't have been possible. Who are they? How the hell did they get so strong? More importantly, why have they only appeared *now*?

I have to track them down. If I don't, then Tanner comes for me, and I'll spend the rest of my short life locked in a government black site. But if I actually do it, then the same thing will happen to whoever this person is. I'll never see them again. Tanner will make sure of that.

The only person out there who knows what it's like to be me will be gone.

You might not have realised it from my sunny demeanour, but being the only one of your kind sucks. And not the everyone-is-special-in-their-own-way kind of thing. I mean *literally* the only one of your kind. I want to find out how this person got their abilities. How they came to exist when everything my parents ever did was destroyed. But more than that, I just want to talk to them. If I could get them alone… just for a minute…

I make sure the Batmobile is locked and head north up San Pedro.

Skid Row isn't a camp with fences and gates. It's just an area of the city where the homeless congregate. Across 7th Street, the tents start appearing: grey and green and blue, torn in places, the early-morning sunlight bouncing off the fabric. They're pushed up against walls and chain-link fences next to vacant lots, buttressed against the outside world with barricades of shopping carts and black plastic bags. The shopping carts are all the same kind: bright red. A charity must have handed them out. And there's trash everywhere: torn flyers, used condoms, discarded cigarette packs. The sharp smell of urine winds its way up my nostrils, squats there.

There are surprisingly few people on the street. An old woman, leaning against a tree, lined face turned up to the sun. A man on the corner, rocking back and forth as he hugs himself, squatting on a piece of cardboard. As I approach, there's a figure coming in the opposite direction—a young Asian guy in clean jeans and a red button-up, sleeves rolled. I'm surprised to see him. He looks out of place on the grimy street. Then I remember how the start-ups and hacker spaces are moving in, taking advantage of the low rents. He's probably a tech-bro coder, working on an app that he thinks is going to make him millions.

The dude on the cardboard says something to him, and the guy just ignores it, even though he has to step sideways to avoid him, passing me without a glance. He's wearing a chain, thin metal links under his shirt. I can feel it. It would be so, so satisfying to give it a good *yoink* right now…

I don't carry a purse, just a little stash pocket in my phone's flip case for my cards and cash. I hold out a few coins, and the homeless man flashes me a toothless smile as he takes them, bobbing his head. He's not someone I know. The very faint burned-plastic smell of crack wafts up from him.

"You doing OK?" I say.

He shrugs, already starting to rock back and forth again.

I jerk my chin at the intersection. "Africa still over by the Mission?"

"*Africa?*" His voice is deep, sonorous, like that of an opera singer. "Africa over in Africa! You on the wrong continent!" Opera voice or not, it comes out as *connent*. He flicks his hands at me, as if gesturing me to get lost, then resumes his rocking.

No point arguing. I keep walking, leaving him behind, heading deeper into Skid Row.

There's more activity as I turn left onto East 5th, with several clusters of people huddled on the sidewalks, smoking, eyeing the block. A cop car rolls by, a meaty arm hanging out the window. It's impossible to miss how the people on the sidewalk turn away, duck their heads.

The sky is a pale blue, made hazy by the smoke. It's already baking hot, but a shiver snakes up my spine anyway. I've never liked cops. And the cops have never liked Skid Row. Everybody I've ever talked to in this place has been rolled up on, had their shit stolen. Everybody knows someone who's been shot.

The Los Angeles Mission is a big concrete complex ringed with tall, spiked railings. It looks like a prison, but it's where a lot of the people on Skid Row go to get help. It might be early, but the gates are wide open, and there are large groups of people milling around the entrance. The street smells of sweat, weed smoke, fried food. The sidewalk is slicked with spilled beer, although there are no smashed bottles anywhere—no litter of any kind, in fact. Even the pee smell isn't as bad here. A couple of kids dash back and forth, laughing, weaving through adult legs and red shopping carts.

On the other side of the street two people dressed for office work march past. Just like the guy before, they don't even look at the people outside the Mission.

I don't know as many people in LA as Annie does. I could live here twenty years and never build a contact list half as deep. But in the two years I've been here, I've got friendly with a few people. And getting some info from them is better than sitting around the office, waiting for something to happen.

Africa is one of those people.

It doesn't take me long to find him. It's kind of surprising I didn't hear him from down the block. He has a big, booming voice, bouncing from one slang word to the next in his thick accent, occasionally breaking into roaring gales of laughter.

He stands head and shoulders and chest above almost everyone in the crowd: a stick-thin seven-footer, wearing a faded dashiki under a ratty purple-and-gold Lakers jacket. He's telling a group of (much shorter) buddies something, and as I pull up he throws back his head to let loose another howl of laughter. Almost immediately, his head bobs forward again like one of those little drinking birds. It's a head that is way too small for his body.

I slide through the crowd, reaching up to tap him on the shoulder. I almost have to jump to do it. "Hey, big guy."

His face creases in a frown, before erupting in a massive smile. "Teggan!" he roars, slapping me on the back, nearly sending me sprawling to the sidewalk. "You *toubab*! What you do here, huh? You bored in Hollywood?"

"How you doing, man?"

The rest of the group makes way for me good-naturedly, although I catch of couple of suspicious glances.

"'M good, huh," he says. "And you? *Yangi noos, yaaw?*"

"Living the dream. Can I talk to you for a sec?"

"'Bout what?"

"Need some help with something."

I don't want to reveal too much in front of the group, most of whom I don't know, but then again what does it matter? All I'm trying to find out is if anyone's spotted anything weird around the Edmonds Building.

Someone calls Africa's name. He lifts his chin, looking towards the Mission gates, yells something in French. "Wait here," he tells me, loping off in the direction of the entrance.

I hang out, leaning against the fence, trying to look casual. Letting my mind drift.

"Spare a cigarette?"

I look up. One of Africa's buddies—a pudgy guy with a single wisp of grey hair hanging off his balding scalp—is standing in front of me, looking pissy.

"Nah, sorry. I don't smoke."

He doesn't miss a beat. "Change, then. Help a brother out."

"I...I can't. I gave it to someone already."

"Come on, man. I gotta eat." He steps closer, getting into my space. "I know you got—"

"*Hey.*" Africa pushes him away, hip-checking him. Africa being Africa, his hip is about level with the guy's shoulder. "Derek! Leave her, *sai sai!*"

The balding guy grumbles but moves away.

"Here." Africa shoves something into my hands—something hot and greasy, wrapped in parchment paper. Then he takes off, striding away from the Mission, beckoning me to follow. He's chowing down on half a sandwich, one he must have got from the Mission kitchen. What I'm holding is the other half.

"Hey, dude, I can't take this," I say, jogging to keep up with his massive strides. Even as I say it, I get the smell of the sandwich, and my stomach wakes up with a jolt.

"You look tired," he says over his shoulder. "Breakfast get you going, huh?"

There's got to be someone I can give the sandwich to. But we're away from the crowd now, and in any case not eating food given to you by a homeless guy would be shitty in the extreme. The bread is fried, filled with eggs and mayonnaise and something sharp and spicy. It tastes fantastic, even if it comes with a side order of guilt.

Africa heads over onto Wall Street, which might have the most ironic name in history. It's a sea of tents pushed up against each other like balls in a ballpit, surging out over the edge of the sidewalk. Africa moves between them like they aren't even there, alternately taking bits of his sandwich and reaching out to grip hands, fist-bump. I jog to keep up, only just managing to stop dots of mayo dribbling onto my chest.

Africa's tent is dark grey, one side with a square of rough neon-green fabric duct-taped across it. There's a mountain of bags next to the tent: backpacks, black garbage bags, duffels. A couple of cardboard boxes. All of them overflowing with clothes and knick-knacks. There's a nodding cat figure, a pile of old basketball jerseys, a framed portrait of Obama.

Africa's story is amazing. Or would be, if he could stick to it. He's been a cab driver in Portland, New York, Santa Fe. He's logged in Maine, smuggled gold in France, sold guns in Egypt—or smuggled gold into Maine and sold Egyptian prostitutes while logging in France, depending on what day you ask him. He swears blind that he worked in the secret service for Obama, which is about the only thing he's never gone back on.

When I first got to LA, China Shop wasn't quite ready to go. Reggie was there, but she and Tanner were still working out the logistics—Annie, Carlos and Paul hadn't appeared on the scene yet. Tanner had me shacked up in a shitty motel in Carson, and her instructions to me amounted to staying out of trouble and learning how LA worked. I got the sense she wanted to keep me as far away from the organisational stuff as possible—and what better way to keep someone like me in line than to give me a little bit of freedom? Which was just fine by me. I had things to be. Places to do.

I was under strict instructions not to use Uber or Lyft—after all that time in Waco, Tanner had to explain to me what those were. She gave me a debit card, told me to use cabs only and get to know the city while she set things up. I explored LA, eating in weird places and talking to as many people as I could. I took long walks on the beach in Santa Monica and went up to Griffith Observatory and ate at dozens of restaurants. After the time I'd spent in the grey hell of the federal government's care while they figured out what to do with me, LA was an injection of pure sugar into my brain. I walked around with my eyes bugging out of my head.

Africa was a dude I gave some change to, a hulking golem on the sidewalk selling old (definitely stolen) records out of cardboard boxes. We got talking. It was one of those weird, freewheeling conversations you have with someone when you've got nowhere in particular to be, and you're pretty sure you'll never see them again—although I was very, very careful not to mention too much about my past.

He read my palm (he's never mentioned palm reading again since that first meeting) and said that, according to my lifeline,

I was going to live for ever. Then he roared with laughter, cackling and smacking the ground with his open palm. It was hard not to like the guy. Over the next few weeks I found myself thinking about him at odd moments. Seeing that delighted face howling with laughter like we were both in on a joke that only we understood.

And I did see him again. Obviously. Ran into him as I was coming out of a Korean BBQ place. He knew who I was straight away and picked up our conversation right where we left off. His turf was the area around the Mission, and over the past couple of years we've run into each other quite a few times.

He's not a contact in the traditional sense—I've never used him to help with China Shop jobs. But he's not part of Annie's Army, and I've always kept him in the back of my mind. Just in case I should ever be woken up at 4 a.m. and be accused of murder.

There's a portable radio playing in Africa's tent as he unzips and clambers in, long legs stretching out behind him. "... latest reports coming in, with marshals saying that they may need to evacuate parts of Burbank and Glendale as fires continue to rage..."

Africa snaps the radio off, beckoning me inside. We squeeze into the tent. It's not easy, and not just because Africa takes up nearly all the floor space. There's another pile of bags inside, along with a dirty sleeping bag. The cold sidewalk leaks through the thin base of the tent, despite the growing morning heat.

"OK." Africa sits cross-legged, gulping down the last of his breakfast. "What you need?"

"You hear anything about what happened at the Edmonds last night?"

He frowns. "Bad things. Bad *gris-gris*."

"Right. I need to know who was there. If you saw or anyone around here saw anything."

"Why you asking?"

I meet his eyes. "I just need to know."

He makes the sign of the cross, muttering something. "Teggan, why you ask me this?"

"*Please*, Africa. It's important."

He bites his lip. It makes him look like a little kid.

"OK, sure, OK. I ask around. But you gotta do something for me, *yaaw*."

"What?" I don't dare look at my phone to find out how much time I have left.

He digs in one of the backpacks piled against the side of the tent, withdrawing a small battered cardboard box. "There's a woman on Main and Winston..." He sees the look on my face and gives me a huge grin. "Relax, *yaaw*? 'S not drugs. Nothing bad."

His words are drowned out by a helicopter passing above us. LAPD, no doubt, a black-and-white buzz saw, flying low over the city.

"Main and Winston," says Africa once the chopper is gone. "Her name is Jeannette. She got a red tent. Give to her, then you come back here this afternoon. Maybe have something for you 'bout four clock."

Four? That's ages away. No point arguing—it's not like I have a Plan B.

The box is about the size of my palm, the edges weathered and fraying. Inside something rattles. I debate looking, then decide against it.

"Main and Winston? That's like three blocks from here. Why don't you just go yourself?"

The cheerful glint in his eyes falls away. For a second there's something cold and hard looking out.

"You a clean white girl," he says slowly. "You look like you work at a job. Police don't like me. Don't like any of us." He lifts his hand, waving an imaginary pistol. "They not stop you."

"But if it's not drugs…"

His eyes narrow, and I trail off. There's nothing I could say here that wouldn't sound wrong.

The silence goes on a little too long. I clear my throat, stuffing the box in my jacket pocket. "Jeannette. Red tent. Got it."

He grins, the cold look vanishing. "Good, good."

It takes less than ten minutes to walk the three blocks. The streets are already starting to cook under the early-morning sun. The few businesses in this part of town are starting to roll up their shutters, and there are more cops rolling past. One of their cars is ramped up on the kerb just where Winston meets South Los Angeles Street, a man with dreads bent over the hood as a navy-clad cop frisks him.

Turning the corner from South Los Angeles Street onto Winston, I have a sudden urge to text Nic, to confirm N/Naka, to tell him that I'm sorry about last night—even if I have absolutely no idea how to say it. But of course he's probably still asleep.

Confirm N/Naka? Yeah, OK. I'll just wrap up this whole being framed-for-murder thing by half four this afternoon. Hell, if I work really fast, I'll even have some time to put on make-up.

I'm so lost in my thoughts that I almost don't notice how quiet the street is. There's exactly one guy behind me—someone I've been aware of, but not paying attention to, like the car that was following me last night. I'm aware of the keys and cellphone in his pocket, the chain around his neck—

Chain?

—and the gun in his hand.

I spin round. It's the Asian guy from before, the one who ignored the homeless man at the edge of Skid Row.

Before I can do anything, he fires.

SIXTEEN

Teagan

I bet you're thinking, *Pfft, big deal. Just stop the bullet in mid-air. Then turn it around and fly it up this idiot's nose with your mind.*

Ha. Oh, ha ha. Let me tell you something. A bullet travels at close to the speed of sound. I'm good, but I'm not that good.

And if it *had* been a gun he was firing, it would have been goodnight, Teagan. Turns out it's not a gun. It's a taser, something I realise a split-second before he fires.

Not that it helps. A taser prong launches at around a hundred and eighty feet per second. Still way too fast for me to stop. The frustrating thing is, I *almost* do it. In the moment before the guy fires I get the tiniest grip on the taser itself, manage to jerk it just enough that one of the prongs misses me.

The other one? That buries itself in my shoulder. Direct hit.

Every single cell in my body goes fucking insane.

I snap rigid, body trembling, unable to even blink. Thinking is impossible. Electric agony holds me in a vice grip.

I'm on my back, looking at the sky. The building next to me is a costume shop, painted a cheerful yellow. If I wasn't in more pain than I've ever been in, it'd actually be nice.

This isn't a mugging. Muggers don't use tasers. And I can't

defend myself. There are plenty of objects around me, chips of sidewalk concrete, trash in a nearby garbage can, the taser itself, but my PK has checked out. A billion volts will do that to you.

The guy comes into view, looking way too satisfied with himself. He glances up and down the block, checking for cops, probably—and of course there aren't any because there never are when shit goes really bad. They're probably off arresting one of Africa's buddies for being poor.

Police don't like me. Don't like any of us. But they not stop you.

Guess he didn't take into consideration douchebag hipsters with tasers. They're the ones you *really* gotta watch out for. The douchebag hipster in question reaches down and rips the taser prong out of my shoulder.

Fucking *ow.*

He flips me over, working silently, kneeling on my back and pulling my hands behind me. A car screeches to a halt close by. An accomplice maybe, here to take me to God knows where. Who the hell are these people?

Everything is fuzzy. I can't focus. There's the sound of duct tape being pulled from a roll. If I don't do something soon, I'm toast. If they know what I can do, they'll have more permanent ways of keeping me under control. If they don't, and I *do* use my PK around them, I'll just get tasered again. Being tasered, I can now officially confirm, sucks.

But that thought is followed by another. Tasers aren't guns. They don't have clips. You have to reload them after each shot. Which means I have a very, very short window where they can't zap me.

I have to move. Right fucking now.

It's like trying to jump-start a car on a freezing Wyoming morning. He's got my hands now, getting ready to tape them up. I bite my lip, focusing on the sharp jolt of pain, and buck him off. Or try to. He's got me jammed down, and my move is less of a buck and more of a wiggle, like a pinned snake.

No. The hell with that. I try again, determined to get rid of him. Of course I can be as determined as I want, but I am also recovering from a taser hit. So all I get is another feeble little wiggle.

He plants an elbow in the centre of my back, leans on it. "Don't move."

Duct tape sticks to my right wrist. I try one more time, squeezing my eyes shut and putting everything I can into just rolling over. Let me look this dickhead in the eye. Make him work for it.

This time I catch him at just the right moment. He loses his balance, has to put out a hand on the ground to steady himself, and with one more lurch, he's off my back. I manage to roll over, a pained grunt forcing its way out of my throat, morphing into a hacking cough before it's halfway out.

OK. Now what?

The glare from the hot blue sky makes me wince. The hipster is back almost immediately, knees planted either side of me. A look of annoyance crosses his face, and it's not just me this time. He assumes the same position without thinking, and of course he now has to flip me back over to get to work on my wrists again.

I work my mouth, lips trembling, trying to get enough saliva to the front so I can hock it into the guy's face. He sees what I'm doing and gives me a pitying smile. "Spit all you want," he says.

And at that moment, right when his attention is distracted, I drive a knee into his scrotum.

Drive is maybe a little too strong. I'm still in beached-fish mode, and there's not a lot of muscle control going on. But what I'm doing is a little like golf. It might be a very dumb sport, but golfers have at least one thing right: sometimes, angle beats power. And when I jackhammer my right knee up towards my head, my angle is perfect.

He sucks in a gulp of air, hissing, leaning back automatically. His hands fly to his injured manhood. I buck, and he topples off me.

With more effort than I've ever summoned in my entire life, I scramble to my feet. I'm leaning forward now, like a runner out of the blocks, body trembling. The street blurs, my vision doubling.

What if the other guy has a taser? Or—shit—what if there's a back-up shot? Some tasers have that now, don't they? I didn't think about it before, my mind too fuzzy to work on the details. Nothing I can do now. If they taser me, they taser me.

I put my head down and run.

I get about ten feet before I collide with a large squashy pointy thing. It's a tent, with someone inside it yelling at me to get off. I roll away, stumble to my feet just as a skeleton with thinning white hair pokes its head out of the tent door, fixing me with a bug-eyed glare. "What the fuck?" it screeches.

No time to apologise. Two blurs are racing up behind me, one with a red shirt and a yellow taser-shaped object in his hand. I lurch away, hyperventilating, teeth chattering like I'm freezing cold.

Suddenly there's a goddamn horse.

It's looming up in front of me, and it doesn't look like any horse I've ever seen. It's ten feet tall and bright yellow and has teeth the size of clenched fists. Next to the horse someone has written DECOLONISE AND CHILL.

It's a mural, painted on the wall that doglegs off Winston

Street. I lurch into it, doing my zombie-with-a-broken-leg impression. If I keep going onto Main, there might—*might*—be people who will intervene before these dickheads drag me away. In the alley there won't be, but that's better. There'll be nobody around to witness me beat these idiots to death with a flying brick or two.

Assuming I actually have enough energy to make them fly in the first place.

Despite the blue sky, the alley itself is deep in shade. There's more graffiti, a little less coherent than our woke yellow horse, along with dumpsters and endless stacks of cardboard boxes. Along one side, a high wall is bordered by a fence covered in razor wire. The alley smells of pee and fryer oil, and there are no tents, no homeless people—no sign of anybody. And no cameras that I can see. Perfect.

But when I reach out, try to find things in the alley I can use as weapons, I get back almost nothing. It's like trying to pick something up after your arm has gone to sleep. I can sense objects, feel their form, but I can't get a grip on them.

The surface of the alley is potholed, with a dribble of water in a central gutter. My feet aren't working well enough to keep my balance. I faceplant, ripping skin off my cheek. A fire-alarm burst of pain blares through my skull.

Someone has painted a silhouette of an oversized spray can on the wall, the face of an Indian shaman in a headdress superimposed on it. Next to it are the words WAR PAINT.

My jacket is gone. I don't even know when that happened. I must have shrugged out of it, or had it pulled off me. I roll over, legs twitching. Taser guy and his buddy—a thickset bald dude in a white T who looks like a gangbanger—are slowly approaching.

Wait. I know him. The second one, the bald dude. He was

in the car last night. The one I thought was following me, and zoomed off when Nic came up behind me.

"Stay down," says taser guy. His voice is ever so slightly hoarse, and he's moving with a weird, bow-legged gait.

"Come on, man." I push myself up on my elbows—or try to, anyway. My lips have gone numb, and the words slur together. "I got stuff to do. You'll have to get your buddy to kiss it better."

"Oh, y'all got jokes, huh?" Baldy nods to taser guy. "Yo, don't miss this time."

I shouldn't be here. I should be in bed in Leimert Park, deliciously half-asleep. Instead, I'm tired, aching, framed for murder and I've just been tasered while running an errand for a homeless guy. I don't know what these two want, but if I don't do something right now, it's over.

My PK gives me nothing. It slips off the taser like it isn't there. There's a broken bottle under the dumpster, the perfect weapon, but I can barely feel it.

Taser guy starts to reload. And that's when I get really scared.

SEVENTEEN

Teagan

Nope. Nuh-uh. Not today. Not in this shitty alley, at the hands of two goons with a taser.

I throw everything I can into one final push. I am going to Fort Minor this bitch. The feeling is ninety per cent anger, five per cent pain and five per cent absolute, cold knowledge that when this is done, they're going to remember my name.

Which is when something... weird... happens.

Athletes talk about how they have to dig deep to find an extra bit of energy at the end of a long race or a game. I always thought it was a conscious thing—that they trained their muscles to draw that energy. Turns out, when it happens it's the body taking over. The internal systems scrambling, shunting conscious control aside and grabbing hold of the wheel.

For half a second I can feel everything in the alley.

And I mean everything.

Every atom in the brick walls, every fragment of paint on the Indian dude on the wall, the prongs on the taser, every tiny fragment of stone and glass and dirt. *Everything.* It's like being surrounded by a million points of light.

The dumpster flips off the ground like a car in an action

movie, its lid gaping, a cascade of garbage exploding out. For a half-second me and taser guy and his friend stare at it in astonishment, watching this giant hunk of metal and trash casually break the laws of physics.

At the very last instant taser guy shoves his buddy out of the way. The dumpster lands where he was with a stomach-shaking crunch, the sound echoing off the buildings around us. There's a huge roaring hollow in my gut, a titanic headache blossoming at the base of my skull.

Somehow taser guy keeps control of the situation. He didn't let go of his weapon after all, and he takes aim at me, ignoring his friend. But my lizard brain survival instinct still has hold of the dumpster. I might not be fully in control of what I do with it, but at this point mine is bigger than his.

I give the dumpster a ferocious push, one that sends an aftershock thudding into the back of my skull. The dumpster rockets along the ground with a squeal of tortured metal. It takes taser guy out at the knees, flipping him over the top. He cartwheels, crashing to the ground with a head-splitting shriek of pain. His right leg is bent at an angle that no leg should ever be bent at. His friend drags him out of the alley, hauling him like a sack of grain.

And, just like that, I lose my grip on the dumpster. I lean over and retch fried-egg sandwich into the alley.

I sit there for what feels like a very long time. My mind is a howling, roaring blank.

The dumpster. When it was full of trash, it had to have weighed five hundred pounds. More. There is no way, at all, that I should have been able to lift it.

The alley doubles in front of me, triples. I sneeze, sharp and violent. What just happened...it's not possible. It can't be. Even during the stress tests the government put me through, I never got *close* to this.

Who were those guys? Did they know what I could do? They must have done—they wanted to immobilise me with that taser, not kill me. Then again, that might not mean anything. A taser is a pretty efficient way of putting someone down, whether or not they can move shit with their mind.

It's too big to take in. Too much with the headache currently gnawing at my temples. I have to call Reggie. That's the only thing that matters right now. Call Reggie, and everything will be all right.

Getting to my feet takes a really long time. Then I have to stand for a minute, trying to talk myself into moving. There are clicking footsteps at the mouth of the alley and a well-dressed woman with a big Louis Vuitton bag passes by. She gives it, and me, a quick glance before hurrying on. Probably thinks the place always looks like that.

Every step I take reverberates up into my jaw. I've never felt like this. It's like the worst PK hangover I've ever had made love to the worst *actual* hangover I've ever had, and they made a baby, and that baby won't stop screaming.

It takes me five minutes just to get back onto Winston Street. On my way past the dumpster I reach out and touch it, hesitant, as if it'll give me an electric shock. It's cold and heavy. Very heavy. I try to grab it again with my PK and get a fuzzy burst of static at the back of my mind.

A lance of sunlight blinds me as I step onto the sidewalk. The cars on Main are way too loud. I need my phone, which is in my jacket...

Which isn't there. It's gone. There's nothing on the sidewalk—no jacket, no phone, no cash, not even my car keys. The only thing left is the little cardboard box Africa gave me, lying discarded in the gutter. Whatever's inside obviously wasn't worth stealing.

I scoop up the box, holding it in both hands, head hanging. I lower myself to the kerb, trying to ignore the sensation of someone banging a fist against the side of my head.

Movement, to my right. It's the person whose tent I crushed. It's a woman. She's a skin-cover skeleton with wispy blonde hair and a deeply lined face. Track marks dot her arms. She's wearing a very old T-shirt with a McDonald's logo over faded stonewash jeans. The tent has been rebuilt, mostly, and the woman sits cross-legged next to it, stuffing potato chips into her mouth.

Maybe she stole my jacket. My phone. Payback for when I ran into her. But the front door of her tent is open, and inside is...nothing. Zippo. Not even a sleeping bag.

Well, OK, maybe she hid them somewhere. But where? And what am I going to do? Demand she give them back? She'll just laugh at me. I can barely walk.

Come to think of it, how the hell did she not hear what was happening in the alley? Come and investigate? Or are there routine dumpster explosions in this part of town?

Her tent.

It's bright red.

"Hey."

She looks up, scowling. There's a fear there, a nervousness behind the angry scowl. Like she's expecting me to lunge forward and slap her. It's a fear that says, *Don't get involved. Not unless you have to.* That's probably why she didn't check out the alley.

"You Jeannette?" I ask.

She actually flinches, then sticks her chin out like she can tough her way through whatever's coming. "You ruined my tent," she says.

"Here," I say, tossing her the box.

She snatches it out of the air, eyes narrowed in confusion.
"Courtesy of Africa."

There's an awful taste in my mouth: blood and dirt and
something sour. I spit, not caring what it looks like.

"Africa?" Jeannette opens the box, and her face transforms.
It's lit from within by an absolutely gigantic smile that her
missing teeth do nothing to spoil.

Carefully, almost reverently, she lifts the contents out. It's a
tiny origami crane folded out of what looks like a club flyer.
And underneath it a small homemade card—corny as hell,
with little red cut-out hearts on the cover.

I look past them, at the stunned, delighted smile on her face.
Thinking about Africa.

Thinking about Nic.

Reggie. Call. Now. I automatically dip my hand in my pocket
for my phone. Then I close my eyes and concentrate very hard
on just doing nothing for a few seconds.

I dig into my jeans again. I'm usually too lazy to stash any
coins in my phone case—I just shove them into whatever
pocket is handy. My fingers close on some change: five quarters
and a nickel.

"Is there a payphone round here?" I ask Jeannette.

She flicks a glance at me, as if annoyed to be pulled away
from her gift. "Just use your cellphone."

I'm about to say something rude when she says, "Over on
Boyd. By the Bodega."

Boyd. OK. After a long moment I get to my feet, swaying
like I'm drunk. My fingertips are numb.

Just before I start moving, Jeannette says, "His name isn't
Africa, you know."

"What?"

"It's Idriss. He's from Senegal."

"Then why do they call him Africa?"

She shrugs. "Easier to remember, I guess."

I look long and hard at her, not sure if I want to hug her, give her the finger, or just start screaming.

In the end I settle for a nod, then take off back in the direction of South Los Angeles Street.

It takes me a fucking *age* to find the payphone. I get lost trying to find Boyd, taking a right when I should go left and getting into the mess of streets around Maple and Wall. I half hope I'll find Africa—*Idriss*—but he's nowhere to be seen.

And there's no Bodega on Boyd. There are like thirty closed-down stores that might have *been* Bodegas, once upon a time, but what there definitely isn't is a payphone. Every person I talk to just gives me a pitying look and asks why I don't use my cellphone.

The sun is much higher in the sky now. I'm dripping sweat, my stomach roaring and growling, my eyes scratchy from the smoke in the air. My head feels like NWA are holding a reunion tour inside it, and they brought Eazy E back from the dead as a fucking banshee. I keep looking over my shoulder, worried that the two douchetards who attacked me are going to come back for seconds. But they're nowhere to be seen, and in any case there are more people on the streets here. I should be OK.

I showed them my PK. Actually, I gave them the IMAX-Dolby-surround-sound version of my PK, which means Tanner is not going to be thrilled. Not that I had a goddamn choice in the matter.

Eventually, just as I'm about to abandon Boyd and look elsewhere, I spot the phone, tucked in the shadows of a doorway. The cord has been stripped right down to the wire, the box covered with graffiti. The handset is sticky on my skin, which is something I'd rather not think about now.

I stand there, relishing the shade, relishing just being able to be still for a second.

According to the ancient signs behind the graffiti, the rate is fifty cents for two minutes. I drop in two of the five quarters I have on me, wait for the dial tone and call the China Shop offices. A long time ago, Reggie and Tanner made me memorise the number, which at the time I thought was lame but now makes it look like they predicted the future.

It's a long time before anyone answers. "Hello?"

"Paul?"

A long silence. Then: "No, sorry."

Huh. Obviously my memory isn't as good as I thought it was. "My bad. Wrong number."

"May I ask who's calling?"

That's a weird thing to say when someone dials a wrong number. "Um...yeah. Sorry, I was trying to call a company called China Shop Movers?"

"Are you a client? Or an employee?"

The shaded doorway suddenly feels too cold. "Who's asking?"

"Ma'am, this is Sergeant D'Antoni from the LAPD. I need you to identify yourself."

"What the hell are you doing in our office?"

"*Your* office?"

Shit.

"OK, ma'am, now I *really* need you to identify yourself. If you're an employee, you should know that we're here with a warrant, and—"

I slam the phone back into its cradle hard enough for it to crack. I actually take a step back like it had burned me.

First Steven Chase. Then I get attacked. Then a cop answers when I call the office.

What in the almighty storm of fuck is going on?

EIGHTEEN

Jake

It should have been over by now.

Three targets. Three locations. Downtown, West Hollywood, Burbank. Taken care of by 6 a.m. tops. Traffic was never
going to be an issue, not when his Enfield can slip through it
like a knife through ribs.

What it can't slip through is an accident on the 405—a
snarled spot on the Sepulveda Pass as he heads into the Valley.
An overturned truck which closes all but one lane, filling the
others with emergency vehicles and squeezing traffic all the
way up to Van Nuys.

Jake straddles his bike, sandwiched between a delivery van
and the concrete barrier at the edge of the freeway, grinding
his teeth. Clenching and unclenching his jaw as if he can
crush the problem into paste. In the east the sun is starting to
brighten the sky.

Chuy had explained the connection between the three
targets, and why that meant that Jake had to do them all in
a single night. If any of them got wind of the fact that the
others were gone, they'd take off for sure. It would make

them harder to track down, expose Jake to more attention, give the cops more time to gather evidence. Not good.

The congested highway, thick with fumes and horns. The driver of the van beside him is picking his nose, finger in halfway to the second knuckle. He takes a sip from a cardboard coffee cup as he digs, barely pausing. He glances at Jake, bleary uninterested eyes sweeping over him. Jake gets the insane urge to shatter the glass, drive a shard into one of those sleepy eyes.

He has spent over two decades in a kind of furious, focused control of his power, and he has never been closer to letting it go than right now. Just unleashing it: shattering glass, twisting metal, breaking bones and crushing skulls, anything within reach. The traffic jam constricts his entire body, crushing him from all sides.

If he can't get this done, Chuy will never help him.

On the day he'd used his power at the LA Mission, after the woman had seen him, he'd sat and eaten his food in a kind of stupor, relief and terror nearly paralysing him, his hands shaking, spilling soup from his spoon. He'd eaten and left as fast as he could.

It had been a few days before he'd returned to the Mission. He didn't see the man he would come to know as Chuy inside while he ate his food. But as he walked back down the block to where he had parked his bike, a car drew up alongside, headlights piercing the darkened Skid Row street.

The window had rolled down, and the man had said, "You the guy who can move shit without picking it up?"

The sentence didn't make sense. The words did, but together they pinballed around Jake's mind. When they finally stopped, he felt the bottom drop out of his stomach. Maybe the woman didn't *believe* what she'd seen, but she'd mentioned it to someone. Who had maybe mentioned it to someone else. Who was now in front of him, ready to destroy everything.

"Get in," the man said.

He'd almost ran. Just fucking booked it out of there, out of LA, out of California, away from the only other person who realised what he could do.

Instead, half-believing he was dreaming, he'd got in the car.

It was an old Honda Civic; the floor a drift of flyers and burger wrappers and soft-drink cups. The man wore an old flannel shirt, untucked, buttoned to the neck, like gangsters Jake had seen in East LA. Without a word the man pulled the car away from the kerb, heading north, away from the Row.

Jake had sat, hands gripping his knees, knuckles bloodless. Twenty years he'd kept his Gift a secret, *twenty goddamn years*, and then he'd thrown it all away. Because, what? He'd got careless? What a stupid, pointless thing to do. What a waste. It was going to cost him everything.

The silence had gone on a little too long, the guy driving like Jake wasn't in the car. They were just entering Chinatown.

"Look, man," he'd said eventually. "I don't want any trouble. If I disappear, there're gonna be people looking for me. I got friends at the Mission."

He'd hardly talked to anybody at the Mission, just shown up, ate and left. But this guy might not know that.

The driver had said nothing. He'd glanced at Jake briefly, then looked back at the road. Neon washed across his face.

Jake licked his lips. They felt like bones in the desert, dry and smooth and hard. "I'm serious." A sudden flicker of anger, eclipsing the fear. "Let me out. Right fucking now."

The man looked over almost lazily. His voice was cold and calm. "Relax, homie. I wanted to rat you out to someone, that woulda happened a long time ago."

"Rat me out? For what? I didn't do nothing."

"Come on, dude. Really?" The car turned left, heading for 110. "This ain't a shakedown. We cool. I'm just curious, that's all."

"Curious about what?"

The man gave him an amused look and said nothing. They'd turned onto the freeway, almost immediately getting locked up in traffic.

"It's just this... thing I do," Jake had said.

"Moving shit without using your hands is just a thing you do." A shake of the head. "Damn, man."

Jake stared out across the highway, heart hammering. Across the way, Dodger Stadium lit up the night. He wondered briefly if there was a game on: a hundred thousand cheering fans, none of whom knew or cared about the predicament he was in. What he wouldn't give to be there, lost in the crowd, anonymous.

The thought didn't sit quite right. He wanted out of this car, true... but there was something appealing about being the centre of attention. Even from a man he didn't know.

Dimly Jake realised he knew nothing about the history of Dodger Stadium. Didn't have a single clue when it was built, or by whom, or even why. For some reason, this bothered him more than the situation he was in.

"You must have killed it in talent shows when you were a kid," the man was saying.

"What?"

"Or like, being lazy. Fuck getting off the couch; just bring the remote over here, beer out the fridge. Most people gotta train dogs or some shit, but not you, homie."

Jake couldn't believe how calm the man was, like he was mentioning something he'd seen in a movie somewhere.

He said so, and the man laughed. It was a throaty sound, rich and full.

He reached over and put the radio on, real low. A salsa station, one of the dozen or so in the LA area. Jake hated salsa usually, but at that moment it fitted right in, just another part of the dream.

"So what happened? You get bitten by a radioactive spider, some shit like that?"

"No. Nah, no spider."

"What then?"

"My mom, I guess. Or my dad, whoever he was. I don't know."

"She have it too? The mind-moving thing?"

"I...No. I don't think so."

"For real? Y'all don't know?" The man's face had creased, half amusement, half disbelief. "Ain't that a bitch."

"I tried to find out," Jake heard himself say. "But...well, I couldn't."

"Hmm." The man had suddenly thrust a meaty hand across the console. "Name's Chuy."

"Jake. Listen, where we going? My bike—"

"Your bike'll be fine. That spot you always park it in is on one of the LAPD patrol routes. Nobody's jacking shit along there." He either ignored or didn't notice Jake's look of surprise. "I'll be real with you. I'm not gonna blab to nobody. Like I said, we cool. But in return, you gotta be straight with me too. I wanna know what you can do."

Jake jerks out of the memories as the traffic begins to move. He guns the Enfield's motor, and before long he's past the accident and cruising through the streets of Burbank.

The fires burning in La Tuna and Wildwood Canyons to the north haven't reached the city—yet—but the hills are a mass of drifting smoke edged with a pale, sickly orange. The air is thick, almost viscous. More than once a fire engine rushes past him, siren wailing. The buzzing of the aerial firefighting planes is almost constant. *The new normal*, someone on a TV at the Mission called it, some Fox News talking head, the word HELLSTORM burning below her. Which is the most insane thing he's ever heard.

A surge of panic—what if they've evacuated already? What if his target is gone? But the few people he does see look calm, almost bored. No cars being jammed with possessions, no one running down the sidewalk, no panicked shouts. He passes a jogger, a young woman with a bright orange headband, chest hitching as she breathes in the smoky air.

The house is a prosperous-looking single-storey on East Orange Grove, painted yellow, set back from the street behind a huge knobbly jacaranda tree. Low-cut hedges border the property, and the pot plants around the front door look green and healthy. As he parks the bike a few blocks away, he checks his backpack. Two pieces of rebar left. That should be more than enough, especially if he's careful. He has no desire to get surprised a second time.

His watch—an ancient G-Shock he got at a yard sale in, where was it, Victorville?—reads 6:27. At that time on a weekend most people will still be sleeping—including, hopefully, his target.

I did it, Chuy.

He uses the same approach as before, sauntering up the walk towards the house, hands in his pockets. Just a kid coming back from a night on the town, a barista heading off to an early shift.

One more. One more task, and he gets everything he ever wanted. He finds he's so excited that he can barely keep a thought in his head. He's never been this close, not ever. All those dead-end towns, all those cold trails, the endless nights under highways and in fleabag motels, and he's finally about to find out who he is. Why he can do what he does. And after that...after that he can write himself into history. He can become someone.

He's just approaching the front door of the house, starting to eye his path around to the back, when it opens.

The woman standing there is alert, fully awake, dressed in jogging pants and an orange tank top. Her brown hair is tied back in a ponytail. She's in her late forties, and the sight of her is so startling that he stops cold, six feet from the front door.

She doesn't notice him at first, putting a hand on the door frame to steady herself, stretching out her right leg. Getting ready for a morning run herself, maybe.

Jake freezes. It's Saturday. The target and his wife should still be asleep—he and Chuy have spent plenty of time watching them, and she's never gone for a run in the morning. Certainly not on a weekend.

Before he can act on the thought, she spots him. "Yes?"

He forces a smile onto his face, the same smile that got him beds on cold nights and spots on work crews. It worked then, and it had damn well better work now. "Sorry to bother you, ma'am. Is Javier here?"

A dark shadow crosses her face. "No. Sorry."

"Do you know where I could find him? It's important."

It's the wrong thing to say. "Sorry," she says again. "I don't know you."

She starts to shut the door, and the drumbeat goes into double time. He takes a step towards her, unsure what he intends to do but knowing he has to do *something*.

She freezes, suddenly wary, the door half-closed. "I *said*, he's not here."

"Yeah, but if you could just—"

"You can try his office on Monday."

"Mommy?"

A girl appears behind the woman's legs. Batman pyjamas, bare feet, the same freckles as her mother. She eyes Jake, blinking away sleep.

With one last glance at him, the woman shuts the door in his face. There's the click of a deadbolt snapping in the still air.

Jake looks around him as if expecting a neighbour to intervene, vouch for him. The stupid, dull feeling grows, threatening to overwhelm him. In that instant he has no idea what to do. Not a single one.

He starts towards the house, stops, starts again. Then he turns, moving unsteadily as if he's drunk, and begins walking back towards his bike. Thoughts crash and collide in his head, shattering and splintering into jagged fragments.

They'd known about the wife and kid, of course they had, but he and Chuy had spent plenty of time observing their routine. They were never up this early on the weekend. And the way the woman had looked at him when he'd said her husband's name...

He stops in the middle of the sidewalk, grinds the heel of his hand into his forehead. Turns back towards the house. Stops. Resumes the walk back to his bike.

No. No way. He has not come this far, worked this hard, to let it all end here. Not on the home stretch. He swings back towards the house a second time. He can do this. It'll just take a little bit more effort, that's all.

This time the door remains closed when he raps on it.

"Who is it?" The voice is muffled, coming from just behind the door, and it only stokes his anger. She must know who it is, she can see him through the peephole.

"Ma'am, I really need to talk to Javier."

"And I said I don't know you." Annoyed now, her voice fracturing. "If you don't go away I'm going to call the police." "Please don't do that." Fists clenching and unclenching. He makes himself smile, aware that he's doing a very poor job. "It will only take a second."

Silence. No, not quite. Muffled footsteps, heading away from the door. And was that the almost inaudible beep of a cellphone?

He's not supposed to touch anyone else. He doesn't want to. His three targets, including Javier, deserve to die—Chuy told him what they had done, showed him all the evidence he had. Jake is doing this because Chuy has promised to dig into his past, which he has proved he can do—but he, Jake, would never have agreed to kill anybody unless there was a very good reason for it. He would never use his Gift like that.

None of which stops him from focusing on the lock, reaching inside it, snapping it open.

He opens the door. The woman is just inside, a phone held tight in her grip. Stunned surprise gives way to fury. "What are you doing? Get away!"

He steps into the house. Her eyes are huge, panicked. She tries to scramble away, slipping to the floor, reaching up to the slim table that runs along the wall to Jake's left. She's going for a set of keys nestled in a small copper bowl, with the distinctive black cylinder of pepper spray attached to the ring.

Without thinking, Jake snags them with his mind, zipping them into his outstretched hand. She goes still, hand frozen in mid-air, watching him like one might watch a cobra with a flared hood. Her eyes—enormous, disbelieving, confused—meet his.

The anger takes him by surprise, roaring up from a dark pit

inside him. She made him do it. She *made* him. If she'd just told him where Javier was, he wouldn't have had to show her.

"You're not Daddy," says the little girl in the Batman pyjamas, huddled at the foot of the stairs.

The wife throws herself at him. She might not understand what he is or what he can do, but her child is enough to get her on the attack. She claws at his face, his neck, shoving him back against the wall and opening up a gash in his cheek with a nail. He growls in surprise, backhands her, sending her sprawling. The girl screams.

For a second time, he almost turns and runs. This isn't him. He doesn't threaten, doesn't hurt people. He's only killing because of a few very specific reasons. And yet, what does it matter? They know who he is now. He's shown them his Gift. Which means he has even more reason to talk to them; they have to tell him where Javier is, and he has to make them understand that they can't tell anybody about what they saw. Ever. He can't run—running would mean that he's failed.

Regret and anger and every other feeling rocketing around his mind are suddenly drowned by a flood of cold logic. This is fine. He'll make it work.

The smile he thinks of as friendly and welcoming slips onto his face again. He reaches behind him with his mind and gently closes the door.

NINETEEN

Teagan

Three quarters left.

Hands shaking, I dial Reggie's cell—another number I have etched on my brain. The voice on the other end this time is Hispanic, annoyed, and I hang up without even bothering to say wrong number.

I get my money back, dial Carlos's number. That I *definitely* have memorised—God knows, I've called it plenty of times. But it rings and rings before going to voicemail, a message in Carlos's rapid-fire Mexican-accented Spanish.

The phone spits back my two quarters, and I try Reggie again, dialling slowly. This time not only do I get a wrong number—a terse, automated, "If you wish to make a claim, our office hours are between 9 a.m. and 3 p.m."—but the phone only spits back one quarter.

I take three very deep breaths, head down, eyes closed. If it pulls that trick again, I won't have enough to make another call.

Very slowly, I dial her number a third time.

And Reggie answers. "Hello?"

"Reggie!" I stand bolt upright, ignoring the queasy

roll-over in my guts. "I'm in Skid Row. I got mugged or something, and—"

"Teagan?"

"—two guys with a taser, and then something happened with my PK, and I lost my phone, and—"

"Stop talking." She's in a car—engines and traffic hum in the background. "We've been compromised. Do *not* go back to the office."

"Yeah, I know. I already tried calling. What the fuck are the cops doing there? Are you OK?"

Paul's voice reaches me, the words inaudible. He must be driving.

"Skid Row?" Reggie asks.

"Yeah."

"Go to Jojo's Diner on Main. We'll be there soon." She hangs up before I can say anything else.

Jojo's. Main. The exact opposite direction from where I came, past Winston Street. I take another three deep breaths then set out, squinting against the glaring sun. The irony is, despite everything else being stolen, I still have a pair of sunglasses; they're just in a completely different part of the city.

This is turning out to be a fun morning.

I hate Jojo's on sight. It's the kind of place where the menu has a chequered border and the logo is in a half-assed 1950s font and the burger description has words like "mouth-watering" and "world-famous" in it. The kind that takes zero imagination or skill to run. On the few times Mom and Dad did take us out to eat back in Wyoming, it was usually to a place called the Rocket, which was exactly like Jojo's, only without the level of class and refinement. It's a place I would love to go back to, so I could burn it down.

Not that I care right now, because Jojo's has food. So despite the fact that it smells of grease and despair, and despite the waitress giving me a skeevy look as I walk in, I sit myself down—somehow—and order the biggest breakfast on the menu, along with a massive mug of refillable coffee. Then I sit for a while, eyes closed, trying not to start bleeding out of my ears. Also trying not to think about the clock above the bar, which is probably the nicest thing in the place: a big, antique number with the little hand just past the nine.

The breakfast dropped in front of me is hot, greasy and tastes like it was cooked in sweat from Rick Ross's ass crack. Every bite probably takes a month off my life. But by the time I'm on my second cup of coffee, I'm feeling a tiny bit more human.

Except, I'm not really human, am I?

The waitress refills my coffee. There are liver spots on her fingers, a bracelet tan on her wrist. We look the same. Have the same shape and skin tone. But I'm not like her.

This isn't a completely new thought. I *know* I'm different. But up until this morning it was a difference with limits. I thought I'd reached the boundaries of my ability, and that meant I never had to work at it. Not really.

I never had to think about my PK. It was just a thing I did, and it left me free to fill up my brain with...well, human shit. People and food and restaurants and the Batmobile and rap and maybe getting a dog and new movies and just being *me*.

The most I've ever pushed my ability was during that fake kidnapping in Texas. Age nineteen. And the conclusion was that was about as powerful as I was going to get. But that isn't true. It can't be true. Not only is there someone out there like me, who can do shit with their PK that I could never have dreamed of, but I just did something with *my* PK that I could never have dreamed of.

Over the past few years, without even realising it, I've increased the limits of my power. Under certain circumstances—like when my body is injecting a huge whack of adrenaline and fight-or-flight chemicals into my body—I can push myself further. Like a normal woman being able to lift a car off her son.

What if I could control what I just did? Stop it from draining me the way it did this morning? What if I could *enhance* it?

There's a stovetop range behind the counter, eight feet away. My PK is still very, very fuzzy, and I only just manage to reach out and wrap my mind around the metal frame. I don't try to lift it, and it doesn't feel like I could...but that isn't true, isn't it? Under the right circumstances, I could rip that range right out of the wall.

Steven Chase. Whoever killed him has some of this figured out already—how else would they have been able to bend the rebar like that? There's a lot I don't know here, but finding whoever did this, talking to them, is a good start.

Of course I have another motivation to find them. I am *pissed.*

It's one thing to mess with me. It's another to mess with my team. I might not get along with people like Annie and Paul a lot of the time, but—along with Reggie and Carlos—they are the closest thing to family I have.

Right now I have a slightly more pressing problem. I've been here for over an hour, and Reggie hasn't shown up yet. How the hell am I going to pay?

I'm on my third cup of coffee. The waitress is giving me even more pointed looks than usual. I have twenty-five cents to my name, which in Los Angeles will buy me around an eighth of a cup of a coffee, even in this shithole. Which means I have to come up with a solution. It'd be a real shame to survive being kidnapped only to get arrested because I couldn't pay for breakfast.

I'm just contemplating ordering a fourth cup of coffee to stall for time when the door opens and Reggie rolls in. Paul is right behind her, looking like the entire world is taking a personal dump on him.

"Hey, Regina." The waitress strides over, bending down to embrace Reggie. I blink in astonishment.

Reggie nudges the waitress with her good arm. "Sorry I ain't been in too long."

"'S all good. How's Moira doing?"

Moira? Tanner was here? The thought of her sitting in this café, eating crappy food, is weird as hell.

The waitress sees where Paul is going, frowns. "Y'all with her?"

"Yeah," I say loudly. "They're with me."

The frown mutates into a smile. "I'll get some more coffee," she says, bustling away. "Sorry," she says, half turning back to Reggie. "You're tea, right?"

"Chamomile, darling. Thank you."

"Not gonna help you with the tip," I mutter.

Paul puts his elbows on the table, wrapping his hands around the back of his neck. "They raided the office," he says.

"Yeah, I got that. Why?"

Reggie scoots up. "Honey, you look like you slept in a woodpile."

"Gee, thanks. Glad we had this talk. I feel so much better now."

"She's not kidding. You got dirt on your..." Paul waves a hand around his face.

"No shi—" Which is when I actually catch a glimpse of myself in the metal salt shaker, something I'd been too zonked to notice before. I don't just have some dirt; I have a massive streak of it, running from forehead to cheekbone. No wonder the waitress was giving me the stink-eye.

"What happened?" Reggie asks.

I'm about to tell them the truth, when I stop.

If they knew what I could do with my PK...wouldn't that give them even *more* of a reason not to trust me? Lifting a dumpster and strangling someone with a piece of rebar must take the same amount of energy, or close to it. I can't afford to have them turn on me. Not right now.

I don't completely lie. I tell them about the attack, the taser. That I managed to chase them away. It doesn't feel good, lying to them, but I don't see what other choice I have.

"And the men who attacked you," Reggie says. She looks both sick and angry at the same time. "Where are they?

"Gone."

"They saw you," Paul says hotly. "You know how Tanner feels about that."

"Didn't exactly get a choice," I say, all but snarling the words. "If I didn't use my PK, they would have—"

"*Please* don't call it that. I've told you before, in Cantonese, it means—"

"Yeah, don't care. Anyway, look, it doesn't matter. We can worry about me later. What the hell happened at the office?"

"We don't know," Paul says.

"What do you mean, you don't know? Why are there cops answering our phones?"

"Because they've got an arrest warrant out for you, Annie and Carlos."

"*What*? Why?"

"Steven Chase."

"Are you shitting me?"

"I only found out because the police logged the warrant on their system," Reggie says.

I pick up the salt shaker, turning it in my hands, trying to keep my voice level. "I had nothing to do with it. *Nobody* had anything to do with it."

The events of the night before run through my head, every moment of the operation, from start to terminal-velocity finish. "It must have been the security guards." I swallow, fighting with my dry mouth. "And there was this lawyer. At least, I think he was a lawyer. We ran into him in the elevator. Would they have told the cops about us?"

"Of course they would have," Reggie says. "But I don't think that's it. They'd have a description, but that wouldn't be enough. Police these days don't like relying on eyewitnesses. And Carlos never went inside."

"So what, then? You're saying we were caught on camera somewhere?"

"Maybe."

"I thought you killed all the cameras. On every floor we—"

"I did."

"You must have missed one. It's the only explanation."

"I didn't miss any," she says, a dangerous edge to her voice. "It had to have been a camera *outside* the building. Paul wasn't on the warrant, so my guess is he was out of view."

"Hang on. Why would the cops raid Paul's Boutique? Even if they got us on camera'—"

"Really?" says Paul. "You're still calling it that? Even now?"

"The fucking *office*, whatever. How did the cops know about China Shop?"

"If they found out who Annie was, or even you and Carlos, they'd be able to dig up the records. They'd see you worked for a company called China Shop. We do have tax returns, after all."

A chill settles on me then. "They don't...I mean, do the cops know who *we* are? Like, what we do?"

Reggie gives me a look. "Honey, please. You think this is my first rodeo? Purged the whole system the moment I heard about the warrant. Got out before the first cop car rolled into Brooks Court." She takes a distracted sip of her tea. "And I still can't figure out *how* you were caught on camera. There was nothing in that alley, no external surveillance. I checked."

"So Annie and Carlos...are they..."

"They were out hunting down some of Annie's contacts. They're ditching the van now."

"Ditching it?"

"Cops have an arrest warrant out for a woman of Annie's description, driving a white van. They need to hide it."

"You think Annie's just going to tool around LA in a hot car?" The words *hot car* sound strange coming from Paul, like it's a phrase he heard in some movie, and he's decided to try it out. "She's smarter than that. You don't give her credit, but she is."

"We're waiting for them to call," Reggie says.

"OK. Then what?"

"Then we pick them up. See how this all shakes out."

Paul says nothing. Toying with his coffee. He looks out the window, giving a very gentle shake of his head.

"What?" I say.

No response.

"Paul," says Reggie. "We talked about this."

"I just think that—"

"*Paul.*"

He pauses then gives her a tight nod.

I almost turn on him. Demand that he finish his sentence. *You just think what, Paul? That I really did kill Steven Chase? Go ahead and say it.*

But it wouldn't do any good. And right now I don't know what else I can do to prove that it wasn't me. If I wanted, I could have run any time in the past two hours, but here I am. If he can't respect that, then...I don't know.

Then I get an urge. A very powerful need to do just that: bug out. Stand up, walk out the door, hop a bus or a train or steal a goddamn car and just go. Get away from everything, find a new place, somewhere small and out-of-the-way, start fresh...

Ha. OK. And how long before Tanner catches up to me? Spending the rest of my life looking over my shoulder? No thanks. And that isn't even talking about what I'd leaving behind. Nic, never knowing what happened to me. Carlos, sent back to Mexico. Annie, in prison. Reggie and Paul... God knows what Tanner will do to them. And all of them will think I did it—that I killed Steven Chase. Whoever *actually* did it will still be out there.

And I'll never get to talk to them. Never find out who they are.

Reggie calls the waitress over and orders more tea. Paul and I get more terrible coffee. Fifteen minutes goes by. Half an hour. There are longer and longer periods of silence. I'm torn between wanting to just sit in this chair for ever, mostly because it would mean I never have to move again, and just tearing out of the diner and doing something, *anything*, no matter how stupid, because it would mean I didn't have to sit in this chair for ever.

I could wait for Africa to dig something up, but that's hours away—if he gets anything at all beyond more declarations of bad *gris-gris*. I could talk to people I've run into on previous jobs, but in all probability that'll turn up zip. Every option feels fluffy, half-assed. I can't afford to be half-assed right now. Whatever Annie has, it's the best lead we've got.

And Reggie, at least, has my back. Paul listens to her, which means he's on side. For now. It's as good as I'm going to get.

Reggie and Paul take another look at the data from the coupler we planted, the one supposedly hoovering up Chase's email data. He is—was—a busy guy, sending well over a hundred emails in the time between when we planted the coupler and when he was killed. "Probably trying to clear his inbox," Paul mutters.

The email content is all encrypted of course, but the addresses aren't. Problem is, there's nothing useful there. Chase didn't contact anybody we wouldn't have expected him to; most of the emails are internal, to others at the Ultra fashion label. The ones that aren't don't help, either. There's one to his wife, a few that went off to media contacts—CNN, MSNBC, Twitter. A couple of charity emails. One to a restaurant in NYC—I don't recognise the name, which annoys me more than it should. Nothing we can use, and nothing you wouldn't expect the CEO of a large clothing label to send.

"Nothing to or from Saudi either," Reggie says.

Paul grunts.

They give up, and pretty soon we're just sitting in silence. It's awkward. Unnatural. And it's not hard to guess why. Reggie might have told everyone that she doesn't believe I killed Steven Chase, but there's still that little nugget of doubt. And as for Paul? I'm pretty sure he's only here because Reggie is.

Ten minutes later, just as the desire to start throwing things has grown so powerful that I'm having to work real hard to restrain myself, Reggie's phone lights up.

It's nestled in a slot on the arm of her chair. There's a special ring on the back of the phone that allows her to hold it, and she slips her fingers through with practised ease. "Hello?"

Paul and I glance at each other, the hostility temporarily fading.

"OK, good," Reggie says after a few moments. "We'll meet you there. How are you folks doing?" Another pause. "Stay out of sight. We'll be in Paul's truck…OK. Yeah, OK. Thanks."

She hangs up. Slowly puts the phone back in its cradle.

"And?" I say.

"The van's safe. They're waiting for us in Cypress Park."

Paul grips the edge of the table. "Is Annie all right?"

"Fine." Reggie doesn't look at him. "She may need a little…soothing."

"Yay." I drain the last of my coffee and push my way out the booth. We can go see Annie, see if she's dug up anything. And won't the restaurant I got takeout from last night be open soon? We can go talk to them. They'll confirm I was there. If nothing else, that might get Tanner off our backs.

"Hey," the waitress says, looking over her shoulder as her hands work the coffee machine. "You haven't paid yet."

I point at Paul. "Technically, I'm on the clock. Put it on his tab."

TWENTY

Jake

Jake sits on the short end of the L-shaped couch in the sunlit living room, using the floating rebar to direct the woman and her child onto the long end. Neither of them can tear their eyes away from the twisted steel. The little girl is crying silent tears, clutched to her mother's chest.

The living room is an airy open-plan space, the kitchen behind the short bar of the couch's L. Sliding glass doors look out onto a fenced backyard littered with toys. A plastic jungle gym stands sentinel in one corner, next to the thick trunk of a palm tree.

Jake is more tired than he thought he'd be. He's used a lot of energy through the night, and now he has to burn even more here. He needs food and sleep, and that makes him angrier than he already is. If Javier had just *been here*, like he was supposed to...

There's a low bookcase set along the wall to his right, filled with framed photos. He settles on one in the middle, and with a thought sends it flipping lazily through the air towards the couch. The woman moans, soft and horrified.

"This Javier?" he says, pointing at the centre figure in the hovering picture. The woman and her daughter are on either side of the man: a big, balding guy with what DeSoto from the Vegas road crew might have called a shit-face grin.

The woman swallows, nods.

"Mommy!"

"Ssh, baby. It'll be OK."

"Just tell me where he is." The photo joins the two pieces of rebar, hovering between him and the woman.

"Just take what you want. We won't stop you."

"I want him."

"How is he doing that?" the little girl says, pointing to the floating photo. Terror and curiosity mix in her voice. "Why can't I do that?"

"*Hush*, baby."

"I'm going to ask again." He leans forward. "Where's Javier?"

No response. Her mouth opens and closes, but no sound comes out. Her wide eyes keep flicking between him and the pieces of floating rebar.

Jake sighs and sends one of them winding towards her head. She yelps, nearly skitters right off the couch. Her daughter squirms.

She speaks quickly. "We...There was a fight. He doesn't live here any more, he moved away a few days ago. I don't know where he's staying. I—"

"Yes, you do."

"No. He didn't tell me."

The rebar twitches. The woman actually yelps this time, eyes squeezed shut.

With a real effort of will, Jake pushes his anger down. Getting angry won't help. He has to approach this calmly. Rationally.

They know what you can do. They know about your Gift.

No. It won't come to that. He'll think of something else.

He spreads his hands. "Nobody's going to get hurt here, OK? We're just having a conversation. I wouldn't have had to use my Gift if you'd just let me in. You know that, right?"

The woman's breaths are coming quickly now. She's almost panting. Her eyes never leave the floating rebar.

"I don't want you to think I'm a bad guy." Suddenly it seems very important that he explain this. He has to make her understand. "I don't have a family like yours. I don't even know where I got my Gift. That's the only reason I'm here, otherwise I would never have bothered you. I'm just trying to find out where I came from, you know?"

He scratches his nose, which has gone stuffy in the still air. "And like, I'm really sorry about all of this, but that's why I need to speak to Javier. He's the guy who...Once I've spoken to him, then my buddy Chuy will help me figure it all out. You know what I mean?"

"Please just go." The woman's voice is barely a whisper, her face a mess of tear tracks.

"You're not listening to me." The anger is back, burning a hole in his gut. "It's like I said. I really didn't mean to bother you. And I'm not just doing this for me. I know you want to protect Javier, but if you knew what he and his friends did in El Agujero, then you'd just..."

He comes to a stop, gnawing on his lower lip. His eyes never leave the woman. She won't care. She won't give a shit what Javier and the other two did. Maybe she even knows already. Maybe she was in on it. How can she live with herself? How can she live in this house with its picture-perfect backyard and it's pretty kitchen, and not wonder about where the money came from? She must know. She *has* to.

And still he manages to keep himself under control. The

smile that crosses his face at that moment is a grimace, a twisted fake. He makes it stay where it is.

"I'm trying to be nice here." Hands folded in his lap. "I really am. All you have to give me is an address. Then I'll never—"

They know about your Gift.

"—bother you again. I swear. Just talk to me. That's all we're doing. Just talking."

Five seconds pass. Ten. A hummingbird flitters up to the window, takes in the scene, zips away as quickly as it arrived.

"Give her to me."

"What?" It's more breath than word.

"Your daughter. Give her here."

The little girl's sobs become wails. The muscles on the woman's bare arms stand out like cords.

Jake pushes himself off the couch. With the rebar hovering in the air above them, he takes the girl, patiently winkling her out of her mother's arms. The woman doesn't want to let go, and Jake has to pull quite hard. When he finally has the kid, the woman just collapses in on herself, shoulders shaking, begging him not to hurt her daughter. In the kitchen the coffee machine gives a cheerful beep as it finishes brewing.

The brat tries to twist out of his arms, mewling with fear. He holds her very tightly as he sits back down on the couch, propping her on his lap, ignoring the mother's choked sobs, her frantic instructions to her daughter to stay still. The picture frame floats between them.

"Do you know the story of Maud de Braose?" Jake says.

The kid won't sit still, so he squeezes her tight. "I do. I like reading about history. I like knowing what happened before we got here. Now Maud, she was born in twelfth-century

France. Noblewoman. And King John…" He bends down, addressing the kid in his lap. "Hey, sweetie, you ever watch Robin Hood? That Disney cartoon?"

"Mommy?"

"Shhh. Shhh, honey. Just…just don't look at him."

"Maybe you haven't seen it yet." Jake gives her an indulgent smile. "Anyway, King John—the real one, not the one in the cartoon—wasn't the nicest guy. He needed money, and he wanted Maud's castle. She wouldn't give it to him, so he took Maud and her son prisoner. Brought them back to Windsor Castle in chains."

In chains. Another one of those stupid writer expressions, like *died screaming.* How did they know?

"Kelly," the woman is saying—moaning, really. "Kelly, look at me. It's going to be OK."

"That's right," he whispers in the girl's ear. "Listen to your mommy. Keep looking right at her. Hope that she's smarter than old Maud was. See, when John got Maud and her son back to Windsor Castle, he put them in a dungeon, then bricked up the door. When they eventually pulled it down a few years later, it turns out old Maud had taken a bite out of her son's cheek."

He snaps the picture frame into pieces, keeping the largest shard of glass airborne. In half a second, he has its point floating less than an inch from Kelly's eye.

The woman shakes her head. The movement is a stiff jerk, as if the muscles in her neck have locked in place. She tries to speak, but the only thing that comes out is a soft, helpless, wheezing breath.

"You know why I like reading about history?" Jake says. "Because of what you can learn from it. Imagine what would have happened, for example, if Maud had just decided her castle wasn't worth it. Do you think King John *really* would have bricked her and her son up if she'd done that?"

At that instant Kelly decides she's had enough. She tries to jerk away from him, worm her way out from under his arm. He grunts, distracted, which is when the mother launches herself off the couch, fear and rage twisting her face.

Jake sends the two pieces of rebar whipping through the air, crashing sidelong into the woman's chest, slamming her back. At the same time, he snags Kelly around the waist with his free arm, gripping as tight he can.

"I didn't want to do this," he says. "No one else was supposed to get hurt. I'm not that kind of guy." The anger is still there, but now it feels good. Righteous, even. As if he's done his duty. "I'm only doing it because you wouldn't listen. This is your fault."

And, on the last word, sends the glass shard right into Kelly's throat.

Well…not all the way. Just the tip. Blood begins to leak down the little girl's neck, and she stops moving. Jake expects her to gasp with the pain, but she goes dead silent.

"Let's try again," he says, addressing the writhing, gasping woman sprawled across the coffee table, the rebar pinning her chest and right arm to it. "Tell me where Javier is."

"Please…"

Anger flares. "If you knew what he'd done, you wouldn't be protecting him. Now, I don't give a fuck if you're divorced, separated, whatever. So you have to—hey, look at me—you have to decide. Him or your daughter."

When she doesn't respond, he claps a hand over Kelly's mouth and drives the glass a little deeper into the soft flesh of her neck.

This time the little girl screams.

TWENTY-ONE

Teagan

Paul has this thing for really sappy 90s pop: Vanessa Williams, Bryan McKnight, Shania Twain, Celine Dion. The kind of music that makes me want to rip the entire audio system out of his truck. Then burn it. Then jump up and down on the ashes. Did he listen to that shit when he was in the navy? They must have loved him.

Thankfully, the ride to Cypress Park is short, and we don't see a single cop car on the way. I can't help jumping at every car horn, scanning the streets rolling by outside the window. I've got the back seat to myself; Reggie's in the passenger seat, her chair folded up and stored in the truck's cargo well.

Cypress Park is a neighbourhood to the north of downtown, along the LA River. Paul winds the truck through rundown neighbourhoods with potholed streets, eventually reaching North San Fernando Road. I'm curious to see where Annie and Carlos stashed the van—I have this image of them driving it into the dense foliage around the river, covering it with dirt and leaves to make it blend in.

When we roll up on them, they're waiting on a street corner. Carlos gives us a lazy wave. Annie doesn't. She's ditched the security-guard outfit—smart—and is in jeans and a plain white T under a blue windbreaker. I have no idea where she got the clothes—from the van, perhaps. She has her hands jammed into the pockets of the jeans. She's also found sunglasses. Big mirror shades. She couldn't be less happy to see us if we were Donald Trump's motorcade.

The second Paul brings the truck to a stop—the very second—I'm out the door and barrelling into Carlos, wrapping my arms around him. I'm not usually an emotional person, but it's been kind of a stressful day.

"Yo." He sounds almost surprised, as if he didn't expect me to be here, but he hugs me back without hesitation "'S all good. Cops didn't get us."

"God, I'm sorry." I don't know why I'm apologising. It's not my fault the cops figured us out—or at least I'm pretty sure it's not my fault. But the thought of him getting arrested… He'd be sent back to Mexico the moment they realised he was illegal. Even the thought of that is enough to make my gorge rise.

"Hey, no, it's cool, Teags. It's cool. We're fine."

I let go of him then go back in for another hug. "We should have gone to Point Reyes," I say, voice muffled against his shoulder. "I should have listened to you."

"Everybody should listen to me, all the time. They should teach it to kids in school."

"Hey, why didn't you answer your phone?" I ask, pulling away.

He looks embarrassed. "Left it in the office."

"You tool."

"Yeah, I was kind of in a hurry this morning. Annie had hers, though."

"The van?" Paul is out of the truck now. He moves to get Reggie's chair out of the cargo well, but she waves him away.

"Out of sight." Carlos points back towards the river. Annie still hasn't said anything.

Paul massages his jaw, like someone hit him. "Good. That's good. Annie, did you have any luck with your people?"

Annie mutters something, not looking at us.

"Annie," I say, thinking she didn't hear him. "Did you—"

"Oh, I got something." Her voice is low and even, almost a monotone. "Or someone, anyway. Maybe he'll help, maybe he won't."

"Everything OK?" Paul says. "You look kind of—"

"No," says Annie. "Tell you the truth, things are not OK." She looks in my direction, the sunglasses reflecting both me and Carlos. "I didn't mind helping when it was just us trying to figure this shit out. But now we got the cops on our ass. They know who we are. So yeah, very much not fucking OK."

I try very hard not to point out that she very much minded helping before. "We'll figure this out," I tell her. "I promise."

"We talked about this, Annie." Reggie sounds strained. She's still in the truck and has to raise her voice to be heard.

"Yeah, but we didn't talk about the cops figuring out we were there. That shit wasn't supposed to happen. How the *fuck* did they know about us?"

Reggie coughs, harsh and brittle. "I don't know."

"I'm not getting arrested again," Annie says. She points at Reggie. "Not for you." At me. "You neither. And definitely not for Tanner. I got family. I did some stupid shit in the past, and there is no way I'm going back to jail. I'm not putting them through that. So you call Tanner and tell her I'm done. I don't give a shit."

"Annie." Paul sounds wounded.

"Nah, man. Nah. I'm getting the hell out of town."

There's a long moment when nobody says anything. In

the distance the river murmurs, almost inaudible under the hum of traffic. On the other side of the street a kid on a little BMX rides past. He gives us a mildly curious glance but doesn't stop. Why would he? There must be a dozen gatherings like ours just in this part of LA alone. Labourers and contractors and other poor bastards unlucky enough to be working a Saturday, hanging around trucks and waiting for their jobs to start. Cyclists and runners, up early, meeting at intersections and planning their routes. All we're missing is the takeaway coffee.

Annie gives us a tight nod. Then she jams her hands in her pockets and walks away.

There's a part of me that just wants to let her go. She doesn't want to be here, and I'm not sure I want her around anyway—not if she's going to hate me for it. But the other part...the other part knows that if she walks away, she won't be coming back. Not this time.

"Hey!" I shout.

"Yo, Annie," Carlos says. "What about—"

"North Western Ave," she says over her shoulder. "Ask for Nando."

"Paul?" says Reggie.

Paul makes a noise that is half-sigh, half-groan. "Hang on," he says, taking off after her. "Annie, hold on. Annie!"

She's halfway down the street when he catches up to her, reaching out to grab her shoulder. At first she shrugs him off but then comes to a halt. I can't make out what they're saying, but it's then that I understand that Annie isn't just angry. She's scared. It's something about the set of her shoulders, the way her hands are held at her sides, open, as if she's forcing them not to clench into fists.

I want to be mad at her. I don't have the energy. And if I

had her record, I wouldn't want to be within a million miles of an arrest warrant.

I got family, she said. Strange. I don't know who she means. She's not exactly been forthcoming about her personal life. Even thinking about her outside of China Shop and the Boutique is...weird.

Reggie has her eyes closed, head back against the seat rest. She looks drained. Carlos shifts next to me, one foot to the other, and my thoughts about Annie are blotted out by another. A much scarier one.

"You're staying, right?" I ask him. "You don't wanna..."

"Course I'm staying." He sounds faintly disgusted. "Who else is gonna make sure you don't get yourself killed?"

"Thank fuck." I force a smile. "Otherwise it'd just be me and Agent Whiteboard."

"Who?"

"Oh. Paul. Just a stupid nickname."

"I don't get it."

"It's...Never mind. Who's this Nando person?"

"I dunno. We were heading over there when Reggie called. Annie's been on the phone all morning." He takes a breath. "Yo, listen. I've been thinking..."

He doesn't get a chance to tell me what he's been thinking. Paul walks up, Annie trailing just behind him. She still looks angry—angry and terrified—but there's a determination there too. Whatever Paul said to her, it looks like it worked. To our right, Reggie lifts her head.

The sun is already hammering down, beating a drum on the back of my neck. We're all sweating. Paul's head gleams in the sunlight.

"Let's get one thing straight," Annie says, pointing at me. "I'm not here for you. Only reason I'm not heading to Canada right now is cos Paul thinks we got a better chance of clearing our names if we stick together." She glances his way. "I don't trust any of you motherfuckers, but I trust him."

Reggie looks put out but nods. "Thank you, Annie."

"So you don't think I killed Chase?" I say.

She bites her lip, chewing on it for a long moment. "Paul doesn't."

"I didn't ask that."

"Fuck you, Teagan." She hops into the truck's back seat. "Come on. You want to figure this out, we best get moving."

Her response isn't what I was hoping for, but at this point I'll take what I can get. I climb into the middle, Carlos on the other side.

"OK," I say, trying to put the conversation back on track. "Let's go see this Nando person. Where is he?"

Annie gives her phone another sour look. "The worst place on earth."

TWENTY-TWO

Teagan

North Western Avenue does not look like the worst place on earth.

It's in Hollywood—not the movie star part, sure, but it's not exactly Compton or Watts either. The houses are shabby, slightly rough around the edges, but the streets are clean. It's a Latino neighbourhood, and this being Saturday morning the streets are full of people. Kids playing in noisy groups, battered BMX bikes riding in circles. *Abuelas* and *abuelos* sitting on stoops and drinking coffee. Hell, there's even an ice cream van on one corner. It's beat to shit and looks like a serial killer lives in it, but there's a noisy crowd of kids outside, cones dripping.

"This where I think it is?" Reggie murmurs.

"Uh-huh."

"Um, where are we exactly?" I ask. Nobody answers me. I nudge Carlos, but he's looking out the window and doesn't respond. I shiver, and it has nothing to do with the truck's aircon.

Annie tells Paul to pull up on the corner of Garrison Street, a little way off the main drag. I'm starting to notice a few things by now. The groups of young men hanging out on the corners, wearing denim shirts buttoned to the neck and doo rags wrapped around their heads. The kids standing on the rooftops—not many but a few, evenly spaced, eyeing us as we pass. One puts his fingers in his mouth as we pass, and his whistle reaches us over the sound of the truck's engine.

I've been watching for police ever since we left Cypress Park. I'm not *too* worried: for one thing, they'll be looking for a white van, not a black pickup truck. Paul drives well under the speed limit, and the few times we see a cop car, he makes sure to give them a very wide berth.

"Is this a good idea?" he says now. His fingers are tight on the wheel.

"No." Annie unbuckles her belt. "But if anybody knows about what happened to Chase, it's Nando."

"All the same..."

She ignores him. "When I get out, lock the doors."

"Uh...OK?"

Annie pops the door, a tongue of heat licking into the car, steps onto the sidewalk. Almost before her feet hit the ground, a man is there. He appears as if from nowhere and doesn't look happy, and neither do his three friends, standing behind him.

Annie says something, and it's like a magic word. His face lights up, and he pulls her in for a handshake-hug. As he does so, his shirt lifts up, revealing a gun tucked in his waistband.

The man leads Annie a little way down the street, towards one of the houses set back from the sidewalk. From where I'm sitting, in the back seat of the truck, I can't quite make out the figures sitting in the shade of the stoop.

The man's friends have surrounded the car with the casual power of a pack of lions protecting a kill. One of them, a fat bastard with a sweat-stained denim shirt, leans on the hood, fingers drumming on the hot metal.

Despite the aircon, the inside of the car feels stuffy. There's a plastic bottle in the seat pocket, still a quarter full. I drain it, making a face. The water is warm, almost sticky. The dashboard clock reads 10:49.

If this were a regular Saturday morning, I might be getting started on my second cup of coffee. Third, if I woke up early, On the couch, still in my PJs, music on—some classic soul or Native Tongues-era rap. Stuff from the early 90s, with easy-going drums and lyrics about peace and love and good weed. I'd be thinking about putting brunch together: French toast, an omelette, maybe even a benny if I was feeling it, a poached egg lapped with a coating of soft sauce. Making hollandaise is a giant pain in the ass of course, and I'd probably be feeling a little lazy. If I really did want a benny, I'd have to head down to Jacko's or Over-Easy, two of the closest brunch spots, and—

My stomach gives a horrible, violent lurch, the greasy breakfast from Jojo's threatening to come right back up. I have to get out. I have to get out of this car right fucking now.

My sticky hands fumble at the door lock, eyes stinging with sudden, nervous sweat. Paul turns in his seat. "What are you doing? Annie said stay in the car."

"Nope. Uh-uh." There's a horrible moment where I'm convinced Paul has activated the child locks. Which means he's about three seconds from a broken passenger window.

"Teags." Carlos's hand on my shoulder. But at that moment the lock pops, and I tumble out onto the sidewalk.

The heat doesn't settle on me, like when you walk outside on a summer's day. It grabs me in a fist, coming from all directions, beating down from the sky and baking up from the concrete. High above us there's another LAPD chopper, floating in the sky like a malevolent god.

The man closest to the back of the car is on high alert, straightening his shoulders as he looks me up and down. Eyes invisible behind wraparound shades. I lift a hand. "'Sup."

"*Como está?*"

"Um. *Muy bien.*"

Mercifully he says nothing else, saving me from having to fumble through a conversation in my shitty Spanish. I straighten up, taking in the rest of the street. On the other side of the car a couple of kids are chanting something in Spanish, a children's song, the lyrics impossible to make out as they sing over each other in loud, joyful voices.

At the very far end of the avenue a black-and-white cop car rolls past. Too far away to make out, but it conspicuously avoids coming in our direction. Which is just fine by me. We've got lucky so far—we've run into plenty of cop cars, but none that have taken more than a passing interest in us.

The house Annie was led to is a little way up from the truck. She's sitting on the steps leading up to the porch, deep in shade, talking to a man I don't recognise. Shaved head, old wifebeater, cut-off cargo shorts. He looks old, sixties at least.

There's a long, low whistle. Carlos is standing next to me—I didn't even hear him get out the car. "Shit, Annie."

"What?"

He nods to the porch. "That's Nando Aguilar."

"Yeah, so? She said we needed to talk to Nando. Guess that's him."

"Didn't know she meant *that* Nando."

I shield my eyes from the sun. It's easier to pick out the details now. The man isn't as old as I thought he was—late forties rather than sixties. It's the stoop in his shoulders that makes him look older, the crow's feet around his eyes. He and Annie are speaking in low voices, too quiet to make out. A gentle smile plays across the man's face as he gestures to something on the street.

Carlos frowns. "Y'all don't know who that is?"

"Should I?"

"He runs the largest MS-13 *clica* in Los Angeles."

MS-13. *Mara Salvatrucha.*

Shit, Annie.

When people think of gangs in LA, they think of the Crips and the Bloods. Blue and Red. But there are plenty of others—Mexican, Armenian, Cambodian, Chinese triads. And Salvadoran. MS-13 aren't the biggest gang in LA, but they are easily the scariest.

A lot of the gangs here are more bark than bite—the kind of outfits that give rich white people a thrill when they talk about crime waves at dinner parties, and the LAPD an excuse to go break down some doors. MS-13, though? They're the real deal. Kidnap. Torture. Ritual beatings. Just a regular day at the office for your friendly Mara Salvatrucha representative.

I glance back at the soldier with the wraparound shades. He inclines his head very slightly. There's a knife in his waistband, at the small of his back. And not a pocket knife either. A fucking machete. I can't see it, but I can feel it.

"Nando'll know what's happening, that's for sure," Carlos mutters.

"Yeah, and what's that gonna cost? I can't see him just doling out info for free."

"Seems like he's getting along with Annie."

I look back over at the stoop. Nando is cackling at something Annie said, head tilted back, mouth open to reveal a couple of missing teeth.

The heat holding me in a closed fist is forced back by a sudden chill. Annie's record is pretty gnarly, even if I don't know the details…but it's supposed to be behind her now. Having contacts is one thing; being *this* friendly with a gang like MS-13, though…

"Well," I say. "If she pisses them off, at least I know I can handle myself." Thinking about the alley earlier this morning. The dumpster I flipped over like it was made of cardboard.

"What?"

"If they start some shit. I can just…"

My eyes go wide. I haven't told him. Or Annie. With everything that's happened, with Annie nearly ditching us, and the cops, I got it into my head that Carlos already knew. What happened in that alley was so insane that it felt like *everyone* knew. I didn't even think to say anything in the ride over here.

I fill him in, talking quickly, careful to keep my voice down so machete boy can't hear us.

"The fuck?" Carlos says when I tell him how I was tasered. As I continue, his eyes narrow, his forehead knitting in barely concealed rage. I debate not telling him about the dumpster, hiding it from him like I did with Reggie and Paul. But this is Carlos. He trusts me, *believes* me, and that's not going to change if I tell him I'm stronger than I thought I was.

I finish with my delivery to Jeannette, the woman in the red tent who Africa is in love with. When I'm done, Carlos wipes his mouth, looking around him as if he's expecting another person to contradict me, say that my story is bullshit.

"Someone did this to you?"

"Yup."

"And you don't know who they were?"

"Yup."

He spits something in Spanish, rapid and ugly.

"Dude, I'm OK. Really."

"It's not that." He steps in a little closer, lowering his voice even more. "This is getting too much. We got the cops, we got people after you, Annie talking to fucking MS-13. Not to mention there's another *you* out there."

"What are you saying?"

"Just…" He looks around him as if afraid that he's going to be overheard. But Reggie and Paul are still in the truck, and even the MS-13 soldiers assigned to watch us are barely paying attention, looking bored.

"I still got friends," Carlos says. "Over the border. What if we just left?"

I shake my head. "Can't do that."

"Why not? Annie and Paul and Reggie…they can take care of themselves. You and me? We got the most to lose. And I can make it so Tanner never finds us."

The same feeling I had at Jojo's swoops back in. The urge to bug out. To run as far and as fast as possible.

I open my mouth to reply, close it again. How do I even start? How do I tell Carlos that I have to find this person, talk to them, hear their story? He'd call me insane, and he'd probably be right.

"Teagan, please." He grips my shoulder. "I don't want you to get hurt."

"I told you stay in the truck."

It's Annie, striding up the sidewalk towards us. Behind her, Nando Anguilar reclines in the shade.

I don't have a smart remark this time. I just shrug, hot and helpless.

"Got something," Annie says, popping the back door. "Let's go."

Just before she climbs in, there's a shout from the stoop: "Annie!"

Nando's voice is rich and deep. He sits up, spreading his hands wide. His arms are covered with black tattoos.

"We straight?" he says.

Annie lifts a hand. "We straight," she yells back. "I got you."

He laughs, waving a hand at her as if to say *Get outta here.*

"Think about it, OK?" Carlos whispers to me as we follow Annie back into the truck. The soldiers watch us go, one of them moseying out into the street as Paul does an awkward three-point turn. It would be wrong to say he speeds back to North Western Avenue, but he goes very light on the brake.

"Success?" Reggie asks. She sounds as if she asked Annie to go and see if there were more sodas in the fridge. On the truck's sound system Luther Vandross is singing about endless love.

Annie slowly shakes her head. "He don't know anything. Or he knows as much as we do, anyway."

"What are you talking about?" I say. "He *must* know who did it."

"Why?"

"Because..." I flounder. What I want to say is, *He's a scary Salvadoran gangster boss and so he must know everything that happens in LA.* But it sounds so stupid, even thinking it, that I don't know how to put it into words.

"That's how this shit works," Annie says, squinting in the glare coming through the windshield. "Sometimes you get lucky; sometimes..." She shrugs.

"What did you even talk about then? You were there for ever."

"I was there for like five minutes. And we just vibed. You gotta ease these dudes into it. You can't just straight-up ask them. They tend to get...kind of antsy."

"Then what are we even doing here? Why—"

"We're shaking trees," she snaps. "It's not an exact science. It's a lot harder than just doing your fucking voodoo." She snaps her fingers by her head.

"How the hell would you know?" I spit back.

Carlos talks over both of us. "OK. OK. Was there anything he knew that might help us? Anything at all?"

Annie puffs out her cheeks. "Whatever it is, it's got the cops freaked out. They're doing everything they can to control what gets to the media."

"Could he have been hiding anything from you?" Reggie asks.

"Maybe. I don't see why, though. If he had any juice, he'd probably have asked me for something in return." She shrugs. "I don't know what to tell you. Some leads just don't pan out."

The dashboard clock says it's 11:04. We've got just under thirteen hours. And we have nothing. We've wasted two hours on this pointless lead.

I tilt my head back, rubbing my eyes. Being mad at Annie isn't going to help. She's an asshole, but she's right. And going to someone as connected as this Nando Aguilar made sense. If anybody would know what's going down, he would.

The problem is, he doesn't. And somehow that scares me a lot more than it should. What are we dealing with here?

"So what's next?" Paul says. The Luther Vandross track ends, another song taking its place. Shania Twain, I think.

Annie exhales through her nose as if thinking hard. "We're going south," she says to Paul. "Stay off the 110, though. Take Jefferson and South Central Ave. It'll be quicker."

Paul frowns. "We're going to Watts?"

"Uh-huh."

"Is going home a good idea if the cops are—"

"We're not going home. We're going to find Mo-Mo."

"Who's Mo-Mo?" Carlos says.

"Maurice Saunders. Dude I know from back when. Used to run with the Circle City Pirus on the East Side."

"He's a Blood?"

"Was. Got out. I ain't seen him in a while, so I don't know what he's doing now, but it ain't with the Pirus. He still got friends all over LA, and—"

"Another gangbanger?" I say. "Won't it be Nando all over again?"

She turns to face me, more tired than angry. "*Gangbanger?* What are you, Teagan, a fucking district attorney from the nineties?"

"Then what—"

"What I was *going to say* before you talked shit about my boy, was that his mom works in the ME's office. Only accounts, but..."

"ME?"

"Medical Examiner, man," she says, exasperated. "The coroner. She might have seen the body, or she'll know somebody who has. And she and her son talk all the time, so if she knows, he will too. Maybe they've got an angle we're not seeing yet."

"Oh." I'm still not convinced, not completely, but it's better than doing nothing.

"All right." Paul turns up the music, twangy guitar filling the cab. "Let's go find Maurice."

TWENTY-THREE

Teagan

Maurice Saunders is not in Watts.

Maurice Saunders is nowhere.

We spend four hours driving around Watts and Compton and Lynwood and South Gate looking for him. We knock on doors, make phone calls, talk to store owners and dudes on basketball courts and groups of kids hanging out on street corners. All useless. Either they have no idea who we're talking about, or they just flat-out won't talk to us. Every listed address we hit is a dud—vacant lots, or just the wrong people living there.

We call the ME's office too. There's no one called Saunders there, and they are understandably reluctant to answer when we ask if anybody in their department lives in Watts.

Reggie hacks into their system, naturally; she's a demon, even with just a phone to work with. It's not as quick as it would be if she was using her Rig—she has to use what she calls rooting APKs, whatever the hell those are—but she gets there. The problem? There's nothing we can use. Just an entry about an adult male deceased from ligature strangulation. If there's a detailed report, it hasn't been uploaded yet.

After a while, we give up on Mo-Mo Saunders. Annie leads us to a couple of other contacts, but not a single one knows what we're talking about. It's around 3 p.m. when we take a break, pulling into a 7/11 just off El Segundo and Crenshaw. The fires in Burbank are a long way away, but even this far south the air is thick, heavy.

Paul leaves the ignition on and the aircon running but at least has the good grace to kill the music. "I'm going to get a soda. Anybody want anything?"

Reggie shakes her head no.

"Hold up, Paul." Annie nods to Carlos to scooch over. "I'm coming too."

"Is that a good idea?" Paul asks. "The police—"

"Unless you'd like me to pee in your truck," she says brightly.

Paul, wisely, doesn't reply.

"Me too," Carlos says. He's got crankier as the day has gone on, less talkative.

"Teagan?" says Paul.

Speaking is an effort. "Ramen, please. Extra egg. Extra garlic. Thick noodles."

With a final side-eye in my direction, Paul pops the door, letting a blast of heat into the car. He, Carlos and Annie climb out, leaving Reggie and me alone in the chilly air-conditioned cab.

Too chilly, actually. As I reach over the seat to adjust the flow, Reggie says, "Would you mind leaving it on?"

"I'm just gonna turn it down a li—Shit. Sorry, Reggie. Forgot."

Fun fact: some people with spinal cord injuries can't sweat very well. Reggie is one of them. Keeping cool isn't usually an issue—the office in Venice Beach is climate-controlled—but even with the aircon blasting, she looks uncomfortable.

"Don't worry about it," she says.

The stupid clock on the wall of Jojo's has taken up residence in my head, and it's impossible to stop thinking about it. "Reggie, is there any way you could talk to Tanner? Ask her to give me a little more time?"

Reggie uses her arm to adjust her position on the seat. "Let me tell you a little story about Moira Tanner."

It's a few seconds before she starts speaking again. "She and I were together in Bosnia when we were both a lot younger. Moira and I were seconded to NATO, working with the UN peacekeepers. That was the official cover, anyway, but what she and I were supposed to do was destabilise the Serbs from the inside."

"I thought you were a pilot?"

"That was later." She gives a weak cough. "As it turned out, she was much better at the whole spook thing than I was, because I got myself caught. I'd managed to steal a list of people the Serbs wanted to take out in Sarajevo. They picked me up before I could make the drop, brought me to this...I don't know, farmhouse or something outside Nemila. They were just getting started on me—"

"Jesus, Reggie."

She's looking out past the windshield, somewhere in the distance. "Moira comes up to Nemila. She tried to round up a couple of her contacts, but by that point nobody wanted to touch the Serbs. So she goes up there by herself. They've got guards on the perimeter, of course, which is what she was counting on."

A car alarm goes off somewhere behind us blaring for a couple of seconds before the owner kills it.

"She ties a guard's hands, puts tape on his mouth. Then she cuts out his eyes."

"She *what now?*"

"You heard. Points the poor bastard in the direction of the farmhouse and tells him to get moving. So he does, and they all come running out, which is when Moira triggers the six pounds of C4 she'd taped to his chest."

A grim smile slides onto her face, and for an instant there's a different Reggie in the passenger seat. One twenty years younger, with coiled muscles and eyes on the horizon. It doesn't make sense—this should be a bad memory for her, and yet the way she's telling it, it's like she wants to relive it.

"She took a bullet in the shoulder during the attack, but she gets me out anyway. Sets fire to the farmhouse first, of course, then puts an arm around my shoulders and leads me into the woods.

"Six days we were out there. I don't remember most of it, only that there were plenty of people still after us. Next thing I know, we're in a hospital in Graz, getting patched up. First person I see when I open my eyes is her."

"That must have felt good."

"Like hell. She didn't go through all that because she wanted to save me. She wanted the information. They'd torched my copy of the list, but they hadn't torched me yet. In Moira's view, she needed those names to do her job, which meant she needed me. If I hadn't seen the info, I'm pretty sure she would have forgot I existed."

"Well, that's pretty fucking cold."

"Maybe. Point is, she saved lives. Mine and the people on that list. She might have done it for the wrong reasons, but she still did it. If I didn't have the information, or she thought there was any other way she could protect people, well... maybe I'd still be in Nemila. Because what it is, Moira has and will always have one goal only: saving as many lives as possible. If you get in the way of that, you're in her way too. And you never, ever want to be in her way."

"That makes no sense at all."

"Doesn't it?"

"You're telling me a woman who does that to someone— with the eyes and the C4—is all about saving lives?"

"And why not? Think about it. If your goal is to save as many lives as possible and to protect the interests of this country, then how does it help you to get wrapped up in the details of those lives? Look at them as numbers, and you'll never hesitate when you're making any decision. As long as the number saved is larger than the number lost, you've won. I'm not saying I agree with it, but it's worked out pretty well for her so far. Her, and a lot of other people who will never, ever know her name."

"Yeah, well." I stare out the window, trying to ignore the fear twisting in my gut. "She doesn't seem too interested in saving my life right now."

She sighs. "You know, I am getting mighty tired of your smart-ass remarks, darling."

"Huh?"

"Seems like every five minutes I'm having to break up a fight between you and Paul, or you and Annie. Now you're acting out at me. You need to get your damn head in the game."

"Reggie, I swear to God, I will reach over that seat and—"

"I beg your pardon?"

"No, you know what? I don't need this from you. I get dragged out of bed at 4 a.m. and accused of killing some- one. Then I get fucking tasered and have to use my PK to get out of it. And now I have to sit here, trying to figure out how the hell I'm gonna make it through the day, and you wanna talk to me about saving lives? Getting my *head in the game?*"

I give her the finger. No flair. No smart-ass remark. Just a good old-fashioned middle finger like Mama used to make.

Then I sit back, arms folded. Half of me is ashamed at the outburst, like I really am a kid throwing a temper tantrum. The other half doesn't care. Not one little bit.

"You finished?" Reggie says.

I don't reply.

"Well, darling, tell me when you are. It's not like we're out here trying to clear your name or anything."

"And go right back to saving lives."

"Bingo. Owning a restaurant is all well and fine, but you're making a real impact here. More than most people can even dream of."

Her words take a second to catch up. "Wait. How do you know about the restaurant?"

"It's..."

"Have you been going through my stuff?"

"Teagan," she says, exasperated, "it's kind of hard to miss when you leave your notebook on the office coffee table."

"Even so, you can't just flip thr—"

"With the book open to a page that has 'Restaurant Name Ideas' written in big letters at the top."

Oh, goddammit.

I drop my eyes from hers. "Yeah, well."

"*Steaks Is High* is terrible, by the way. I much prefer *Pasta in Numbers.*"

"Actually, the number-one contender right now is *Grillmatic.*"

She smiles. For a few moments neither of us says anything.

"What happened to you..." she says "...what you are,

you didn't choose any of it. And God knows, the situation with Tanner isn't something I'd wish on anybody. But we *are* making a difference. The people we...disrupt...on our jobs really are the bad guys."

"You put a lot of trust in Tanner to decide who's a bad guy."

"Because I know how her mind works. We may not always know the exact effect we're having on a particular situation, but I can tell you right here and now that we're making a difference. I know you didn't choose any of it, or us. But we have to make the best of the situation, and that means focus. No more fighting with me or with Annie and Paul. Like I said, get your head in the game."

We fall back into silence. An easier one this time. I let my mind drift, thinking restaurants and PK and this whole insane mess. Thinking about Carlos. About our conversation last night.

Thinking about Nic.

I'm going to miss N/Naka. No question. I can't even call Nic and apologise because I don't know his number off the top of my head. I have a momentary fantasy of getting this all wrapped up by five o'clock, catching the killer, getting Tanner off my back, somehow making it home to change into the one decent dress in my closet—which I look damn good in, thank you very much—then sliding into the restaurant and sitting down in front of a startled Nic. *What? Like I'd miss this.*

Paul and Carlos climb back into the van, Paul turning the music back up a little, buckling his seat belt. Behind them Annie comes out of the store, looking even more pissed than usual. Her shades are pushed back on her forehead, her face gleaming with sweat.

"You know what?" I say. "I think I'm gonna get a Coke or something. Anybody want—"

Which is when a cop car pulls into the parking lot.

A big black-and-white Dodge Charger, tyres hissing on the rough surface. It's not moving at speed; the two cops inside are probably mid-shift, taking a break to get a soda, just like us. Their path takes them past Annie, who is right in the middle of the parking lot, utterly exposed.

She doesn't react. Just keeps walking, head down, as if deep in thought. Moves as if to detour around the approaching car. The two cops inside are visible now, both in dark blue LAPD uniforms. A female officer driving, her mirrored aviators reflecting the hot tarmac; her partner, a beefy dude with tribal tattoos peeking out from under his shirtsleeve, busy winding up the window as they prepare to park.

Annie walks right past them. The driver turns her head to look. As she does so, the car slows down a little.

"Oh fuck," Carlos murmurs.

The cop in the driver's seat angles the Charger towards a parking space in front of the store. Annie keeps moseying towards us, calm and easy. In the truck Reggie and Paul stare in frozen horror.

After what seems like years, Annie reaches us. "Let's go," she says out the side of her mouth.

Past her, the cop in the passenger seat is just climbing out. As he does so, he glances in our direction. He looks away, then looks back, frowning.

Annie opens the door, starts to climb into the truck.

"Hey," the cop says. His partner, halfway out the car herself, turns in his direction.

"Get in the car," I hiss at Carlos as I clamber in after Annie. It feels like the air is trying to trap me, hold me tight to the tarmac.

"Hey!" Now the cop has his gun out. His partner too. They're charging across the lot towards us. "Stop!"

"*Mierda.*" Carlos gives me a shove, pushing me into the truck's back seat, launching himself in after me.

"Go," Reggie hisses at Paul.

"Shouldn't we—"

"Go!" Annie yells.

TWENTY-FOUR

Teagan

You know how in movie car chases: all the sound is perfectly mixed, and you can hear every crunch and bang and tyre skid, and everything the main character says?

Yeah. It's not like that in real life.

Everyone in the car is yelling at everyone else. Carlos is shouting at Paul to switch to semi-auto transmission, work the gears, Paul replying that he doesn't know how, he's always driven automatic, his words dissolving in a strangled scream as an oncoming bus nearly smears us all over El Segundo Boulevard. Annie yelling that this isn't her fault, she didn't do this shit. Reggie gasping at everyone to shut up. I think I'm the only one who *isn't* talking.

It's amazing I can hear any of it because Paul still has Celine Dion playing, singing about how her heart will go on.

Oh, and the cops are now following us, barking over their PA system, ordering us to pull over. You know, just to make things interesting.

"Paul, just fucking go to manual, man!" Carlos leans over his seat, jabs at something on the steering column.

"Get off!" Paul bats his hand away.

"Then at least kill the music."

"It helps me think."

"For real?"

"Yo, Teagan." Annie twists round, eyeing the chasing cop car. "Shut 'em down."

"No good," I spit. It's true that I could fuck with the engine, maybe, twist some delicate little component and stop the car in its tracks. But it's way out of my range—matching our speed but still around thirty feet behind us. Not exactly surprising: unlike movies, cops don't ram people off the road in the middle of a city.

Could I drop something in their path? Spin another car into theirs, maybe? But I'd have to do it without hurting the cops or anyone else. I can't think of a single way to pull that off.

Annie curses. "Keep heading straight," she tells Paul. "There's a—*Whoa!*"

A second cop car explodes out of a cross-street. Paul yanks the wheel, only just managing not to hit it. As he does, the truck's back tailgate pops open. Reggie's chair, on its side in the rear, is sent sliding. It bounces off the side, then pops off the back edge of the truck like a diver from a high board, shearing itself to pieces on the blacktop. A chunk of plastic whizzes straight up in the air.

"Go to sport mode at least," Carlos says.

"OK, yeah!" Paul's voice sounds several octaves higher than normal. He pushes something on the dashboard, and the truck's engine pitch changes, Paul swinging us away from the cop car right into the second lane. There's nothing immediately ahead of us, but there's a car in the distance, flashing its lights as if trying to gently inform us that we're out of our lane.

"Don't turn off El Segundo." Reggie is tapping at her phone. "We can take Continental."

"Where?"

"Up ahead, the blue building? Just past it."

"What about roadblocks?"

"Not in the city," Annie says. "That's not how they work."

"Hang on then!" Paul guns the truck, swerving through honking traffic, tapping the brake to turn right onto Continental—only to yank the wheel with a grunt of surprise as Continental reveals itself to be blocked solid with traffic, bumper-to-bumper. None of us in the back seat is wearing a safety belt, and Annie and Carlos squash me against the door.

"Any other ideas?"

"Sepulveda?" says Reggie.

The traffic has thickened, slicing past on both sides, horns blaring.

"They're dropping back," Carlos shouts over the music. "The cops."

"You sure?" Annie says.

"Take a look." He claps Paul on the shoulder. "Keep going, man. You got this."

I don't get it. We're in a big heavy truck loaded with five people—how are they not keeping pace with us?

"OK," Reggie says. "Sepulveda, then I think we can hang a left onto Grand. Then we—Is that a *helicopter*?"

It's a helicopter. Hovering over the sunlit street ahead of us, the wind from its rotor blades pushing back the palms on the side of the road, the *whup-whup-whup* penetrating the car.

"LAX is two miles away," Reggie says. "They're in the no-fly zone!"

"Don't think they got the memo," says Carlos.

"How the hell did they get here so fast?" Paul says.

But how many helicopters have I seen today alone, buzzing over Skid Row and North Hollywood? The LAPD, patrolling the skies. There was probably one nearby, available the second the cops called in air support. Hell, they're probably happy to get some action.

We roar underneath the chopper. It banks, following us close, less than a hundred feet off the deck. Excellent.

Annie leans back into the headrest. "Oh, we're so fucked."

"Not yet," Paul says.

"You don't get it. You can't lose an LAPD chopper—believe me, I've tried. There's nowhere for us to go."

"What about like an underpass?" I say. "Or a garage?"

"Won't mean a goddamn thing if they see us go in." She points up through the roof. "Why you think the LAPD use them? No matter where you go, they got you. They got infra-red, ultraviolet, all types of shit."

The surroundings are getting more industrial, with fewer cars on the road and fewer pedestrians, but there's no telling how long that'll last. El Segundo doesn't go all the way to the Pacific. Soon we'll either dead-end or turn up into the suburbs below LAX. Nowhere to hide.

"Teagan," Carlos says. "You gotta do something."

"Her ability doesn't go that far," Reggie says. "Not for something a hundred feet up."

"You threw a dumpster this morning." Carlos is almost pleading with me. "You gotta try."

"I beg your pardon?" Reggie says.

Oh, Carlos, I wish you hadn't told them that.

"What do you mean, she threw a dumpster?" Annie says.

"When did that happen?" says Paul.

"It doesn't matter." My voice is almost a shout. "Yes, I can lift heavy shit now. But I can't just throw something a hundred feet. I've got strength, not range."

"How do you know?" Carlos says.

"Because—"

"Have you tried?"

"Do you mean to say you can lift past your limit?" Reggie sounds furious. "And you didn't tell us?"

"Jesus! Shit! Yes! I'm sorry! But I can't just—"

"Everybody shut up," Annie says. "Teagan, whatever it is you can do, you've gotta do it now."

"Do *what*? It's like ten times my normal limit."

"Then throw something at it. Knock them off course."

"Great idea. No one will suspect anything. I'm sure psychokinetics get into police chases all the time."

There's the sudden, piercing blast of a horn, invading the cab, nearly blowing my ears apart. Paul swings past a truck: a big Mack, gleaming red. The driver leans on the horn, letting us know exactly what he thinks of our driving. My PK skids across the side of the truck's cab, plays along its oversized wing mirrors.

"What kind of helicopter is it?" Reggie says.

"How the hell should I know?" Annie spits back. "One with a big-ass LAPD sign on it."

"What does the front end look like?"

"*Huh?*"

"Look at the front of the cockpit. From the edge of the roof to the tip of the nose. Does it run down straight or is there an angle?"

"Reggie," I say. "This isn't the time for—"

"Someone talk to me. I can't see a damn thing from here. Is there an angle? Or does it run down straight, cockpit to nose tip?"

"Um…" Carlos has his head craned out the window. "I think it's an angle…"

"Are you sure?"

"Yeah…yeah, it's angled," Annie says. "Like three degrees, but it ain't straight."

"OK," says Reggie. "The LAPD uses two types of choppers: Bell 206s and Eurocopters. That's a 206. How fast is it going?"

"Our speed?" Annie's veins stand out on her neck, like they're about to pop.

"Paul?" Reggie says.

"Seventy-five miles an hour? Give or take?"

"Good. Now the height. How high up is the chopper?"

"What the fuck are we doing?" Annie hisses.

"Just tell me. Give me the chopper's altitude."

"A hundred feet," Carlos replies. "Maybe hundred-ten."

Reggie bows her head as if thinking deeply. "206… hundred feet…seventy knots…the curve would be…" Her eyes snap open. "OK. Teagan, there are fuel pumps in the hump below the rotor mast, next to the tanks. Crush the pumps, and they'll just coast right down."

"Is anybody listening to me?" I shout. "Anybody at all? It's out of my range."

"Teagan."

Carlos looks me dead in the eyes, gripping my hand. "You can do this."

"I can't…"

A smile flickers across his face. "Course you can, *cabrón*. I don't know how you do what you do, but I believe in you."

It doesn't matter how much he believes in me. I can't even push past ten feet. How am I supposed to manipulate an object a hundred feet up? There's too much saliva in my mouth, like I'm going to throw up.

"It'll kill them," I say. It's hard not to picture Steven Chase laid out, rebar wrapped around his neck like garrotte wire. Whoever did it might not have a problem taking lives, but that's not me. And last I checked, you can't crash a chopper without killing the pilot and the passengers.

"I used to be a pilot, remember?" Reggie replies. "The rotors'll keep spinning even if the engine cuts. At that height and speed, the chopper can autorotate down."

"Auto-what?" Annie says.

"They've got the entire street to land on," Reggie says. "It'll damage the chopper, but they'll be OK."

She's looking at me as she speaks over her shoulder. There's the strangest expression on her face—a kind of horrified determination.

She's not trying to convince me or anyone else in the truck. She's trying to convince herself.

Her eyes might be on mine, but the person behind them is far away: above a scorched desert in a far-flung corner of the world, wrestling with the controls of a chopper that wouldn't listen to her. She knows the consequences of getting this wrong. If I do this, and whatever calculations she did are off, then the people in the chopper will be hurt. Badly. Maybe even killed. And if they survive, Reggie knows *exactly* what they'll go through to be whole again.

"There's gotta be another way," I say. I don't know whether I'm addressing her or myself.

"There isn't," she says through gritted teeth. She closes her eyes. "Fuel pumps. Under the rotor mast. LAPD pilots are some of the best in the world. They'll know what to do."

A swell of that old, familiar panic. The same panic of watching the flames ripple across the walls in that farmhouse, hearing the insane, hysterical laughter. But then again, what does it matter? Reggie can tell me to take out the fuel pumps all she wants, but I can't just *make* my PK go supercharged.

And then I get an idea.

One that lands in my mind like a live grenade.

"Hit me," I tell Annie.

She goggles at me. "Say what?"

"I said, hit me."

"*Hit* you?"

"You wanna lose that chopper? Do it!"

Annie turns to Carlos. "Don't look at me," he says, sounding as stunned as she looks. "I ain't fuckin" hitting her!"

"I'm sorry," says Paul. "Teagan, why are we hitting you?"

"Could someone just please *do it*?"

"I don't understand," Reggie says.

"Oh my fucking God." I reach over and slap Annie across the face.

If I'd stopped to think, I'd never have actually done it. It's not a hard slap, but the expression that follows it would scare Moira Tanner back to whatever spy school hellhole she crawled out of. Annie draws her fist back, twisting on the seat. I close my eyes.

"Annie, no!" Carlos shouts.

Her fist takes me across the jaw, snapping my head back. Blood floods my mouth, my ears ringing, pain flashing across my face in jagged bursts of lightning.

Whatever chemicals flood my body when I'm in danger, they obviously jack my PK, giving me strength I didn't even know I had. And I don't know for sure if it translates to range instead of power—I'm still figuring this out. But right now it's the only option we've got.

I dig deep.

Touch the raw, electric energy.

Ask it to go further than it's ever gone before.

I reach up through the back window of the truck, sending the tendrils of invisible energy through the air, right at the chopper above our heads.

Not far enough.

Going from ten feet to a hundred is a big, big ask. I don't know how far I actually get with my PK—there's nothing to grab on to, nothing to feel.

I dig deeper, clenching every muscle in my body like it'll help, willing my energy to go further. It does...but it's still not enough.

"Again," I hiss.

"What the fuck is this?" Annie sounds like she is *this close* to freaking out. Probably not used to someone she punches asking for more.

My voice is almost a snarl. "Hit. Me. *Again.*"

The punch, when it comes, isn't as strong as the first. Annie's anger is draining away, replaced by terrified confusion. But even at half-strength the hit is enough to cut my lip, bloody my teeth. My cheek goes numb, then wakes with a jolt, sending ragged bursts of pain through my skull.

My energy leaps, a volcano flowing through me. Reaching the chopper. I can feel the shape of its hull, the texture of the skids. I can sense the whirring machinery inside it, the contours of the cockpit windshield, the pen in the pilot's shirt pocket. The subtle curve of her sunglasses.

I follow Reggie's directions, sliding my PK into the hump under the spinning blades. I find the fuel tanks, one on each side: sloshing, hot, sticky. The lines running off them. And the lumpy metal cylinders alongside them, running at full bore. The fuel pumps.

I wrap my mind around them and *squeeze.*

Even inside the truck, the change in the chopper's engine noise is audible. The *whup-whup* of the blades is still there, but there's nothing behind it. The subsonic rumble of the engines has vanished.

I crane my head back, looking out the window, mind still wrapped around the fuel pumps. They're nothing more than crushed lumps of metal now, completely destroyed.

The chopper wobbles, like the pilot can't decide what to do. It starts to fall...

...and the second it does, the pilot flares the nose, tilting it up. The chopper comes in crazy fast, but the rotors keep spinning. It lands square, skids thudding off the tarmac, the body bouncing once, turning ninety degrees in a full slide before coming to a shaky stop. The pilot is just visible, still at the controls, still moving. We're too far away for me to see the expression on her face, but I imagine it's some variant of *What the shit just happened*?

"Is it still there?" yells Paul.

"Yeah, but it's on the ground," Carlos says like he can't quite believe what he's seeing.

I let go of the chopper, and my PK energy dissipates like it was never there. I collapse back onto the seat, body slick with sweat, barely able to open my mouth to speak—and not just because my lip is starting to swell from Annie's punch.

"You're welcome."

There's a half-second silence, then the truck erupts.

Reggie murmurs, "Thank God," over and over again. Paul grips her hand, squeezing it, his other smacking the wheel. Carlos is saying, "I knew it! I fucking knew you could do it!" He's slapping the seat over and over again, reaching around the headrest to grab Paul's shoulders. Only Annie is silent, staring down at her hands.

"No cops behind us," Carlos flips a mock salute. "*Adiós, pendejos.*"

Annie looks up at me. She's wide-eyed, mouth slightly open. It makes her look younger than she is. "Teagan, I...I didn't mean to..."

I don't hear the rest because that's when I really do pass out.

TWENTY-FIVE

Jake

Jake sits at the island in the kitchen of the yellow house on East Orange Grove, eating a grilled cheese sandwich.

He let it sit too long in the pan, not used to cooking with a gas flame. Most of it is burned, turned black and greasy. He's managed to eat most of one half, but the other sits abandoned, nudging up against a slick of ketchup.

The woman who owns the house is locked in the pantry, just off the kitchen. With her kid. They stopped sobbing a while ago, which was a relief. He really didn't feel like going in there, not in the mood he's in.

He's been in the house for over twelve hours. He's napped, eaten, watched TV, played games on his phone. He wants nothing more to than get the hell out of here, get on his Enfield, finish what he started. He doesn't dare. If he's going to pull this off, he has to be careful.

It hadn't taken long for the woman to give in. The sight of her child—Katie? Carey?—being hurt was enough to do it. She'd begged him to stop, all but dropped to her knees in front of him. Jake had hated to do it, hated the idea of hurting a kid. But a little cut wasn't the end of the world, and there was no way he was going to let this little family stop him. Not when he was so close to the finish line. And it had worked: the woman had given him the address where Javier, his final target, now lived. He was south, near Long Beach.

Which was a problem.

He had to be sure. He couldn't risk driving all the way up there only for Javier to be somewhere else. So he had held Katie or whatever her name is close, the glass no longer digging into her neck but still hovering nearby, a hand over her mouth. Whispering to her that if she made another sound, even one, he'd kill her mom.

He'd felt a thread of remorse at that, wondered for a moment what the hell he was doing. But it vanished almost immediately. They'd get over this—the woman and the girl both. It was nothing compared to what he'd been through: a few minutes of pain in a perfect life, compared to everything he'd endured.

He'd made the woman get her phone, call Javier. She was shaking so badly that she kept misdialling. Jake had made her stop, told her to take a few deep breaths, then a few more. He needed her calm. Composed. *Normal.* So she'd sat, inhaling and exhaling in shaky bursts at his command, hands folded in her lap, eyes never leaving her daughter. When she'd stopped, after a minute or so, Jake made her keep going.

Eventually she managed to dial the right number, put it on speaker. When Javier answered, groggy from sleep, her voice had sounded almost normal. "It's me."

"Sandy?" There'd been a hiss, as if he was sitting up in bed. "What time is it?"

"It's... um, it's early."

He was suddenly alert. "Is the Bean OK?"

Jake had smiled at that. While Sandy was struggling to dial,

he'd toyed with the idea of having her tell her husband that
their daughter was hurt, get him to rush to the house immediately. He'd rejected that; if the girl was hurt, the expected
place to meet would be at a hospital. He couldn't afford to
have Javier suspicious.

Ditto for telling Javier that he, Jake, had his wife and daughter. It was a more promising possibility, one which would
definitely speed things up a little. But after a moment he'd
rejected that too. The only hostage situation in history that
had ever gone even close to smooth was when D. B. Cooper
hijacked an airliner in 1971—and you couldn't even really call
that a hostage situation.

Sure, he could tell Javier not to call the police, but people
did stupid things under pressure. Or the man could panic, get
himself into a car accident on the way over. No, that was a bad
idea—especially when he (or Sandy anyway) could get Javier
to come to the house willingly, walk right in here. If he was
only prepared to wait.

Sandy had to take another shaky breath before she answered,
force some cheer into her voice. "She's fine. She's sleeping."

"Did they issue an evac order? I saw the fires on Fox last
night. They—"

"No. No, it's just a warning for now. The fire's still a
ways away."

Jake had smirked at that. The people here treat fires the same
way they treat earth tremors: things as normal as sunshine.
Even a fire as severe as the one ripping through the canyons
above Burbank won't get them moving until the evacuation
warning turns into an actual evacuation order. All the same,
the fire hasn't backed off. It's intensified, eating up the hills
above Burbank and Glendale. He'll have to keep an eye on it.

"Oh. OK," Javier had replied. "Uh, I don't... What's up?"

She said exactly what he told her to say: "I just want to know if you could come by the house?"

"Why?" He came a little more awake, suspicion entering his voice.

Jake had shifted his position on the couch, still holding tight to her daughter. The child hadn't made a sound, despite the tears staining his hand. *Smart girl.*

"We...I...well, we miss you," Sandy had said.

A few seconds passed before Javier answered. "You can't do this, Sand."

"What do you mean?"

"Last week you told me you never wanted to see me again. Told me to go talk to your lawyer. Now you want to meet up? Like everything's OK?" He sighed—the sigh of a man who has been asked to deal with far too much. "I told you I'm sorry about a thousand times. I made a mistake. I know that. But it doesn't give you the right to...to torture me like this."

A flash of anger. "I'm not."

"What else would you call it? First you're angry at me, and now you just call out of the blue? I don't know what you want me to do here."

Jake had found, to his surprise, that he was bored. He didn't come here for this. He wasn't interested in whatever bullshit fight they had going on.

He'd gestured with his free hand to Sandy to move it along and floated the bloody shard of glass a little closer to the child to make the point. The girl had given a soft moan, exactly one, so quiet it was almost inaudible.

A note of steel had entered Sandy's voice. "Do you want to see your daughter or not?"

"Don't you dare. Don't you dare use her to get to me." A thud, as if he was standing up. "For your information, I'm

working today. The project out in Chino Hills. I'm only supposed to be there at nine, so I was kind of planning on sleeping
off my hangover for a little bit. Of course, now I'm awake, I
guess I'll get some coffee and stare at my bank account to see
how long I'll be able to rent this place. Maybe check my email
to see if you've sent the divorce proceedings. Is that OK, Sand?
Is that info *sufficient* for you?"

Sandy's fear had given way to anger, her face turning dark.
"You don't get to talk to me that way."

"Then what way would you *like* me to talk?"

It came as a shout, the call distorting. Sandy's face had collapsed, and she'd given Jake a helpless look.

"Wait. Hold on." The anger had left Javier's voice, replaced
by desperation. "I'm sorry, Sands. I didn't mean it. I just...I
didn't sleep too well last night."

"Me neither."

"Can I speak to the Bean? Can you put her on?"

"She's still in bed."

"Oh. Right. I'm sorry I yelled at you, Sands, I didn't mean
to get...get like..."

"It's OK. Can you come?"

A few seconds' silence, as if he was trying to decide whether
the offer was real or not.

"I gotta be in Chino Hills," he'd said, sounding genuinely
torn. "Mariposa's off sick, so they got nobody else to run point,
and I can't risk my job right now. I'll try see if I can get off
this afternoon."

Jake had gritted his teeth. *This afternoon.* Was the man going
to be this difficult? He'd felt impotent suddenly, emasculated.
He was supposed to have this under control.

"I'll be there, though," Javier had said. "Count on it. Maybe
we can get tacos or something? Poquito Más?"

"Sure. OK."

It would have to do. It was the safest, most effective method of finishing the job. Sure, maybe Javier would find out what happened to the other two targets at some point today—but even if he was spooked enough to run, he wouldn't just leave his wife and daughter. He'd be here sooner or later.

Jake had given her another, more firm gesture, slicing at the air.

"I'll see you soon," the woman had said and hung up.

But they hadn't.

Jake had kept the phone and had been getting occasional text messages from Javier all day. The job had taken longer than they thought. A delivery hadn't arrived. There was a problem with the readings. Apologies and excuses. More than once it had made him doubt his plan to get Javier to the house by telling him that he had his family. He'd managed to hold back—just. He'd waited years to find out who he was; he could wait a few hours more.

It's nearly 7 p.m. When Jake first came to LA, he was enthralled with what the people who lived here called the magic hour, when the sun hits the hills just right and the air turns gold and syrupy. No magic hour today—the smoke has got worse, choking off the sunlight, painting the sky a sickly yellow.

He's been staring into space for the past forty-five minutes. Thinking about Chuy and about the mother lode of information he's holding.

The night of that first car ride, Chuy had taken him to a junkyard in Northeast LA. He'd managed to coax a little more out of Jake by the time they got there, including his time spent in foster care. Jake hadn't wanted to reveal too much at first, but Chuy had this way about him: like he was in a joke that nobody else was, and that nothing anybody did could surprise him.

Chuy knew the guy who ran the junkyard, an enormous bearded white guy with a torn biker jacket. The man had emerged from a trailer, fist-bumped Chuy and then vanished. Chuy had led Jake through the stacks of crushed cars, their heels kicking against tiny shards of smashed headlight. It was surprisingly quiet, despite being close to the freeway.

When they reached a clearing in the maze of metal, Chuy had lit a cigarette, offered one to Jake, who shook his head. It was cooler here, the baking LA night softened by the cars stacked in piles like ancient monoliths.

"OK," said Chuy, expelling a blast of smoke. "Let's see."

"I'm not a dancing monkey."

Chuy smiled. "Nobody here but you and me, homes. No test, no grades, no audience. I'm just curious, like I said." He took another drag of the cigarette, looking faintly embarrassed. "'Sides, I figure you might be a good dude to know, you know? This town gets to you after a while. You gotta have friends."

He'd clapped his hands, leaned against a crushed car. Looked at Jake expectantly.

Jake had taken a deep breath, glanced around him. Settled on a broken headlamp nudging up against an old pile of rags. He reached out, grabbed it, floated it over to Chuy and dropped it in his outstretched hand.

Chuy had whistled, long and low. "Well, shit. OK." He'd flashed a smile at Jake, open and delighted, like a kid who'd been given a present. "Not bad. What else you got?"

He began to move other things: an old steering wheel, a hubcap, a few pieces of shredded tyre. First one at a time, then all together, making them form a slow circle in the air. Then he'd stacked them, mimicking the cars around the edge of the circle. This last one took a little more effort than normal—the pieces kept wanting to drift off to the side, and he had to focus to keep them still. He'd held the stack for a few seconds, then lowered it to the ground, turning to Chuy with a smile on his face.

It wasn't returned. Chuy rubbed his nose, absently tapped out another cigarette from the packet. "OK. Nice. Keep going."

"What do you mean?"

"Lift something different." He waved in the direction of one of the stacks, lighting the smoke. "One of the cars or something."

"I can't."

"Sure you can. How hard can it be?"

"It doesn't work like that."

That had earned him an annoyed look. "The hubcaps and shit? It's a cute trick. But I think you're holding out on me, man."

He'd flushed. "Fine." He couldn't lift the car, but he'd grabbed one of the hubcaps, thrown it as hard as he can with his mind into the darkness.

Chuy had actually laughed. "What's that supposed to be?"

"If I threw that, and it hit someone, it could—"

"Big deal. I got a nine mil can do that, and I don't have to carry round hubcaps to use it, neither." He lit the cigarette, the lighter sketching shadows on his face.

Jake had started to shake his head, which is when Chuy had sprung off the car. The cigarette waggled in his mouth as he strode towards Jake, burning only a little brighter than his eyes. For a crazy second, Jake had been sure Chuy was about to hit him, but he'd stopped short, his shoulders shaking with what Jake saw was raw fury.

"You fucking pussy."

Jake had stared at him, too stunned to be angry.

Chuy spread his arms. "Look around you, man. Look where you are. You could make as much noise as you want and wreck as much shit as you want, and nobody would notice. That's what I gave you. And what do you do? You throw fucking hubcaps around." He marched over to the nearest car pile, whanged his fist on the metal. "Stop being an asshole. Do it."

Jake had stammered something, he doesn't remember what. But he does remember the shame, the sullen anger.

"*Come on.*" In the tight ring of cars Chuy's voice was a metallic bellow.

And then, all at once, he'd deflated. The energy ran out of him like water from a jug, and when he'd looked up at Jake the expression on his face had been unreadable.

"You know what, man? Forget it."

"Chuy, I—"

"Nah, that's my bad. We only just met. I shouldn't have yelled at you like that."

He'd taken a deep draw from his cigarette, tilting his head back to blow the smoke skywards as if contemplating the deepest mysteries of the universe.

The drive back to Skid Row was done mostly in silence, and when he'd dropped Jake back at the spot the bike was parked, all Chuy had said was "We'll talk soon."

Jake barely remembers the ride back to the shelter in Monterey, an indifferent building of stuffy dorm rooms where he'd managed to beg a spot for the night. What he does remember is not being able to sleep, getting up and going round to the alley behind the building and finding the heaviest thing he could—an old bag of dusty cement, left over from some ancient building works. He focused all his energy on it, trying as hard as he could to not just get it off the ground but hold it in the air, turn it, make it dance.

Part of him felt resentful. How could Chuy, a guy he just met, possibly understand a single thing about how his ability worked? And yet he kept at it, trying to manipulate this thing that was far too heavy for him, straining until the muscles on his neck stood out hard as wood. The headache the next day had been brutal, like the world's worst hangover, and yet he'd been strangely proud.

Jake blinks. The plate, with its ruined grilled cheese sandwich, hovers in the air in front of his face.

For a long moment he stares at it, his face slack. Then he sends it whirling across the kitchen, the sandwich disintegrating, the plate detonating against the wall. There's a startled yell from the pantry, one which could be either the woman or her kid.

Jake throws out a wave of energy from his mind, grabbing everything and everything: the plates in the sink, the coffee machine, the utensils in the pot by the microwave. He howls— an almost joyous sound—jack-knifing himself off the stool he's sitting on, the space around him filled with whirling metal.

All at once he's furious with himself. Plates? Utensils? He could do those in his sleep. *You're not trying hard enough.*

He grabs the microwave, launches it through the plate-glass window separating the living area from the yard. The dishwasher is next—it takes an effort, a little more focus, but he rips it out, sends it crashing into the couch. With a look, Jake overturns what's left of the couch, going from there to the TV, the pictures on the wall.

Now he's no longer angry with himself; he's angry with the people who live here. The wife and kid in the pantry, the husband, wherever the fuck he is. They don't know what it's like. They've got everything, more than they could ever want. When the little girl grows up, she won't just have money, she'll have memories. She'll know where she came from. Fuck them. Fuck them, and their perfect life, and their perfect house. Fuck their perfect memories.

When he comes back, he's sitting up against one of the kitchen cabinets, head slumped. He blinks again, long and slow, smacking his lips like he's just waking up from a nap. There are no noises from the pantry.

The oven has been pulled out but hasn't quite been yanked from its power point, as if he lost interest halfway through. The clock on the front is still alive, reading 19:21.

The outburst has drained him. Stupid. He should save his strength. He gets to his feet, digs in the fridge, pulls out a carton of milk. It goes down cold, oil-thick. Taking the carton of milk with him, he walks into the living area, settling down on what remains of the couch to wait.

TWENTY-SIX

Teagan

Waking up this time is exactly like it was when I fell out of bed at 4 a.m. And by *exactly*, I mean a million times worse.

My head is pounding, my stomach a roaring hollow. My bottom lip is swollen from Annie's punch, like my face has been injected with helium.

I open one eye, then wish I hadn't. We're in an industrial area: gravel underfoot, pipes everywhere, surrounded by huge cylindrical tanks. We're out of the truck, which is parked deep in the shadow of one of them. The sun, wherever it is, is a lot lower in the sky. I'm propped against the tank, next to Reggie.

Paul, Carlos and Annie are standing by the truck, talking in low voices. Carlos glances my way, sees that I'm awake and lopes over.

"*Holá*," he says, crouching down. "How you holding up?"

"Like the morning after you brought that expensive whiskey to the office." My voice is barely above a whisper. I sit up, wincing as my head lets me know that it violently disagrees with this course of action.

The corners of his mouth twitch. "Don't blame me. Four of us, and you had like half the bottle."

I give him the finger. "Where are we?"

"The old Chevron plant," says Paul. "Just south of the Boulevard."

"Cops?"

"Nah." Carlos smirks. "Lost 'em. Been hiding out here for a couple hours, just in case."

"Still probably gonna be some heat when we get outta here," Annie says. "We need another car. This one's licence is in their system now."

"Just finished paying it off too." Paul smacks the back of the cab. "Quite a situation you've landed us in, Teagan."

"Go die in the street, dude."

"How did you do that?" Paul folds his arms, frowning at me. "The chopper. Your psychokinesis shouldn't be that powerful."

"Yeah," Annie says. "That was some major shit."

"I..."

"Thought you weren't that strong, man." She isn't looking at me. "Isn't that what you said? When you came in this morning?"

"I thought I wasn't," I mumble, more to myself than to her. This is why I didn't want to tell them. One of the few things I had going for me was that I wasn't strong enough to bend rebar like the killer does, an alibi which is now out the window.

I retell the story about the alley in Skid Row, this time leaving in the part where I discovered that I could lift five hundred pounds. When I'm done, Annie lets out a low whistle. "And this happens when someone hits you? That's kinda fucked up, Teagan."

My lip is throbbing, sending low waves of pain across my face.

"No," I say. "It's not that. It's like a...a fight-or-flight thing. My mind senses I'm in danger and just like quadruples its energy output. Quadruples the hangover too." I spit, a globule of saliva arcing through the air. Gross. "That's why Annie had to hit me—convince my brain to use some more juice."

"Does Tanner know about this?" Paul says quietly.

"No." Reggie, who hasn't said a word up until now, speaks without opening her eyes. "They tested her under stress, but they never saw anything close to this. This is something else."

Propped against the tank, she looks impossibly small and frail. She's gritting her teeth, her jaw locked.

"Are you OK?" Paul says.

"Damn nerve pain." Her eyes flicker open, then slam shut again. "Happens sometimes after a long day."

"Long day is right," Annie mutters. She squats down in front of Reggie. "You want some deep tissue?"

"Doesn't really help."

"Yeah, well, better than nothing." Annie starts to work on Reggie's wasted legs, powerful hands squeezing and kneading. Reggie has zero real sensation below her shoulders, but sometimes she gets phantom pain: burning heat, freezing cold. Pins and needles. She can't feel the deep-tissue massage, but it doesn't stop Annie from trying.

"So what do we do now?" Carlos says.

"Keep looking." I nod to Annie. "She must have more contacts, right? Other than this Mo-Mo Saunders guy?"

"Yeah, about that." Annie sits back on her heels. "Phone's dead."

"What?"

"Forgot to plug it in, with everything that's been happening." She pulls it out her pocket, frowning down at the black screen. "All the numbers I got, they're on here."

"I'll find what you need," Reggie says. She speaks quietly as if every word costs her. "Someone hand me a phone. It's not my Rig, but..."

"Where's yours?" Paul asks.

She winces. "It was in my chair."

Which is now scattered in pieces across El Segundo Boulevard.

"Carlos?" I say.

"Left it at the office. You tried to call me, remember?"

"You know—" Paul pulls his phone out of his pocket "—you folks really ought to take better care of—"

"Zip it," I say. "Anyway, we're not getting online with that."

"What about yours?" Annie asks me.

"Gone."

"What? How?"

"Afraid so." I close my eyes. So. Most of our phones are either stolen or destroyed. The phones we *do* have are dead or from 1975. Same thing, really, if we're talking about tech.

A wave of nausea slithers up my throat, and I lean my head back against the tank, willing it to pass. Willing myself not to think about any of it. It's not just about having a phone. We might work for the government, but we're not special forces. We can't keep going for ever. We need to take a breath.

It's as if Paul senses my thoughts. "OK, so we get somewhere with a computer." He leans back against the truck, spreading his arms out on the metal. "In any case, it'll be dark soon. This place doesn't have heavy security, not since they built the new plant in Fresno, but there'll still be a nightwatchman."

"Yeah." I get a foot underneath me, planning for a future in which I'm actually able to stand up. "Plus, we need to eat."

"Where, then?" Paul looks around. "We can't go back to Venice Beach. Annie, Carlos and myself—all on the police systems." He ticks us off on his fingers, looking more morose by the second. "They're probably staking out our homes right now. Annie, do you have anybody—"

"Nobody whose numbers I know off the top of my head."

"Carlos?"

He puffs out his cheeks. "I mean, we could go over to Pomona. I got fam out there."

"Way too far," Reggie mutters. She sounds as if she isn't in as much pain now. Maybe Annie's massage really did help.

I slowly get to my feet. Reggie's right: it'll take at least an hour and a half to get over to Pomona, and that's assuming we get lucky with the traffic, which we won't. That's not time we have. The sun is already—

"Wait. What time is it?" I say.

"Um..." Paul looks at his watch, a chunky piece of metal that looks like it could control a space station. "Six fifty-one. Why?"

I lean back against the tank. Then I thump my head against it, then do it again, letting out a disgusted groan.

"You OK?" Paul asks.

"I know where we can go."

"Great. Where?"

I raise a finger. "Before I tell you, question: if you stand someone up on a date, what's the best way to apologise? I mean it's not technically a *date*, per se, but let's say it's definitely something you shouldn't have missed. Are flowers enough, or—"

"The fuck are you talking about?" Annie says.

"Never mind. I have a friend who can help us out. You'll like him. Assuming he doesn't actually slam the door in my face."

TWENTY-SEVEN

Teagan

But first we have to steal a car.

We can't Uber, thanks to the sudden lack of phones built in the twenty-first century. We *could* call a cab, but even if we got one sent out to us—which could take anywhere from twenty minutes to an hour in this city—we don't really have a way to pay for it. The only one of us who still has their wallet is Paul, and of course he never carries cash.

We can't take the risk that the cops aren't watching his bank accounts. Even a quick withdrawal would lead them right to us. That's *if* we could actually find an ATM and *if* a cab would even take us; we don't exactly look like the safest passengers to have in your ride. So car theft it is.

The neighbourhood is a little way to the north, but it takes us for ever to find the right car—one that won't immediately be reported stolen. We have to be careful: scouting for cops, zipping across the still-busy El Segundo Boulevard, checking out various side streets . . . it all adds up. It takes us half an hour to go half a mile and to find a car we can use. We pick a beat-to-shit green Corolla with rust on the door panels, parked on a side street. The buildings around it are low-rise apartments and flat-top warehouses, most of them looking like they haven't been visited in a while.

Fortunately, the car looks the same way. There's a good amount of dust on the windows, and the building it's parked front of looked unoccupied. Whoever owns the car probably hasn't used it in a while and definitely won't have bothered to install a tracker.

Opening a locked car isn't exactly hard when you have PK. The only problem is, I can't do it.

I am so badly out of juice that it takes me a full minute just to wrap my mind around the door mechanism. I have to focus hard, block out everything around me. That's not easy with Paul fretting and Reggie (who is being carried by Carlos) telling him to can it. It's the first thing she's said since we left the industrial zone. She's drawn into herself, blocking everything out. I'm guessing only some of it is pain. The rest is probably her replaying the chopper crash over and over. Doesn't matter that it came out OK or that no one got hurt.

And I don't have the faintest idea what to say to her.

Another five minutes go by, everyone standing awkwardly while I try to winkle up the lock. Paul is just asking about maybe breaking the window when I finally get inside.

Carlos knows how to hot-wire a car, and before long we're on our way, skirting LAX as we head north. The clock on the dash reads 7:37.

Nic lives in Sawtelle, a suburb just south of UCLA. It's a twenty-minute drive, if you take the 405 and get really lucky with the traffic. We don't even bother. We zigzag through Del Rey and Mar Vista, adding another fifteen minutes to the trip, easily.

My shoulder muscles tense every time we hear a siren or

spot a cop car rolling past at the end of a distant block. Our only hope is that they won't recognise the car we're in.

I've got out from under worse before. I survived my parents. I survived Wyoming. I am going to figure this out. Yes, Tanner's deadline is ticking closer and closer, and yes, there's a killer with identical powers still running around, but I can do it.

All I have to do is convince Nic. I focus on that, take this one step at a time, and it'll all work out.

As we move further into Sawtelle, heading up a side street lined with double-storey apartment buildings, the Corolla starts to cough. Carlos swears, working the gas, but it doesn't help. The engine dies with a long, wheezing sigh, and we coast to a stop, Carlos pulling us in at the kerb.

We sit for a moment in the silent car, none of us willing to move. Or too exhausted to.

"What you expect?" says Annie eventually, popping the door. "Damn thing's a lemon. Amazed we even got this far. Yo, Teagan, where we going again?"

"Westgate Ave. Just off Wilshire."

"Maybe we should try another car." Paul looks around as if a likely candidate is just sitting there, waiting for us.

"Nah." Carlos squints out the windshield. "Round here? People'll report that shit stolen in like ten seconds. We gotta walk. Westgate ain't far."

The sun has set. There's still a little light in the sky, edging the cloudless horizon in purple and blue. The street lights are on, just starting to dapple the sidewalk. There aren't many people around, and for once there are no cops. The odd office worker arriving home, a group of kids messing around by a big tree on Missouri Avenue. I'm worried that we look out of place, but nobody gives us a second glance.

I'm lost in my own thoughts, so much so that the group has got ahead of me. All except Annie.

She's walking alongside me, staring straight ahead. There are dark circles under her eyes, and she's moving with a deliberate, focused stride. Like she's just got to keep going, and everything will work out. Can't blame her. I'm feeling the same way myself.

"Annie," I say.

She doesn't respond at first—I have to say her name a couple of times before she looks my way. I don't think she planned to end up walking alongside me. "Huh?"

"You OK?"

No response. Beyond the low-rise buildings a thumping bassline reaches us: a car driving past in the distance, system cranked, the sound fading almost as soon as we notice it.

We're at the end of the block when Annie says, "Please don't make me do that again."

She sounds so sincere, so polite. I blink in surprise. "I don't—"

"Hitting you. I didn't want to."

"Um...sure. I won't. Promise."

"Thank you."

Another few moments of silence. Then: "My dad used to do it to my mom."

"Oh, Annie..."

She continues as if I hadn't spoken. "He never hit me. Always my mom, though, and it'd come outta nowhere. One second fine, the next second boom. She serve his food wrong, say something he didn't like, not answer him fast enough, that was it."

Her tone of voice doesn't change. The whole way through, she sounds like she's talking about the weather.

"He worked at a children's library over in Carson. You believe that shit? Guy spends his whole day working with kids, giving 'em books, talking to 'em, then comes home and beats the shit out of his wife. Like it was nothing."

"I didn't know," I say quietly.

"That's cos I never told anybody. Not till now, anyway. That's why I'm not mad at you for it."

"He still with your mom?"

"That asshole? Got himself killed back in '03. Drank too much and went for a ride down the 110 to San Pedro. Lost control on an off ramp, and it's a miracle he didn't kill anybody else. You wanna know the most fucked-up thing?"

My voice is barely there. "What?"

"I take after him." It's as if she's swallowed something rotten. "I got his face. And I get angry like this." She snaps her fingers.

Her expression when I slapped her in the back of Paul's truck, to make her hit me. She was furious—like a completely different person had taken her place at that second. What must it have been like for her, knowing what was happening, knowing she couldn't do a damn thing to stop it? And afterwards...

"Please don't ask me to hit you again," Annie says. "I know your voodoo, your thing, whatever, you gotta give yourself that fight or flight now to get it working...but I don't wanna do that again."

"I won't." I mean it too. "I only did it because—"

"I know. Like I said, 's aight."

We walk in silence for a few minutes. We're passing a school now—a low rectangular building with blinds down in the windows. There's a fenced-off soccer field to our right, a tattered banner hanging from the chain-link. GO TIGERS!

"Your mom. She still around?"

"What? Oh. Yeah. She still out in Watts. Got emphysema and can't walk more than three steps without huffing oxygen, but she here. Got a mouth on her too. You don't take your shoes off when you come in the house, you'll be hearing about it for months."

"Sounds like it's not just your dad who passed things down."

"Watch yourself." But there's no anger in her words, and the ghost of a smile plays across her face, caught in the glow of a street light. It's almost full dark now. "Anyway, we get by. Folks in the neighbourhood look after her when I ain't around. She got good days and bad days, but it all evens out."

"Insurance?"

One of the weirder things about our arrangement with Tanner: we actually get federal health benefits, same as any other government worker. Don't ask me how Tanner pulled that little trick off. I keep meaning to ask Reggie, but I haven't got around to it.

"Doesn't cover parents," Annie says.

"What about—"

"Private's too expensive."

"You couldn't ask Tanner for help?" Our insurance might not cover family, but surely our supreme commander could pull a few strings…

The look on Annie's face is one of absolute disgust. "I ain't asking that bitch for a goddamn thing."

"But—"

"I *work* for mine. I don't do charity. Never have, never will."

Her eyes are fixed on the road ahead, and there's an edge to her voice, one that warns me not to push it.

Another long silence. In the distance Paul yawns.

"Annie?"

"Mm-hmm?"

"I swear to you," I say. "I didn't kill Steven Chase. I know I can do some crazy shit, but I would *never*—"

"I know."

"You do?"

"Yeah." It's a few seconds before she continues; she's quiet for so long that I'm about to prompt her. "I admit, I thought you was lying about it, but that was...Look, now it's different. You could have gone on the run a million times over, but you're still here. That counts for something. At least to me. I didn't wanna see it before but...anyway. You're here, and that's what matters."

"Thanks," I murmur.

A few blocks later Annie speaks again.

"What I said last night..." She clears her throat. "I didn't mean it like that. I was just kind of freaked out, is all."

For a second, I struggle to even remember where I *was* last night. Then her words come back to me: *I think you wanted to use your power. Your ability. Whatever the fuck it is. I think you were looking for an excuse.* It sounds like something said to a different version of me. When Annie first went off, it stung, but now? Nothing. After all that's happened, it's impossible for me to stay angry.

And in the last twelve hours I've found out exactly what happens if I push my ability. I can do things—things I never thought were possible. I am *stronger* than I thought was possible. Sure, it kills me every time I do it, but if I can find a way past that...

"It's cool," I tell her. "I *did* just throw you out a window."

She grunts.

"Hey," I say, "Did you ever—"

"Oh, the fear of heights I *did* tell you about. Your ass just forgot."

I blush. "My bad."

Another ghost of a smile. "Forget it."

My stomach growls, knotting in on itself in a painful cramp. It's impossible not to start thinking about food. Smashed burgers wrapped in grease paper, dripping sauce, curly fries on the side. A Vietnamese *bahn mi*, jammed so full of spices and crisp veggies that the baguette can hardly close. Sushi. Oh my God, *sushi*. Nigiri, the fish relaxing onto a soft pillow of rice. Sashimi: a hit of straight, clean, healthy protein, the tuna so fresh it almost snaps between my teeth.

Nic's apartment is on the second floor of a concrete apartment building—a corner spot overlooking the intersection of Westgate and Ashton. The building itself is a dull grey, clearly designed by someone who really wanted to make an art-deco masterpiece and didn't have the budget. It's all weird swirls and curves and arches. The first time I came here, I thought it looked like an alien spacecraft—one which had landed on earth and was trying to blend in, but the aliens had only studied humans for about five minutes before coming. It's one of several identical blocks on this street.

As we approach, I clear my throat. "Guys, maybe let me go in first?"

"Is that a good idea? Splitting up?" says Carlos. He's still carrying Reggie and hasn't shown any signs of getting tired.

"No. But he's probably already pissed at me, so seeing a bunch of people on his doorstep isn't really gonna help."

The complex next to Nic's has a path straight through to the inner courtyard, but of course the one *we* want to get into has an outer security gate made of thick white metal. I hit the buzzer.

No response.

I hit it again, then lean on it, willing him to answer. Please,

God or Buddha or Satan or whoever happens to be listening, let him be home. Don't make us have to break in or go somewhere else. Let one thing in this clusterfuck of a day go right. Let—

"Hello?"

His voice is tinny, distorted, but there's no mistaking the annoyance in his voice.

"Nic? It's me. It's Teagan."

Nothing for a moment. Then: "Not right now, Teagan."

"Nic, please. I just wanna talk, that's all. Just for a minute. Can I come up?"

No answer.

"Look, I'm *really* sorry about N/Naka. I can explain everything."

He laughs. "Yeah, I bet you can. Get out of here, Teagan."

I blink. That stings.

"No way." I say. "*Please.* Just five minutes, that's all I ask."

Something's not right. He might be pissed at me about N/Naka—I definitely would be—but he wouldn't just…shut me out like this.

When he doesn't respond, I lean on the buzzer. When he *still* doesn't respond, I turn round, giving everyone a confident smile. "OK. Plan B."

"And what would that be?" Paul says.

I gesture to the top of the gate. "Give me a boost."

TWENTY-EIGHT

Teagan

There's a big central courtyard and parking area behind the complex gate, half-filled with cars. An old rusty sign informing residents that garbage pick-up is on Mondays and Thursdays is bolted to the wall. Big terracotta pots are dotted between the cars; some of them even have plants in them, big ferns with spiky leaves.

My PK brushes the pots, running along the grainy surface of the terracotta. I've got a little strength back since we stole the car—not much, true, but enough that I could probably lift small objects now.

Nic's apartment is on the second floor. The opaque window next to the front door—the bathroom window—is dark. I listen hard but can't hear anything from inside. Doesn't mean much; he's probably in the living room at the back.

I raise my hand to knock...and hesitate.

I'm putting him at risk by coming here. He'll be in danger from the cops, from Tanner. From whoever sent those two goons to kick my ass this morning, an event that feels like it happened years ago. Can I really do that to him? Should I?

I don't have a choice: we need to stop somewhere, catch our breath. I can't just back out after coming all this way.

I knock on the door. Nothing. No answer. I try again and get the same result. OK. There's no way I can go back down to the others and tell them we've come all this way for nothing. Annie's head will probably explode.

I'm about to knock a third time when the door opens.

Nic wears jeans and an untucked black dress shirt, sleeves rolled up. The smile that makes him so much fun to hang out with is gone, and what's left is cold and hard and angry.

"Hi," I say.

Without a word he turns and marches back into the apartment.

At least he didn't slam the door in my face. That's a start. I hover on the threshold for a second, then step inside.

The apartment has a long entrance hall, with the bathroom on one side and Nic's bedroom on the other. He lives alone— he got lucky with the rent and decided that he could afford not to have a roommate. As I pass, I catch a glimpse of his unmade bed, the pile of books on the nightstand.

The living room is open plan. One wall has a counter with a tiny stove on top and a fridge underneath. There's a sink the size of a hip flask, currently drowning in dirty dishes. A couple of worn cupboards take up the space above it.

The room has the unfinished feel of someone who isn't really interested in furniture. There's no dining table, and the coffee table is basic Ikea. The only decent piece in the room is a big couch covered in buttery black leather, opposite a good-sized TV. An Xbox sits on the floor beneath it. More attention has been given to his surfboard and snowboard, which rest on special wall racks on the far side of the room, rubber draining mats beneath.

The walls are unpainted, but there are two huge, stacked bookshelves running along the one to my right. I might worship music and food, but Nic worships books. He has a real thing for old mysteries—Raymond Carver, Jeffery Deaver, Ed McBain—along with a serious non-fiction boner. The shelves are stacked with dog-eared paperbacks. His Kindle balances on the arm of the couch. Plus plenty of legal textbooks, filed in neat rows.

He's over by the sink, rooting around in one of the cupboards, his back to me. His plastic kettle is just coming to the boil.

"Um, look," I say. "I'm so sorry about—"

"I'm making coffee." He glances over his shoulder at me. "You want some?"

It's like he's speaking Russian. "Coffee?"

"I forgot to buy cream. You OK with black?"

"Yeah," I say, feeling dazed. "I mean, no. Nic, look, I just need to talk to you."

"There you are." He shakes out instant coffee and a little clumpy sugar into a mug, then adds the just-boiled water. "You sure you don't want?"

"Nic. Please just look at me. I can explain. I really wanted to be at N/Naka, but—"

"N/Naka?"

He turns towards me, slowly stirring his coffee, the spoon clinking against the side. He's a long way from taking the lead on a case, but it's easy to see him doing it, easy to see him standing in a courtroom, chin raised like it is now, calmly making his arguments.

"N/Naka doesn't bother me," he says, still stirring. "What bothers me is you vanishing for an entire day and not answering any of my calls or texts." *Clink. Clink.* "What *bothers* me is

that you somehow end up in a police chase across Hawthorne
that ended up with a helicopter crash."

Wait. *What?*

He can't know. It isn't possible. The only witnesses were
those cops.

Nic walks over to the couch, lowering himself onto it.
"What bothers me is that my friend, who I thought worked
at a moving company and who wants to open a restaurant one
day and tells me she grew up on a farm in Wyoming—"

"I *did*! That's the truth!"

"I don't care." He's grinning now, a horrible grin, and he
hasn't stopped stirring the coffee. "I really don't. You're hanging out with a bunch of suspects for a murder that shouldn't
technically be possible, and I'm suddenly living in one of those
Netflix series, and then you show up at my front door and
expect me to be cool with things. *That's* what's bothering me.
Thanks for asking."

Oh fuck.

He works in the district attorney's office. The chase with
the chopper must have made some waves.

"OK." I spread my hands. "I don't know what you heard—"

"*Heard?* I didn't have to hear. I saw." He points two forked
fingers at me like he's warding off a curse. Or casting one.

What does he mean, he saw? I might have been scared out
of my mind, but I'm pretty sure I would have noticed Nic
wandering around Hawthorne.

"Oh yeah. There's video."

Nic taps his chest twice, over his heart. It takes me a
second to understand, and when I do, the blood in my veins
freezes solid.

A bodycam.

The cops at the 7/11. They were wearing bodycams. They

have to, in the LAPD. They don't like releasing the videos to the public, but they still wear the things. One of the cams must have been rolling as the officers got out of their car. It made its way through the LAPD right into the DA's office.

"I wasn't even supposed to be in the room," he says. "I think Grace forgot I was in her office. I saw the whole thing. They watched it about ten times. Really got your good side. Yours, Annie's, everybody who works with you. You were all on it."

I can't move. My feet are welded to the floor.

He finally, finally takes a sip of his coffee, slurping a little. "The cops found your van in Cypress Park, by the way. Someone tipped them off. Prints all over it, from what I hear."

Goddammit.

I take a step towards him. "Look…"

He doesn't jerk away, not exactly, but he freezes, eyes darting towards the front door.

He's scared. Of *me.*

"No." The word is barely a whisper. "Nic, please, I would never—"

"Never what?" He doesn't move. "What is it you do, exactly? Since when do moving companies kill people?"

My stomach feels like it drops a full two inches. "Nic…"

"Stop saying my name like it's going to change things. Someone is dead, and the cops think you did it, and I want to know why."

"We didn't kill Steven Chase!"

"So you *do* know who he is."

"Yeah, but—"

"Explain it to me, then. If your friend Annie didn't kill him, then why do the cops have you on video outside the guy's building?"

He sees my confusion. "Yeah, didn't I mention that?

Bodega got you folks on camera. You really ought to be
more careful."

My mouth goes dry. *Bodega.* The convenience store on the
corner. An oasis of light opposite the dark alley below the
Edmonds Building, the neon open sign flashing. The store would
have had cameras. And of course neither Annie nor I thought
to tell Reggie to hack in and shut them down. Why would we?

Nic frowns. "Come to think of it, you told me you were
having dinner at Annie's last night. More bullshit."

"It's... it's kind of hard to..."

He takes another sip of coffee, his hand actually shaking a
little. "Jesus, this explains so much. Why you keep this *distance*
all the time."

That hurts. "Distance?"

"Yeah, Teagan. Distance."

"You had a girlfriend!"

"Emphasis on *had*." He doesn't sound angry. Just resigned.
"You told me to give Marissa another chance. You wanted me
to keep going with a shitty relationship so you wouldn't have
to actually make a decision about us."

"That is *not* fair. This isn't about us."

"Tell me I'm lying then." He raises his voice for the first
time, spreads his arms like he's inviting me to take a swing.

"You don't think I wanted you?" My cheeks are hot. "If
I'd told you, you would have been in danger. I wasn't gonna
do that to you."

"So you just made the call."

"*Yes.*"

But he's full steam ahead now. "No, see, what I'm starting
to get is, like, you never corrected me. I thought you were just
normal, and the whole time you were involved in... whatever
the hell this is. Murder. Running from the cops. How long

were you going to keep me in the dark before you actually told me this? Even if it would have put me in danger or whatever, you think you were just gonna keep it a secret?"

"*Fuck you!*" I don't mean to shout, but it happens anyway. "You're right—I never lied to you. I just wanted to live my life. I wanted you in it, and there are things I'm not supposed to tell you. If you can't deal with that, then that's your problem not mine."

He half smiles. "Touched a nerve, did I?"

In the silence that follows I swear the ringing in my ears is louder than my voice was.

"You know what?" I say, the words tasting bitter. "I . . ."

I can't finish. I'm crying again. I throw my hands up, start heading back down the passage. I barely make it four steps. Because where are we going to go? We *need* to stop. We've got no car, no computer, no food and we're running out of time. My eyes find the digital clock on the front of Nic's oven before I can stop myself: 8:02.

Six hours left.

"OK," I say, slowly turning to face him. "I'm sorry."

He says nothing.

"I wasn't kidding when I said telling you would put you in danger . . . but that doesn't change the fact that I kept you in the dark. That's on me. And if I'd figured out any other way to do it, I would have." I can't get the words right—the feelings are too conflicted, the anger and frustration threatening to overwhelm me. I can't let that happen. I need him to take us in. And more than that, I need *him*.

"But Nic, listen to me. I'm in a lot of trouble. It's not just the cops. There's . . . other stuff going on too. And I can't even tell you the day I've had, which started off with me getting tasered, and then—"

"*Tasered?* Jesus."

His eyes widen with automatic concern, and that's when I know it might be OK. Emphasis on *might*.

"Yeah. And I promise I will explain everything. But right now everyone's waiting downstairs, and we're in bad shape. We could really use a place to crash."

"What do you mean, everyone?"

"As in the guys. China Shop."

"You're joking."

"Afraid not."

He sits back on the couch, lacing his hands behind his head. Lets out a long breath. In that moment the apartment is frozen in time. No sound. No movement. I don't even want to blink.

I am so goddamn tired.

"Fine," he says. "Yeah. Bring 'em up."

TWENTY-NINE

Teagan

I head down to tell the others they're OK to come in. "'Bout time," Annie mutters as they move in single file through the gate.

"Oh, by the way," I say, not meeting anyone's eyes, "he knows about the chopper."

"What?" Reggie looks like she's about to leap out of Carlos's arms and throttle me. "You told him?"

I explain about the bodycam video. As I finish, Paul pulls Annie aside and they have a muttered conversation.

"Cops found the van too," I tell Carlos.

He winces. "Shit."

"Yeah."

"With your prints all over it, no doubt," Reggie murmurs. "Well, can't be helped. Let's go."

In the apartment Nic has switched his black shirt for a grey UCLA hoodie. He's turned the hall lights on and is leaning against the kitchen counter. He gives everyone stiff nods as they come in. "There's some chips, if you want," he says, nodding to a plastic bowl on the table which he's filled with Doritos. "Help yourself."

"Very kind," murmurs Reggie.

"Nice place." Paul looks around, swinging his arms. "Good neighbourhood too. What do you pay per square foot, you don't mind me asking?"

Nic looks at him like he asked if he could take a shit on the carpet.

I put a hand on his shoulder, stand on tiptoe to hug him, meaning it as a thank you. He turns his head away. I hover for a moment, then drop back, not trusting myself.

"Would you mind if I rustled up something to go with the chips?" I ask him. "Been kind of a long day."

"Chips?"

"Yeah."

He lets out a long, slow breath. "Yeah. Get some chips. Help yourself"

I clear my throat. "No, I meant, can I cook something? To eat with the—"

"*Yes*. Fucking...I don't care. Whatever. Do what you need to do."

It might seem crazy, taking time out among all this insanity to bumble around a kitchen. But we won't be able to do a damn thing—or at least *I* won't be able to—if we don't get some food inside us. And give me this: the one thing I can do in a crisis is cook.

Nic doesn't have much in his fridge, but he's got cheese, mustard, some butter and a loaf of white bread. Everything I need. I stick a pan on the electric burner as I prep for grilled cheese sandwiches, calculating how many slices of bread I'll need to feed six of us. Of course, cooking in a home kitchen for a few people isn't quite the same as churning out multiple meals for a full service, but when I eventually open my restaurant, I'm going to—

I stop for a second, letting the block of cheese rest against the grater. Open my restaurant? I'll be lucky if I ever open the front door of my apartment again.

I make the sandwiches, almost attacking them. I mix the grated cheese with grain mustard, sandwiching gooey piles of it between slices of bread, buttered on the outside. Cooking is good. It distracts me not just from the events of today, but also from the world's most awkward party, currently happening six feet away.

"Thanks again for letting us come up," Paul says eventually.

"No problem."

Carlos clears his throat, staring down at his shoes.

"So." Nic says. "What's the deal here?"

"We're not going to be here long," Paul says. "We'll eat, we'll do a little research and then we'll be out of your hair. We just need to—"

"Um, 'scuse me." Nic raises a finger. "That doesn't really answer my question. I want to know exactly why the cops think you killed Steven Chase."

Reggie glances at Paul.

"We had nothing to do with that," Paul says slowly.

"Then why do they think you did? Why are they chasing you?"

"They spotted our company van outside the Edmonds Building last night. It was nothing, just a job we were on, a late moving assignment."

"Really?" The familiar smile dashes across Nic's face. "A moving assignment for...who, exactly?"

Paul shrugs. "We've got a client in downtown. Insurance company, if you can believe that, right next to the Edmonds Building."

It's amazing how smoothly the lie rolls out of him. "They

had a burst water line around six o'clock last night," he continues, smiling as if to say *These things happen.* "Got a call from their head guy, whole disaster, they had to move all the furniture out so the rug could be taken up and replaced. You know, I asked him if they themselves had insurance, and if it was from another company, or if they insured their own stuff…"

Nic raises an eyebrow.

"Anyway, that's what we were doing." Paul says. "This whole thing is a case of mistaken identity."

"Then why did Teagan tell me you were all at Annie's for dinner last night?"

Behind him Annie mouths at me, *What the fuck?*

"Yeah, Teagan." Paul's voice shoots up an octave or two. "Why would you tell him that?" He turns back to Nic. "Whatever Teagan says we did, we really and truly were on a job."

"Cut the shit," Nic says.

"Excuse me?"

"There was no client, and you weren't on a moving job. If you can't be straight with me, you can get the hell out."

"I can assure you—"

"Shut up." This is the other Nic. The one his friends outside work almost never see. The one that he locks away when he's sneaking onto a no-swim beach or wolfing down something tasty and exotic. This is the Nic that works in the twisting, convoluted world of LA's legal system, and that Nic does not fuck around.

"There are so many holes in your story, I don't even know where to start," he says. He's holding his hands together as if in prayer, fingertips resting against his nose. "I need to know why you were at the Edmonds Building, why the cops think you committed the murder and why you would run from them instead of turning yourselves in and trying to figure this all out."

Paul opens his mouth, closes it again. It's impossible to miss how exhausted he is. I badly want to intervene, but I don't have the first clue what to say. I'd only make things worse.

"Nic."

Reggie speaks quietly as if it takes real effort to say the words. "I'm truly, truly sorry you got caught up in all this. We wouldn't have come here if we had any other choice."

He tries to reply, but she speaks over him.

"I need you to extend us a little faith here. We're in serious trouble, and it's going to be very bad for everyone if we can't get out from underneath it. We won't be here long, and I promise, when this is over, I'll explain everything."

"Nope. Not good enough."

Annie mutters something unintelligible. Nic swings to face her, suddenly angry. "No, no, no. Don't just talk shit like I'm not sitting right here."

"There are things..." Reggie takes a deep, laboured breath. "Things that we aren't authorised to tell you about."

"*Authorised?*"

"Trust me, homes," Carlos says. "It's better if you don't know."

"Do you know what I'm doing, letting you guys in here? I'm putting everything on the line. Not just getting arrested for harbouring fugitives. I'll lose my fucking job."

"That's not going to happen," Paul says.

"You know what?" Nic jabs a finger at Paul. "Don't even speak to me, man. You don't know shit."

"Hey." Annie wakes up. "Don't you talk to him like that."

Nic ignores her. "You're in charge, right?" he asks Reggie. "That's your job? You the head of China Shop, or whatever this company is?" His voice is rising. "OK. So you tell me what's going on, right now."

"Nic, your sandwich is ready," I say.

Reggie glares at him. "As I *said*, we will explain everything to you once this is—"

"*Nic*. Your sandwich."

"Jesus, Teagan." He turns to face me. "I don't want a—"

He stops talking.

Along with everyone else.

They're all staring at the frying pan, a sandwich still in it. It's hovering in front of my face, along with a plate. I've got my hand underneath the floating pan—not because I need to, but because I want there to be zero ambiguity. I'm doing this. It's me making the frying pan defy gravity, me who tilts the pan so the sandwich plops onto the plate, me who floats it over and deposits it on Nic's lap.

THIRTY

Teagan

"Teagan," Reggie breathes. "What have you done?"

What have I done? Interesting question, Reggie.

"So here's what I see happening," I say. "We were gonna keep telling Nic that we couldn't tell him anything, and he was gonna keep getting angrier and angrier and then try and kick us out for real. And so you'd give him a few more details to try, I don't know, to keep him happy or whatever, but he'd keep digging because what you don't understand about him is that he doesn't quit, even when he really should."

I step past the pan, floating it slightly to one side. Nic blinks. He still hasn't said a single word.

"*Then,*" I continue, "he'd wanna know why we were in the Edmonds Building, and you'd lie to him, and we'd go round and round in circles, and eventually you'd tell him that we work for the government—"

Paul buries his head in his hands.

"—and then he'd wanna know if we were special forces or spies or the Illuminati or something, and you'd tell him yes. He'd start asking for details, so you'd make something up, and he'd figure it out and tell us to leave again, and by the time we've gotten to the fact that I can move things with my mind the cops will be here and *we still won't have had anything to eat.*" I grab another plate from the counter, one holding a sandwich I'd already made, and take a jagged bite. "*Fuck,* that's delicious. Anyway, that's what I've done, Reggie. Can we move on already?"

They gape at me.

"You've made a mistake," Reggie whispers. "You're putting him in danger."

"If he lets us stay, he's in danger anyway."

Nic looks like he's just woken up from a really weird dream. What he said when he told me how I always kept at a distance, left him in the dark…that hurt. A lot more than it should have.

"I am sick and tired of lying to people," I say. "You ever think about that, Reggie? I don't care how many bad guys we help put away, we still have to lie to do it."

Reggie opens her mouth to reply, but Annie gets there first. "You are so full of shit. You know how many people I talk to? Every single day, for China Shop? I let everybody know what we do, that's half of LA."

"You're not listening. You never listen. I get that we *have* to lie to some people. It sucks, and I hate it, and I don't have a solution for it. It's just that…Annie, aren't you tired of it? Don't you wish there was another way? At the very least, we shouldn't have to do it with people we care about. Not if we're asking them to help us, like we are now."

Annie says nothing, just shares a look with Paul.

"And the worst is," I say, "we lie to each other too. I lied to you guys when I didn't tell you about how strong I'd got, because I was scared you'd think I really did kill Chase. I don't wanna do it any more."

The words bring back memories I'd rather ignore. A boy called Travis and the night we spent in that park. I lied to him, and I'm not going to lie now.

Not to Nic.

"Teags," Carlos says. "Just think for a second…"

"Nic." I make him meet my eyes. "This is what I can do. This is why we were in the Edmonds Building. We're gonna tell you everything. If you still want us to leave afterwards, that's fine.

"Now." I send more plates floating across the room, setting them down on people's laps. "I made food. It's rude not to eat when someone cooks for you."

"What the fuck," says Nic. It comes out as one long, blurred word. *Whathefuck.*

"Yeah. I know. The world isn't what you thought it was and blah blah blah."

His eyes are going to swallow his face. "What…"

"It's called psychokinesis. PK for short. I can only move inorganic objects—I don't really know why—and only up to about three hundred pounds. Well, five hundred, I guess. Now, I mean. I'm a lot stronger than I used to be. And it's just me, by the way—Paul and Carlos don't have superpowers, although they both probably want to."

"OK." Annie gets to her feet, sounding resigned. "You guys have fun with this. I'm gonna do some real work. Nic?"

"Huh?"

"You got a USB-C phone charger? Or a laptop?"

"Uh…yeah." He doesn't look away from me, gesturing to the bedroom. "Nightstand."

Annie nods thanks, slipping away and quietly shutting the bedroom door. She leaves behind a pregnant, uncomfortable silence.

"Reggie?" I say, putting a sandwich in her hand. "Why don't we start with Steven Chase?"

She gives me a Look. But after a few moments she starts talking.

As we eat, she and Paul fill Nic in on what's happened in the past twelve hours. Mostly, he listens in stunned silence. I sit on one end of the couch, ploughing through a second sandwich. They're not my best—they're a little undercooked, the bread not as crispy as it should be—but right now I'd pick them over *anything* Niki Nakayama could make in her kitchen at N/Naka.

When Reggie finishes the story, Nic sits back. He raises a hand to his face, drops it again. Looking over at me, he says, "This all true?"

"Yeah."

"OK." The hands get all the way this time, coming to rest on his chin. In the quiet, Paul delicately munches the last of his crust.

"I know it's a lot to take in," Reggie says. "Usually, you'd need high-level clearance to even get told that we work for the government." She raises an eyebrow at me. "These are not the usual circumstances."

"Wait. Hang on." Nic turns in my direction. "Before we do anything...I need to know how you can do what you do. I get that doing jobs for this Tanner person keeps you free, but how'd you hook up with her in the first place? Is your... power, ability, whatever it is, really genetic? How the hell does that even work?"

"Long story," I say, swallowing a mouthful of cheese sandwich.

"I bet."

He isn't going to be swayed. I set my plate down. "Well, my parents—"

"OK." Annie comes marching back into the living room, clutching her cellphone, Nic's laptop held under one arm. "Think we got something."

"Hold that thought," I say to Nic.

"You get hold of Mo-Mo?" Carlos asks.

"Uh-huh. You know what that motherfucker's doing now?" She points at Nic's hoodie with its university lettering. "Works for UCLA. In the goddamn library too. I didn't even know dude could read."

"Did he have anything we could use?" I say.

"Yep. Took me for fucking ever to convince him the cops weren't gonna bust through his front window just cos he was talking to me." She puts her hands on her hips. "But I got him to talk to his moms. Steven Chase wasn't the only victim."

"What?" I spin in my seat so fast I nearly smash Carlos in the face with an elbow. "Who?"

"Bryan Hayden, B-R-Y. Killed at his house over in West Hollywood, same way as Chase. Cops kept it quiet."

"Killed last night?"

"They don't know. They aren't sure about time of death yet. But he was killed with a rebar, same as Chase."

We crowd around the laptop. Even Nic gets involved. Carlos pilots, running Google search after Google search. There are no less than eight Bryan Haydens living in West Hollywood, and the info on most of them is sparse. One works for a movie studio. One runs a home air-conditioner business. A third turns out to be a reserve pitcher for a minor league baseball team.

Which is super-helpful when trying to connect them to a clothing company, as you can imagine.

"Wait a minute." Reggie narrows her eyes. "Hayden. Hayden. I've seen that name. Carlos, let's pull up the coupler data."

"Shit. *Yes.*" I'd forgotten about that. The coupler we planted in the Edmonds building is still transmitting.

Reggie and Annie and Carlos go to work, accessing the coupler's feed, filling the laptop screen with gibberish. It doesn't take them long to find what they're looking for. Chase sent a hundred emails before he died, and one of them happens to be to bhayden@oceansafe.com.

"What's Ocean Safe?" I ask.

"Charity," Paul replies. "That's why we didn't spot it before. Carlos, can you…"

But Carlos is already there, opening up a website that looks like it was designed in the 1990s. It's an environmental charity, the page covered with donate buttons. Carlos clicks on a few links, lingering on projects, photos of demonstrations. One of them shows Hayden—the caption says he's Ocean Safe's CEO—above a sea of protest signs, holding a megaphone and looking righteous. He's bearded, with long hair and an electric-blue Hawaiian shirt.

"I don't get it." Paul rubs his temples. "What's the connection?"

"Got me," Reggie replies.

I lean over, squinting at the screen. "Were they maybe working together? Some initiative or something?"

"One hell of an initiative," Annie says.

There's nothing. No mention of the Ultra clothing label on Ocean Safe's page. Ditto for the reverse. Googling Steven Chase and Bryan Hayden together turns up nothing. The closest we get is an outdoor summer movie screening they both told Facebook they were going to: a showing of *La La Land* at a spot in Brentwood. Given that they were among five hundred people who responded, I don't think it's a very good lead.

"Unless Ryan Gosling killed them," I murmur.

"What's that?" says Nic.

"Never mind. Maybe Ultra had a factory. Maybe they were, I dunno, pumping shit into the ocean or something..."

Carlos's fingers are a blur on the keys. It doesn't take long—there are plenty of stories about how Steven Chase built Ultra from the ground up, plenty of long profiles and business reports. Annie wasn't kidding about not using overseas factories, which would have been a lot cheaper. Ultra's three factories are all stateside, and they made a big deal about using only local materials.

Problem is, the factories are in Nebraska and Colorado. Neither of which have any coastlines. There aren't even any rivers or lakes near them.

"There's gotta be something," I murmur. "Something in the supply chain, maybe. Pumping industrial waste, or..."

"To where, though?" Annie spreads her hands. "And even if they were, wouldn't this Hayden guy be trying to *stop* that from happening? Why kill him too?"

"Maybe they were connected some other way," Nic says. He's not as stiff as before, one knee up on the couch as he peers down at the laptop. The dazed look he had is gone. "Maybe they both owed money to someone..."

Annie rolls her eyes. "Who just happened to have a psychokinetic on payroll? You don't find a dude like that on Craigslist."

I bite my lip, getting to my feet and wandering over to the kitchen, trying to think. I rest my elbows on the counter, which feels good, then I wrap my hands around the back of my neck, which feels better.

Chase. Hayden. Ultra.

"OK," I say, turning and leaning back against the counter. "Reggie, can you maybe go through Chase's emails some more. Maybe some weren't encrypted, or—"

"Yes, Teagan," Reggie says patiently. "We're already doing it."

"Oh. Right. Good job."

"Little slow without my Rig, but Carlos should be able to—"

There's a piercing crash. The window next to the couch blows inward, followed by the sound of tinkling glass. Nic and Carlos yelp in unison, scrambling across the couch.

I stumble back, almost tripping on the uneven kitchen floor. My first thought is that someone's shooting at us, but then I see what came through the glass: a small black cylinder with a complicated rectangular section sprouting from one end.

Annie's eyes go wide. "Flash—"

—*bang.*

THIRTY-ONE

Teagan

Light.
   Noise.
   Heat. Close.
   Down.
   Noise. Shouts.
   Nic.
   Carlos.
   Annie.
   Crawl. Elbow. Elbow. Can't hear. Can't see. Ears ringing.
Tile. *Noise.* Front door. Crashing open.
   Go back. Help. Can't hear. Can't see. Get out. Get out.
Door. Close. Elbow. Elbow. Nearly. Reach.
   Footsteps. Running. Closer. *Reach.*
   Gun. Back of neck. Barrel cold. "Don't move." Barely hear
it. Ringing. Ringing everywhere.
   Hands pulled behind. Cable-tied. Gun barrel still on my
neck. Blinking, but the world is too bright. Annie swearing.
Thud. Reggie screaming.
   Arms under my elbows. Pulled up. Guys from the alley?
This morning? Come back? Spun round, afterimages

glaring. Black. Everywhere black. Black armour, black helmet. White teeth.

Mouth moving, but I can't hear. He's shaking me. Over and over again. Huge white smile. Big black wraparound sunglasses, reflecting my stunned face. Stubble crusted on his cheeks. Black gloves moving. Around my neck. Pulling tight. Tight. *Tight.*

Can't breathe. A burning line at the my throat. Can't think.

My hearing slowly, slowly, slowly comes back. "...what I'm saying?" His voice is wrapped in cotton wool. "We see a single thing move, and I'll choke the life out of you. Got it?"

I nod. Then shake my head. I still can't breathe.

"*Got it?*" he roars in my face.

He's strangling me, a length of rope in his fists, digging into my throat. Without thinking, I try to grab it with my PK, only to have my mind slide right off it. It's organic, thin and strong.

His grin widens. "Spider cord, bitch. Like I said, you move anything, anything at all..."

I don't know what spider cord is, but it doesn't sound fun. Grey feathers the edges of my vision for a moment before he relaxes, flipping me over onto my stomach.

The flash-bang has had the same effect as the taser this morning. It hasn't wiped my PK, but it's made it fuzzy and useless. I can just, *just* get a grip on other objects in the room, but I probably couldn't move anything very far.

"That Tanner's lady?" someone else says.

"Yeah, it's her. Get the others."

Tanner.

Then I'm back in the living room, down on my stomach with the others, their hands bound like mine. Even Reggie— Annie, bleeding from the mouth, is trying to tell them that she's a quad, that she can't move. They just ignore her. Paul is yelling that we're American citizens, that they have no right, that we're entitled to legal representation. A boot in the stomach shuts him up.

There are too many of them, black shapes thundering through the room, shouting at each other. Nic's terrified eyes meet mine.

There's a knee on my back. "Give me a reason," the man says. "Move anything, even an inch, and I'll end you. Those are literally my orders, and I would be *very* happy to carry them out."

"Burr." It comes from of the others, a giant of a man with a huge grey beard. "Quit the chatter."

"Copy," says the man called Burr.

The apartment is a hurricane of noise: soldiers yelling, radios crackling, orders to lock down the perimeter, confirmations that the package is secure.

The package. Me. Has to be. Tanner might have given me a 2 a.m. deadline, but that was before I took down a helicopter, got the whole DA's office and LAPD in a frenzy. She must have decided that we weren't worth the trouble.

"Leave her alone!" Nic yells. Like Paul, he gets a boot in his stomach. What I feel for him at that moment can't be described. I want to wrap my arms around him. I want to tell him how sorry I am. And then grab the soldier who just kicked him and bash his head against the countertop until there's nothing but red paste.

Reggie's eyes meet mine. There's real panic on her face, her breathing coming in quick, harsh rasps. Seeing her fear—on a face that has always been calm and cool and collected—is enough to jack my own terror up into the stratosphere. She's groaning, low and long, shaking her head from side to side.

The jumble of thoughts collides and throws up a word: *dose.*

They're going to sedate me. Knock me out. If I'm unconscious, I can't use my PK, and I'll be easy to handle.

It doesn't make sense. Why not just have one of the soldiers dose me? Or better yet, dart me from a sniper rifle, like an elephant from a chopper?

The answer comes before I've even finished asking the question. Sure, they could dart me, but it's hard to get the dose right. Too little, and I could fight back. Too much, and my heart stops—not ideal when your mission is to capture not kill. Plus, no matter what movies and video games show you, sedatives aren't instant. They take time to work. Better to subdue me—give them this, the spider cord is clever—*then* dose me up. Right into a blood vessel.

If they do put me under...that's it. It's over. I'll take the fall for both Bryan Hayden and Steven Chase. By the time whoever killed them does it again—*if* they do it again, because we still know nothing about who they are, or what they want—Tanner's bosses will have made sure that I'm in a five-star suite in a government black site. And by five-star suite, I mean a padded cell where they put me after they've finished their experiments. Maybe they'll release me after it turns out I didn't kill anybody. Then again, would they risk it? Now that they know how strong I am?

I can't let that happen. I won't.

I try to go nuclear. Try to pull out some of the energy that saved me this morning in the alley, because if there was ever a fight-or-flight situation, it's this one. I feel the objects in the room, my PK wrapping around the pots in the sink, the lightbulbs in the ceiling sockets, the metal lighter in Burr's pants pocket.

Which doesn't change the fact that all Burr has to do is pull hard on the cord: the one thing I can do nothing about.

At the very first sign of PK, he'll choke me to death. It won't
even take much—the wire is that tight around my throat, my
air supply shrunk down to a tiny pinhole. And even if I do
start throwing shit, I don't know how much control I'll have.
Enough to stop Carlos or Nic or anyone else getting hurt?

Maybe.

Maybe not.

"Burr, listen to me," I say, my voice harsh and papery. I
don't even know what I'm doing—getting him talking is the
only thing I can think of.

"Shut up." He sounds bored.

"We got something. OK?" I turn my head a little. "A connection between the victims. If you do this, I'll never—"

"Please. Pretty sure that if you could find it, won't be an
issue for us. You're going back where you belong."

"*Burr.*" It's greybeard, and he's not happy. "I told you
to stow it."

"Come on, boss," Burr says, eyes never leaving me. "You
want me to be nice to this freak show?"

Freak show?

Reggie is struggling. She's breathing faster, her shoulders
shaking. And the sounds she's making: those groans, with a
tiny, hitching cough at the end of each one.

Something's wrong. She shouldn't be doing that.

"Yeah, I heard about you." Burr's voice is soft, too soft for
his commander to hear. He tugs the wire around my throat.
"You're going back in a hole, freak show."

Buddy, you are so lucky I am out of juice right now.

"What's wrong?" Greybeard has noticed Reggie. "Hey."
He nudges Paul's shoulder with his foot. "What's wrong
with her?"

"She's an incomplete quadriplegic," Paul spits back.

He has to twist his head to look up at the man. "Her diaphragm's weak."

Greybeard gives a jerk of his chin, and he and one of the others haul the coughing Reggie upright, plant her on the couch. She's still shaking.

I turn my head a little, just as another soldier come through the door. He's dressed in much the same way as the others, all in black. I can't see his face from my position on the carpet, but he's carrying a black case, like one you'd use to hold a microphone, and his boots are polished to a mirror shine

He makes his way over, squats down next to us, placing the case in front of me.

"'Bout time," Burr mutters as the soldier flips open the case, revealing a syringe nestled next to three vials of liquid, all of them held in shaped slots cut into the interior foam. The wire tightens again. "Little reminder," Burr hisses in my ear. "I'll be watching that syringe. I see it move in any way it's not supposed to..." He gives the wire another tug.

"She's heavier than we were briefed on," the doc says.

Oh, fuck you, man.

"She'll need a couple of doses."

"Just get it done, doc," says Burr.

"Burr..." My mouth is too dry. "Take me if you want. Just let them go."

"Teagan, no." Nic twists to face us and gets a foot on his neck for his trouble.

The doc fills the syringe. I still haven't seen his face, but his hands are that of an older man, lined and calloused, speckled with liver spots. "They aren't involved. They can't do what I do. Please."

"Sorry," Burr says, not sounding sorry at all. "Orders are

clear: capture if you can, kill if you can't, but everybody gets brought in."

"She's getting worse," Greybeard says. Reggie is jerking now, the weak coughs coming more and more frequently. "Doc, need you over here."

"Just a second." The syringe is full. He taps it, squirts a little out the end. I twist away, only to be forced to stop as Burr leans into my back with his knee. I almost grab the syringe with my PK on instinct—the syringe, and everything else in the room. Just wanting to lash out, throw anything, go fucking bananas. I don't. I can't. Desperately, I try to grab hold of the wire at my throat, hoping against hope that it'll listen to me. Nothing. It's like trying to reach out and pinch the air.

"Doc!"

"What?" He's pulled up my overall sleeve, fingers hunting for a vein. The tip of the needle is just, just touching my skin.

"She can't breathe, for God's sake," Paul shouts.

The doc growls. "Watch her," he says to Burr, getting to his feet and striding across to the couch. I get a look at the back of his head, his salt-and-pepper hair. There's an ugly fold of skin at the back of his neck.

"C7?" he says.

"C6," Annie says. "She gets neuropathic pain—stress makes it worse."

"Any breathing issues?" The doc bends over Reggie.

It doesn't make sense. Reggie doesn't *have* breathing issues. Her lungs work fine. Colds can be dangerous—her diaphragm isn't as strong as it should be, which can be an issue if she has a cough. She's coughing now, but she wasn't before. What...

She's faking.

I don't know how, or what she thinks is going to happen, but she's trying to distract them. Trying to get them to stop looking at us and start looking at her, getting them to drop their guard. Maybe she doesn't understand—she won't know what the wire at my throat is made of, won't know that I can't manipulate it.

There must be something I can do. Reggie's giving us a chance, and I am *not* going to waste it.

I scan the room with my PK, tracking over guns and metal buttons, the pots in the sink, the kettle, the zippers on the couch cushions. Nothing—nothing that won't make Burr slice my head clean off with a single tug of the wire. Nothing that—

Oh.

Oh, Burr.

You stupid motherfucker.

The wire is crossed once at the base of my neck, the ends held in Burr's hands. And on his left one: a metal wedding ring.

He probably didn't even think about it. Probably doesn't even remember it's there. He was so focused on the organic wire, on capturing and/or killing the freak show himself, that he didn't stop to think about his ring.

"Hey, Burr," I say.

He leans in close, his breath hot on the back of my neck.

"Till death do us part."

Then I grab hold of the ring and break his finger.

THIRTY-TWO

Teagan

Burr howls, jerking back as he tries to strangle me. Which he can't do because I've pulled his left hand all the way over to the right, and I've already twisted out of it.

I don't waste time taking a breath. I twist sideways, bucking Burr off me.

Then I let go.

The flash-bang made me fuzzy, but I'm not aiming for precision. I am pissed and motivated and grabbing everything I can get my hands on. Pots, pans, pictures, knives, forks, coffee cups. The bowl of chips flips through the air, cascading Doritos. Every single rifle and knife and sidearm gets ripped away, slammed into the ceiling, out of reach.

I don't worry about direction. I just throw everything I can, upending the contents of the apartment over greybeard, the doc, Burr, the other two members of the tac team. I make it happen at head level, way above everyone on the floor, way above even Reggie. She's not shaking any more. She's looking right at me, a delighted, almost evil smile on her face.

The fuzziness starts to fade. It's like a car starting on a cold morning: takes a while to catch, but once it gets going, you can put foot to floor. The walls start to come apart, the individual panels of synthetic drywall ripped out through their layers of paint, whirring through the air. Less than a second later, there's a huge, crunching smash as a plant pot from the courtyard explodes through the window, filling the air with flying soil, terracotta shattering.

Holy *fuck*. I didn't even know I'd grabbed hold of that.

And while all this is happening—and all of it only takes about four or five seconds—I'm reaching down, wrapping my PK around the plastic cable ties binding everyone's hands and snapping them in two. My own included.

"*Let's go!*" I yell. Or try to. It kind of comes out as "Let's grrrrk" because that's when Burr manages to get the wire around my neck again.

Broken finger or not, he's still special forces. I reach out for the ring only to find that it isn't there. The son of a bitch actually managed to rip it off his broken finger. It's behind him, discarded in the kitchen.

This time Burr isn't playing. He yanks me backwards, my head banging on the tiles, a burning line of agony around my throat. I can't get air. Not a single atom of it. I claw at the noose, the one thing here I can't touch with my PK, my fingers scrabbling at it, unable to get a grip.

Which is when Carlos kicks Burr in the face.

It's a championship-winning, full-run-up, top-of-the-foot fifty-yard-field-goal monster. He could try out for the Rams with that kick. When his foot whips past my face, I actually feel the blowback.

There's a wet *crack*, and the wire goes loose. I rip it away, scramble to my feet. I'm losing energy fast—hardly surprising, given what I've been through today. There's still stuff spinning through the air, but it's sluggish now, not moving with nearly the same speed as before. And the weapons: they're still held against the ceiling, but I'm not going to be able to keep them there for long.

Not that it matters. The door's right there, and once we're out, we can lose these assholes. Nic grabs me, pulling me down the hallway, Carlos and Paul just behind him. Annie bringing up the rear, swearing, hands covering her head, like she's the one I'm trying to beat to death. And—

"Reggie!" I yell. "Where's Reggie?"

Nobody's carrying her. Not Carlos, not Nic. I turn back, feet stutter-stepping as I switch direction. She's still right where they put her, on the couch.

Her eyes lock on mine. And with what looks like every ounce of strength she has, she bellows, "*Run!*"

I've lost control of the weapons on the ceiling. Most of the other stuff too. I'm running out of power fast, losing my ability to move things, and if we go back for Reggie now . . .

The rational part of my brain knows it's a bad idea. The rest of my brain tells that part to go fuck itself, and sends my body sprinting back towards Reggie because like hell am I leaving her with these douchebags.

If Nic hadn't been there, I would have run right back into the middle of it. He pulls me up short, hauling me along with him.

"Reggie!" I yell.

"Come on!" Annie barrels into Nic and me, accelerating us towards the door. We explode out onto the balcony walkway, her name still on my lips. I get one last look at her, collapsed on the couch, and then we're gone.

I twist away from Nic. "We can't just leave her!" Knowing we have to. Knowing we can't go back in there. On the one hand, I'm furious with them for not picking her up; on the other, what were they supposed to do? Risk getting brained by whatever shit I was throwing around? Fight their way past the soldiers?

I don't get a chance to think too hard about this, because that's when Paul crashes headlong into another member of the special forces team.

It's a younger guy with a Mohawk—probably left behind to make sure no neighbours interfered. He comes roaring round the corner, slamming right into Paul. They go down in a tangle of limbs. I use the last dregs of my PK to grab the guy's rifle, tearing it out of his hands and smashing it against the wall.

After that I'm not really sure what happens. I just put my head down and run.

I blink, and we're in the courtyard of the complex, surrounded by cars and plant pots.

"Where's your ride?" Nic says.

"Don't have one," Annie replies. She's out of breath, her words run ragged.

"What do you mean you don't have one?"

"It broke down."

"Are you serious?"

"Forget that," Carlos says. "Where's *your* car?"

"Doesn't matter. I don't have the keys."

"Are *you* serious?"

"They're up there." Nic points back towards the apartment.

A gunshot splits the air, the report ricocheting off the buildings. We don't see where the bullet goes, but all of us hit the deck anyway. Gravel grinds into my hands as a second shot rings out. It's greybeard, silhouetted in the window of Nic's apartment, rifle in hand.

So much for taking us alive.

Hands on my back. Nic. We take off across the courtyard as greybeard fires again. This time the bullet digs a chunk out of the ground, sending up a drifting spray of dirt. I reach out for his rifle, but it's too far away. I could push it, extend my range, just like I did for the helicopter. Of course, if I do, I'm pretty sure I'll pass out again.

Why aren't they hitting us? This isn't an action movie—the good guys don't get away because the bad guys can't hit anything. Then again, they're aiming at moving targets in low light. All the same, if we don't get out of this courtyard soon, they're going to find their range.

There's a grey Prius parked on one side of the courtyard, next to a six-foot wall. Carlos barely breaks his stride, vaulting onto it, running up the windshield and onto the roof, touching the top of the wall as he flies over it.

Paul and Annie aren't quite as graceful. She makes it OK, just, but he has to actually clamber up right as a second rifle burst joins the first. Bullets puncture the engine, dinging off the car's paintwork, the front lights shattering. About three feet from us.

Looks like they found their range.

"This way." I grab Nic's hand, and we tear across the courtyard, heading for the exit to the street. Annie shouts my name from the other side of the wall—she probably thinks I've been hit. "I'm OK!" I yell back.

We hit the narrow alley leading to the security gate, meaning we're out of the line of fire—for now. Fortunately, these kinds of gates don't need a key to open up—you can just push right through them from our side.

"*Come on!*" I grab his hand, bolt across the street—just in time to see Annie, Carlos and Paul emerge to our right.

"You OK?" Carlos says.

"Fine. Let's get the hell out of here."

"Up there." Annie points. "Onto Wilshire."

"Wh—"

"Traffic. People. Cars."

She's right. Wilshire is right at the top of the block, a fifteen-mile-long street that bisects Los Angeles, east to west. Burr and his buddies might think twice about firing at us if there are other people around. Or at least, I *hope* they'll think twice.

We bolt up Westgate. Halfway there, I look back over my shoulder, knowing I shouldn't but unable to stop myself.

Burr is chasing us.

The rest of the squad are nowhere to be seen. It's just him. His face is a bloody ruin, his left ring finger bent at a strange angle. It's like he doesn't even notice—and despite his size, he's *fast*. He's sprinting to catch up with us, head down, rifle slung on his back and arms pumping. He's gaining, and I yell at the others to hurry. What the hell are we going to do when we reach Wilshire?

The street isn't gridlocked, but there are plenty of cars whooshing past: ten lanes of traffic, vehicles moving in both directions. A giant billboard looms over one corner of the intersection, Ryan Reynolds' shit-eating grin towering over us.

Paul gets there first. He comes to a halt on the sidewalk whipping his gaze left and right. I barrel into him from behind, shoving him onto the tarmac.

"The traffic!" he says.

"Just keep moving!" Burr is closing fast, barely fifty yards away now.

"Teagan," Nic yells. "Watch ou—"

A car screeches to a halt, the driver slamming the horn. I

don't bother apologising, slaloming past it into the next lane of traffic. The cars around me are going nuts, horns dopplering as we pick our way through.

The surface of the road isn't flat—it's pocked with potholes. My foot catches in one of them as I reach the halfway point, and I drop to one knee, cursing.

Nic is a few feet away, just ahead of me. He half turns, trying to double back—and a car zips between us, hooting like crazy. Then another one. An unbroken line of traffic whizzing past. He can't get back. He tries to dodge through, but there's no space.

I turn my head, looking down the street, trying to find a gap, which is when the car ploughs right into me.

THIRTY-THREE

Teagan

It's an old Nissan, green paint, rust on the bumper. I know this because I get a real good look right before it sends me flying.

If the driver hadn't already been leaning on the brakes, it would have creamed me. As it is, it still sends me bouncing across the tarmac. I skid to a halt on my back, ears ringing. My shoulder took the full force of the hit, and it's letting me know just how much of an asshole I am for putting it in this situation.

The driver pops her door, screaming at me, wanting to know if I'm OK and what the hell was I thinking and should she call 911. She has a high-pitched, screechy voice, and a serious valley girl accent. Her right headlight is cracked from where it hit me, a thin spiderweb radiating out from the centre.

Burr. Ten feet away, weaving through the line of cars to get to me. His white grin has turned dark red.

"Teagan!"

Nic and Carlos are both trying to get to me from the other side, Annie and Paul behind them, everyone yelling my name. The traffic has picked up, cars whizzing past on both sides, leaving me stuck in the middle. If there's a gap for Burr, he'll be on me in seconds.

Slowly I get to my feet. Nic and company are still shouting for me. I put a hand out to tell them I'm OK, my eyes finding Burr's, not looking away from him. The valley girl has stopped screeching, hands gripping the top of her car door, looking between us and probably wondering what the hell she's got herself into.

"There's a gap." Paul's voice cuts through the sound of the traffic. "Teagan, behind you. You can make it."

And Burr will just keep chasing us. He won't stop. Not unless I make him.

I face Burr head-on. Throw my arms out like I'm inviting him to step outside.

Valley girl is about to get one *hell* of a surprise.

I have almost zero PK energy left. But I still have enough to do something simple. It doesn't take a lot of pressure to break glass that's already cracked; snapping a big shard out of valley girl's broken headlight is easy. I snag it, pull it towards me and zip it up to hover in front of my face.

The remaining headlight on valley girl's car illuminates the shard perfectly. She makes a really strange sound, a kind of breathy *whuh*, like someone hit her softly in the gut.

Oh, I'm just letting *everybody* know what I can do today.

Burr pauses, his grin faltering. I make the glass twitch, dancing in the air in front of me. The message is clear: *Take one more step, and this goes in your eye. Then maybe I break your other fingers.*

His grin is gone now. What's left is raw hatred.

Freak show.

If he decides to move anyway, if he rushes me, there's no way I'll be able to fight him off. My PK is starting to falter, just like before, the very last dregs of my energy draining away.

There's still a gap in the traffic behind me, all the way to the sidewalk. To Nic, and Carlos, and the others. I take a step back. Then another. Never looking away from Burr. He doesn't move.

As I reach the sidewalk, I drop the glass shard into my hand. Then I point a quivering finger at Burr.

In that moment I know he won't stop coming. For him this isn't just a simple mission with an objective and a target. He took this one personally. Like I'm an affront to everything he stands for.

And next time I might not be able to stop him.

Carlos, voice urgent in my ear. "We gotta go."

THIRTY-FOUR

Jake

After their first meeting, when Jake showed Chuy what he could do, the other man had cut off contact for three months.

That was how Jake saw it. Like Chuy had taken a long hard look at their relationship and decided he didn't like what he saw. Taken a knife and delivered a single, clean cut.

It was agony. Jake didn't have Chuy's number—he'd never got it, never even thought to ask. He spent whole nights wide awake in the shelter, staring at the bulging mattress above his head, wondering if the clunk of a footstep from the corridor outside was the cops. Or worse.

It occurred to him that he could track down the woman at the Mission—the one who had spotted him using his ability in the first place. It made sense. But he couldn't bring himself to do it. A dozen times he promised himself that he'd visit the next day, and a dozen times he found an excuse not to.

The nights that followed those promises were the worst. They were the nights he abandoned sleep and retreated to the alley behind the building, honed his Gift, not sure what he was doing but doing it nonetheless.

He'd already been up to the junkyard in Northeast LA—or

parked across the street from it anyway, waiting for the guy with the beard to show himself. That hadn't happened. A bald man with lidded eyes and a badly fitting suit had come out of the office at the front of the property and stared at him, expressionless. Jake had ridden off.

The leaden feeling in his gut hadn't gone away. He'd thought it was worry, but he knew what it really was. Disgust. Disgust at Chuy for vanishing. At Los Angeles, a city that had seemed to offer so much when he drove into it and which had given him absolutely nothing. Most of all at himself for not knowing what to do next.

Then again, was he really to blame? Hadn't he been down this road before, hunting for a trail only to get nothing? What was the point?

His ability couldn't help him. It would just get him noticed. Maybe, he'd thought, it would be better if he vanished too. After all, it wouldn't matter who Chuy told if they couldn't find him.

But they will find you. They'll use computers and tracking programs and informants and everything you don't have. They'll find you.

He'd bent his first piece of metal that night. Ripped the lid off a dumpster and bent it in two, grunting with the effort, sweat bucketing down his face. In the end he'd collapsed, dry-heaving, the lid clattering to the ground. He'd crawled back inside, somehow got into bed, shivering and shaking.

The only way he got to sleep any more was by running through stories from history in his head. The stories he liked best. The Battle of Changping, in 262 BC, where two of the greatest kingdoms the world had ever seen, Zhao and Qin, went head to head. Alexander the Great. Hannibal crossing the Alps with his war elephants. The inquisition. The sacking of Rome. He had their details memorised, but it was different now. The images were thin. Insubstantial. Like a shirt that has seen too many hot days and not enough dry closets.

He would never take his place in history. Not ever. He would never find out who he was or where he came from. For the thousandth time he thought about walking into a records office, taking the people there hostage, *making* them find out for him. Only, what if they couldn't? What then?

He didn't think he could kill. And if he did, they would hunt him down. He was strong, stronger than he thought was possible...but he wasn't strong enough. They'd wipe him out.

And then, on a day so hot the walls themselves seemed to sweat, Chuy had shown up at the hostel.

Jake had been about to go to work—he'd picked up a gig in Pomona, handing out flyers for some car rental place—and was climbing onto his bike when there'd been the impatient noise of a horn behind him. Chuy, in the same beat-up Civic, wearing the same flannel shirt. He hadn't parked—had just stopped in the middle of the street, backing up traffic behind him.

"You coming or what?" he'd said, then flipped a lazy finger at the honking cars behind him.

Jake had stared, sure he was about to start sobbing uncontrollably. He hadn't. He'd scooted round to the other side of the car, ducked inside, squashing a takeout container underneath him. Chuy had taken off with a squeal of wheels, rocketing away from the line of cars.

They hadn't gone to the junkyard that day; they'd just driven, moving in a loose circle up through Glendale and San Fernando, all the way down to Santa Monica. At first they'd just listened to music, Chuy pumping salsa and Latino rap and old-school rock through the Civic's crackly speakers. But after a while he'd begun to talk.

Nothing important: sports, politics, the shit he'd seen

in LA, how everyone here was a fucking actor. Jake hadn't said much, merely nodding, occasionally giving a grunt of agreement or laughing at Chuy's jokes. He didn't trust himself to talk yet.

They'd ended up in Playa Del Rey, watching the sun set over the ocean, drinking a six-pack of Budweiser that Chuy had had in his trunk. It was piss-warm, but Jake would later think that he'd never been happier, sitting in the shotgun seat of that car with Chuy, having a beer, talking about nothing. When was the last time he'd done that? Just...relaxed?

"I've been practising," he'd said after his third beer.

Chuy had given him a sideways look. "Practising what, man?"

"You know...my Gift."

The beer muddied his thoughts, made it hard to focus. Certainly, if he tried to lift anything now, it would wobble up into the air, barely in control—if he could get it up in the first place. The choice of words nearly made him giggle, and he only just managed to stop himself.

"OK," Chuy had said, not sounding very interested. He'd taken another swig of the warm beer, eyes on a woman in a bathing suit roller-skating past.

"I'm serious. I can do stuff now."

"Yeah? Good for you."

"No, listen. The other night—"

"Dude." Chuy had waved the bottle out at the ocean. "We gotta talk about this now? About work and shit?"

"Work?"

"Whatever, man. We can't just hang out? Talk like normal people? I mean, I know you an X-Man or whatever, but you don't gotta be an X-Man all the time, right? You can't just kick back, have a beer?"

They'd done just that, getting more and more drunk. After

a while Chuy had plied Jake with questions: where he grew up, what he'd done before he got to LA, where he'd got the bike. Jake found himself telling it all, talking for longer than he'd done in years.

For his part, Chuy told him he was from Venezula—Caracas. He'd been in the States four years, owned a car service up in Canoga Park. "You gotta give back, man," he'd told Jake, staring out onto the darkening ocean. He'd tapped his chest. "Get right here." Pointed to the sky. "Get right there. You gotta try make the world a better place, even when it doesn't want to be."

"Right on." Jake took another pull of Budweiser, his third.

Whatever Chuy had said, Jake had figured that one night in the junkyard wasn't going to be enough. He'd been right. Chuy had shown up at the hostel two nights later, one of the Bud cans from the beach still rattling around in the car's passenger footwell.

They made their way deeper into the junkyard—the bearded dude was back at his post as if Chuy had conjured him. For all Jake knew, maybe he had.

Chuy had joked about Jake's ability. "We gotta find a spot with plenty of hubcaps right? You want me to set up a couple bullseyes, keep score?"

The jokes had trailed off when Jake lifted a rusty V8 engine block out of a destroyed pickup. He'd held it for a moment, floating it above them, then launched it. The block vanished into the maze of cars, the crunch of its impact echoing. He'd torn off a car door, bent it in half, doing everything he could to keep his expression neutral, trying very hard not to reveal the strain he was putting himself under.

Chuy watched, barely blinking, sitting on the hood of a crushed car with his elbows on his knees. Eventually, he'd nodded, sprung off the car, clapping Jake on the shoulder and telling him they'd go get a beer.

At first Jake had been confused—wasn't this what Chuy had wanted? But as soon as they'd got back in the car, Chuy had started talking. Slowly at first, then more animated: about how special Jake was, about how he could change the world if he wanted, about how *they* were going to change the world. At one point he'd pulled into the parking area of a gas station on La Brea, moving way too fast, squealing to a halt just before he would have rammed the car into a concrete barrier.

Jake had lurched forward in his seat and hadn't even had time to fall back before Chuy had grasped him by the shoulders, looking at him with burning, almost pleading eyes.

"I fucking knew it," he said, spittle showering Jake's face. "You didn't have it all at first, nah, you didn't, but you fucking had it inside you, didn't you, *hijo de puta*?"

He'd grabbed Jake's hand, holding it tight, almost massaging it. "You don't know what this means, man. To me, to everyone. You gonna change everything. We gonna set this whole city right, and they aren't even *close* to ready for it, you know what I'm saying?"

Jake had grinned, amazed and delighted. All that practice, all those hard nights in the alley...it had paid off. He might not know what Chuy was saying, not really, but in that moment it didn't matter.

Chuy had sat back, breathing hard, stroking his chin. Then he'd started nodding to himself. "OK. OK. Here's what we're gonna do. We gonna help each other. Tell me again."

"About what?"

"*You*, motherfucker. Your story. Wait. In fact, hold on."

He'd pulled out his phone, opened up a note app. "OK.

From the beginning. Where you grew up, your moms, all of it."

"I don't ... Why?"

Chuy had looked at him like he was dense. "You want to find out where you came from. Shit, I do too. Maybe I can help."

Jake had sighed, the good mood starting to slip away. "Look, man, like ... I appreciate that. I do. But I searched for years, and I came up with nothing."

Those burning eyes had found his, feeling like the only points of light in the darkened car. "I know people," Chuy had said, suddenly deadly serious. "I got friends who got friends. Who got friends who got friends who got friends. I hustle. Now I'm trying to help you out here, and you being mighty ungrateful all of a sudden. So come on. Spill it."

Jake had.

The phone in his hand beeps again. Sandy's phone, receiving another text from Javier. It takes every ounce of control he can muster not to crush it right then and there.

The man was supposed to arrive at five o'clock. Then it was five forty-five. Then eight. The job he was on had gone badly: crew not arriving, parts defective, a hold-up while a particular map was located. He'd apologised over and over again, saying he knew how it looked, that he had no choice: *xoxo Sands plz tell the Bean i'll c her soon.*

The latest message is yet another apology: *Still going. Plz put Kelly to bed and I'll give her a kiss when I arrive k? xoxo*

He debates whether or not to respond, decides not to. He might be able to pull off Sandy's diction or, at worst, get her to do it—she and her daughter were still locked in the kitchen pantry, their sobs long since gone silent—but it was far more effective to stay silent. Let Javier wonder. It would make him get over here faster.

The doorbell rings, the chime echoing through the house. It's followed by a sharp, urgent knock.

Jake blinks, a sour taste trickling through his mouth. Then he's off the couch, marching over to the the pantry, cracking the lock with his mind and ripping open the door. The two captives inside yelp in surprise, shrinking back into the darkness. Sandy's daughter is clutched tight in her arms.

"Who's at the door?" he says.

She doesn't respond. Her eyes dart between his face and the phone.

He snaps a kitchen knife into the air from somewhere behind him, dances it into the pantry. The woman recoils like she's spotted a venomous snake. The girl has started sobbing again, face buried in her mother's shoulder.

"The door," he says. "You didn't say anybody was coming round." It can't be Javier—not after he just texted that he was still running late.

"I don't know," the woman says. "Please…"

The anger is a tight band around his head, crushing his temples. He storms into the pantry, lifts Sandy up, using the knife for a little extra encouragement. Getting Kelly out of her arms takes longer than he would have liked, the girl almost hysterical, kicking at him. Her mother has to soothe her, begging her to be quiet. And all the while the knocking at the front door gets more and more urgent.

Jake sends Sandy into the front hall. He and Kelly wait just round the corner, out of sight, his hand clamped over the girl's mouth, and the knife hovering over her head. He jerks his head at the front door. "Open it."

He crouches down, still holding the trembling girl, as Sandy opens the door.

"Thank God," says a male voice. Old, gravelly—the voice of someone who goes through a pack a day.

"Is...is everything OK, Mr....." Sandy says.

"It's Alan. From number 281? Two houses down?"

"Right. Sorry, yes. Hi." Under the circumstances she manages to sound calm. Relaxed, even. Under Jake's hand the girl moans softly.

"I saw your car in the driveway. And the lights were still on."

"OK?"

Alan pauses. "They've issued the evac warning. I just wanted to check you were all right? We're hearing the winds have shifted, so this whole area might get the actual order later on, and..."

"Oh." She actually sounds upbeat. "Yeah, no, we're good, yeah. Thanks for checking."

"Are you sure? I just know with your husband not...I mean..."

The man trails off as if he realises he's overstepped the mark.

"We're fine." Sandy's voice is a little less steady this time. "We're getting ready, I promise. Thanks for checking though." A slight creak as the door starts to close.

"Are you sure?" Alan says again. "I'm not sure I'm comfortable leaving if—"

Jake hears the man's sharp intake of breath.

The knife, the one he was holding over Kelly's head, has drifted very slightly out into the hall.

He lost focus. The lack of sleep, the continued use of his Gift—it's all taking a toll on him. He didn't let the knife drift far, but it doesn't matter.

Alan has seen it.

Jake doesn't hesitate. Still holding Kelly, he puts his head round the corner. Sandy has realised something is wrong, is looking back over her shoulder. Alan is framed in the open doorway: an overweight man of about sixty with a messy goatee and a sweat-stained T-shirt. Behind his thick glasses, his eyes are huge.

His watch is a big digital model, a clunky Casio with a thousand buttons. Jake grabs it with a thought. Alan is jerked forward, a startled "Hey!" on his lips, arm out in front of him, as if Sandy had taken him by the hand.

Jake darts the knife through the air. Alan's eyes meet his— just for a split-second—then the knife is buried up to the hilt in his ear.

Sandy starts to scream.

THIRTY-FIVE

Teagan

"So what now?"

Nic sits on the edge of the empty pool, arms straight, fingers splayed on the brick. Annie, Carlos and I are opposite, at the bottom, leaning up against the damp wall.

The pool is kidney-shaped, completely drained save for a single tiny puddle of water at the very bottom, a lone leaf floating in it. Above us Paul paces. He looks like a pissed-off principal.

We're somewhere east of UCLA. It took us a while to find a place we could stop without getting the cops called or having Burr and his goon squad find us. Even here, in one of the better parts of the city, there are empty houses. The one we found was down a quiet side street, a two-storey building covered in Tyvek paper. Some professor renovating his place maybe. Kids have been skating in the pool; there's an old wheel bearing, logo smeared with dirt, at the edge of the puddle. Good place to skate if the owner isn't going to stop you.

Don't ask me how we ended up *in* the pool. We were sitting on the edge at first, and then we kind of just ended up sliding down.

It's been a weird day.

The backyard is hemmed in on all sides with thick foliage, and the pool itself is next to a half-assed wooden gazebo, a rectangular structure with old wooden slats. At the north end of the yard, just beyond the trees, the sky glows orange from the fires. We're still a ways from Burbank by car, but it's only a few miles as the crow flies. I can't look at the sky without shivering.

Reggie's absence is like a missing tooth. We should have gone back for her. I should have been able to control my PK enough to clear a path. I grind the back of my head against the pool wall for the hundredth time, furious with myself.

"Because I'm just trying to get a handle on this." Nic's voice is light, but there's an undercurrent to it.

"So are we, man." Annie says, head tilted back. "Shit, my moms is gonna be worried sick. Cops probably been up in her place already." The words are more to herself than to us.

"Not to mention my kids." Paul sounds resigned. "It's Cole's soccer game tonight. I told him I'd be there."

"You got a phone," Annie tells him. "Just call."

It's a few seconds before Paul answers. When he does, it's impossible to miss the defeat in his voice. "I'm trying to figure out what to say."

Annie gets to her feet, which takes her more than one try. She's just tall enough to put her folded arms on the side of the pool. "Yo. Sam around?"

"Who's Sam?" I whisper to Carlos.

"His wife. Ex-wife."

"I think so," Paul tells Annie.

"Then it's cool." Her voice is unexpectedly tender. "Cole'll be OK. He's a good kid."

I frown, wondering when exactly they would have met. I

try to imagine Annie hanging out with Paul and his kids at Chuck E. Cheese and can't do it. It's too strange.

I look up at Nic. "Well, we know two of the victims. We still need to figure out the link between them." Another pang: how the hell are we going to do that without Reggie?

"We need a computer," Carlos mumbles.

"No, but OK, let's say we figure that out." Nic hops off the edge, slides down onto the opposite side of the pool. A plane rumbles overhead, headed for the distant LAX. "How do we actually stop whoever this...other person is?"

"Well, you do have a psychokinetic." I push a tiny bit of confidence into my voice. "Although there's never been two of us in the same room together, so who knows what'll happen?" I flush. "Sorry, by the way. Didn't mean to wreck your place."

He lets out a sound that is somewhere between a sigh and a laugh. "Who needs a security deposit anyway?"

It's kind of amazing he's able to joke at all. It's been an insane day for me, sure, but at least I haven't had my friend show up, trailed by both the cops and a black-ops team, and had her destroy my apartment using her mind. That's one hell of a thing to happen to you on the same day you find out that such people actually exist.

"I'm so sorry about N/Naka," I say. "I really did want to be there."

"You still mad about that stupid restaurant?" Annie says over her shoulder.

Another one of those sigh-laugh noises from Nic. "N/Naka. Shit. Well, you *were* mixed up in whatever the hell this is, so you get a pass this once. Although I gotta say, the plum granita was fucking delicious."

"The...You went anyway?"

"Yeah."

"Wait, hold on. So you know I'm on the run from the cops…and you don't miss our dinner date?"

"Didn't exactly expect you to show up. I figured whatever nonsense you'd gotten involved in, I was probably never hearing from you ever again."

Ouch.

"Besides, like I'm going to burn a reservation at N/Naka," he continues. "Took a buddy from work. From the look on his face, it was like they moved the Superbowl to Christmas Day, and the Rams won."

"I thought the granita was off the menu?"

A twitch at the corner of his mouth. "Served it as an *amuse* when I sat down." He leans forward. "It was *amazing.*"

I give him a half-hearted finger.

"How'd you do that?" Carlos says. "The apartment, I mean. I figured the thing around your neck was organic fibre, so…"

I lift my left hand, waggling the fingers. "Used the power of the one ring, Frodo."

"Huh?"

"Doesn't matter." I exhale long and slow, trying to sort my messy thoughts. "You're right. We might not have Reggie, but we can still…"

I fumble the words. Saying her name, voicing it, is like admitting to a horrible secret.

"Don't worry about Reggie," Paul says.

"Don't *worry*? Oh, OK. Thanks, Paul. I'm so relieved. After all, it's not like she's in the hands of a psychotic bunch of murderous soldiers who she, I don't know, just fucked with to help us escape."

"What I mean is—" Paul carries on as if I hadn't spoken. "—they won't hurt her."

"How do you—"

"Because it wouldn't help them. If they can't find us, they can't use the threat of hurting her to get us to turn you over. They won't be able to dictate the terms of the exchange." He sounds like a professor lecturing a class. "They'll keep her safe for the time being."

"And if they do find us?"

He says nothing.

"Is she going to be OK though?" Nic asks Paul.

"I just said—"

"No, I mean, like, she had a fit or something. Before Teagan…"

"Guess the acting lessons paid off," Annie says.

"What acting lessons?" I ask.

"She's been taking 'em for a while. Playhouse over in Anaheim."

"Reggie wants to be an *actor*?"

"Yeah." She fixes me with a glare. "Is that a problem?"

"No, I just…" I falter, not quite sure what I was about to say. I admit, it's hard for me to imagine wheelchair-bound Reggie as an actor. Then again, why the hell not? Why can't she be?

I don't meet Annie's eyes, embarrassed, staring into the silent puddle at the centre of the pool. If Burr touches her, if he so much as looks at her funny while I'm around, I'll take that ring of his and put it somewhere very, very personal.

"I think we should run," Carlos says.

We all look over at him.

"Just get out of here," he continues. "We ain't got Reggie, and we don't actually know anything about anything."

"That's not true," I say. "We know what the two victims did, we just don't know—"

"How we we gonna find out? We got no computer, nowhere else to go, cops'll probably find us—'specially since everybody knows what you look like now, cos of that bodycam video."

"Where we gonna run to, exactly?" Annie says.

"Anywhere. Doesn't matter. We just scatter, go our separate ways. We'll be harder to track if we aren't together." His eyes meet mine. "We could go up to Point Reyes. Or even over the border—I still got some buddies in Tijuana who could help us."

"No. Fuck that. We're not running." I put as much force into the words as I can, trying not to reveal just how scared they make me. Not the running, although God knows that sticks in my gut. It's the way Carlos suggested splitting up.

Whoever went with who, I know that if we did that, we'd never see each other again. Not just Reggie—nobody. The thought of that, of losing everyone like that...

Paul's phone rings. He still has it set to the default Nokia ringtone.

"That'll be Sam." He clambers to his feet, moves away from the pool. He sounds like he'd rather throw himself in, head first.

"OK." Annie is trying to sound reasonable, which is never a good sign. "What do you suggest we do then?"

"We find a connection between the victims. We know one of them was in fashion, and the other one was—"

"You keep saying that, but you don't actually say *how* we're supposed to get that done."

Paul, speaking in the background, has changed his tone of voice. "No," he says, sounding annoyed. "I think you got the wrong number. There's no one of that name here...Look, if you would *please* lower your voice. I can barely understand you."

I tune him out. "We go somewhere," I say. Yes, *that* will convince them. I keep going. "Somewhere with a computer. Where we can do some more research without grenades and shit getting thrown at us."

"We lost our hacker," Annie says.

"I know, but—"

"No hacker, whole LAPD after you, not to mention those soldiers..."

"Could we go to your offices?" I ask Nic.

He grimaces. "I don't really feel like getting fired on the same day my apartment blows up."

"You're not gonna get fired. And this is kind of a life-or-death situation here."

"Yeah, I got that. But I'm not sure having the people in that video show up at the office of the district attorney is a good idea, is what I'm saying."

"Ugh. Fine. Be that way."

"And if the connection was online, we would have found it."

Carlos cuts in. "That's what I'm saying. We need to start thinking about getting the hell away from—"

"Teagan." Paul says my name like he's offended I even exist. "It's for you."

I'm still thinking about our options, not really paying attention. "What's for me?"

"The phone."

"I...What?"

"It's for *you*." He dangles the phone over the edge of the pool. "Good luck getting any sense out of him, though."

I take the phone, staring up at him in confusion. "Um...hello?"

The reply almost takes my head off. "*Teggan!*"

"Who is this?"

"I say come back four o'clock, you never arrive! You not wanna see me?"

"I don't... Wait, *Africa?*"

He bellows laughter. Now I'm almost certain that I'm actually dreaming this whole day—one of those dreams where people you know from your past appear at random. Next to me, Annie mutters, "Who the fuck is Africa?"

"How did you get this number?" I ask.

"Got your phone."

"My phone was stolen. How—"

"Ya ya. I saw Derek got it. He try sell it but I *catch him.*"

"Who the hell is—"

Derek. The pudgy dude who tried to bum a cigarette from me outside the LA Mission. Bald head with the single wisp of grey hair. He must have followed me when I was delivering Africa's package to Jeannette. It feels like it happened a thousand years ago.

Nic spreads his hands in a *Who is it?* gesture. I wave him off.

"Stupid *sai sai.* You got the horse on the back, so I know it's yours."

My little stoned unicorn sticker. I am *never* getting rid of that thing. I don't care how old it gets.

"I hear you got in bad news. But no one know where you are, so I pull up your call list and start there. You gotta put a lock on your phone. When I was guarding Barack, we have to take away his Blackberry, he—"

"Yeah, yeah, got it."

"Well, I got sometin for *you,* Teggan. Someone see sometin."

I sit up a little straighter. Everyone else is looking at me now. "Tell me. Actually, hang on, let me put you on speaker."

Paul has to do it for me, skidding down into the pool, nearly soaking himself in the puddle. Africa's voice sounds tinny and echoey in the confined space. "I got a friend. She go sit at Pershing Square to play guitar. Next to this café, *yaaw*? Edmonds is maybe three, four blocks. I go there, I ask her, "'Tiana, you see anytin?' You know what she say?"

"What?"

There's a pause. One I'm almost certain he's leaving in for dramatic effect. "She say she see a dead man."

"You mean Steven Chase?"

"The man from Edmonds. The bad juju. She see him go in the café, more than once."

"She sure it was him?"

A dark note comes into his voice. "You think we see nothing, know nothing. Tiana tell the truth."

"So what?" Carlos says.

"Hold on, Africa." I cover the phone's mic with my hand. "What's that?"

"She sees our guy go into a café. Maybe he's getting a cup of coffee. We can't use this."

I bite my lip, wishing he was wrong. "Africa," I say, lifting my hand from the mic and trying to ignore the sinking feeling in my chest. "Was there anything—"

"Oh, you want more now? You too greedy, you bloody *toubab*. Course there is more. You think I call you for nothing?" A volcanic clearing of his throat. "Tiana say he go there two, maybe three time. She ask him for money, he give her ten dollar. Ten dollar! And he have a bag with him, all times. She see him go in...but he not have the bag when he come out."

"She sure?" I say again.

"You want to know or not?" he replies, annoyed.

"Yeah. No, of course." I ignore the sceptical look on both Annie and Carlos's faces.

"He not have the bag. But later someone else come out with it. She say she remember because both people with the bag give her money, *yaaw*?"

Was Chase bribing people? Was that what was in the bag? It makes sense. If he was going to pay off someone, he wouldn't want an electronic record of it...

"What'd they look like?" Annie says.

"Who is that?" says Africa.

"Name's Annie Cruz. Don't feel like we've been introduced." A half-smile. "Maybe when this is over, you let me come buy you a coffee, man. Sounds like you're a good dude to know."

I shoot her an evil look, suddenly jealous—he's *my* source.

Africa belches a laugh. "Annie Cruz. OK, OK. Ya, maybe."

"What *did* they look like?" Paul says.

"Hol' on." There's a muffled conversation on his end with a woman—we can't hear her voice clearly. Tiana, I'm guessing.

"OK, she say, one look like a heepee." *Hippie*, I'm guessing. "Long hair. Glasses. Old man."

"Hayden," I mouth. Annie nods.

"And the other guy?" I say.

"Tall. Very tall. Big, you know. Maybe fifty, fifty-five. Bald." Another muffled exchange. "She say he nice to her. Gave her *fifty* dollar."

Carlos shakes his head, and I can see why. It's not enough. "Africa, was there...like...Did Tiana see anything else?"

This time the muffled conversation goes on for a good minute. A few times Africa actually raises his voice, scolding the person I assume is Tiana.

"She say he dress smart. He wearing this uniform...His shirt has a logo on it."

"What kind of logo?"

"Like a lot of faces. Like shadows. Looking the same direction."

"Fuck does that mean?" Carlos mutters.

"Hm," Paul says.

We all look at him. When he doesn't respond, Annie spreads her hands, raising her eyebrows.

"Los Angeles County Department of Public Health," he says with a lopsided grin.

"How do you even know—" I stop myself. "Never mind. Of course you know. Was there anything else?"

"Tiana say that's all."

"OK, thanks. And hey...Idriss?"

A long pause like I said something I wasn't supposed to. "Ya?"

"When this is all over, I am gonna buy you the biggest steak dinner you've ever had in your entire life. You and Jeannette. And Tiana. All of you."

He roars with laughter. "We be here! I see you soon, Teggan."

"So your guy had someone on the health department on payroll," Nic says after I hang up. "Why?"

"Yeah, maybe." Annie looks dubious. "But I don't get it. Victim one runs a clothing company. Victim two—" She ticks them off on her fingers. "—works at an environment charity. And this third guy...LA County health. What's the connection?"

"Well..." Nic has moved into a crouch. "The public health department *does* handle the water in LA County."

"You sure?" Carlos says.

"Dude, I work for lawyers. You pick things up. They do all the water testing for the beaches."

"Yeah, but that's assuming they weren't connected some other way, man. Gambling debt or whatever. Something we can't see."

"We've been over this already," Paul says, sounding doubtful. "Ultra's factories aren't near any bodies of water. They don't even *have* any in California. So what would Chase need to bribe people for? And even if this…health department official *was* getting a bribe from Chase, I don't see how it gets us anywhere."

"What do you mean?"

"We don't know who they were. And we have no way of finding out."

"Sure we do," Nic says, a note of excitement creeping into his voice. "Health department's staff list will be online. Just find the guy responsible for ocean health, who also happens to be big and bald."

"With what computer?" Carlos replies.

Annie starts laughing. It's the exhausted, can-you-believe-this-shit laughter of someone reaching the very end of her rope. She clutches her stomach, howling with glee. "Sorry," she says. She's under control for half a second, then erupts into another guffaw.

"What is your problem?" Carlos says.

Annie gets herself under control. "How far are we from UCLA?" she asks Nic.

"Maybe half an hour? On foot, anyway."

She holds out her hand to Paul, who passes her his phone.

"No," I say.

"Yup."

"No fucking way."

"Yes fucking way,"

"You're telling me he's—"

"Evening shift." She grins. "Son of a bitch got out the Bloods, started working at UCLA."

Nic spreads his hands. "Is that supposed to mean something? Who are we talking about?"

I rest my head against the side of the pool. "Mo-Mo."

Paul groans, and Carlos rolls his eyes, unable to keep the smile off his face. I fill Nic in, telling him about our quest to find Maurice Saunders.

"But you don't have his number any more, do you?" Paul says to Annie.

"Don't have to. Directory enquiries gave the UCLA library number straight off, so—Oh, hello? Yes, hi, could I speak to Maurice, please?"

"Should we really be walking that way?" Paul asks. "With the police looking for us?"

"I could steal another car," I say, even though the thought of using my PK so soon after I destroyed Nic's apartment isn't exactly happy-fun-good-times.

"*Another* car?" says Nic. "When was the first one?"

Goddammit, I hadn't actually mentioned that we stole one the first time. All the same, there's a little beat of excitement in my chest. *Finally*, a lead we can use.

"They'd have trackers anyhow." Annie says, hanging up. "Last thing we need. Anyway, he'll wait for us."

"Is this really a good idea?" Carlos says quietly.

We all fall silent. It's that uncomfortable quiet you get when you know you have to make a big decision, and nobody wants to be the first to commit.

"This is getting kind of crazy," he says. "I just think that... I dunno, man. If we bug out now, we might have a shot. They can't chase all of us."

"We can't just run," I say. But how true is that? Up until now I'm pretty sure everyone's been staying together because they needed China Shop. Then the cops got involved, and Burr's team showed up. And it's like Carlos's question has opened a box that can't be closed again. If we run now, it'll be hard—but it might be easier than plunging ahead, when we're certain of almost nothing.

I don't want that to happen. I might have my PK, but without these people—without China Shop—I'd never have survived. Annie's connections, Paul's brain, Reggie's leadership and computer skills. We're hanging on by a thread already, and if everybody decides to go, I don't know if I'll make it.

"He has a point." Paul nods at Carlos. "That spec ops team wasn't more than four or five people. My guess is, they probably don't have the manpower or resources to hunt all of us, if we go our separate ways."

"That's what I'm saying." Carlos pounds a fist into open palm. "We don't even know if the health department guy is still alive—or if the killer knows about him."

Nic frowns. "There are pros and cons, I guess…"

"Plus, even if we do find him, we gotta find another car. Because I guarantee you that he's not just living down the block. The longer we stay out there—"

"We're doing it," I say. But Carlos doesn't even look at me. I feel sick. Africa's call gave me a tiny bit of hope, but if it wasn't enough to convince them, then I've got nothing else. There is no Plan B.

"I think we need to put this to a vote," says Paul.

"What, like, stay or go?" Nic says, glancing at me.

"Guys," I say. "Come on…"

"Yes." Paul puffs out his chest. "We vote on it. Annie, what do you think? How about it?"

Annie mutters something, looking at her feet.

"Beg pardon?" Paul says.

"OK, well, I vote we split up," Carlos says, raising his hand. "Sorry, Teags—you kind of knew I was going to."

"Annie, I didn't hear you," Paul says. "What do you think about a—"

"Cut the shit." Annie's fists are clenched, held tight at her sides.

"I'm sorry?"

"You heard me. Shut the fuck up."

She looks around, taking us all in. "You're trying to make this whole thing logical, like any of this makes sense. You wanna talk about pros and cons and voting, and whether it's worth doing this and yadda yadda, when *none of you* wanna admit how scared you are."

Her words are forceful, but the way she's saying them is strange. She's not looking at anyone, and the way she's clenching her fists... I thought it was because she was angry, but it's more than that. It's like she's doing it to steel herself.

Nic tilts his head. "We're not—"

"Nope." She shakes her head. Hard. "You're scared. You're fucking terrified, and you just don't wanna admit it. You wanna pretend like we can solve everything if we just talk about it enough, and that's just bullshit."

"Now just hold on," Paul says, taking a step towards her.

"Teagan." She turns to me. "I don't like you. You do stupid shit, you act like a five-year-old and you never take anything seriously."

I blink at her. "Yeah, well...you..."

"Shut up, I wasn't finished. You might be a pain in the ass, but you were right about one thing: none of us are straight with each other." She levels a finger at me, rounding on everyone else. "This bitch got the balls to speak her mind. With that cheese-sandwich stunt back at the apartment—she didn't know that shit was gonna work. She didn't know how you—" The finger finds Nic. "—were gonna react. What does that make *us*, if we can't even admit why we don't wanna do this?"

Paul is giving Annie the strangest look—like she's turned round and casually stated that the earth is flat.

"You want honesty, Teagan? You want the truth? Here it is. I'm scared too. I'm scared my mom is gonna wake up tomorrow and find out her only daughter got sent back to prison. Or got killed. How about you, Teagan? You scared?

My tongue feels odd in my mouth, heavy and thick. "Yeah."

"Good. You should be. You're in way over your head, and you're probably gonna get yourself shot. But I'm not gonna leave you to do it and tell myself there was a good reason. I've done..."

She closes her eyes suddenly, lets out a long, slow breath.

"I've done some shit I'm not proud of. Things I haven't told you guys. When this is over, maybe I can set it straight, same way you did with him." She nods at me, then waves a hand at Nic. "But right now? We're gonna do this. We're gonna stand up for each other, no matter how scared we are."

I am an ugly crier. I am talking snot everywhere, fire-engine face, honking sobs. So it is a damn good thing that I manage to keep my emotions in check.

Paul lets out a long sigh. "I go where Annie goes." His eyes meet mine. "We're with you."

Carlos gets to his feet, a look of deep discomfort on his face. He still wants us to run. Him, me, everybody. But instead of pushing the point, he just nods and says, "OK. We'll do it your way."

"How about you, man?" Annie asks Nic.

He hasn't said a word since he asked about the stolen car. He looks away, staring into the distance.

If he wants to take off, I won't stop him. It'll kill me—it really will—but I can't force him to stay. He's had his entire world turned upside down, the laws of physics broken right in front of him. That'll do a mind job on anybody.

He looks back at me. Holds my gaze for the longest time.

"What are you going to tell...Mo-Mo? That his name?" he says.

"What do you mean?" Paul asks.

"Are you going to tell him the truth? About what you guys do?"

I open my mouth to reply, but what the hell am I supposed to say? *Should* we tell Mo-Mo the whole truth, after my big speech? Do I show off my ability again? What if...

"No."

Annie looks a little calmer now. More determined. As if she'd been squaring up to take a punch, and when it landed, it turned out whoever threw it can't hit for shit.

"We can't tell him," she says.

Carlos frowns. "You said—"

"I know. It's not right, and I know I just gave you all that stuff about being straight, but we need to be smart before we tell the whole world. I don't have a solution for it right now, but we'll figure it out."

She sees our blank looks. "You know what I'm trying to say. We have to lie...but we can at least be honest about why we're doing it."

A slow, exhausted smile creeps across Nic's face. "I'm a lawyer. That should have been my line."

Which is when I know it's going to be OK. Not for ever. Maybe not even for the next hour. But right now? Just for a little bit? Yeah.

I put a closed fist to my mouth, mostly because those

emotions I mentioned are about to come tumbling out of me. The urge to hug Nic is enormous, but if I do that, I really will start bawling. Instead, I give him a very grateful nod.

"OK." Annie gives a brisk nod. "I'm tired of playing defence. Let's go get this asshole."

As we climb out of the pool, Paul coughs. "Teagan?"

It's still hard to talk. "Yeah?"

"Am I saved in your phone as 'Agent Whiteboard'?"

"What? No. Absolutely not."

"Really."

"Yeah. For sure."

"Because your friend Africa seems to think—"

"Can we *please* just take this shit seriously?" Annie is already over by the side of the house. "At least until we're not running for our lives?"

THIRTY-SIX

Teagan

We don't speak much on the way to UCLA. We stick to the shadows, even when we reach the campus. The place is quiet, its wide avenues lit by soft yellow street lights. There's no sign of the cops or Burr. No sign of anybody.

We pass a building with two towers bracketing a set of swooping arches, lit from below by spots. It's peaceful—like I could curl up on the grass and just close my eyes, without a care in the world. *Wouldn't that be nice.*

The library is in the north part of the campus—a big brick building set back from the street. And it's there, after checking in at reception, that we finally meet Mo-Mo Saunders. At this point I'm not sure whether I want to hug him or beat him to death.

He's Annie's age, wearing jeans and a neat blue button-down. The shirt is open over a white T, with a weird acronym on it, UCLA IOES, under a green and blue circle. He looks like he should be holding court in a philosophy seminar.

Until he opens his mouth. "Annie Cruz," he says, leaning against the door frame. His eyes are huge, his pupils rattling around like pachinko balls. He is stoned out of his mind.

"Hey, Mo–Mo," Annie says. "You're a hard man to track down."

"Who this?" he says, nodding at us. Or he tries to nod, anyway—the movement kind of carries him forward, nearly spilling him down the steps he's standing on.

"Friends." She steps past him, gesturing at us to follow. Mo–Mo turns his head to look at her, which almost sends him stumbling in the opposite direction. There's a huge gentle grin on his face.

The inside of the library makes me wish, for the second time, that I could just stop. It's beautiful: high vaulted ceilings, intricate columns, winding staircases. Hogwarts, if one of Harry's wacko spells teleported it to California. It's just as quiet here as it was outside, with no more than a handful of students around, most of them reading under low lamps at big wooden tables. None of them looks up as we walk past—the only time one of them notices us is when Mo–Mo tries to make a turn by a desk and smashes his hip right into it.

He leads us to an office off the main reading room. The door is ornate, made of wood, but the space behind it is cramped and cluttered, lit by grimy fluorescent lighting. The walls are covered with ancient posters, and the computer on the desk—an old-school monitor with the extended back end—is surrounded by piles of dog-eared paper.

The place stinks of weed and is only just big enough for the six of us. As we crowd inside, Annie squeezes into the chair in front of the computer, pulls up the browser. "Won't take me a minute," she says to no one in particular. Her voice betrays her exhaustion, ragged at the edges.

"Yo, you doing OK?" Mo–Mo says.

"Fine, why?"

"Heard Nando Aguilar was looking for you."

"Never mind that. Me and Nando are cool."

"No one's cool with Nando."

"Nando?" I say. "You mean the MS-13 guy."

"Yeah," says Annie. "It's no big thing. We're good."

"What's your deal with him anyway? You guys used to run together?"

"More than that," says Mo-Mo. "They—"

He stops when Annie gives him a very poisonous look.

"OK, hold up." I plonk my butt down on the edge of the desk. "Annie..."

"Don't worry about it."

"No, I am kind of worried about it, actually. You're acting weird all of a sudden."

"It's a long fucking story."

"Which I'd really appreciate hearing."

"Now." She leans back, waving a hand at the computer. "You wanna hear this now? Because seriously, it's not important."

"Yeah, kind of."

"Ladies." Mo-Mo tries to step between us. "Let's just..." He trails off as if he isn't quite sure what he was about to suggest.

Annie's gaze is needle-sharp. "*Nando* is my own business. Him and I have our own shit to deal with, but it's got nothing to do with do with Chase and Hayden and whoever this other dude is."

"Didn't you just do that whole big speech about being straight with each other?"

"Uh-huh. And I *said* that my own shit wasn't an issue right now. I'll tell you guys after this over. Until then? It doesn't matter."

"I'm not saying—"

"If I could just cut in here." Paul puts a hand on my shoulder. "We have more pressing things to deal with at the moment, no?"

"Damn right," Annie spits.

My instinct is to push it. I don't because Paul is right. We have bigger fish to fry, and then to eat with a squeeze of lemon and a little parsley.

"Respect each other!" Mo-Mo blurts out. "That's what I'm saying. Let's just respect each other."

Annie goes back to work without a word. Soon she's got the LA County public health website up, along with its logo: the silhouetted faces Africa was talking about.

With Paul's help, we find the staff directory. The department has district offices and only two of them cover ocean territory: Santa Monica and Coastal Cities. We crowd around the monitor as Mo-Mo leans against the wall, briefly sliding sideways before catching himself.

Santa Monica's chief is a woman, Angela Baxter, while Coastal Cities is run by a guy called Javier Salinas. I scan the list of areas he's responsible for: Carson, Redondo Beach, San Pedro, Torrance, Harbor City, Wilmington. Most of them areas along the ocean.

"Gotta be him," I say.

"I dunno, man." Carlos's voice is a low mutter. "Could have been anybody in that department."

"Nope." Annie's way ahead of him. She's already googled a photo. Salinas is in his late forties or early fifties, bald, with a bullet-shaped head and a big smile.

"And—" Annie flicks back a tab, pulling up a page titled AnyWho. "—I already got his address."

"Well, well," Paul murmurs.

I reach over, grab the back of Annie's head with both hands

and plant a huge kiss on it, forgetting for a moment about Nando Aguilar. "I will never throw you off a building again. I promise."

"Promise never to kiss me again, neither, then we're square." She taps the screen. "Dude lives in Burbank."

The smile drops from my face. Burbank. *Fire.*

Annie doesn't notice. "Got a home number. Can someone—"

"On it." Nic picks up the handset next to the computer, his fingers dancing across the pad. He listen for a moment, then grimaces. "Answering machine. His wife, sounds like."

"But what's the connection?" Carlos says. He moves his hands in front of him like he's trying to solve an imaginary puzzle. "You got all these pieces—the health department guy, the clothing guy, the ocean charity guy—and you don't know how they all fit together."

"What about microfibres?" Mo-Mo says.

We all turn to look at him.

He blinks back at us, suddenly lucid. "Microfibres. Little bits of synthetic material. Millions of 'em come off clothes in the wash, then get swept out to sea and end up in the food chain."

"What?" Nic says.

"Y'all don't know about this?" Mo-Mo spreads his hands. "Y'all need to read more, man. A single piece of clothing can shed nearly two thousand fibres. Toxic shit too. It ends up in microorganisms, which end up in the fish. Either they die from shredded stomachs, or we eat them first, and *we* get—"

"How do you even know that?" Paul says.

Another long blink. "Institute of the Environment and Sustainability," he says, tapping his T-shirt. "Taking some classes there."

"So Ultra's clothes are shedding microfibres..." I say.

"And Steven Chase knows about it," Paul finishes. "He

bribes Hayden and Salinas to look the other way. Either one of them could have turned him in."

"Yeah," Nic says. "But I mean…is that really it?"

"Is that really it, how?" Annie asks.

"It makes sense, but why would someone kill them? It's not…" He fights for the right word. "It's not *personal*. It's the kind of thing you bring a lawsuit over or stick on WikiLeaks. It's not the biggest issue in the world, right?"

"Only cos you don't pay attention." Mo-Mo has come out of his weed fog in a major way. "You know that the Hudson River in New York dumps three hundred million fibres into the Atlantic every day? That's one river! And here—"

"I get it," Nic says, raising a hand. "I do. But why would somebody start killing people over it? It's not like it's going to stop the problem."

"Killing?" Mo-Mo looks around at us. "The hell are you guys into?"

"And I keep saying—" Carlos points at the screen, at the picture of Javier Salinas. "—it's not enough. We go after the wrong guy or if he's dead already, that's it."

I follow his finger, taking in Salinas. He's right. So is Nic. None of this hangs together—not in a way that makes sense yet. We are navigating in the pitch-dark by holding our hands out in front of us, hoping we aren't about to walk off a cliff.

But when the only alternatives are standing still or just running away, what choice do we have?

I turn to Mo-Mo, hold out my hand. Confused, he takes it.

"The United States government thanks you for your service," I say. "Also, we're gonna need your car."

THIRTY-SEVEN

Teagan

Of course Javier Salinas lives in Burbank.

Of course this insane clusterfuck of a day would end up with us driving right into a towering inferno.

Sweat pools at the small of my back as we walk back outside. Smoky air digs into my eyes and throat and nostrils, thin fingers with long nails.

It doesn't help that fire is what everyone else is talking about. We're just coming out of the library, Mo-Mo's car keys in hand, heading across the manicured lawns towards the side street where his Prius is parked.

"So it's an evac warning only?" Nic is saying. "Not an order?"

"For now," Paul replies.

"Will he even still be up there?"

"We gotta go find out," Annie says. "Only way."

"We can't call ahead?"

"We just did. No one answered, remember?"

I turn the problem over in my head, trying to find an angle, something we haven't thought of. There isn't one. This is the only lead we have, the *only* place we can go. The longer we stall or second-guess ourselves, the better chance Burr and his team will have of catching up to us, and the better the chance the other psychokinetic will kill Salinas.

If it hasn't happened already.

"So what exactly are we gonna do when we get there?" Carlos says as we reach the street.

"We just be careful." Paul sounds resigned but determined. "We identify ourselves to Salinas, let him know why we're there..."

"Yo, Teagan." Carlos turns to me. "What are you gonna do if the dude with the rebars actually shows up?"

"Dunno. Never fought another me before. I'll figure it out."

"*Figure it out?* No. Uh-uh. We go in there with a plan, or we don't go in at all."

"What do you want from me, man? If he does show up, you get Salinas and get out of there."

"We aren't just gonna leave you."

"Second that," says Nic.

"Yeah, Nic, you know that whole thing where I destroyed your apartment with my mind? Imagine two of me. You've seen what I can do when I'm pissed, and I'm pretty sure the other guy can do even worse. You don't bend a metal bar around someone's throat with your mind unless you—"

I stop because right then the sense of disconnect—of *distance*—is so strong that it turns my stomach to lead. I finish the sentence in my head, words I don't even want to think about saying aloud. *Unless you're more powerful than ever. Unless you've become something... more.*

I'm not the same as these people. As Annie, Carlos, Paul. As Nic. I look like them, talk like them... but I'm not them. They know it. I know it. What are we doing, pretending we're all on the same side?

It's a horrible thought. Poisonous. *Wrong.*

"You're still gonna need a plan," Carlos says.

Annie scowls. "Way I see it, we gotta bring this guy down."

"Bring him down," I say. "As in, kill him?"

She shrugs. "Maybe."

"Uh, yeah, we're not doing that."

"Oh, OK. So you got an idea how we deliver him up to Tanner, then?"

"No. But—"

"Why not knock him out?" Nic says. "We can do that, right?"

Suddenly everyone is looking at me. It's not a comfortable feeling.

"A taser would work," I say.

Annie makes a show of patting her pockets. "Think I left mine in my security-guard outfit."

"What if the police are there?" Carlos asks. "They might be ahead of us on this."

"Then we just roll on by. Figure out something else."

"Yeah," Annie says. "Pretty sure they'll just let a carload of escaped fugitives who are probably all over the system just roll on *by*." She looks towards the library and sniffs as if there's a scent she's trying to place. "Gimme the phone," she says to Paul.

"OK?"

"Got someone who might be able to do a drive-by before we get there. Scope the place out."

"You know *his* number by heart?" I say.

"Her. And no. I'm gonna go ask Mo-Mo if I can log into Facebook real quick, see if it's there." She points at me. "Figure out how to stop this guy. Use your voodoo."

She turns, starts striding back towards the library.

"Wait, wait, wait," Paul says to me. "Let's assume you actually subdue this...individual. What then?"

"Um...we go to a bar and get shitface drunk because we'll be in the clear?"

"Be serious. How are you planning to prove to Tanner that this person, whoever they are, is the killer?"

"I'll have a few witnesses," I say, gesturing at him and Nic. Carlos unlocks the car, the *bleep-bleep* too loud against the hush of the campus. Annie is heading across to the library doors.

"Yes, well, none of us is exactly in Moira Tanner's good books any more," Paul says. "And there's the small matter of us still being sought by the the LAPD."

"Paul, come on. I'm figuring this out as I—"

A screech of tyres. Very close, and very loud.

All of us look towards the lawn where Annie is, maybe fifty feet away. It's lit up with headlights, although it's a second before the vehicle comes into view.

It's a van. Gleaming white. It jerks off the road, like a predator switching direction to chase prey, and rumbles up onto the grass, pinning Annie in its headlights.

Even before it comes to a stop, the side door is opening, figures leaping out onto the grass.

Tanner's men. They've found us.

Except it isn't them. They're not in uniform for one thing, and they're wearing...ski masks? *What the hell?*

Annie turns towards us. Despite the distance, her expression is clear. Stunned, angry terror.

"Annie?" Paul goes from a jog to a sprint in half a second. "Annie!"

The first figure reaches her, wraps an arm around her neck. She twists away, shouting, throwing a wild punch that takes the guy in the ribs. By then we're all running, Nic alongside me, Carlos bringing up the rear, all of us yelling Annie's name.

The second figure grabs Annie's legs as the first wraps his arms around her midsection. They're big, both of them, bigger than even she is, and they haul her to the van. She's screaming now, fear mixing with her fury.

I throw out my PK energy, looking for something to grab on to. But I'm not supercharged, and they're too far away. I'm closing the distance, but I'm not going quick enough—Annie is already half inside the van, a third set of hands visible on the door frame, ready to slam it shut. In desperation I grab the first thing I find with my PK, the lid of a trash can, hurling it at them. It lands a good ten feet short.

"*Annie, no!*" Paul yells.

Annie vanishes inside the van, her screams cut off as the door slams shut. With a squeal of tyres, it accelerates away, roaring into the night.

THIRTY-EIGHT

Teagan

As the van disappears, I send out a last urgent burst of PK. I'm twenty feet away, and it takes everything I have to push it that far. If I can grab a wheel, even an axle, stop it from moving...

The PK just brushes the van's back right hubcap. Then it's gone.

As I sprint across the grass, it roars off, heading east. I come to a stop as the van makes a hard right, vanishing down a side street.

"Jesus." Paul has his hands on his head, staring in horror at where the van was.

"Who..." Nic can't finish the sentence, gasping for breath.

The Prius screeches in alongside us, Carlos behind the wheel. "Get in!" he yells, his words audible even through the closed windows.

We pile inside, Nic and I in the back, Paul in the passenger seat. Carlos punches it before the doors close, taking off in the direction the van went.

Those weren't Tanner's people—and if they were, why take Annie hostage when they've already got Reggie? No, this was something else.

Nando Aguilar.

How the hell did they know where to find her?

If anybody can catch up, it's Carlos. He's already locked in, head tilted very slightly forward, hands at ten and two. He reaches down for the stick shift, cursing when he remembers it's an automatic.

"There!" Paul points. The back of the van is visible for a split-second, vanishing into a side street between two buildings that look like smaller versions of the campus library.

"On it." Carlos's voice is a low growl. He works the wheel and the gas, skidding us into the narrow alley. A parked truck looms in the windshield, coming fast enough to make me lean back in my seat.

"Watch out!" Nic yells.

Carlos slides past it without slowing, the back of the car fishtailing. We rip past the truck with maybe an inch to spare. "Front-wheel drive," Carlos shouts back. "We're fine."

But we're not. The van is gone.

We zip down a few more streets, navigating through the narrow confines of the campus, but it's nowhere to be seen. Eventually Carlos brings the car to the kerb.

"Shit," Paul murmurs. "Oh, shit."

I don't think I've ever heard him swear. Not once, in the entire time I've known him.

I lean forward, head between the seats, still breathless. "We can't stop." I swallow hard. "They might still be in the area. If we—"

"That was MS-13, wasn't it?" Carlos says.

The car falls silent. For a good five seconds.

Nic: "Who were those people?"

Paul says nothing, staring into the distance.

"Paul?" Nic says.

"I told her not to." He doesn't move. "I said I could help her, but she wouldn't listen."

Carlos cuts the engine, turning the key with a very precise, almost decisive movement. He looks like he wants to smash Paul's face against the dashboard. "Why the *fuck* did they just grab Annie?"

"It doesn't make sense," Paul says. "We hid the van. Yeah, we would have been late, but—"

"Been late?" Carlos almost snarls.

"And what are you talking about?" I say. "I told you the cops found the..."

Except I didn't tell him.

I told Carlos and Reggie.

I didn't even think to mention it to Annie and Paul. At that point, it didn't seem important. Who cared if the cops had the van, when they were after us anyway?

"Are you sure?" Paul says.

"Yeah." Nic closes his eyes. "Pretty sure."

"Teagan, why didn't you tell—"

"Doesn't matter. What the hell is going on here, Paul?"

Paul leans back against the headrest. "You don't understand. She needed money. Her mother has cancer, and they don't have health insurance."

"She could have asked us." Carlos is almost pleading. "Asked you. Or Tanner. She—"

"I told her to. She wouldn't."

Annie's words, from before. *I ain't asking that bitch for a god-damn thing.*

"She wanted to earn it," Paul says. "She's always been like that, ever since I've known her. Annie doesn't take charity."

"Except from MS-13." Nic is rubbing his eyes with the heels of his hands.

"Nah," Carlos says. "The MS don't just lend money. That's not how they work. What did she do for them? What was she getting a cut of?"

Paul sighs. It's almost a contented sigh, like he's relieved to have this off his shoulders. He doesn't mean it that way, but now *I* want to smash his face against the dashboard.

"They wanted her to take a shipment up to Bakersfield," he says. "They needed a clean vehicle, one they could hide the drugs in. It was supposed to be an easy job..."

"Oh, man," Nic says.

And the last puzzle piece clicks into place.

The night before, back at Paul's Boutique, Annie and Paul were talking about fixing something in the van. I didn't think much of it at the time, but she must have been about to load up the drugs and take them north—which she never got to do, what with Reggie calling the red light. Maybe she thought she'd have a chance later on, but that was before she and Carlos had to dump the van. And before the cops found it.

This is what Annie was talking about when she said we needed to be straight with each other. She thought it didn't matter right now, because she thought MS-13 wouldn't be a problem until later.

"What was it?" Carlos says. "Heroin? Coke?"

"Heroin." He sounds wretched. "I don't know the street price, but—"

"How many bags?"

"Maybe five?" He makes a shape with his hands, like he's holding a basketball.

Carlos whistles. "Two million. More."

"Jesus fuck." I can barely get the words out.

"She was going to get ten per cent," Paul continues. "Now

the van is in an impound lot somewhere. And if the cops look closer . . ."

"How do you know all this?" I ask.

"She asked for my help."

"Yeah, but why? You're telling me she couldn't have just asked to borrow the van for a while, then done this herself? Hid the drugs in the walls or whatever? No way. Why did she even involve you?"

"You think Annie knows how to take a van apart and put it back together?"

"One of her contacts then. Someone must have had a car or a truck or—"

"Nothing clean. Nothing that could have slipped by the cops, which was how she sold it to MS-13."

"*Pinche pendejo,*" Carlos says through gritted teeth.

"I don't get it." I sit back, trying to run this all through my head. "Why'd you help her in the first place? She came to you because she needed the van, but why'd you say yes? If I'd come to you with this, you'd have gone fucking *nuts.* You'd never have let me do it."

Paul says nothing. He turns his head, looking out the window.

"Hey. Paul."

"I trust her."

"You *trust her*? She's using our van to ship drugs. How in the hell are you cool with that?"

"I didn't say I was *cool* with it." I've never seen him this uncomfortable. Like he wants a sinkhole to open up and swallow him, us, the car, the whole world.

Carlos punches the steering wheel. Hard. A sharp, jagged blast of the horn echoes into the night, making me jump. He turns to Paul. "You know what these people do?"

"Of course I—"

"They cut you. Over and over again. I seen it in Mexico. They don't stop, even if you give them what they want. Everybody they take out is a warning."

"I was just trying to help her." Paul's voice is a shaking whisper.

"Help her?" Carlos shakes her head. "Motherfucker, you just killed her."

"And I still don't get *why*," I say. "Why didn't you tell Reggie? Why—"

"*Because I'm in love with her!*" Paul twists in his seat, bellowing the words.

In the silence that follows I can just hear the car's engine ticking as it cools.

"OK," Nic murmurs.

"Paul," I say. "That's—"

"That's what?" He looks over his shoulder at me. "That's what, Teagan? What were you going to say?"

I don't know *what* I was going to say. I try to put Paul and Annie together in my brain and can't do it. They're just too different.

"How long?" Carlos says quietly.

"A few months." Paul sags in his seat. "Remember the Thousand Oaks job?"

A vague memory: black limos, a scowling bodyguard, a listening device I ghosted through the shadows towards the underside of one of the cars. A job that went off without a hitch, and which I'd forgotten about almost as soon as it happened.

"I gave her a ride home," Paul continues. "She...I mean, we passed this diner where they do pancakes. Du-pars, on Fairfax."

Du-pars. I've been there before, more than once. A white house with a big red-lettered sign in front of it, looking like time travellers from the 1950s dropped it there.

"She asked if I'd been there before, I said no, and suddenly she was insisting we pull in and get some food." He shakes his head. "I think she was just hungry, to be honest, but we... we got to talking. More than we had before."

"So since that night?"

"Not really. Not for a while after, actually. It just... Having pancakes at that stupid diner became like our thing. We'd go there sometimes, just talk."

"You never told us." I don't mean to sound so insulted. It just pops out.

Paul either doesn't hear or pretends not to. "Anyway, we did get together, after a bit. Pretty good pancakes, I guess." The tiniest flicker of a smile plays at the corners of his lips. "We decided to keep it outside work until we could figure things out, see if it was serious—we'd probably have to work together still, even if we didn't *stay* together. That was her saying that, by the way, not me. I know she can be tough to deal with sometimes, but she's... I don't know. She has all these plans. Things she wants to do. She wants to look after her mom more than anything. And like I said, she wouldn't take charity. If she couldn't earn it through Tanner, she'd earn it some other way. That's what she told me."

"But couldn't you have just... I don't know, given her money?"

A bitter laugh. "Not with my credit rating. Or my child support payments."

"So the moving jobs," I say. "The ones you had us do. You wanted to help Annie out?"

"What, with money? No. God no. They pay terribly. But

I wanted her to have something—something that wasn't government work or moving drugs. Something she could be proud of. And for the record, they *do* make us look more legit. That's part of it too."

That is both the sweetest and the dumbest thing I have ever heard.

I stare at the back of Carlos's seat, not seeing it. Instead, what I see is Annie. See her pride when she talked about her mom. See her grinning in excitement after she found Salinas. See her massaging Reggie's wasted legs.

She always put others first. The whole time. I never realised it before now, but nothing she's done has ever really been about her.

We have to go get her. We have to. Except…

Except, if we do, then Salinas dies.

Nobody's talking any more. Nobody's looking at each other. They're all having the same thoughts I am. I take a deep breath. Then another.

"You go to Salinas," Paul says. He sounds miserable. "I'll get Annie back."

I blink. "Not an option."

"I'm not leaving her."

"I get that, but we are *not* splitting up." Suddenly I'm furious, although I don't know whether I'm genuinely angry at him, or at any one of the thousand-odd people who want us gone.

"Try and stop me." Paul doesn't meet my eye as he pops the car door, turning sideways to step out.

"Wh—Hey, Paul!" I clamber out the car too, and then we're all the sidewalk, all of us talking at once, Paul saying that there's no way he's letting Annie go, me asking him how he plans to break into a gang compound by himself, how he even plans to *get* there when we only have one car, Nic and Carlos trying to get between us.

"Hold on. Hold *on*." Carlos shoves his way between Paul and me, hands out. "Let's just think. Splitting up may not be the worst idea."

This again. "Nope," I say. "That actually is the worst idea."

"Yeah," he says. A shocked, disbelieving smile flashes across his face. "This whole day, man. It's all been bad ideas. This is just one more."

I don't know what to say to that. He's right. There are no good options here. None.

"We can't win this one, man," he says. And we shouldn't be trying to."

"What are you saying?" Nic asks.

"I'm saying…I'm saying we cut and run. Fuck Salinas. Let's just go."

"We can't just leave him," Paul says. "Or Annie."

"That's not what I mean." He points to Paul. "Go get Annie. I can take Teagan across the border, get her somewhere safe."

I try to interrupt him, but he talks over me.

"Every minute you're in LA, you're in danger," Carlos says. "From Tanner, from the cops, from whatever psycho's after Salinas now. I can help you get out." He looks over at Nic. "You take off, dude. We got this."

"Look, my man," says Nic. "I don't know what you got going on here, but she's the only one of you I actually knew before today. You think I'm leaving her now, you out your goddamn mind."

"*Listen to me*," Carlos roars at him. "You don't have the first clue what—"

I've had enough. I grab hold of Carlos, pulling him along the sidewalk.

"Stop," I say. "Right now. Just fucking stop."

"A whole year years now I've had your back. Every step of the way I been there. Why won't you listen to me?"

I shut my eyes, hating that he's right. Salinas or Annie. I can do one but not both. No, that's wrong: I *could* do both, assuming that all the luck in the world is on my side. Assuming that the killer doesn't get to Salinas while we're off rescuing Annie, in which case we can just give up.

And I'd lose every chance of finding out who this person is.

Is that selfish? Leaving Annie with MS-13? Letting other people put themselves in danger? Yes. Maybe. I don't know. There are no good choices here, but one has to be made. And it has to be made right now.

"You're right," I say. "We're gonna split up. But we're not gonna run. Nic is gonna drive me up to Burbank, and then get the hell out of there while I handle things. You and Paul need to find Annie. I need you to do that for me, OK?"

"And what about you? What about your chances?"

"I can move shit with my mind, genius."

I smile. He doesn't return it.

"I'll be OK," I say. "I can't go up to Burbank by myself—I'll probably fall asleep and crash the goddamn car. But if Nic can drive me, I can figure it out when I get up there."

He looks at me for a long moment. Behind us, Paul and Nic have gone quiet.

"Just run," he whispers. "Please. Teagan, I'm begging you. You don't have to tell any of us where you're going. Just disappear."

I open my mouth to reply, and no sound comes out.

He puts a hand on my head, pulls me close so his forehead touches the top of mine. "You're my little sister, Teags. *Mi hermanita.*" The words are almost hissed. "I'd rather have you safe and never see you again than... than this. I know you're strong, but this guy, he's stronger. I don't want you to fight him. *Please*."

I wrap my arms around him, hold tight.

"Do this for me, *cabrón*," I say. "Just... help Paul. Find Annie. Keep them safe."

We hold each other, rocking back and forth.

And after a long time he nods.

"Yeah," he says. "OK."

THIRTY-NINE

Jake

The neighbour's body lies in the hall, the blood soaking into the cracks between the hardwood floorboards. Sandy and her brat are back in the pantry, and it's a goddamn miracle that nobody heard their screams. And Javier is *still not here*.

Jake paces in the ruined living room, Sandy's phone in his hand. He can't go find Javier—the man could be anywhere, and killing him in a public place is not an option. He doesn't dare urge the man to hurry; he can't afford for him to get suspicious. He needs him here, needs him to walk in unsuspecting, and that means he has to wait.

He brings up Javier's message chain, looking for the three blinking dots, listening out for the telltale sound of a car pulling into the drive. It's now nearly midnight—what could possibly be taking him so long?

No wonder you and Sandy split. The thought is bitter, satisfying.

Chuy. He should call Chuy. No, he doesn't dare. He has to handle this himself. Sun Tzu wrote, *One who is prepared and waits for the unprepared will be victorious. They offer bait that which the enemy must take, manipulating the enemy to move while they wait*

in ambush. In ancient times, those skilled in warfare made themselves
invincible and then waited for the enemy to become vulnerable for steep
ground if you occupy it first occupy the high on the sunny side and wait
for the enemy when the rainwater rises and descends down to where
you want to cross...

Behind him a cluster of debris floats through the air, shattered frames and cutlery and chunks of wood from the ruined
couches. He doesn't notice. Nor does he notice how thick the
air is, or how the horizon above the backyard fence has turned
a vicious red. He doesn't hear the sirens in the distance, the
ones which have become almost constant now.

Call Chuy.

No.

Jake wasn't stupid. He'd told Chuy everything he knew
about his past, but he understood that it wouldn't come to
anything. Chuy was a friend—a good friend, the very best—
but he wasn't God. He'd either get bored once the trail started
to grow a little frosty, or keep going and run into the exact
same problem Jake had: there simply wasn't any information
out there.

All the same, it felt good. Having someone to listen—no,
having someone who *wanted* to listen, there was a big difference. Watching Chuy bent over his phone, focused and intent,
made Jake's heart feel like it was going to explode out of his
chest. In that moment he would have killed for Chuy. With a
smile on his face. He relived every detail he could remember,
along with the scraps he'd manage to gather over the past few
years. That night, after Chuy dropped him back home, his
sleep had been deep and dreamless, the best he could remember in years.

Chuy had vanished for a second time. Dropped right off the
grid. This time there was no leaden feeling in Jake's gut—or at

least, nothing like before. Chuy wasn't going to betray him; he knew that now. It was amazing of him to try to find out what Jake had long given up on discovering, but he didn't expect Chuy to actually do it. He even, with a kind of satisfaction, realised he knew what would happen: Chuy would show up in a few weeks, in that musty-smelling Civic, and they'd go toss shit around the junkyard for a while and then go hang out by the beach.

That didn't sound so bad.

Four nights later, just as he was coming in from a long shift—washing dishes or manning a checkout counter, by then they were all blending into one—his phone leaped to life in his pocket. He dug for it, swearing quietly, knowing that at any second Garrett from the other part of the hostel was going to yell at him to shut the fuck up. He didn't even look at the screen before answering. "Yeah? Wha—"

"Outside." Chuy sounded relaxed, laconic. "Let's go."

It had been a long day. A long shift. Under normal circumstances, Jake would have told Chuy that he'd see him tomorrow. But there was something in Chuy's voice. A note of eagerness behind the laid-back tone.

Jake smiled to himself. Chuy'd probably got that thing from Bucktail, an old relative of his mother. Still, couldn't blame a guy for trying. He owed Chuy a beer, if nothing else—he'd just been paid for that week's work, which wasn't much but surely enough to buy a sixpack or two.

He'd sauntered out to the car, which was idling at the kerb round the corner. As he'd swung into the front seat, he'd said, "Hey, man, it's good to see you and all, but it's kinda late, so—"

Which is when Chuy dropped the picture on his lap.

For a moment his mind blanked. He didn't—couldn't—understand what he was seeing.

It was a photo, colour-printed on flimsy paper. The printer must have been old, leaving streaky white lines across the image, but Jake could still see what it was. A little kid with blonde hair, bundled up warm, held tight to the chest of a smiling woman, both of them in a park somewhere. And the woman...there was no mistaking who she was.

It was a photo he'd never seen before.

"Told you," Chuy said. His voice seemed to come from a great distance. "I got friends."

Jake hadn't even been aware that the car was moving. He couldn't look away from the photo. Could barely blink. He held the paper tight as if it would be caught by the wind and torn from him.

"How?" he'd said eventually, his voice barely above a whisper.

Chuy had grinned. "That's my business. Took a while to dig that up—you didn't give me much to go on—but there's plenty out there if you know where to look."

"There's...there's more?"

"A lot more."

"Chuy, I don't...How did you..." He was almost gasping, unable to tear his eyes away from the photo in his lap.

Chuy turned on the radio, more tinny salsa music flooding the car. They were on the freeway, and when Jake looked up, he realised they were heading north.

"Tell me everything," he'd somehow managed to say.

"Hold on now," Chuy had replied. "You gotta do something for me first."

No matter how many questions Jake asked, Chuy hadn't answered. Just let them wash over him. Jake was delighted, furious, confused, terrified, all at the same time. His body felt like it was generating its own electrical field, one that would fry him, Chuy, the car, the whole world.

He'd kept asking questions as they pulled into the junkyard, not even realising that they weren't parking until they were already deep in the maze of cars. Chuy had winked, then got out, pausing for a minute to stretch, cricking his back as he gazed up at the stars. He could have been standing in his backyard, cup of coffee in hand, gazing out the sunrise and ready to face the day.

Jake nearly fell when he tried to get out of the car. His body didn't appear to be listening to him very much. "You went to College Springs, right?" he said, almost babbling as he came round the back of the car, where Chuy was now standing. "You must have done. But I checked there, and the records office said they had nothing. There was this one diner, and I thought someone might remember something, so—"

Which was when Chuy popped the trunk. And for the second time that night, Jake's words left him in a great hitching breath.

Tonight—this night, in this house in Burbank—represents the end of something. A process. One that started when Chuy first opened that trunk.

Jean Grey met Charles Xavier almost right after she started showing her powers. Spider-Man didn't get bitten by a spider, then have to wait for eighteen years in a series of grey, dry foster homes.

Jake wants to find out who he is, how he got his abilities. Who his mother was, his father—if that's even possible. That's still more important to him than anything. But that's not his origin story, and maybe tonight is. The night that he, Jake, criss-crossed a burning Los Angeles and took down the bad guys in one fell swoop.

The night he found out who he really is, once and for all.

FORTY

Teagan

You know how sometimes you get so tired that you can't actually fall asleep?

It should be the simplest thing in the world, just close your eyes and *boom*. But you can't. You just lie there, trying to think calm thoughts, knowing that it's not going to work and cursing evolution for giving you a brain.

That is me. Right now.

It's a forty-minute drive up to Burbank from UCLA, and I'm going over the plan again. One: get Javier Salinas out of there. Two: wait for the other psychokinetic to show up and stop him. Somehow. I'll be honest, neither Nic nor I could figure out how that was going to go.

Of course, none of this matters if Salinas is already dead. Or if the cops are watching the place. Or if Salinas shoots us when we walk in the door. Every part of this plan feels like a Hail Mary, but what the hell else are we supposed to do?

And the whole time, the fire burns on the horizon. Fire we're driving straight towards.

"Can't sleep?" Nic says after I change position for the seventh time.

"Yeah. Think we can find like a Motel 6 and get some shut-eye for a few hours? Maybe order pizza?"

He gives me a sideways look, his mouth slightly open like he's trying to decide on the best way to answer.

"Nic. I'm kidding."

"Sorry." He shakes his head, eyes back on the freeway. "Long day."

"Yeah, well, *someone* had plum granita at N/Naka. You should have more than enough energy. Suck it up, buttercup."

He smiles, and for a second he looks like the Nic from before. Before he found out about the PK and the special forces and how I'm being framed for murder.

The car slows as we negotiate a snarl of traffic.

"So are you gonna tell me?" Nic says.

"Am I gonna tell you what?"

But of course I know what.

We're on 405 now, heading north, just outside Sherman Oaks—and for once the traffic is actually moving. I stare out the window, watching the lights pass by. The radio's on, music playing, although I can't tell which song—something with a very low, almost inaudible beat, like a human pulse.

I don't want to talk about this. I don't want to relive the memories. Ones I've spent a very long time walling away, brick by brick.

Then again, just because I don't like talking about them doesn't mean they didn't happen.

"You said your parents gave you your..." He waves his hand. "Your thing."

"My ability, yeah. They genetically engineered me while I was in the womb."

"You can't just...give someone superpowers by messing with their genes. Otherwise everybody'd have them."

"Everybody didn't have my parents."

We're heading east on the 101 now, running alongside the LA River. Out the window, headlights glitter in the dark.

"My mom and dad got together at Harvard," I tell him. "They were in the genetics department, two of the top students. They were so good the Department of Energy stole them to work on the Human Genome Project."

"How does that—"

"I'm getting there. So, my mom had a twin brother. He didn't have her brains, but they were super-close. He was a soldier, and in 1991 he got deployed to Kuwait."

A place I've only seen in pictures. Mom and Dad wouldn't talk about it. Ever. They talked about the man they called Uncle Tony, a lot, but never about the war itself.

"He was killed. And it...did something to my mom. Changed her. She became obsessed with trying to end wars— her and my dad both. They wanted to create a—"

"Super-soldier," he says at the same time as me.

We look at each other, Nic briefly taking his eyes off the road.

"Kind of, although they never really called it that. They wanted to build a person who could end a battle before it even started." The words aren't mine—they're mom's. It's all too easy to picture her saying them, see the way her eyes shone. I push on, not wanting to think too hard about this. "But the government wouldn't let them just go experiment on humans. Maybe they might have pulled it off now, but there was no way they were getting permission then. So they quit."

"Yeah, but...I mean, Teagan, you can't just mess with someone's genes like that, no matter how smart you are."

"Really? I throw a giant flowerpot through your apartment window with my mind, and you're still not convinced?"

He grimaces. "Fine. OK."

"You don't get how smart my parents were. Or how determined my mom was after they dropped off the genome project. Money wasn't an issue—my dad's dad made a lot of it, back in the 70s, and he wasn't around any more. They had a lot of connections with the people who made the equipment from their work on the project. They bought a place in Wyoming, a big ranch, and got to work."

"Got to work with…what?" Nic looks like he's struggling to take this all in. "I don't know about a ton about gene science, but don't you need, like, subjects? Embryos or whatever?"

"Yeah."

"So what—"

"You have to understand, they wanted this more than anything in the world. Mom most of all."

His voice is quiet. "What did they do?"

"They—"

I stop dead.

"They…what?" Nic says. When I don't answer, he says, "Don't leave me hanging."

"Holy shit." My words are a whisper. It's all fitting into place. All of it.

"I know how the killer can do what I can," I say. "I know how they got their ability."

FORTY-ONE

Teagan

"Wait, what? How?"

I can't believe I didn't see it before. "You're right. My mom and dad needed embryos to experiment on. So they...they'd find women. Prostitutes, women who couldn't afford to have a kid. They'd offer them money."

The car is dead silent. On the radio the Eagles are singing very, very softly about Hotel California.

"They didn't have ethics committees to oversee them. They had plenty of money, and subjects. That was how they ironed out a lot of the early errors, before they figured out how to do it for real. And what if—"

"—one of them wasn't an error," he says quietly. He still hasn't looked at me. "So what, they just let this woman go?"

"Makes sense, right? If they thought they'd failed, and the mother had been paid...Maybe they did something with the foetus in the womb...Fuck, I don't know, Nic, but it makes sense. And she gave birth to someone with my ability..."

"Hell no," Nic says. "I still don't buy it. I'm not denying that you can definitely do some shit. But genetics? You're telling me your mom and dad switched a few genes around, and suddenly you've got telekinesis?"

"*Psycho*kinesis."

"*Whatever.* It doesn't make any sense. Like, at all. That's not how genes work. Has it occurred to you that maybe there was some other explanation?"

"Like what?" I can't keep the weariness out of my voice, and this time it has nothing to do with physical exhaustion.

"I don't know."

"Neither did the government. After they pulled me out, they spent months grilling me, trying to understand how I existed. They kept saying the same thing: that there was no way genetics could create kids like us."

"So how—"

"Mom and Dad always told us they'd modified our genes. They had a genetics lab in their barn. They had backgrounds in high-level genetics. If it looks like a genetic experiment and quacks like a genetic experiment..."

"But you don't know for sure." He changes lanes quickly, jerking the wheel. "Didn't you ever want to find out?"

I don't know how to answer that.

For my entire life with them, Mom and Dad stuck to the gene story. It's not that I never thought to question it—it's that I didn't know enough to tell them they were wrong. And by the time Moira Tanner got me out, Mom and Dad and almost all their material were gone for ever.

I've spent a lot of time thinking about how they did it—thinking, and reading, trying to wrap my head around plasmids, drug-resistant cassettes, CRISPR, ex-vivo modification. It got me precisely nowhere. All I know is that at some point before I was born, my parents had a breakthrough that sent their research in a new direction—and led to me.

It took a long time of me banging my head against a wall before I decided that it wasn't worth it. The simplest answer was the original one: that my parents were way ahead of their time. If there was something else, there was no way I was going to find it, and I discovered that I wasn't willing to try any more. I didn't want to live in the past. That part of my life was done.

"You said *kids*."

"Huh?"

Nic shifts in his seat. "You said *kids like us*. You had siblings?"

"Yeah. Brother and sister."

"Older? Younger?"

"Both older. They were twins. Two years ahead."

"They were tele—psychokinetic too?"

"No." In the window my reflection looks like a ghost. "Chloe could...she could sense infrared. She had these pits in her skin that could detect body heat. It looked like really bad acne, actually. And Adam, he—

I stop, my memory filled with burning smoke, dry heat baking onto my skin. The pop of wood as the roof beams burned. The smell of flesh cooking.

"Adam never needed to sleep."

"For real?"

"Mom said they altered his..." It takes real effort to recall the words. "His sleep-wake homeostasis. His body could function without it." *And it made him completely, homicidally insane.*

"Why those powers?"

"What do you mean?"

"You can move things with your mind, your sister sees infrared, your brother doesn't sleep. Why those?"

"Imagine a soldier who doesn't need to carry ammo or

night-vision goggles. One who never has to rest. You have those, you could end a war before it started."

A car pulls up next to us at a light: a group of teenagers, laughing like they don't have a single thing in the world to worry about. I make myself look away. "Mom and Dad couldn't put all of it in one of us—*that* was too complicated, even for them. But they wanted to show the world that it could be done."

"What was it like?" Nic says.

"What was what like?"

"Growing up with your mom and dad. Your siblings."

"You know what homeschooling is, right?"

He gives me a look.

"Well, we were, obviously. Can't have three superpowered kids running around kindergarten. But my mom and dad... they weren't *evil*."

"Seriously? They—"

"I *know*. I know what I said before, about the babies and everything. And yes, it was messed up. But you gotta understand, after they had us..."

I've gone through this in my head so many times, and I still struggle with it. "They weren't bad parents. They didn't mistreat us. It wasn't a cult. We didn't get to hang out with other kids or anything, but when you're seven years old and you've got a brother and sister and ten thousand acres of countryside to mess around in, you don't really know what you're missing."

"You didn't ever *want* to hang out with other kids?"

"The one thing Mom and Dad drilled into us, from like age three, was that we could never show anybody our powers without telling them. That if we did, people would come and hurt us. Hurt us, and take them away."

"That *is* messed up."

"Also true. But they made us believe we were all special, and gave us a huge wilderness to play in. Like I said, kind of hard to know what you're missing."

"And nobody came along? Nobody ever visited?"

"Of course they visited. We weren't completely isolated, and we still had to go into town for groceries or whatever. We just never showed what we could do in front of strangers."

"And you were homeschooled." He nods to himself. "Nobody from the government ever came by, said maybe you should get these kids into a classroom?"

"Wyoming, dude. Nobody gives a fuck."

"Fair enough."

"And like, Mom and Dad looked after us. Yeah, it was homeschooling, but we could read and write. We didn't think Jesus was coming to murder all the gay people. And they taught us about our abilities too—plenty of tests in the lab, out in the barn. Well, tests for Chloe and me—Adam's power wasn't really something he did, it was more like something he *was*. He was smarter than me and my sister, mostly because he could stay up all night reading. Mom and Dad couldn't buy enough books for him."

If memories have a taste, these are dark chocolate: bittersweet, mysterious. Mom in her usual jeans and flannel shirt, sitting with us at the big table, a stack of books in front of her and her greying hair pulled back in a ponytail. Dad in the kitchen behind her, whistling very quietly, shoulders hunched over something hot and bubbling on the stove. The windows behind him steamed up, hiding the outside world. Cooking chilli con carne with homemade chilli paste. Venison from the elk that sometimes wandered onto the property. Then fruit salad, rough-cut, tossed with mint and brown sugar.

He'd let me cook with him—neither Chloe nor Adam was ever interested. I would stand next to him at the kitchen counter, hulling strawberries or trimming sinew or chopping herbs.

Those memories open up more. The ones that hurt the most because they're so good.

What Mom and Dad did to us was awful, and what Chloe and Adam became was...even worse. But it doesn't change the fact that I still rode horses with Adam and Chloe, played tag, shot air rifles, the three of us tearing across our little chunk of paradise. It doesn't change how good Dad's food tasted, or how it felt to hug my mom.

"So why'd you leave?" Nic says, jerking me out of my thoughts.

"Puberty."

"Come on."

"I'm not actually kidding. All three of us were fine until we were about twelve or thirteen. Then it's like something inside us just...woke up. Chloe and I had the usual teen bullshit, but Adam..."

Nic flicks me a glance, not saying anything.

I swallow. "They had to lock him up. He stopped being able to tell what was real and what wasn't. He...he hurt Mom."

Nic says nothing.

"Mom and Dad started to fight. About everything. About us. Chloe hated them for what they had done to Adam, because they were twins and all, and it just got worse and worse, you know? Mom and Dad were still testing us, or trying to, and they started to get angry when we couldn't do stuff."

I can feel tears pricking at my eyes—even now, years after the fact. "I can't move anything organic with my mind. I don't know why. It doesn't listen to me. When I was little it didn't matter, but as I got older Mom started making out like it was my fault...like I wasn't trying. She said the same things to Chloe, when she couldn't see far enough or deep enough."

I'm clenching my fists and have to make myself relax. "The one time, Mom got this cat. A kitten, really. She told me to move it, or she was gonna kill it."

"Jesus."

"She didn't, in the end. Just let it go. But she would never have done that before. And that's when they *really* started to lean on the whole super-soldier thing. End all wars. Greater purpose. Problem was, none of us wanted that any more."

"Why didn't you just leave?"

"I thought about it. A lot. Nearly ran a couple of times too. But they were still my mom and dad, so I told myself it would get better."

"And Chloe?"

"She'd never have left Adam. And that was the problem. Mom and Dad fucked up—they kept the two of them separated after Adam lost it. She didn't know how bad he'd got, so when she let him out—"

"She *let him out*?"

"He got in the house." My voice is a dull monotone. "If it hadn't been my day to chop the firewood, I would've been inside too. Mom was dead. Dad was dead. Chloe was...He'd broken her leg, I think. The fire had reached the top floor by then, and he was just...laughing."

I rub my face as if I can shield myself from the flames. When I pull my hand away, he's there. Adam. Grinning back at me, eyes horribly bright, face ringed in fire. I blink, and he's gone.

"He came for me, and I just ran. Bolted. I wanted to save Chloe, but it was like...like I didn't have a choice. Before he could get to me, the whole roof collapsed. Crushed them both. Missed me by like half an inch.

"I don't remember a ton of what happened next, but some- one must have spotted the smoke. By the time the fire brigade got there, the house and most of the barn were gone. Nearly all of my folks' research was destroyed, all except one or two computer towers. One of those towers had video files on it."

He whistles long and low. "Tanner?"

"Not right then. But once they realised what had been happening, the government took over pretty fast. They put me in this facility. In Waco. Every test my mom and dad had ever done, they made me do again, and again."

I don't remember a lot about the place they kept me. I do remember crying a lot. And the two psychologists they assigned to me: an older guy with round glasses who had a way of looking down his nose at me, and a young woman with red hair who always seemed like she was about to start screaming just because we were in the same room. Most of all, I remember grey. Everything grey. Walls, ceiling, my bed frame. The rocks in the tiny fenced off garden.

"They didn't hurt me," I say. "But they wouldn't let me leave. Every time I asked, they'd just throw more shit at me— comic books and video games and fucking *Seventeen* magazine. Like I was a zoo animal they had to keep fed. Of course, after a while I realised I didn't have to put up with their shit any more. Broke a few locks. A jaw or two. Made it all the way to the end of the driveway before they tasered me. After that they got smarter. Kept me dosed."

As I talk, Nic's eyes get wider and wider. We've come to a stop in the tangle of roads where the Ventura and Hollywood Freeways meet. We've stopped because the traffic has got worse. So has the hooting. And despite the fact that the win- dows are closed and the aircon is off, smoke digs into the back of my throat.

"How long were you there for?" he asks.

"Four years? Give or take?"

"*Four*? Holy fuck."

"I don't remember a lot of it. And of course being dosed didn't do wonders for my PK control. I don't how long I was there for, but I guess at some point they decided I wasn't worth keeping. The problem was, they couldn't just pop me back into society because that might lead to all kinds of uncomfortable questions."

There's a sick, curdled feeling in the pit of my stomach. "Anyway, about that time Moira Tanner came by, introduced herself, said the government wanted to euthanise me and cut me open."

"She . . . *what?*"

"I know. Kind of a downer."

"Teagan, that's . . . Jesus, you're a U.S. citizen. They can't do that."

"Yeah, because the government is really good at taking care of its citizens. Point is, it didn't happen—obviously. Tanner offered me a deal."

And all at once I'm back in that tiny grey interrogation room, with a camera in each corner of the ceiling and the metal table with a big dent in the middle, like someone a lot larger than me had punched it in frustration. Tanner sitting opposite me, hands clasped, dark suit, white shirt buttoned to the neck. Hair pulled back. Eyes the colour of the room, and face as hard as the walls.

Here's how it's going to work. You'll do the jobs I tell you to do, work with who I tell you to, live where I tell you to. In return, you'll be my responsibility and under my protection. So long as you never reveal your abilities to anyone without security clearance, you can live a normal life.

"She'd keep the government off my back," I tell Nic. "In return, I do whatever covert bullshit she needed done."

"And you could never quit?"

"Nope."

"Or live outside LA."

"Nope."

"But..." His face contorts like he's struggling to put it all together. "You wanted to open a *restaurant*. How were you planning on—"

"Please. How hard could it be to run a kitchen *and* do black-ops shit on the side? Gotta admit, that's a hell of a secret identity."

"How are you still doing that?"

"Doing what?"

"Making jokes. All the shit that's happened, and you still..."

"You're right. I should totally be crying and screaming right now. Sorry, I'll get on that."

"No." I look over to see that there's genuine frustration on his face. "That's not what I mean. You...you're...*normal*."

"Gee, thanks."

He gives an exasperated growl. "What I mean is, I've known you for a while now. I've spent time with you. What you're describing...it's like you're talking about a different person. If even half of what had happened to you happened to me, I'd be in an institution."

He realises what he's just said and drops his eyes. "Sorry. That kind of came out wrong."

"Kind of."

"But just—"

"Number one: it's rude to diagnose someone like you just did. You should stop that. Number two: just because I *look* totally normal doesn't mean everything's OK. Number three..."

I don't actually get to number three. Once more, I'm back in the facility—not just seeing it but *feeling* it. Feeling the awful, awful despair, the sense that everything had gone to shit and there was no way out. And then, worse, the numbness from the drugs after my escape attempt.

Nic's voice brings me back. "If I was in your situation, I'd be angry. At everyone. Your mom and dad, the government, your brother. None of what happened was your fault, and you've got every right to be furious. But you're not angry."

"How do *you* know?"

"Maybe I don't. But Teags... you're the most straight-up person I've ever met. You're kind and smart, and funny as hell. Your forward-planning skills are all over the place, but... you're you. I mean... Fuck, I don't..." He closes his eyes. Takes a very deep breath. "I know I'm not saying this right, and I know it's probably simplifying the situation like a billion times over. So I'm just going to say it. What you went through would have broken most people. It would have broken me. How did it not break you?"

We're under the interchange now. Concrete above and below us.

"You're right," I say after a minute. "I should be angry. I was for a long time. Years, even. But..."

This memory is something I've kept close, returning to it often, polishing it like a precious jewel. I am so, so scared of losing it. Forgetting it, or changing the details in my mind, or letting it slip away. Even telling it to someone feels like I'm putting it in danger.

"But then I came to LA," I say, still looking out the window at the passing lights. "Tanner set me up here. I didn't know anybody, and the whole thing with the…with Reggie and everyone was still being worked out, and I just…didn't know what to do. She just told me to wait, you know? Shacked me up in a crappy hotel and said she'd be in touch.

"I was on Hollywood Boulevard. Where the Walk of Fame is. It was like five o'clock, and I was hungry, so I bought a taco from this little food stand—I'd never eaten one before."

"You didn't know what a taco was?"

"I did, just hadn't had one. Not exactly a Wyoming specialty."

"Right. Sorry."

"So I'm standing on the corner with this taco, which is leaking out its cardboard holder all over my hands, and there's all these tourists around, just huge crowds, gawking at the stupid stars on the sidewalk, and the sun is going down, and the palm trees are like, silhouetted against the sky, and…"

I trail off. When I speak again, my voice is very steady. "And suddenly it was *real*. I could do whatever I wanted. *Be* whoever I wanted. I was a million miles from Wyoming and Waco, and I was never going back."

"I don't get it."

"Get what?"

"You say you could do whatever you wanted, but you couldn't. You had to work for Tanner. She wouldn't have let you open a restaurant, or even be with someone, and—"

"I know all that. Tanner's deal was—*is*—deeply fucked up. But it got me here. I think she knew that—knew that after Waco being made to live somewhere like LA would be enough to keep me sweet. I'd been in the worst situation you can imagine, and it ended. Things got better. If it could happen once, it could happen again."

He reaches over, takes my hand. It's the one I wiped my face with, but he doesn't care, squeezing hard despite my wet skin.

"So I'm standing there with this stupid taco," I say, "and I just decided...I decided that I didn't want to be angry. The people who hurt me were gone. I wasn't gonna let them fuck with me any more. I was somewhere I thought I'd never even see, and I had to make the most of it. What happened to me? It wasn't gonna define me. I wasn't gonna let it. My parents took so much from me, and I was *not* gonna let them take this too.

"Yeah, it's been hard sometimes. Working under Moira Tanner sucks. And yeah, I'll probably never own a restaurant. But I am never gonna stop trying because things can *always* get better. People are stupid, things go wrong, plans fall apart. Shit doesn't work like you want it to. But there's always a way out."

He doesn't say anything for a long time. The traffic slowly crawls along around us, heading for the glowing sky.

"How was it?" he says eventually.

"What?"

"Your first taco."

I pull a face. "Tasted terrible. I threw it in the trash."

He snorts. Then I snort. Then we're both laughing, then we're both howling until my stomach feels like it's going to explode. The pressure of the entire day just rolls out of us, filling the car with absurd, hysterical laughter.

"Oh shit," he says, wiping his face when we stop laughing a thousand years later.

"Yeah." My stomach aches, but it's a good ache. "Nic, listen. I—"

"Oh, *shit*." He leans forward, peering out the windshield.

Flashing red and blue lights. Just out of sight around the curve of the freeway.

FORTY-TWO

Jake

Jake is no longer in the house on East Orange Grove. He's back in the junkyard with Chuy, lost in the memory.

The man in the trunk had stared up at them with lidded, rheumy eyes, breathing through his mouth. Drugged with something. His straggly days-old beard was crusted with what looked like dried blood, a rivulet of spit leaking from the corner of his trembling mouth. He was in his late fifties, body hunched and bent, wearing a hoodie with carolina basketball across the front. The hoodie had gone grey with age, and was threadbare, holed in a dozen spots. Ancient cargo pants and torn trainers with flapping tongues completed the picture.

The man's hands and feet were bound. Chuy reached inside and with a grunt rolled the man up and out of the trunk. He'd thumped to the ground, giving off a pitiful mewling sound. Under the junkyard's floodlights, he'd looked shrunken like a mummy, the greying hoodie shrouding him.

"You got a decision to make," Chuy had murmured.

He'd squatted down, head tilted to one side, considering the wheezing man.

"What are you talking about?" Jake had said. But he'd

known. Of course he'd known. He'd known the second Chuy had lifted the trunk lid.

"You can spend the rest of your life pretending you ain't different, like you're just another one of us poor motherfuckers wandering around with our thumbs up our asses. You can keep hiding."

He'd turned his head towards Jake.

"Or you can man up. Use your power, your ability, whatever the fuck it is. Use it like it was meant to be used."

"You want me to k—" He couldn't say it. Couldn't quite get the word out. His palms were cold and damp, and he wiped them unconsciously on his shirt.

Chuy had glanced at him as if he hadn't realised Jake was standing there, then all at once had rocketed to his feet, delivering a kick to the bound man's stomach. The air had left him in a great, lurching heave, and he'd curled into a ball, trembling.

"See, what I did," Chuy had said, wiping his mouth, "is I went digging for the scummiest dude I could find. Took me longer than I thought, considering the amount of scumbags in this town. But I found him. This asshole..." He'd nodded down at the man. "This asshole used to touch little kids back in the day. Wasn't too clever about it either—got himself ten years in Pelican Bay.

"Hangs out on Figueroa most days, but lately he's been going past this school. Just posting up on the corner, watching. Staying there longer and longer, every day."

"I can't."

The response was automatic. But even as he'd said it, Jake could hear the uncertainty. He felt terror, yes, and a surprising, startling anger at Chuy, but...yes, wasn't there something else behind the fear? Something that might or might not have been curiosity? It had been building ever since he'd first shown

Chuy what he could do, when he'd thrown that hubcap into the darkness. *I got a nine mil can do that, and I don't have to carry round hubcaps to use it, neither.*

"Of course you can," Chuy had said. "You just don't want to."

He could walk away. Right now. Just head right into that gap in the maze of cars and go home, hitch a ride, fuck it.

Except, then Chuy would vanish. And so would the picture.

"It's blackmail," he'd said.

"Blackmail." Chuy had actually laughed. "You know what happens if you don't do it? Nothing. Not a goddamn thing. You get to go on living your life. Hell, I'll even drive you home. That ain't blackmail. No one's forcing you to do anything. I'm *asking*."

The man on the ground had tried to roll away then. Chuy had glanced down, delivered another rib kick, doing it almost absently. The noises coming out of the man's throat had started to take on a raspy, reedy quality, like a sleeper about to start snoring.

"Blackmailers lie," he'd said. "They lie and they cheat and steal. Have I lied to you? Cheated you? I'm your fuckin' friend, man. Friends don't lie to each other. I'd never do that. Never, d'you hear me?"

Jake had turned then, walked around the side of the car, stood with his hands by his sides. His palms felt like they'd been dipped in warm, runny oil.

Chuy's voice from behind him. "What I found on you? It's the real deal. It doesn't paint the full picture—my guess is there's a ton of stuff that didn't leave a paper trail, which isn't surprising, not with what you do—but it gives you one hell of a starting point."

Chuy had stepped closer, his voice dropping to a conspirational rumble. "This guy? He's nothing, J. Nobody. Not a single person would even notice he's gone. I got a bigger target in mind. Bunch of guys much worse than the dude back there. The shit they into...you can't even believe. I thought about doing it myself, thought about it a bunch of times, but I always stopped. You know why?"

He'd held a finger to his temple. "Fucking cops. The things they can do with bullet matching and ballistics and residue, I can't even tell you. Maybe one guy, OK, I get away, but more than one? And you gotta do it quick, or they'll scatter. But *you*..." A smile had crept onto his face. "With what you can do? You could take care of all of 'em, leave zero trace. Can you imagine the cops trying to figure out how you did it? With no fingerprints, no contact between you and any of these dudes? No gun, no ammo? No bullet residue? Hell, you don't even have to be in the same room; you could be watching them through the window of the next building over. And who says you have to use an actual weapon? Fuck it. Knock a bookcase over. Rip the brakes out of their car. And even if you *did* somehow get caught, how the fuck are the cops going to prove it? Let's see 'em argue that one in court."

"Jesus Christ, Chuy. I can't just..." He had to force the words out, almost yell them. "I can't just *kill* someone."

Chuy had given him a baleful look. "I'm not saying turn into a serial killer. You're smarter than that. I'm saying, what if you could use your Gift to do some real good? Take out the trash? But before that happens, I gotta know you can do it. I gotta know you got the stones."

"I...I can't..."

"Why not? Who the fuck is he to you?"

"He's a human being!"

Chuy had given Jake a sad, almost pitying look. He'd glanced back towards the shaking, moaning thing on the ground staring at them with uncomprehending, terrified eyes. Vaguely, Jake had wondered what Chuy had drugged the man with, where he'd got it.

The photo was still in Jake's hand. Chuy had taken it, held it up as if seeing it for the first time. Then he'd handed it back with a shrug and started walking away, heading for the edge of the circle of cars.

"Ch—wait. Chuy. Chuy!"

"Your decision, man," Chuy had said over his shoulder. He'd almost vanished into the darkness between the cars. "No blackmail. No forcing."

"Hey!"

But Chuy was gone. The junkyard had swallowed him.

Jake doesn't remember much of the next few minutes. He remembers standing by the car, clutching the photo to his chest. Then he was standing over the man, looking down at him. The drugs must have been starting to wear off, because the man's eyes were a little more focused now, his mouth trying to form words. His lips had come together, separated with a faint pop, as if trying to form the letter P. For *please*, perhaps.

Jake had been getting stronger. Much stronger. Strong enough that he could easily force a piece of metal through someone, or move an engine block over their head and...

There was no way. He couldn't just kill someone. Nothing was worth that.

He'd paced the circle of cars, prowling like a tiger, scrunching the photo in his fist. He told himself a dozen times to stop, not wanting to damage the photo, telling himself it was all there was...Only that wasn't true, was it? Chuy said he had more. And that was the question here, wasn't it? Did he trust Chuy?

The fear and confusion were almost too great, almost over-whelming him, sweeping him from the circle like a rising tide. Chuy was...complicated. He was the kind of person who could switch from warm good humour to cold hard fury in half a second.

But was he a liar?

When you got down to it, at the very core of it all, he'd always been straight with Jake. He'd kept his secret. He said he was going to dig up info on Jake's past and he had. Chuy wouldn't lie, Jake was sure of it.

His gaze landed on something at the edge of the circle of cars: a pile of steel rebars. Each one four feet long, rusted and warped, undisturbed perhaps for years. Without fully under-standing what he was doing, he'd reached out for one, pulled it out, the others clattering off it as it shook loose a pall of dust. Dimly he was aware of the moaning from the bound man getting more and more frantic.

He looked down at the photo in his hand. It was crumpled, a crease bisecting his mom's face. He felt like he was at the very centre of the world at that moment: like every other person on the planet was watching him, billions of people, no one daring to breathe.

His past stretched before him, a landscape shrouded in fog. Who he was. How he got his abilities. Why his mother had given him up. Who she was, who her parents were. How could he move forward if he didn't know any of it? If he didn't lift that fog? He had a chance to blow it away, clear the air in a single breath—was he really going to pass that up?

He's a human being.

He'd watched expressionless as he moved the rebar over to the space above the man's body. Ignoring his gasps, the half-formed, pleading words. The man tried to wriggle away, rolling across the packed dirt, and Jake had made the rebar follow him almost without thinking about it.

He didn't have to do it. He could walk away. If there was more out there, he could find it too. He didn't need Chuy, he just had to work harder at it...

Then the rebar was buried in the man's chest.

Jake wasn't even aware of having driven it down. He could feel that it hadn't gone all the way through to the ground—it had penetrated a couple of inches into the flesh, no more. A curious squirming sensation registered in his mind—feedback from his grip on the rebar as the man coughed and gurgled and twisted.

Blood gouted. Jake pulled the rebar out, then forced it down again, harder this time. More blood, the man's howls rising to a wild warbling shriek. Again and again, eyes huge and heart slamming, Jake drove the rebar into the man's chest.

And when the man failed to die, when he kept right on screaming even after the ground around him was almost black with blood, Jake ripped the rebar out and, with a thought, bent it around the man's throat.

Bent it, and tightened.

Which is when Chuy had come sprinting out of the darkness and grabbed him, enveloping him in a bear hug. "Easy. Easy!"

Jake was screaming too. The screams devolved into sobs, and he collapsed in Chuy's arms. He let go of the rebar, which stayed in place, wrapped around the man's neck like a garrotte, one end sticking straight up in the air.

"You're OK, man. Just breathe." Chuy put a hand on the back of Jake's head, bent it so their foreheads were touching. His next words were a low, almost satisfied growl. "Proud of you, brother. You fucking did it. That's why I believe in you. It's like I said, man, we gonna change the fucking *world* with this shit."

In the nights to come Jake would think back to the

junkyard. It was the first thing on his mind when he woke up and the last thing he thought of before he went to sleep. But strangely, it wasn't the feeling of murdering the man that he remembered; it was the sensation of touching foreheads with Chuy, that burning intensity, the *connection*. And those words. *I believe in you.*

Later, when Chuy had laid out why Steven Chase, Bryan Hayden and Javier Salinas deserved to die, he'd felt that same intensity. That same sense of rightness. He was no serial killer. He took no pleasure in doing it. But it had to be done, and nobody was better placed than him.

There's no way in hell he's letting Chuy down. He can finally make that call, the one when he tells Chuy it's handled. That all three of the people responsible for El Agujero are out of the picture. He can imagine the look on Chuy's face: the relief, the huge grin. The fierce gratitude.

His attention is jerked from his thoughts. A sound has washed into the ruined living room of the house on East Orange Grove, a sound that separates itself from the rest.

A car. Close. Underscored by the crunch of gravel as it pulls into the driveway.

Jake pads into the hall, Sandy's cellphone still clutched in his hand. A rebar follows him, jangling as it flips its way out of his backpack.

A car door slams. It's followed by the click of footsteps coming up the walk.

Jake positions himself directly opposite the front door. The hallway is dark, and he slides into the shadows at the far end, being sure to keep the rebar below the mirror.

Not that it matters. The second Javier Salinas steps inside, the second the door closes behind him, Jake will jam the rebar through his skull.

FORTY-THREE

Teagan

"Here." Nic pulls off his hoodie, fighting with the belt. "Put this on."

I pull the hood over my head, crossing my arms and leaning against the window as Nic crawls around the curve. They can't be looking for me. Us. Why would they roadblock all the way up here? Has the fire spread that far?

I risk a glance. There are multiple officers walking in and out of the traffic, along with one or two firemen. A cop car is parked across the lane to our left, lights flashing.

Torchlight flickers through Nic's window, and I bury my head in the hoodie. Which probably isn't going to help, but I don't know what the hell else I'm supposed to do.

The window slides down, letting in the stench of smoke.

"Everything OK here?" Nic says.

"Where you headed today, sir?" The cop has a voice like old wood: textured, deep and very hard.

"Just Burbank."

"Yeah, where in Burbank, please?"

"Uh...East Orange Grove. It's north of the 5."

"East Orange and?"

"What?"

"The cross-street, sir."

"Ninth? Yeah."

"You live up there?" The cop sounds sceptical. And why wouldn't he be? We're driving a shitty, dirty Prius. Burbank isn't the richest neighbourhood in LA, but if you can afford to live there, you're probably driving something a little nicer than this wreck.

"My mom." Nic actually manages to sound bored. "Just going to check on her."

"She should be gone already, sir. They've issued an evac order."

"When?"

"Maybe a half-hour ago. The wind changed, and the marshals are pulling back. Can I see your licence, sir?"

"Uh, OK? Why?"

"Just procedure."

Nic doesn't respond, but there's a rasp of fabric as he pulls his wallet from his jeans.

"Thank you," the cop says. "Hernández! Is south of Bel Aire still good?"

The officer he yells for wears a thick bulletproof vest over her uniform shirt, a white undershirt peaking out the collar, a radio clipped to her shoulder. Her dark hair is pulled back in a severe ponytail.

I stay very, very still and keep my eyes closed. I am half a second from yelling at Nic to just floor it, but we are *never* going to be able to bully our way through the traffic. They'll run us right down.

"Our man here's going to Orange Grove. Just south of Bel Aire. Did they evacuate there?"

Any second now they're going to tell me to turn round.

Show my face. Maybe they'll just cut right to it and start shooting.

"No, Orange Grove's OK," the lady cop says. "Fire hasn't got that far yet."

I risk another glance around the edge of the hood. She's a little closer now, a few feet to the right of Nic's car. She looks exhausted. There are dark rings under her eyes, and the slump of her shoulders speaks of someone who has had a very, *very* long day.

My eyes meet hers.

It's a split-second glance, no more. It's like I can't help it— like it was inevitable. The breath in my lungs freezes solid.

The set of her shoulders changes, her hand straying to the pistol on her hip. She might not know what she saw, not consciously, but she knows she saw something.

I can't breathe. Every muscle responsible for getting air into my lungs has locked up tight.

A loud blast of a horn from the car behind us. Whoever it is really *leans* on it.

"Let's keep it moving, Hernández," the first cop rumbles. "We backed up all the way to Los Feliz by now."

The next few seconds take years. The cop holds her position, scanning the line of cars.

Then she nods. Stalks off.

"Do *not* go north of Bel Aire," the cop says. "If you can, get your mother and take her somewhere safe. It's OK now, but it might not be later."

"I will," Nic says. "Thank you."

The window whirrs up. I stay very, very still, counting slowly to thirty in my head. Then, still without moving, I open my eyes.

Nic glances at me. "You OK?"

"What? Oh. Yeah. I think so."

"Sure? You look like you're about to have a heart attack."

The fires are visible now, turning the horizon an angry red. Not to mention the giant plumes of black smoke choking the night sky. No stars tonight.

I would give anything, absolutely anything, to know if Carlos, Annie and Reggie are OK. Hell, even Paul. No way of finding out. I don't even have a phone to call them on.

My tongue feels like it's coated in grease, a coppery taste that won't go away no matter how often I swallow. I'm light-headed, and it isn't just with exhaustion. It's fear. Raw, slippery fear.

The last time I felt like this was when I was with Travis. On the one night we spent together.

Telling Nic about my past was easier than I thought it would be. My parents, my brother and sister, Tanner: I came to terms with it all a long time ago. But I don't dare speak about what happened with Travis. I don't even know how to begin. What I did to him on that night...the way it all turned out...

I don't really do regret. I don't spend time dwelling on my past fuck-ups—it just wastes energy and time. Time is better spent eating and reading and listening to good music and doing fun shit. But just because I force myself not to think about those regrets doesn't mean they don't exist. And Travis? Travis is the biggest regret there is.

I'm lost in my thoughts when Nic says, "Scooch down."

"Huh?"

He points to the street sign illuminated by his headlights: East Orange Grove.

"I want to do a pass of the house," Nic says. "Make sure nobody's watching."

"And if they are?"

"Well, you wanted to come up here. I'm sure you'll have a few ideas."

"Yeah, OK." I slide down in the seat, pulling the hoodie over my head again. Willing myself to stay calm.

He's close.

The killer. The second psychokinetic.

I can't know this for sure, but it doesn't matter. It's starting to feel real. I haven't even thought about what I'm going to say to him if we *do* meet. Assuming he doesn't try to kill me first. I've got so many questions, and asking any of them is going to be almost impossible—at least at first.

"All clear," Nic says.

I sit up, blinking. Nic is mid-U-turn, pulling us back onto North Parish. We're at a leafy intersection, the north end of which is a railway line separated from the street by a long stretch of gravel. "No cops?"

"Nobody. I think I know where the house is—didn't see anyone there." He points to one of the houses, hidden behind a tall wooden fence. On the other side of the fence an American flag hangs limp. "That's it, I think."

"Isn't that kind of odd if they're evacuating people?"

"Not really. They don't exactly have the manpower to go door to door." A pause. Then: "How do you want to do this?"

"Park a little way away. Probably better if I approach on foot."

"We, you mean."

The car is just rolling up to an intersection. I choose my next words carefully. "No. I. Singular. You are not coming in there."

"'Scuse me?"

"Stick around for a couple of minutes—I might need an exit if we're too late. But if Salinas is still there, I want you to get the hell away."

"Fuck no."

"I'm not kidding, Nic. If the other psychokinetic arrives…"

"Which part of *Fuck no* didn't you get? The *Fuck* part or the *no* part?"

"I don't want you to get hurt." How can he be this dense?

"Sure. I'll just head on out of here and leave you to do this by yourself. Great idea."

"*Nic.*"

"No, no, no. You're not—"

Which is when Javier Salinas comes smashing through the windshield.

FORTY-FOUR

Jake

Jake explodes out onto the street. He's so angry that the edge of his vision has actually gone grey.

Javier Salinas was supposed to come right through the front door. He was supposed to open it, step inside and get a piece of rebar right between the eyes. Quick. Clean. Simple.

He didn't come inside.

He knocked.

Jake stared at the door, mouth hanging open. What was Javier doing? This was his house!

Except it wasn't. He and Sandy had split up. He was living somewhere else. He might not even have a key any more.

"Sands?" Javier's muffled voice was threaded with panic. More frantic knocking. "Sands, it's me!"

Carefully Jake reached out, grabbed the lock, clicked the door open.

"Hey," Javier said, pushing inside. "I'm so sorry I'm late, the job was—"

He trailed off, confused as to why the hallway was dark, why Sandy wasn't there to greet him.

Jake made himself wait. He wanted Javier fully inside, silhouetted against the dimly lit street. The perfect target.

"Sandy?"

Javier took another step—and stopped dead.

He was looking down at the floor.

Jake followed his gaze. Alan—the neighbour. His body was still there, along with the patch of blood, grown tacky but still unmistakable.

"*Sands! Kelly!*" Javier Salinas shoved the front door open, barging into the house, and that's when Jake sent the rebar flying at him.

He should have waited. He was trying to hit a moving target and had acted out of panic—panic and anger. The metal shot past Javier's head, burying itself in the door frame. The man yelled, dancing backwards, falling down the front steps, getting to his feet and bolting back down the drive. Then he turned, eyes huge as if suddenly remembering his wife and daughter. Torn between blind terror and protecting his family.

Which is when the furious Jake came through the front door, the rebar whistling through the air ahead of him. Salinas ducked, and the rebar shattered the driver-side window of his truck, a big Ford F150. Under the dim street lights, the health department logo on the door gleamed a dull white.

Javier bolted, the terror taking over. He took off, sprinting into the street, moving with a gait that said he wasn't used to running.

Jake was dimly aware how thick the smoke had got. The air had a hot syrupy quality, like he'd have to swim through it to make any progress. Salinas was going to run? From him? Running wasn't going to help. It was way, way too late for that.

Jake reached out with his Gift, picking up the first thing it touched: the tall metal flagpole embedded in the dirt. His intention was to throw it point first—a bigger version of the rebar—but at the last instant, as Javier turned left, he had a flash of inspiration. He swung the flagpole in a wide arc, putting so much force into it that he felt the metal torque.

The pole hit the running man right at the base of his spine. By then it was moving with so much speed that it swept Javier up into the air, sent him tumbling end over end as if he'd been hit by a moving car.

Jake feels bitter joy flood through him. Shoot at him? Try to kill him? Forget quick. He's going to impale him with the flagpole. Slowly. He strides out into the road, lungs burning from the smoke, picking up the flagpole as he goes.

FORTY-FIVE

Teagan

I tumble out the car, landing ass first on the asphalt. There's broken glass everywhere: in my hair, down my front, collected in the hoodie at the base of my neck.

Had Salinas—or whoever it is—been moving even a little bit faster, or been a little bit heavier, he probably would have killed both of us. He came butt first through the windshield, embedding himself in it but not dislodging it from its frame. He's still moving, his body twitching. Still alive.

"*Teagan!*" Nic is up, shaking glass out of his hair, coming around the front of the car.

"Fine." I cough, fighting the smoke. "I'm *fine*. Help him."

My mind chooses that moment to reboot. For a second I've got a completely blank slate, then a rush of thoughts nearly knocks me over. Salinas didn't throw himself through our windshield; he was thrown. That means…

He's backlit perfectly by the glowing horizon: a tall figure striding out from behind the wooden fence into the middle of the road. I can't get a good look at his face, silhouetted as he is, but it's him. It has to be.

The strangest thought: this is the first time in the history of the human race that two people with psychokinetic powers have been in the same place.

The moment just crashes over me. I thought I was ready for this. I wasn't. This other person—this killer—is the only one like me.

"*Watch out!*" Nic roars.

The flagpole hovers over the street, whirling like a baton, the American flag flapping. Then the figure cocks his head, and it comes right at Salinas, point first.

If I'd actually been thinking straight, I could probably have deflected it. But I just lie there, watching it come, eyes huge.

It's a good thing Nic is more on the ball than me. He knew what was going to happen the second that flagpole started flying. He reaches over, grabs hold of Salinas and *pulls*. Salinas is heavy, but Nic manages to yank him out of the hole in the windshield a split-second before the flagpole buries itself dead centre. It does so with a loud *whang*, the end of the pole bouncing as it settles.

A horrific, cruel thought: Salinas, a government worker, impaled on an American flag. The image is like a slap to the face. It snaps me awake, and I scramble up, using the side of the car for leverage.

The flagpole rips itself out of the car with a huge crunch. It twitches like it's alive, hunting for its prey. Then it points at Salinas, who is lying on the street on the other side of the car.

This time I get there first. I reach out with my PK and grab the pole before the other dude launches. The pole jerks in mid-air, shuddering.

The man clenches his fists, fighting with me for control. When I don't give it back, he looks first at Nic and then his head snaps towards me.

"Yeah," I say.

Abruptly he releases his hold on the flagpole. I manage to hold it up for perhaps half a second before I let go too. It crashes down on the car's hood, metal screeching on metal as it rolls off.

I'm expecting him to come at us a second time. He doesn't. He just stands there. Long blond hair, an angular face, jutting chin. Young—my age, maybe a little younger. He wears a dirty biker jacket over torn jeans, and he has the strangest expression on his face.

Nic is cradling the unconscious Salinas. It's definitely him. He might not have been impaled by the flagpole, but he's still in bad shape. One leg is turned at a horrific angle at the knee, and there's a huge gash on the side of his neck, his shirt turning dark with blood.

"We gotta help him," Nic says.

"Nic, we—"

"Call 911."

"The—"

"*Call 911!*"

"On what?" I yell back.

He squeezes his eyes shut, and a long angry growl escapes his throat.

I point at the car. "Find a cop."

"Teagan—"

"Just go. I got this."

Our eyes meet. Just for a second.

There's a horrible moment when I think he's going to refuse. If he does, I don't know if I can protect him.

Then his eyes change. It's like he's taken a step back, looked at what he's being asked to do and decided the only way to do it is if he wipes away every trace of emotion.

"OK," he says, not looking at me.

Which is when I reach over, pull him to me and kiss him.

I don't know why I do it. No, that's a fucking lie. I know exactly why I do it. I do it because the blank, focused look on his face terrifies me. It's a look that says he's not sure if I'm going to make it out of this, and the only way he can get through it is by shutting himself down completely.

I don't want him to leave. He has to. And kissing him—his lips on mine, tasting of salt and smoke—is the only thing I can think to do.

I pull away. "Go." My voice is hoarse, the smoke starting to shred it.

There's a flicker of anguish in his eyes, then the shutters come down again. He gets his arms under Salinas, grunting as he lifts him.

I keep expecting the other psychokinetic to attack, but he doesn't. He's just…standing there. Staring at me. Like he's lost all interest in Salinas. Like I'm a bug, or a bacterium under a microscope.

Nic shoves Salinas into the back of the car, slamming the door, clambering into the driver's seat, ignoring the shards of glass. His eyes meet mine one last time.

He reverses, swinging the car round with a squeal of tyres, hitting the gas and roaring off into the smoke. The fire is very close now.

I turn. The movement lasts no more than a second or two, but it feels like it takes years. The other guy is still standing there, in the middle of the road, glowing smoke at his back.

He's killed people. Let me take the blame for it. Taking him out is the only chance I have of making it through the night. And I don't have the first clue how to do it. I don't have a taser, or any other method of knocking him unconscious.

But if I do, if I somehow face off against him and actually

win, and do it without killing him, I'll never see him again. Tanner will make him vanish. She'll tell me I'm lucky that I actually get to stay alive and should be grateful and kiss her pretty little feet.

But out of everyone in Los Angeles—everyone in the entire *world*, for all I know—he's the only one like me. Seven point six billion humans . . . and us.

Even Chloe and Adam didn't know exactly what it was like to have my ability. What would it be like to talk to him? Find out if it's the same for him as it is for me?

He's stronger than I am, that's for sure. But how did he get there? How much can he lift? Did it happen gradually, or did he suddenly realise one day that he was more powerful than he thought? Has he had sex? Does what happens to me happen to him?

Where did he come from?

Still nothing. He doesn't move, not an inch. Outside of the distant sirens and the soft crackle and crunch of fire, the street is silent.

Slowly I lift a hand in greeting. "Hi. My name's Teagan. What's yours?"

Movement. A flicker at the edge of my vision. I turn just in time to see something hurtling out of the darkness.

It hits me so hard that my lungs lock up. Just stop working. Unbelievable, incredible pain rolls up from my diaphragm as I'm sent crashing to the ground. Fireworks explode across my vision. I'm aware of putting out a hand to stop myself falling, aware of it skidding across tarmac, skin ripping from the palm.

FORTY-SIX

Jake

He hadn't meant to hit her. It had been instinct—a decision driven by flat panic, by the sheer, stunned confusion of seeing her do what he can do.

She stopped him. *She stopped him.* His entire life he thought he was the only one who could make things move. As a child he'd had fantasies of hunting for others, finding them, joining forces. But it's been a long, long time since he's thought that way. He'd resigned himself to being alone, putting every atom of energy he had into finding out where he came from.

And then, right at the moment he was about to finish off Salinas...*she* arrives. Salinas was escaping, and this woman was standing in front of him and she could do what he could and—

—he'd panicked.

The car was already out of range and she was standing there looking at him, and she could do what he could and he had to do something. He'd reached out, grabbed a nearby mailbox, ripped it off its post and sent it right into her solar plexus, just as he'd done with Bryan Hayden.

She lies on the tarmac, clawing at it, gasping for breath. As he watches her, he has a single clear thought: *Get her inside.*

He jogs over to her, heaves her to her feet. She doesn't fight. She's drawn every bit of energy she has into herself, focusing on nothing more than getting the next breath into her lungs. She only keeps her feet because he's holding her up. Several times he has to drag her, her sneakers dragging on the street surface. It occurs to him that he could use his ability—get something underneath her, float her into the house. But when he tries to work out how he could do this, he can't. His thoughts are mush.

The orange glow in the sky has got brighter. The crunching, crackling sound of the fire is no longer background noise. Jake barely notices. They reach the driveway of the house, and he kicks open the front door, stepping over the body of Alan the neighbour. Getting her the last few steps into the living room takes almost everything he has. Her breaths come in huge, croaking gasps.

Another sound reaches him. Screaming from the pantry. Sandy, her voice turned ragged, hammering at the door and yelling to be let out.

"Shut up," he mutters.

He lowers the woman to the ground by the remains of the flatscreen TV. She's dressed in jeans and a grey hoodie, with a shock of black spiky hair. His thoughts, which were just beginning to come together in some sort of order, desert him again.

He's furious at himself for lashing out, furious for not knowing that there was another like him—not just in the same country, but the same city. What else has he missed?

Her gasps dissolve into a hideous coughing fit. With what feels like an almost physical effort, he brings himself back. He can't afford to have her attack him, which is almost certainly what she'll do when she can breathe again.

An idea comes to him, fighting through the muck in his mind. He darts back into the hall, rips the rebar out of the door frame and floats it back into the lounge. He aims it like a gun in front of him, pointing it right at her head.

One way or another, he'll get answers.

FORTY-SEVEN

Teagan

I have never been hit that hard before. Not even when the car ploughed into me when we were running from Burr and his team. That was a love tap compared to what this jerk-off did.

After what feels like thirty years I'm finally able to get some air into my lungs. It's a trickle, no more, but even a trickle can be enough after thirty years without water. I raise myself up on my elbows, thoughts starting to clear. *OK, fucker. Let's see if you can take hits as hard as you give them out.*

There's a smashed TV behind me with lots of loose shards of glass and metal in its frame. I reach, grab hold of it, very slowly start to lift—

"Don't."

He's got one of his rebars less than two feet from my face, twitching in mid-air. No way I'll be able to do anything with the TV before he skewers me.

The air is actually hazy with smoke now. I control the fear, lock it down, make my eyes meet his as I drop the TV. It lands with a muffled thump.

"Yeah." I groan the word, finally sitting up. My voice is a wreck. "I've seen what you can do with that."

"How did you get your Gift?" he says. And yes, from the way he says it, the capital letter is obvious.

"My . . . what?"

"Your Gift. You can do what I do."

My side throbs, sending rolling waves of pain through my torso. I take a closer look at him. There's a weird look in his eyes. A hunger. No, a *longing*.

Someone is screaming. Screaming *and* hammering. It's coming from behind me. "What is that?"

"Don't worry about it." But his eyes don't change.

Over my shoulder there's a door leading off the open-plan kitchen, shut tight, vibrating as someone pounds on it. A woman. She's yelling, and underneath that sound there's sobbing. A kid. *Oh shit.*

I almost tell him to let them go—they aren't a part of this. But that never works in movies, and it isn't going to work here. Whoever they are, they're safe—for now. Better in there than out here.

Until the fire hits the house.

"Did you know your parents?" he says.

It's a few seconds before I answer. "Yeah. Yeah, I did."

"Who were they? Tell me."

I don't even know where to begin. He has to be the child of one of the women my parents used. But was he still in the womb when they decided the experiment was a failure?

"They were scientists," I say, slowly moving a knee underneath me. "Geneticists."

"Like Watson and Crick?" he says.

"I don't—"

"They discovered DNA. It was a turning point in the history of genetics."

"OK?"

He reaches up with a trembling hand, scratches at his stubble. The hungry look hasn't left his eyes. "Your parents, were they the only ones doing it?"

"I...I think so."

"Then they must have given me my Gift. Just like they gave it to you." He looks at me. Really looks. "So they experimented on both of us. What did they do? Tell me everything."

I'm really not sure I want to tell this guy his mom was a hooker.

"I don't know the details. I'm not—"

"How can you not *know*?" Now he's angry, the rebar twitching. "Don't you care?"

"Buddy," I say, my temper slipping, "I care more than you know."

"Then do you remember me? When we were little?"

"No."

"You're lying," he says through gritted teeth. "You have to be."

"Just take it easy."

"How can you not *remember*?" Behind me the TV is launched into the air, flipping and spinning, crashing into one of the wrecked cabinets, making me jump.

"Hey!" I shout, more scared than angry. "It was just me, and my brother and sister, OK?"

"Were they like me?"

"No. They had different abili—Gifts." I lick my lips, trying to ignore my scorched throat. "How long have you known what you can do?"

"Since I was a kid. I kept it a secret."

"I kind of had to do that too."

"Doesn't sound like it." He grins suddenly—an awful grin, one that flares across his face like fire licking through gasoline. "Sounds like you had it all figured out."

A shard of glass floats between us, distorting his features, elongating them. I'm not the one floating it, and it's not the only object in the air right now. I don't even think he realises he's doing it.

This isn't working. I can't talk to him. We're not even on the same planet.

"It wasn't like that," I say as I reach out for the heaviest object I can find: a microwave lying against the wall behind him, its door shattered in a spiderweb of cracks.

He looks down as if thinking. I grab hold of the microwave, but I don't lift it. Not yet. If he's like me, he'll be able to sense the objects in the room around him, even now. There's a chance he might realise what I'm doing, stop the microwave in mid-air. He's strong enough. I have to fire it at him, slam it into him when his attention is focused on me.

"We couldn't tell anybody," I say. "And there was no one else like…no one who could do what I could. You're the first, dude."

"No," he says, wagging a finger at me as if I've been naughty. "You're lying. There's no way someone like me lands up in the exact same city at the same time. You knew me. You knew me, and you don't want to say it."

More and more objects are starting to lift into the air. Chunk of shattered plastic and torn metal. Kitchen implements. More glass shards. If I don't do this soon, he might grab the microwave.

OK. If reasoned argument won't work, maybe getting pissy will.

"Hey," I say, bringing his attention back. "Let me tell you something, asshole. I've had one hell of a day. I've been framed for murder, tasered, been chased by the cops, wrecked the apartment of someone who wants to date me, and then you bumble along and smash me in the side hard enough to knock me out. I have had precisely two hours sleep in the last forty-eight, and I am *very* close to completely losing my shit. So how about you stop calling me a liar and *listen to me*."

On the last word, I launch the microwave at his back.

His eyes go wide. The microwave comes to a jarring, shuddering halt three feet from him. It's like I've slammed it into a wall.

And at the same instant the floating rebar rockets towards me. I have just enough time to scream before it wraps itself around my throat.

I can't believe how fast it happens. It's like the rebar is alive. The metal groans, almost squeals, as it twists in on itself. I claw at it, panicking, trying to push it back with my PK. But he's too strong. Way too strong.

I'm jerked into the air. My feet kick and dance, a foot off the ground, fingernails breaking on the steel. *Can't breathe.* The words flash in my mind like a neon sign. *Can't breathe can't breathe can't—*

"I thought you could help me," he says. "But you can't. You're just like everyone else."

Which is when the best and worst thing in the world happens. Carlos.

He's in the doorway behind the killer. Neither of us heard him come in. He's standing there, mouth open, staring at me.

He can't be here. He can't. I have to tell him to run. I have to.

But my face must give it away, because at that instant the killer spins round. I gasp a warning, and nothing comes out. *No!*

He's going to kill him. Right in front of me. He's going to take one of those pieces of glass and bury it in—

With something like wonder, the man says, "Chuy. What are you doing here?"

FORTY-EIGHT

Jake

The Chuy standing in the doorway of the living room is not the Chuy Jake knows.

That Chuy had a look to him: like he was expecting the entire world to come at him and knew he could take it on. This Chuy looks like he's run a marathon. His flannel shirt is streaked with soot.

All the same, there is no one he's happier to see. Yes, Javier Salinas got away—if he's even still alive—but that doesn't matter. They'll find him. And if they can convince this Teagan, the girl who has what he has, who can do what he can do, then…

We gonna set this whole city right.

His whole body is vibrating with an electric energy. Another him. *Another him.* Chuy is going to go fucking insane.

The girl—Teagan—tries to say something. She can't quite do it. Jake realises he pulled the rebar too tight, and a little jolt of guilt shoots through him. Now that Chuy's here, they can convince her. He lets her go, keeping the rebar around her throat but letting her crumple to the carpet.

Chuy looks over Jake's shoulder. "Just stay down, Teagan, OK?"

"Chuy," Jake says. "Oh my God, you have no idea…" But even as he speaks, his mind is catching up. Chuy just called her Teagan… but neither she nor Jake have said her name yet.

"Jake." Chuy coughs so hard it nearly doubles him over. "Homie, we gotta get the fuck outta here."

"I did it. I got Chase and Bryan Hayden. Javier got away, but I hit him pretty hard." *No, she didn't tell him her name, and neither did I, so how…*

"That's fine." Chuy raises his eyes to Jake. "That's all good. We'll get him. But we gotta go."

Teagan manages to choke out a word: "Carlos."

Chuy points to the door. "I got a car. Help me with her."

Slowly Jake says, "Why is she calling you Carlos?"

"Doesn't matter. I'll explain it all later, OK? For now, we gotta—"

"You *know her?*"

It doesn't make sense. How could Chuy possibly know this girl? He's got to be mistaken.

"Carlos," Teagan says. Her voice is a wreck. "Fucking *help me.*"

Jake points, feeling as if he's in a lucid dream. "She can do what I do. She can move things."

"Yeah." Chuy pulls something out his pocket. A taser, black and yellow. "Look, she ain't just gonna come quietly, no matter how hard you choke her." He turns toward her, aims the taser. Jake can feel Teagan's power scrabbling at the bar at her throat even as she stares up at Carlos in disbelief.

Jake tries to marshal his thoughts, force them into some kind of order. "If you knew about her, then why would you—"

Chuy—or Carlos, or whatever his name is—spins round, and this time there's no mistaking his anger. "Shut up. Shut the fuck up right now."

He sticks a finger in Jake's face. "You couldn't finish it. You were supposed to do it all in one night, and now I gotta come in and save your ass." The finger swings towards Teagan. "I'm gonna hit her." He lifts the taser. "You're gonna grab her, I don't care how, and then I'ma drive all of us outta here."

"Why didn't you tell—"

"Because you didn't need to know! Quit hanging around like a fucking pussy."

He turns to Teagan, aims the taser again. He doesn't see Jake's face contort, the anger on it much, much worse than his own.

What Chuy is saying is logical. They can incapacitate Teagan, make their exit, track down Salinas. Finish the job. Chuy kept this from him...but he might have been planning to share it later on, as part of the info he'd promised. These thoughts are rational, calm, logical—and utterly powerless in the face of the furious, betrayed anger coursing through him.

This whole time Chuy knew about Teagan.

And he said *nothing*.

Before he realises what he's doing, Jake has reached back with his mind. He finds another one of his rebars without looking, its shape as familiar as the saddle of his motorcycle. As familiar as the gnawing hunger he took to sleep with him on the many nights he spent under overpasses and on park benches. Thinking he was alone.

In the instant before he launches the rebar the part of his mind that's still thinking straight cries out. But it's too late, much too late.

Chuy lied.

He puts so much energy into throwing the rebar that he feels it actually bend. It doesn't matter. The leading point punctures Chuy's chest, yanks him back off his feet.

FORTY-NINE

Teagan

Carlos knows the killer.

More than that. He wanted to have me take the blame for the murders. He wanted to taser me. Kidnap me.

And right now I can't think about any of that. It's too much, too complicated, *way* too batshit crazy. All I can focus on is how Jake just hurt someone I care about, and I am going to make him pay. No more talk. No more two-of-us-against-the-world bullshit. This fucker is going down.

As the rebar strikes Carlos, slamming him against the wall, my PK goes nuts. It's a marathon runner breaking through the wall, a deadlifter busting through her max weight. It is my body and my mind working as one, channelling every ounce of energy I have into a huge, focused, raging flood.

I grab everything I can. Every piece of glass and metal and plastic in the room. Every object. Chunks of plaster tear themselves from the walls. The light fixtures rip from their sockets, trailing sparking comet-tails of wire. The rebar around my neck doesn't bend. It snaps, the pieces whirling away, then coming back like boomerangs. All of it—metal, wire, glass—aimed right at the killer.

It almost works too.

This time he really is distracted, focused completely on Carlos. A whickering blade of glass slices across his shoulder. A lamp, its shade missing, strikes him in the shin, dropping him to one knee. But then he reacts, meeting my energy with his own, stopping the barrage of objects coming his way. Our opposing energies don't hold them; they ricochet outwards, hurled away, smashing into the walls and ceiling. Somewhere Javier Salinas's wife is screaming.

The killer—*Jake, Carlos called him Jake*—adds his own ammo into the mix, grabbing the flying objects and bringing them back, launching them towards me. I duck behind a table, digging deeper, pushing out more and more energy. The noise is unbelievable. It's a volcano, an earthquake, a hurricane, all of them squashed into a tiny space and raging to get out.

I sweep my energy across the wall behind him, digging through the plaster into the supporting beams. A choked howl bursts out between gritted teeth as I drag at them. This is beyond anything I've done before. I don't have time to pay attention to whether I can actually do it or not; I have to get those beams out. One is buried too deep, but the other two bend and then snap with a sound like bombs going off, crunching through the plaster as they tear out of the wall.

Jake turns, his face twisted in a grimace. He deflects the first beam, but the second one hits him square in the chest. It knocks him onto his back, even as he manages to grab hold of it, sending it bouncing out into the yard through the smashed picture window. I don't waste the advantage, getting to my feet and grabbing everything I can and attacking hard, launching every object in range at the figure on the floor.

Something rises off the ground behind me—an oven, ripped out of the wall and torn in half, all jagged metal and shredded wires. I duck just before it poleaxes me, grab it as it passes over my head. Then I send it in a huge arc towards him, like I'm swinging a warhammer. He rolls away, and the stove buries itself in the floor with a noise like the world ending.

I snarl, reaching for it, trying to pull it out of the ground— Except I can't.

It's not coming. I don't have the energy any more. I pushed myself too hard, and I'm running out.

I ignore the feeling, going for smaller weapons, throwing glass and utensils and jagged shards of metal. They don't fly as fast or as far, and Jake—up one knee, eyes blazing—bats them aside like they were nothing.

I gasp, almost sobbing, push harder. Knowing I can't do it, not caring. There's an awful hollow feeling building inside me now, swelling like a balloon in my chest, nothing inside it but empty air.

And still I keep going. Even as the objects I grab fall to the floor, having travelled no more than a few feet. Even as the insane noise begins to ebb. Even as Jake, slowly getting to his feet, a triumphant smile on his face, rips the torn stove out from the floor.

He floats it over my head. I try to push it aside and get nothing. As the last dregs of my energy drain away, Jake spins the stove so the jagged metal edge is pointing right at me.

FIFTY

Teagan

The seconds stretch into hours.

I'm back on that corner. On Hollywood Boulevard, just as the sun is setting. The smell of grease in the food truck behind me, the scent of sweat and sunscreen and a very faint hint of pot smoke. The chatter from the passing tourists, the taco grease on my fingers. Light from the setting sun, filtering through the palm trees.

Nic and I in the truck on the way over here. Both of us howling with laughter, my stomach aching with it, unable to even breathe. Unbelievably, perfectly happy. Just for a second. Right there. If I have to die with that being my last thought, I'm OK with it.

No.

Actually: no.

I am not OK with that being my last thought. I am very much not fucking OK with it. That memory of Nic? Both of us laughing until we can barely breathe? That's going to be the first of many.

I can't just push the oven away. He'll come at me again and

again, and pretty soon I won't have anything left. I end it now, or it ends me.

I go as deep as I can. I hold the memories uppermost in my mind, really focus on them. I refuse to acknowledge that my PK is almost spent. That's a lie. That's an illusion. It's my body giving me false info, protesting because it's tired. I focus on the memories and think about what it would be like to lose them. To lose everything.

Then I push my PK out.

I'm not even looking for strength. I want range. I want something that isn't in this room, something he won't see coming. My teeth grind together with the effort. Every atom in my body feels like it's trying desperately to get away from the ones around it.

I grab the beams in the walls and the roof. No go. He's got hold of just about everything, wrenching it away from me even as the oven makes one final adjustment, one of the sharper metal points aiming right for my face.

I've got maybe four or five seconds of this energy left. Desperate, I throw my PK as far as it will go, trying to find anything I can use, sending it out past the walls, past the truck in the driveway, past—

The truck.

The one Salinas must have arrived in.

It hasn't moved. Maybe Jake's forgotten it's there. Maybe he knows but doesn't think he needs to use it.

I can't lift it. No way.

I have to.

The oven drops. I push against it with a fraction of my PK, slowing it down, making it shudder as our competing energies meet each other. It slows to a crawl, creeping towards my face, the torn metal getting closer and closer. I'm not going to be to hold it much longer.

My back actually arches as I push the energy out, my eyes flying open. It's like I've stuck my hand in a wall socket, one the size of California.

I wrap the truck with energy. I slide it into the wheel wells, curl it around the chassis, dive deep into the engine. I tangle my mind around the steering wheel, the hubcaps, the tail lights. Above me the oven creeps closer, less than two feet away now.

In the driveway the truck rocks on its wheels. One leaves the ground, just for a second, before dropping back down.

It's heavy. Heavier than anything I've ever lifted. I ask for more energy, somehow get it, feeling it crackle through my body. My *bones* are vibrating.

All four wheels leave the ground, the truck gently rocking from side to side, metal creaking as it settles. I can't lift it further. I can't.

I have to.

I scream. No. I *roar*. It's a deep, animal howl, and in that second I'm not sure if it's me or something else entirely. Inside my shredded, tortured throat, already torn to pieces by the smoke and the rebar, something tears. The lance of pain is bright, sliding right into my stomach. But I don't dare stop. I can't. The metal above my head inches closer.

Six feet. Seven. Just keeping the damn thing level almost kills me. I can see it now, looming through the destroyed wall, a hulking shape in the smoke.

Now. Throw it now!

At the very last instant Jake senses something. His pressure on the oven slackens, and he looks over his shoulder. At that moment I put all my energy under the truck and *shove*.

FIFTY-ONE

Jake

He's got her. She's lost almost all control of her Gift, the objects in the room twitching and jerking like dying animals. She's no threat—not any more. He's laughing—hacking really, his throat and lungs stinging with every hot breath.

Doesn't matter. It's almost over.

A wave of resentment washes over him, fuelling his anger. How could he have thought that Chuy wanted to help him? Chuy—if that was ever his real name—just wanted to use him, use his ability for his own good. He probably would have given Jake up after this was all over—made a call, turned him in. Why wouldn't he?

There is a part of him—small, very distant, like a figure waving on the horizon—that is begging him to stop. He's about to kill the only other person like him. Maybe the only one in the entire world. Has he really been through everything just to have it end here? With this girl dead?

But even if he wanted to listen to this part of him, he's beyond that now. The anger is black, joyous. Smooth as silk and hard as iron.

It's the righteous anger Churchill must have felt as the Allies entered Berlin, the anger that must have coursed through Boudica as she began her uprising. And didn't they face people who wanted to trample on what they'd built? These leaders—these titans of history—they didn't shrink or cower. They faced their enemies head-on. They looked them in the eye and refused to bow.

A sound reaches him. The creaking and groaning of metal under stress. As he turns to look, the wall to his left is obliterated.

The thing on the other side is as big as a meteor: a giant misshapen lump that was once a truck. Its weight punches through the plaster and wood and support beams, breaking them like matchsticks, letting in a gust of hot, horrid air like giant's breath.

In the split-second before it hits him, Jake has a sudden, vivid thought, one that makes absolutely no sense but is as clear as a bell ringing out into crisp air. *Los Angeles is trying to kill me.*

He sends out one last, desperate burst of energy to try and stop it. But it's not enough, not for something so huge, not even to slow it. The truck isn't moving that fast, but the sheer weight of it crushes his bones, turns his internal organs to pulp. It knocks him sideways, and as the full weight of it slams into him, there's an unbelievable, nuclear-bright pop at the base of his spine.

FIFTY-TWO

Teagan

I push the oven to one side with the very last of dregs of my energy. And this time it drains the tank for good. Like tilting back a glass to get the last few drops.

The house is trashed.

What our fight didn't destroy, the truck did. It's a miracle I didn't get crushed. But despite my ripping out some of the wall beams and the truck taking out the wall and ceiling to my right, the house is still standing. The ceiling tilts down at an angle, part of it torn away. It looks like it's ready to just slide right into the floor, but it holds. For now. There's a child's bed poking through one of the gaps, the rainbow-coloured comforter still tucked in.

The truck is on its side, and underneath it...

That gets me to my feet. I scramble up, breath ragged, stumbling across to Jake and dropping to my knees. It occurs to me that I should find Carlos first, but the one part of me that still has the ability to think says he's gone. And then that part shuts down, because the thought is too awful to look at.

The only colour in Jake's face is the splash of blood on his lips: an almost delicate fan of it, flaring up towards his nose, as if an artist had held a brush over his face and given it a flick.

I did this.

It shouldn't matter. He was trying to kill me, and I wouldn't have been the first or the last. But it does. It fucking does matter.

His eyes find mine. And it's like he doesn't know where he is. Or who he is.

I have to save him. Whatever he's done, he doesn't deserve to die like this. I have to make up for what I did. And I can't just let him die—not the only other me, not the one person who might understand.

But I've got *nothing.* My PK is dead, fuzzing static, grey and useless.

I grip his hand as tight as I can. He doesn't have the strength to grip back, but I hold on anyway.

"It's OK." I can barely speak. It takes me more than one try to get the words out; my throat is completely shredded.

His mouth opens slightly, like he's trying to respond.

Then he's gone.

Crying is out of the question. There's no moisture left in me to do it. I can't scream—my throat won't let me. So I ball up a shaking fist. Hit the ground. Hit it again, knuckles aching. Again, skin splitting. A fourth time.

The smoke is thicker than ever, and the air has got hotter. From the flickering light, from the searing waves of heat that wash over me, I don't have to look up to know that the fire is here.

The HELLSTORM has arrived.

And still I don't move—not until I hear footsteps behind me.

It's a woman, clutching a young girl in her arms. The smoke has smeared her skin with soot, and her eyes…Jesus, her eyes. She's in her forties, but her eyes have an age measured in centuries.

The woman who was locked in the room off the kitchen. Salinas's wife. His daughter. How did they get out?

The door to their prison hangs off its hinges. It must have been ripped off in the fight. They stayed down until it was all over. Smart.

"Is he..." She starts to cough, and the girl in her arms whimpers. Behind them there are flames—huge, towering flames, no more than a hundred yards away.

"Yeah," I say. It barely qualifies as a word.

Which is when I hear choked groans coming from somewhere behind the car. A voice calling out for me. A voice I recognise.

Carlos.

"Get out of here," I tell the woman, rasping the words.

"What about you?"

"I'll be fine. Just go."

She hesitates for only a second. Then she's gone, making her way around the debris, holding her daughter tight. The girl's eyes meet mine over her mom's shoulder, just for a second, before they're swallowed by the smoke.

I don't know how I get to my feet, but I do. It feels like it takes years to actually reach Carlos. He's sitting against the wall of the house—or what's left of it. And his chest...

He's been impaled by a piece of rebar. It's pinned him to one of the support beams, driving its way right into the steel. Most of the rebar is straight—all except for the last six inches, which is bent down by a few degrees where it juts out of his chest. The front of his shirt is black with blood.

His eyes are bloodshot from the smoke. "Teagan," he says. Unbelievably, his voice is clear.

He betrayed me. He was working with Jake. And yet, in that moment, it's like something that happened in another universe. The Carlos I know...it can't be this person. It can't be this torn, impaled body.

The Carlos I know was the guy who always brought beef

jerky on our missions so I'd have something to eat afterwards. I never asked him to do it; he just did.

That Carlos made the world's worst coffee and was the only Mexican I ever met who hated tequila. He drank whiskey, malt if he could get it, Jameson's if not, and he'd knock back shot after shot and laugh when I couldn't keep up.

That Carlos had so many boyfriends and hook-ups that I could never keep them straight. He'd grin as he described his encounters in lurid detail, almost licking his lips with glee. But he was never cruel. He painted his lovers in the best light, even when things didn't work out.

That Carlos taught me Spanish swear words and went for walks around the block with me on hot nights in Venice Beach, talking about nothing. That Carlos would never betray me. Not ever. He'd never lie to me.

There's got to be a way to get him off the rebar. If I can do that, stabilise the bleeding…

But I won't be able to. The rebar is probably the only thing keeping him alive. If I remove it or pull him off, he'll bleed to death.

My PK isn't going to help. I reach out, knowing it won't work but doing it anyway, and get nothing but the same dead-TV static.

"Help me," he says. He doesn't have the blood around the mouth, but his face is paper-white. He's going into shock.

He called him Chuy.

Jake. When he was talking to Carlos. Why did he do that?

Because Carlos's full name is Carlos Jesús López Morales. In Mexico, he once told me, Chuy is a nickname for Jesús.

It's a small thing. It doesn't change what I already know. But putting the last piece in place snaps something inside me. I make a fist, rest it against his shoulder. "Why?"

When he doesn't respond, I lift the fist, plant it on him. Not hard, but it still makes him groan. "Why?" I hit him again, harder this time, and now I'm punching his chest, not caring about how much pain he's in. "*Why?*"

But it's all sliding into place. All of it. The whole time, ever since the red light was called this morning, he's been urging me to run. Trying to get me out of the city. Talking about getting me into Mexico, having me vanish. He wanted to make sure I had no alibi for the killings.

That's why he came up here. When he couldn't get me to run after Annie was snatched, he took matters into his own hands. Because he knew that Jake would try to defend himself. He couldn't let that happen—if I was going to take the fall, I needed to be unharmed. Even if that meant Paul was left alone to save Annie.

Which means they're probably both dead.

He used me. He and Jake wanted Steven Chase and Hayden and Salinas and God knows who else out of the way, and decided they would use me to do it. And I still don't know why. I don't know how Carlos came across Jake or where Jake even came from.

I didn't think I had enough moisture left in me for tears. Turns out I was wrong.

"This morning," I manage to say, "two men attacked me in Skid Row. Were they…"

Despite the shock, he's still lucid. "They weren't supposed to hurt you. They were just supposed to keep you safe until this was all over. So you were out of the way."

"You tell me why." My voice sounds like it comes from someone else. *Someone not human.* "You tell me why, right fucking now."

"You don't…" He loses strength for a moment, sagging onto the rebar. Then he raises his head again. "You don't know what they did. Chase, and Salinas, and the rest of them." His mouth curls upwards in a bitter smile. "Look up El Agujero. Look up microfibres in the water. They *deserved* what was coming to them."

Microfibres. Like Mo-Mo said. But that can't have been worth all of...all of this.

"And me?" Tears sting my eyes, worse than the smoke.

"I was trying to help you."

"By...by framing me for murder?"

"By giving you a new life!" He almost yells the words, and a fleck of blood arcs out of his mouth.

Which is when I understand.

The motherfucker.

The arrogant, selfish, stupid mother*fucker*.

He thought he could do both. He thought he could take out these people, the ones he believed deserved to die for whatever reason, and rescue me from Tanner and China Shop all at the same time. He wanted me to run, far away, away from the cops and from Tanner and from all of it. He thought he knew what I needed, whether I wanted it or not. If it hadn't been for my PK suddenly growing major teeth, maybe he would have succeeded. Never mind the fact that it would have put a target on my back for the rest of my short life, or that it would have ripped me away from Nic, or that I'd never be able to live in Los Angeles ever again. He thought he was doing me a favour. I'm sure if I asked him about our friendship, he'd say that he was helping me. That he wanted to get me out of a bad situation, get me to a place I could be free.

"This whole time," I say, "you knew there was someone else like me. Someone with the same abilities. And you never said a word."

"It wasn't like that."

But the look on his face pushes through, despite the pain he must be in, despite the shock. It's a pugnacious, almost childish look: a look that says *I know what I'm doing, and you couldn't possibly understand*. It's raw, boiling arrogance.

I start to back away. His arrogance vanishes, replaced by a wide-eyed fear. "Help me. Teagan, please!"

He clutches at the rebar, his hands slick with blood. Behind him the fire licks at the street. All the houses on the other side are burning, the flames leaning in our direction. The sight of it almost paralyses me, puts me right back in the burning house in Wyoming, Adam screeching with laughter.

I'm shaking my head, but I don't know if I'm saying *I won't* or *I can't*.

"Please." It's almost a whine. It's the sound of an injured animal realising that it might not get out of this one.

If I pull him off the rebar, he'll bleed to death. I won't be able to keep him alive. And even if I can, the two of us won't be fast enough to outpace the fire.

If I run, he'll burn to death. Or suffocate on the smoke.

I wrap my arms around his midsection, the rebar digging into my left side, his blood soaking my clothes. "Hold on," I rasp through gritted teeth, and pull.

His howl of agony nearly blows my head off.

I can't do it. I just don't have the strength. Carlos is big, and I'm trying to pull him off a steel bar. A *bent* steel bar.

I let go, get behind him, squashing myself between him and what's left of the wall. I tell him I'm sorry, not sure if I'm saying it in my head or out loud, and push.

His scream is even louder this time. But he's too heavy, and I am too exhausted, and the rebar is buried too deep.

When I stop pushing, he sags, arms hanging, making these horrible grunting noises. I move to the front, resting my hands on my knees, trying to think. Waves of heat bake against my face.

"Come on," I say. It's almost a prayer.

And it isn't answered.

He's done horrible things. He's lied to me—no, not just me, the whole team. It's because of him that Tanner's men have Reggie. It's because of him that Paul is probably facing the whole of MS-13 by himself. It's because of him that I just murdered someone.

But I can't leave him like this. I can't. If he's lucky, he'll suffocate first. If he's not, he'll—

—*burn*.

I squeeze in behind him again, put my back against his, push as hard as I can. Ignore his screams. And he's not moving. Not even a little bit. And still I keep pushing. It takes me a few seconds to realise what I'm really waiting for: I want him to tell me to run. To save myself.

He doesn't. He's still begging me to help him, almost panting now. He's not going to let me go.

Not even when he's gone. You'll remember this for the rest of your life.

I push harder. I use everything I have. I block out his screams and his panting and his pleading and try to slide him off the rebar. Then I try pulling at the rebar itself, try to yank it out of the wall. It's buried too deep, way too deep.

Either he dies, or we both die.

"I'm sorry, *cabrón*," I tell him, barely able to get the words out.

"Teagan . . . no, Teagan!"

The fire sets my mind alight, sparking the old fear, burning through every fibre of my being.

I turn and run.

And with every step, with every burned breath in my lungs, I hear him screaming my name.

FIFTY-THREE

Teagan

Hell has nothing to do with fire.

It's not about physical pain. It's not about smoke that scorches your lungs or ash gritting your eyes.

It's the lies other people tell you

And the lies you tell yourself.

FIFTY-FOUR

Teagan

I should be sprinting. But all I can do is stumble, zigzagging in an almost drunken lurch down the street.

I take long wobbly strides across the baking tarmac, pausing every now and then to cough, so loud and so intense that it's as if both my lungs are trying to explode out of my mouth. The coughing leaves me bent like an old woman, hands on my knees, almost retching. The muscles in my midsection actually sting with the effort.

And with each cough, with each stride, I see Carlos.

"Come on." I reach up, wiping my face, still tacky with dried tears. "Get it together."

I don't know what happened to push the fire so far into the city, but this is bad. I can't believe how intense the heat is: like I'm standing over a gas range with all eight burners on full blast. I can't get away from it.

A car goes up with a *whoomp*. The fire engulfs it, shattered window glass tinkling onto the tarmac. And the trees ... every single one is ablaze, beacons against the smoke-stained sky. Embers flicker through the air like deadly butterflies. One lands on my neck, making me yelp.

I'm going to die here. I'm going to burn.

I don't know how much smoke a human being can suck in before there's permanent damage, but I have a horrible suspicion I'm a long way past that point. My head feels like it's drifting three feet behind my body. And I don't even want to talk about my throat.

The street ahead of me ends in a T-junction. The fire races across it left to right, the flames growing from tiny flickers to six-foot-tall monsters in seconds. As if sensing me, a tongue of it begins to curl in my direction.

I panic. Blind, flat-out, scorching panic. It clamps me to the spot, locks my feet to the tarmac.

A gap. Between two houses off to my left: a tiny black passage between the walls. The houses are on fire, but the flames haven't got to ground level yet. I force myself to move, sprinting—if you can call what I'm doing a sprint—with my lungs burning and Nic's hoodie held tight across my face.

There's a low wooden fence between me and the passage. I hurdle it, rocketing between the houses, the fire cooking the skin on my hands. Then I'm out into an alley at the rear of the two houses, looking left and right and left again.

The fire catches me.

My right leg burns, the flames sneaking up the fabric of my jeans. The pain is incredible: bright, sharp, vivid. I don't think. I just throw myself forward, rolling on the dry, crunching ground, unable to even scream.

The flames vanishes as I roll, leaving the pain behind, gnawing at my leg. A great wave of heat rolls across my back, and I look over my shoulder to see flames ten feet high coming towards me. The houses spit and crackle as they collapse.

I have never been this scared. Never. It's going to eat me alive.

I spin in a circle, trying to find an exit, find nothing.

Everywhere I look, there's only fire. I moan, paralysed. Rooted to the spot. *It's because you left Carlos. This is your punishment. What happened to him is about to happen to you.*

I drop to my knees. The air is fractionally fresher here than it is at head level, but it's not like it helps me escape the fire. But it's all I can think to do.

If I inhale enough smoke, I'll just suffocate. Maybe it won't even hurt after a while. I'll never see Nic again. Or Reggie, or Annie, or Paul. I'll never own a restaurant, never cook again, never listen to music…

The sound of the fire changes, the roar deepening. Like it knows what I'm thinking.

And then I'm drenched.

It happens so suddenly that I think I'm dreaming. Or dead. I'm immediately soaked to the skin by a giant, hissing cloud of water. The fire retreats, the flames shrinking, the ashen ground turning to slick, gooey mud. For the first time smoke isn't curling its way into my throat and lungs.

I lift my hand to my face, turning it, trying to understand what I'm seeing. It's covered in water droplets. Rivulets run down my face, drip off my chin.

The fire is still roaring. Except it's not the fire. A giant shape passes through the air far above my head, still disgorging water from its enormous belly.

I'm still stuck in a world of monsters and living fire, and my mind isn't exactly in tip-top condition right now. So for a second all I can think is *water dragon*.

But it's not. It's a plane. A goddamn firefighting plane. It came right over Burbank.

I can't scream. I can barely speak. It takes almost everything I have to raise a single fist. I keep it up there for as long as I can, waiting until the plane is out of sight.

Another coughing fit. An even worse one this time. I'm shivering. How is that even possible when a second ago I was scorching? My skin is covered in gritty ash and grime.

And as I lift my head, wiping my mouth, I see something beautiful.

Lights.

Very far away. But lights. Twinkling, glimmering through the puffs of smoke.

Los Angeles. Showing me the way home.

I don't say anything. I can't. I just make myself move, resuming my drunken stumble-lurch, heading for the lights of the city.

I don't know how long I walk for. The streets are blank, smoking spaces. There's more fire, but in the distance this time, racing up another section of the hillside. The plane comes back, roaring overhead. This time I don't even have the energy to lift a hand to it.

I lose track of the lights. There are big palls of smoke drifting across the sky. I keep marching. More than once I fall over. More than once I feel like just lying there. Never moving again. Closing my eyes and letting everything go. Instead, I haul myself to both knees, then one knee, then my feet. And I keep going.

At some point the sound changes.

The roar of the fire dwindles. I look up to see more houses: dark and silent this time, their driveways abandoned, their doors locked shut. Standing sentinel in the smoke.

I keep walking. I don't know what else to do.

I don't even bother trying to work out where I am or where I should go. It doesn't matter. Not right now. All that matters is that I keep walking.

And then, years later, cars.

This is LA. There are always cars.

I'm on a bigger road now, one that's a little wider. There's the highway, and beyond it the city itself, glimmering in the dark.

There's an intersection ahead of me, bordered by yellow crossing lines on all four sides. To my right a vacant lot, blocked off by fencing covered with green mesh fabric. It reminds me of the lot I drove past on my way back home from the Edmonds job, decades ago. And a two-storey apartment block, dark balconies looking out onto the street.

Intersection first. Then maybe find a gas station. Somewhere with a phone. I have no idea who I'll call—it's not like I could dial 911—but I'll figure that out later. For now…

For now. For now I can't go another step. My body just won't let me. I try, and just collapse. The best I can do is stay up on all fours.

The sound of a car. Not from the highway. Approaching the intersection. I don't know how I'm going to hail it when I can't even get on my feet, let alone say anything, but it turns out I don't have to. Whoever it is sees me, and it screeches to a halt.

Very slowly I lift my head.

The car is a huge black SUV. Tyres as big as I am. And in the back seat…

Reggie.

I stare back at her, sure I'm dreaming this. No, I *know* I'm dreaming this because sitting alongside her, leaning forward to look out the window, are Paul and Annie. Their eyes are huge, their mouths moving behind the glass. All three of them look like shit. Paul has a giant shiner, and Annie's got blood crusted on her top lip.

Not that I care right now. They're here. It's not a dream. It's not the afterlife. I didn't get eaten by the fire. They are here, in front of me, and they're real. I know it.

Moving with exaggerated care, I get up onto my knees. It's then that the thought occurs: *If they're all in the back seat, who's driving?*

The front of the car is turned slightly away from me, the driver on the opposite side of the car. As if in answer to my question, there's the clunk of a door. A figure comes around the side, but a drift of smoke obscures who it is.

Nic. He found the others, he kept them safe, and he's here for me. Here to take me somewhere with water, and cool sheets, and sleep. Blissful, dark, dreamless sleep.

But it's not Nic who steps out of the smoke.

It's Burr.

His hand is heavily bandaged, his bulbous nose covered in tape. He's grinning.

There's an object in his hand. A gun. No, not a gun. A taser.

I raise my eyes to his.

"You have got to be *fucking kidding m—*"

He fires.

FIFTY-FIVE

Teagan

LAX.

I know it's LAX because I saw a giant sign on the front of the hangar as we drove in. It read, LAX HANGAR 18. Also, there was a giant cargo plane parked inside. That kind of gave it away.

I wanted to tell someone that there used to be a pretty good rap group called Hangar 18, but I couldn't because I couldn't speak. After Burr tasered me, his crew wasted no time in doping me up to the gills. No Reggie to save me this time—no cute little diversion. Just whammo: needle in the neck, thank you very much and goodnight.

I am really fucking high right now.

They've got me tied to a gurney or stretcher or something, one with heavy leather straps. Even if I had full control of my PK, I couldn't move them. And I really don't have full control of my PK. I'm still conscious, but I can't move. Can't speak. Can barely think. The world is coated in a soft dandelion haze, all the rough edges blurred and fuzzy. Which is just fine by me. Fuzzy is good.

All the same, there's a lot of noise. Mechanical sounds:

clanking metal, hissing hydraulics from the plane, loud
thumps of heavy objects. And voices. Everybody is shouting, and none of them seems to be speaking a recognisable
language. I wish they would be quiet so I could sleep. I tried
to ask them, but I can't move my lips. It's a miracle I'm still
breathing.

Someone turns the gurney or stretcher or whatever it is.
The movement tilts my head to one side, so I'm looking right
out the front of the hangar. The sun is up. Morning sunlight,
a shaft of it piercing my vision and drilling directly down into
my brain. Blinking is an impossibility. Mercifully whoever has
the gurney keeps turning, and the sunlight vanishes.

They wheel me underneath the plane, its giant, distended
belly appearing overhead. Annie is yelling. I can't see her yet,
and it takes me a few seconds to recognise her voice, but I'm
helped along by the fact that she is going absolutely nuclear.
Believe me, I've seen Annie Cruz angry enough times to
recognise the tone.

"I will fucking end you," she's saying. "Hey—don't walk
away from me. Do you hear what I'm saying? You put her on
that plane, I will knock your fucking teeth out, bro."

The gurney passes below a face: concerned, battered, familiar. Paul. A giant bruise turning one side of his face into a
raccoon. Then he's gone. A snatch of Reggie's voice flickers
across the hangar, wheezing and angry: "...didn't do any of
this, just like I told Moira Tanner, and if you..."

Gone. And for the first time a little slimy ball of worry
begins to form deep in my gut. Should I be worried? I dunno.
It's hard to be stressed out when I'm this comfortable.

All the same...

They leave me parked for the longest time, right next to a
giant ramp that leads into the back of the plane. There is no

one around—or at least no one that I can see. I can't exactly turn my head to check.

The ball of worry hasn't gone away. It's got bigger. But I can't remember what happened. Dimly, I'm aware that it's very hard to breathe. My throat is on fire, and my entire body aches.

Movement. Noise. And then Annie, turning my head to face her, talking fast and frantic. "We'll get you out, OK? We can't stop them putting you on the plane, but we'll figure this out. Promise. Just—"

Gone. Annie is snatched away by a hand with a ring finger wrapped in thick bandages.

At some point they wheel me up the ramp and into the plane. There's a lot of bumping, more bright lights lancing into my eyes. And when they bring me to a stop, locking the gurney's wheels with a *clunk*, Burr finally shows himself. His face is a horror show, his nose swollen and bruised.

"Hey, freak show," he says quietly.

Drugged I may be, but it's all coming back. Jake. Carlos. Burbank. The fires. Nic. Nic! Annie was there—how did she get away from Nando Aguilar? MS-13? Paul was there too, and Reggie. But no Nic. Or was he? I don't know, can't be sure. What am I doing in the plane?

"Shhh." Burr actually strokes my forehead. He's grinning down at me, but behind the grin is naked contempt. And why not? He beat me. I was supposed to be a super-soldier, and look who came out on top. Good old Burr. Old school beats new school. This must be one of the greatest moments of his pathetic little life.

"You're done, freak show," he says conversationally. His voice is slightly nasal. "You're going back to Waco. Maybe they'll let me come visit you, if they decide to keep you alive."

Jake is dead. The thought arrives like a thunderbolt. If Jake is dead, then so are my chances of proving there was another psychokinetic. Even his body is probably ash by now, along with Carlos. Tanner is going to let the government have me. They're going to lock me away, cut me open, do what they've been wanting to do for years.

"You know, you should thank your friend Marino," Burr says. It takes me a few seconds to realise he means Paul. "He was the one who told us where to find you."

His face darkens. "Course, we had to beat it out of him. The cripple wouldn't tell us, your pal Annie Cruz neither, but I always said navy boys were a bunch of pussies. Smart, though. When he went after Cruz, he called up every government contact he had in that old-ass phone of his. We got wind of it, came right to him. You know what he said? Said you were holed up in a house in West Hollywood. That you'd made a deal with the Salvadorans."

Paul. You genius.

Burr's grin gets wider. "We had to search the house twice before we figured out what happened. I wanted to let the MS-13 boys we left alive have dear old Annie, but the cap said you were the priority. And like I told you, navy boys are pussies. Couple of minutes alone with me, and Marino told us everything."

I try very hard to spit in his face. All that happens is that I start drooling. Burr leans down, takes the edge of the sheet, and wipes the saliva away. He's surprisingly, horrifyingly gentle.

"They say there was someone like you walking around up in Burbank. Same powers and everything. Maybe there was. Maybe you really didn't kill those folks. But we searched everywhere once it was safe, and we didn't find a damn thing." He taps me on the nose, very gently. "Sorry, darling. This one is on you."

The plane begins to move. A pushback tug, taking us out onto the runway. Burr pats my cheek, then stands up and walks away.

He didn't get all the saliva on my cheek. It's dried to a crust, and it's starting to itch. Maddening, constant. And no matter how hard I try, I can't move my head.

Another soldier walks past me, glances down in silent contempt. Someone—the voice sounds like Burr's grey-bearded captain—tells everyone to strap in. The command isn't urgent. It's bored and routine. Mission accomplished, after all.

Suddenly it seems very important to scratch the itch on my cheek. If I can just do that, then everything will be all right.

I'm so intent on doing it, so focused on just trying to get my stupid head to move a stupid two inches, that I don't realise how stupid I'm being until the plane's engines power up. That's when my fuzz-addled brain finally wakes up. Forget the itch—if I don't do something drastic right now, I am well and truly screwed.

The pitch of the engines rises to a howl. The lights above me go dark for a second, then flick back on. The plane's body shakes as it rumbles down the runway, and no matter how hard I try, I can't move. My PK is toast.

Come on. Come on, you motherfucker. Come on!

Zip. Nada. Nothing.

Tears blur my vision. A hitching half-sob squirms its way out of my chest. Hell no. I did not go through all this just to get shipped off to a government lab without even a squeak of protest. If I can't find a clever way out of this, then I'll find a dumb one. I'll throw something, smash a window, bust a hole in the plane wall. Crash it, I don't care.

But wishing for something doesn't make it true. And the girl who can move shit with her mind is just a girl now. They'll keep me this way until they cut me open: a mute, trembling body that can't fight back.

The plane banks, the engines roaring as they take the strain. Whatever I've been dosed with lets me breathe, but the sobs are coming thick and fast now, my lungs burning as they too take the strain. My throat is torched, black and ruined.

Wait. Wait, wait, wait. I've got something. The barest thread of feedback: a piece of metal, part of the gurney. Down by my right hand. I can just, just make out its shape with my PK. The relief that washes over me is exquisite. I concentrate as hard as I can, willing my energy to go just a little bit further...

And instead it drains away. Like it was never there in the first place.

I picture my friends. Nic. Annie. Paul. Reggie. As clearly and completely as I can. Nic's smile, the smell of his skin. Annie's eyes as she talked about her mom. Paul, standing on the edge of the pool in Sawtelle, holding his phone and wondering what he was going to tell his son—not our logistics guy then, just a dad who didn't want to let his kid down. Reggie, refusing to quit, with no chair and no one to help her, faking a seizure so she could buy us some time.

China Shop. Fucking China Shop.

My people.

It takes a few moments for me to realise that the plane is still banking. That doesn't make sense. It's like we're turning in a full circle. And there are other noises too, like the sound of footsteps thundering through the plane. A low, annoyed groan. Greybeard demanding to know what the hell is going on.

And then Burr appears. He grabs me by the chin, twists my head to face him.

"What did you do, freak show?" he says. Saliva showers me, dots my skin. "Who did you talk to?"

My eyes are still full of tears, and they double his face, turning him into a nightmare. What the hell is he talking about? Talk to anybody? I believe my last words before the taser and the drugs were *You have got to be fucking kidding me.*

My ears pop. We're descending. That can't be right. We only just left LAX.

Burr's grip on my chin is agony. "Captain," he barks over his shoulder, "there's gotta be a mistake."

Without waiting for a response, he bends in close. His breath stinks. "You tell me right fucking now what you did. You hear me?"

Grinning, I stick a raised middle finger right in his face.

Well, actually, I don't. The drugs won't let me. But I picture myself doing it very clearly, and while I might not have the gift of telepathy, it's clear from the look of furious disgust on his face that he knows I'm doing it. We're going back to LA. We're turning round. I don't know why, but we are.

For now, that's enough.

FIFTY-SIX

Teagan

A few months after I started working for China Shop, I found a way onto the roof of the building.

It's not easy to get there, or at least not easy when you're short. To do it, you have to climb onto the big plastic trash cans at the side of the building, trying like hell to keep your balance. Then you have to use that perch to scramble up onto where the roof is slightly lower. It takes a lot of swearing and feet scrabbling at the wall, but you can do it. And it's like that part on Mount Everest. Once you're over the second-to-last bit, it's just a short walk to the summit. Which, in this case, happens to be the peak of the house's pitched roof.

I don't come up too often. But on a day like today, when the Cali weather seems even more perfect than normal and I can see all the way to the ocean, it feels perfect.

I sit just below the apex of the roof, sunnies on. Soaking in the light. It helps, but only a little. There's a lot I still have to figure out, and it's going to take a while, no matter how bright the sun shines.

So, yeah. Didn't end up on the dissection table at a

government black site. And the only reason it didn't happen was because of Nic.

Beautiful, brilliant, amazing Nic.

He did what I said, even though it must have killed him. He took Javier Salinas and drove like hell until he found the emergency services. Then the idiot tried to turn round so he could come get me—or at least help me fight Jake in some unspecified way.

Of course, they wouldn't let him. By then, Burbank, Glendale and even some parts of North Hollywood were on fire. He didn't have any choice but to wait, so he stayed with Salinas while they took him to the nearest hospital, Saint Joseph's. And a while later, guess who gets brought in? None other than Sandy and Kelly Salinas—exhausted, suffering from smoke inhalation but otherwise OK. When they were reunited with Javier, Nic was right there.

The first thing he does is ask them if they saw me. And they—and Javier, who by now is sort-of-mostly awake—start talking about Jake.

Which is when Nic realised that what he had were three witnesses.

He didn't have any sort of agency contacts, obviously, but that didn't stop him. He borrowed a phone from someone and called the China Shop offices. How did he get the number? Because we have a website. We have a goddamn website. The one Paul set up to present China Shop as a legitimate moving business, and which I will never give him shit for doing, ever again. It's the greatest website of all time. Between that and his stunt with Annie and MS-13, Paul deserves a Nobel peace prize. They should carve his name on the moon.

Nic suspected that Tanner might be listening, and he called and called and called, filling up the mailbox. For the first time in history, something good came out of the government tapping a phone line.

Most of the blaze had been pushed back by then, thanks to LA's airborne firefighting division. Once they knew where to look, Tanner's people found the remains of Jake's body, still under the truck. Most of it was burned to ash, along with the house, but there was still a little left.

It was that they eventually took away on the C-17, spiriting it away to whatever black site they wanted to lock me inside.

They still haven't told me who or what he was, and I can't stop thinking about how I killed him. I didn't have a choice, not really, but it still hurts. It's going to hurt for a long time.

That, and the fact that they didn't find Carlos where I left him.

He was gone.

I don't know how he managed to get himself off the rebar he was impaled on. I don't even want to think about the effort it must have taken or how much pain he must have been in. He should have died: from shock, from smoke inhalation, from blood loss. Somehow he didn't. And they never found his body. It's possible it got burned up too, the ash blown away or crushed by a piece of debris.

Possible. Now there's a fun word.

It took a long time to sort everything out. They kept us at LAX—turns out the government has a whole building of their own there. One with a fully equipped hospital. I was still dosed, but they got me on oxygen and gave me some drugs for my throat.

I don't remember much, although I do remember Burr. Staring down at me in my hospital bed, the sick grin still on his face. I couldn't respond, could barely even blink, but he didn't seem to mind.

"You got lucky," he said. "But just so you know, we're going to be watching you. You fuck up again, you do *anything* you're not supposed to, and I'll make sure that I'm the one who gets to bring you in." He lifted his hand, swathed in bandages, and waggled the fingers that were still working. "Be seeing you, freak show."

I was drifting off by then. When I came back, he was gone.

We were at the LAX facility for at least two weeks. All that time Tanner was busy. I'm guessing that the conversations about what to do with me and the team probably took up a lot of her schedule that week. But in the end I guess she decided that we were worth keeping around.

And yes, I find it completely fucked and deeply annoying that the fate of my entire life still depended on Tanner and whoever her bosses might be coming to a consensus. That hasn't changed, even after everything that happened.

But once they *did* decide to keep me, Tanner got busy. I'm still not entirely sure how she dealt with the cops—my guess is she pulled some major strings with the commissioner's office here in LA, got the few actual witnesses not to speak out. The DA's office would have been trickier, but she pulled it off.

I was the last one they let out. Last night they finally brought me out of my drugged-up haze. Realising I'd lost two weeks was...not a fun moment. Reggie, Annie and Paul had already been released, so I didn't even have anyone to talk to—nobody except a very nervous doctor, who handled me like I was radioactive.

They drove me back here this morning. The driver ignored me when I asked him to take me home. He dropped me off at the entrance to Brooks Court and just drove away. The burn on my leg is still healing, and the itch was coming and going in nasty, prickling waves.

They'd found me a pair of jeans. Sneakers a little too big. An LAX employee polo shirt, the collar stiff and uncomfortable. Clean bra and panties, both also slightly too big. I walked up Brooks Court still not a-hundred-per-cent sure I wasn't dreaming this. As I got close, I saw the same poster on the wall opposite the Boutique: the orange and green monstrosity still advertising a club night from three months ago. Same graffiti on the power box, same garbage cans. None of it had changed at all.

The Batmobile was there—my black Jeep. Someone had retrieved him from Skid Row, parked him outside the house. I had an urge to run up to the car and wrap my arms around him, like he was a damn dog that had found his way home. I settled for resting my hand on the side, just for a second.

They were all inside the Boutique. I hugged Reggie. Shook Paul's hand. Nodded at Annie, who flashed me a wan smile. I thought they'd be surprised to see me, but of course Tanner had told them I was coming. Paul even had the coffee on. There was something awkward about it all, and it wasn't hard to see why. Carlos, and what he'd done, hung over the place like a bad smell.

It didn't help that Paul had started talking about him almost immediately, saying they were still doing some digging, still uncovering key facts, but he never would have believed that son of a bitch would have done it, it was unconscionable. That was when I said I needed a minute and headed up to the roof.

I can't go forward until I've drawn a line under the previous two weeks. I have no idea how to do that, but it starts with just taking a breath.

And sitting on the roof in the blazing Cali sunshine is a mighty fine place to do just that.

I'm not OK with what happened. Any of it. I keep trying to

figure out if I could have done anything differently. If I could have saved Jake, or Carlos, or stopped all this from happening in the first place.

I don't know. I just don't know. I'm finding it hard to focus, and it has nothing to do with any after-effects from the drugs.

What a fucking mess.

"Yo."

I didn't even hear Annie come up. I'm about to tell her to give me some space, but there's no energy behind the thought.

"Thought you were afraid of heights," I say.

She side-eyes me. "Bitch, please. Only someone short as you would call this high up."

For a minute the two of us sit in silence, saying nothing, gazing out at the ocean in the distance. From somewhere below us, Paul's voice drifts up as he talks to Reggie. A snatch of music reaches my ears—a car, driving past on 7th, bumping Kendrick Lamar. "Mortal Man." Definitely, with that bassline.

"You and Paul, huh?" My voice still sounds like Scarlett Johansson shaking off the worst cold in history.

"Yeah, well." Annie tilts her head up to the sun, eyes closed.

"Didn't exactly strike me as your type."

"Like you know my type, Frost." But there's a very slight smile on her face. "Nah, he's...I mean, I know he's a pain in the ass sometimes, but..."

"Sometimes?"

"Well. I told him we gotta work on that. But honestly, he's a good guy. Better than most. A lot of dudes will construct this...like, idea of what they think you want. Paul is straight down the line. And one on one, he's kind of a sweetheart."

"You kept it under wraps. I'll give you that much."

"I know. I was planning on telling you guys everything after we figured out your shit. That, and the whole deal with them MS-13 boys. What you said about...you know, with the whole cheese sandwich, and Nic. You were right about something for once."

"So why not tell us then?"

She shrugs. "Me and Paul and MS-13...it didn't feel relevant then. You know what I mean? I thought it would complicate things too much. Although I swear to God I was gonna come clean about all of it when things settled down a little." A guilty look crosses her face. "My bad. I didn't expect them to just pop up like that, get all up in our shit."

"It's OK. Hey, is your...like, your mom, is she..."

"We'll be fine for a while. They gave me half up front, so that'll cover some of the treatment."

Some. But for how long? "You could always ask Tanner. She—"

"Thought you might wanna know about Carlos," she says.

The abrupt change of subject knocks me sideways a little. "Sure. I mean, if you—"

"You ever hear of a place called El Agujero?"

Carlos, impaled. Blood slicking his hands. *Look up El Agujero. Look up microfibres in the water. They deserved what was coming to them.*

"Little town near Puerto Vallarta, in Jalisco. Beautiful beaches, good tequila. Also a massive factory that made synthetic fabrics for clothes. Carlos—only he wasn't called Carlos, by the way, name was Angel Campos—he ever tell you he had a brother?"

I'm having a hell of time trying to keep up with her. "No. Never."

"Well, he did. Rigoberto. Floor boss at this factory. And Rigoberto, he finds out that the clothes they're making got a problem. Sounds small, but like Mo-Mo said, it's some genuinely scary shit."

"When *did* you dig this up? How?"

"You think we been sitting on our asses while you been gone? Just listen. See, the problem was that this fabric, whenever it got turned into clothing and washed, would shoot these synthetic microfibres into the water supply. Billions of them. And that wasn't even talking about the shit this factory was dumping direct into the ocean. This stuff, Teagan..." She shakes her head. "It's making its way into the food chain, killing sea life across the whole planet. It's this massive thing, and nobody even knows about it. Or if they do, they don't care."

"Carlos cared." Even the feel of his name in my mouth sounds wrong.

"Be nice if he was that noble. But he only cared because of what happened after. He and Rigoberto got the workers organised. God knows how the fuck he pulled that off—these people didn't have a lot, and they needed their jobs. But they did it. Started striking, protesting, the whole nine. Until the cops came along.

"Mexican cops don't play. They never report that shit on the news here, maybe not even over there, but it was a massacre. Fifty people dead, including Rigoberto Campos."

"Jesus."

"Yeah. Thing is, cops in that part of the world don't do shit 'less they get paid for it. And as it turns out, the chief in El Agujero received one motherfucker of a wire transfer, just before. Reggie traced it back."

"To Ultra." It's all starting to fall into place.

"Bingo. They were the factory's biggest client, and they couldn't afford for any of this to get out. Steven Chase probably didn't think the massacre would happen, but he must have had some idea of what he was buying."

"What about Hayden and Salinas? I thought Hayden worked for an ocean charity? Wouldn't he have wanted to stop this?"

"Sure. Unless he took a payment too. Probably not the only one."

"And Salinas?"

"Coastal Cities office of the health department handles water quality. Chase paid Salinas to look the other way on the official side, and paid off Hayden in case his charity did their own independent tests. Either way, Salinas is about to have some interesting conversations with the cops."

Salinas's wife and kid come to the front of my mind. I decide not to go there. "So Carlos wanted revenge."

"Uh-huh. Probably why he came across the border to LA in the first place. Course he didn't know how to get to Chase without getting caught, and even then it wasn't just Chase he had to take care of. Must have taken him a long time to dig up what actually happened—who helped cover it up, I mean.

"Meantime Tanner recruits him, he bangs with us and then he meets this Jake kid and realises he's got the perfect opportunity."

"Me."

"You."

"Hold up. Why wait until we did a job at the Edmonds Building? He couldn't have known that was gonna happen."

"He didn't."

I frown at her. "I don't get it." The answer whacks me around the head before I've even finished the sentence. "Chase was never sending money to Saudi, was he?"

"Nope. He'd done some shit but none of that. My guess is Carlos somehow got word to Tanner, anonymously, that this was happening. Of course she wanted evidence herself, which is when we got sent in."

"Why didn't he just tell her about the microfibres? And his brother?"

"You think she'd give a fuck? Anyway, we go in, and Reggie brings down the cameras. Window of opportunity for Carlos's boy to do his thing."

"And we still don't know how Carlos and Jake..."

A guilty look crosses her face. "Sorry, man. With both of 'em out of the picture..."

I take a deep, shaky breath. If I hadn't thrown the truck as hard, if I'd stayed with Carlos a little longer...

Annie reaches over, grips my shoulder. "Hey. Look at me."

I look at her.

"You did the only thing you could. I wasn't even there, and I can figure that out."

"I just...I don't..." I squint at the sky, hunting for the right words. "It sounds like you're talking about another person. Carlos, I mean. I know he really did do all this, logically, but it just doesn't...I don't get it."

"I do."

"Really?"

"Sure. Remember I told you about my dad?"

"Kind of."

"When we were walking up to Nic's spot. I told you about how he worked at the children's library in Carson. Then he'd come home and tune up on my mom?"

"Oh. Yeah."

"Same shit. People wear masks. They lie to each other. You know that more than most. But listen to me: I know you and Carlos were tight, but he doesn't deserve any more energy. He fucked with all of us."

"And how about you and me, Annie?"

"What?"

"Are we tight?"

She doesn't hesitate. "Always, baby girl. Long as you don't throw me out any more buildings."

"No promises."

Annie smiles, turns to go. "We'll be around when you're ready," she says.

As she reaches the edge of the roof, right before the drop onto the lower level, her phone rings in her pocket. That gets me thinking: I need to get a new one. Or at least get my old one back from Africa. Shit—*Africa*! Well, Idriss. I owe him big time, and right now a steak dinner sounds fan-fucking-tastic.

I still don't have the first clue how to fix Skid Row—how to help the hundreds of people living in tents in the middle of one of the richest cities on the planet. But treating them like human beings is probably a good start, and nothing says you respect someone like buying them a meal. Or cooking them one: Idriss and Jeannette can come over to my place, and I can fix up some—

"Yo, Teagan." Annie's back, balancing on the roof's apex.

"Huh?"

She holds out the phone. "Think you'd better take this one."

As she heads back the way she came, she starts to hum something. I just catch it before she drops out of sight. "I'm a Slave 4 U."

I lift the phone to my ear. "Hello, Tanner."

FIFTY-SEVEN

Teagan

"Good afternoon, Ms. Jameson."

She's not in her office; she's in a public place—somewhere with distant voices, traffic. The joyful scream of a child. A park, maybe? It's strange to think of Tanner mingling with people, just sitting there while joggers and hand-holding couples and sprinting kids move past her. Vaguely I wonder how she knew to phone Annie and not Reggie or Paul.

"The doctors tell me there'll be no permanent damage from the smoke," she continues. "And I wanted to check in with you, since you're back on your feet. See how you were holding up."

"Did you now."

There's a pause, as if she's weighing up whether or not to call me out. Instead, she says, "I'm glad you're back. We still have a lot of work to do. I trust you'll keep working with Ms. McCormick's team as before. I know you recently lost a team member, but we should be able to replace—"

"*Lost* a team member?"

Carlos—*Angel*—impaled, begging me to help him. I shake it off.

"Indeed. We're scouting for another driver as we sp—"

"Did you know? About El Agujero?"

"...As I said. We'll be finding you another driver. You'll need to bring them up to speed."

"You didn't, did you?"

It's been dancing around the edges of my mind since Annie told me. If Tanner had known about Angel's background, about what happened with his brother and the factory and the microfibres and Ultra, then she would have viewed him as a suspect in Chase's murder from the start. She would have brought him in—or at the very least, she wouldn't have put it all on me. And if she'd known about what happened at El Agujero, she'd never have hired him to work in the same city as the people who got his brother killed. Tanner would never take that risk.

"No," she says, her tone icicle-cold. "And we'll be re-evaluating our intel gathering mechanisms in Mexico. It appears that Mr. Morales—Campos—used a particularly good information broker. They do exist in that part of the world, if you can pay them. His identity checked out when we investigated it. Our due diligence in that regard was clearly lacking, which won't happen again. Whoever joins the team next will be *rigorously* vetted."

"And Jake?"

"What?"

"He wasn't on your radar." I sit up a little straighter. "When Chase was killed, you didn't even *consider* that there might be someone else out there."

"Careful, Ms. Jameson."

"You missed it. You didn't even know he existed. You thought my parents got lucky, and that I was the only survivor, and you figured you had it all under control. But you didn't. All this time he was out there, and you had *no idea*."

I'm out of breath, and for once it has nothing to do with my damaged throat and lungs. Up until today Tanner's power and reach had seemed infinite. I didn't dare disobey her, because she could do anything. Her office in DC was the centre of a vast spiderweb, a million strands reaching out across the globe. Pluck one, pluck two, listen to the signals that come back, then act, safe in the knowledge that the strands went everywhere.

Except they don't. Even the biggest spiderweb doesn't go on for ever. The strands have to stop somewhere.

What else does she not know? What's out there in the dark places where her web doesn't quite reach? A spider like Tanner might seem terrifying, might be able to hurt you if she wants to. But if you're beyond her web, she won't even know you're there.

"So you're looking now," I say. "If there was one, there might be more, right?"

Now there's real venom in her voice. "Let me remind you, Ms. Jameson: the terms of our arrangement haven't changed. I am still your advocate here. I'm the one keeping you where you are, free as a bird. You would be very wise not to forget that. You are going to keep working for me. You're going to keep up with your assignments. If or when I have information that is relevant to you, I will decide if it is worth sharing. Am I clear?"

I'm about to tell her no. How dare she? How dare she mess up this badly and still try to give me orders? How dare she stop me from finding more of the people my parents... changed? There might be more. Many more. If she thinks I'm not going to search for that, she can...

But I don't tell her, *fuck you*, like I should.

Doing that would mean being on the run, probably for ever. It would mean leaving behind everything: my car, my apartment, my books, my dreams for a restaurant. Nic. And most importantly Annie, Paul and Reggie.

How could I leave them? How could I just vanish after everything we've been through? It's not just that it would be wrong to ditch them; it's that I can't even bear the thought. Throughout that whole insane day, the twenty-four hours—excuse me, twenty-two—when it felt like the entire city wanted us dead, they stuck with me. They helped me and put themselves in harm's way to do it.

Once, a very long time ago, I had a family. People who knew me. Accepted me. Took care of me. That family destroyed itself—destroyed *us*—but I've found another.

And more than that. Reggie's words from before we outran the chopper come back to me, spoken as we were sitting in Paul's truck. *What happened to you . . . what you are, you didn't choose any of it. And God knows, the situation with Tanner isn't something I'd wish on anybody . . . We may not always know the exact effect we're having on a particular situation, but I can tell you . . . we're making a difference.*

I don't trust Tanner. But I trust Reggie.

I'll keep doing the work. I'll make my PK mean something. It means it'll be harder to find out if there are more people like me. Tanner isn't going to share what she discovers—there's no way. Not unless it's to her advantage. I'll have to build my own web. Start sending out my own strands into the dark places. It'll be harder, but I can handle it. I have Annie's connections. Reggie's hacking. Paul's logistical skills. And of course I have my PK. An ability which is way, way more powerful than I thought it was.

I reach out with it. I don't have the energy to really use it, but that doesn't stop me from sending it out anyway. My range has increased, even now. I can feel everything within fifty feet, my energy wrapped around it. The garbage cans. The power lines. The glass in the windows of the houses lining Brooks Court. The basketball being bounced by a kid in a yard across the way. The chain he's wearing.

I bring it all back in and wrap it around the Batmobile.

I don't lift it, but I do give it a very slight tug. The Jeep shifts on its balding tyres, rocking every so slightly.

For everything she can do, and as wide as her web is, Tanner is still human.

I'm not.

"OK," I tell her. "I understand."

"Good. I'll be in touch."

"I wasn't done."

"Excuse me?"

"Just because I'm still working for you doesn't mean it's gonna be like it was before. I'm changing a few things."

"You don't get to give me—"

"Number one: if you ever send a group of black-ops guys my way again, I will send them back to you in body bags. You don't believe me, go ask Burr what I can do. Tell him I hope his finger gets gangrene and falls off."

Dead silence over the line. Even the children in whatever park she's in have stopped playing.

"Number two: you're gonna share what you find. If there are other people with abilities out there, you tell me." She probably won't, and I'll have no way of knowing if she does find anything, but it's worth a shot. "I find out you're not being straight with me, and we're gonna have words."

"Is that so?" She's gone dangerously quiet.

"Number three: Nic Delacourt. He knows about me and about what we do here, but you're not gonna touch him. You're not gonna contact him. You're not gonna put him under surveillance. You're gonna forget he exists. Otherwise, you'll be the one going home in a body bag."

I've pushed it too far. Telling her how it's going to be is one thing; threatening her is something else.

But after a very long moment she says grudgingly, "I suppose an exception can be made."

"Damn straight."

"Anything else I can do for you, Ms. Jameson?"

"Nah. I'm good."

"Well, if that's *all*, then—"

·"Wait. I changed my mind. There is something else."

"What?" It's a single syllable, but I swear if I were standing in front of her, it would turn solid and stab me in the heart.

"Stop calling me Ms. Jameson. My name is Teagan Frost."

I hang up.

I expect her to call back to demand the last word, but she doesn't. I sit for a while, face turned up to the sun, letting the afternoon wash over me.

I need to be careful. Just because Tanner is fallible doesn't mean she isn't dangerous. The cage I'm in is bigger, but it's still a cage. If I'm going to break out one day—live my life, own my restaurant, be more than what my parents made me—then I'm going to have to watch what I do.

Look at me, planning ahead. See, Reggie? I'm learning.

Speaking of which…

They're in the living room when I come down off the roof. Annie and Paul are on the couch, holding hands, talking quietly. It's the first time I've seen them do it, and I kind of hope they don't stop. This place has had enough secrets for a while.

I can't stop myself looking towards the kitchen, as if Carlos is going to be there rooting through the cupboards for the coffee. His absence feels like a missing tooth. After what he did, I should be glad he's gone. Where is he now? Still in California? Did he go back to Mexico? Is he even alive? The thought of him still out there...I can't even begin to figure out how I feel about it. It's too much.

Reggie is off to one side, tapping at something on her phone. She looks up as I come through the door. "Oh, thank God. Someone to distract me from these two lovebirds."

"Please," Annie says. "You been playing *Clash of Clans* for the past ten minutes. You don't even know we here."

"So you didn't know?" I ask Reggie, nodding to Annie and a sheepish, grinning Paul.

"About them? Uh-uh." Reggie shakes her head. "Well, I had my suspicions. They were pretty good at hiding it." She gives me a sly smile.

"Hey," I tell her. "I never said. Thanks for your...well, what you did at Nic's apartment."

"How do you mean?"

"The fake seizure."

"Oh!" Her eyebrows shoot up. "I'd almost forgotten. You're welcome, dear." The smile returns. "You should come see one of our performances some time. I do a mean Blanche DuBois."

"I...I don't know who that is."

"You can't be serious." She turns to Paul. "How does she not know that? Haven't we been teaching her right?"

Paul looks embarrassed.

"You don't know *either*?" Reggie says. "You've come to my shows before!"

"Yeah, but that was Shakespeare. I think. I'm into more modern stuff. *Arrested Development*, that kind of thing."

"Modern my ass." Annie rolls her eyes. "He watches that shit on DVD, if you can believe that. Refuses to get streaming."

"Not true. I don't refuse, I just like having my own copies."

Paul gets to his feet, dusting his hands off, even though all he's been doing is sitting on the couch.

"So I was—" I start.

"Well, I don't about the rest—" he says at the same time.

We stop, and I gesture to him. "You go."

"I was going to say, we've actually got a job lined up this afternoon. A moving job, not a Tanner job," he says as if trying to reassure me. "Just a small one. Some boxes for an old guy up in Santa Monica. Annie and I could do it, but it'd be great if you wanted to join us..."

"Actually, um, I'm kind of gonna head home," I say. "Something I gotta do."

"Oh." He looks a little crestfallen. "Right. Of course. Sure."

"Hey."

I meet his eyes. "I'll be there on the next one. Don't worry about it."

"Take your time," Reggie says quietly. "We'll be here."

Annie's phone is still in my hand. I'm about to pass it back to her when a thought occurs. "Actually, can I make a call real quick?"

She shrugs. "Sure."

A few moments later she looks up to see me still staring at the phone. "You OK?"

"What? Oh. Yeah."

"You don't know his number in your head, do you?"

"No."

"Don't worry," Reggie says. She spins her chair, heads for the door leading to her Rig. "I'll find it for you. I don't what you'd do without us."

Neither do I.

FIFTY-EIGHT

Teagan

Two weeks at the LAX facility, which means two weeks since I've been at my house. The thought of sleeping there again— assuming I *can* sleep the whole night through—is almost too much to think about.

Two weeks. Jesus. At least I don't own a cat.

Nic is waiting for me when I arrive. This time he doesn't bother parking around the block. It's around 2:15 when I pull the Batmobile up to the kerb behind his blue Corolla. He's wearing dark jeans, a pair of old Tims, a grey button-down with the sleeves folded to mid-arm, leaning on the hood with his eyes hidden behind big Ray-Bans.

I climb out of the Batmobile and just stand there for a second, savouring how normal it all is. The quiet Leimert Park street, middle of the day, sun beaming through the jacaranda trees. Distant traffic. A retiree walking her just-as-ancient Dalmatian on the far sidewalk. The air smells of jasmine with just the faintest hint of wildfire smoke. The world has that amazing hot, liquid light you get at around two o'clock on a summer's day.

A clinking, clattering noise from the far end of the block:

Harry, pushing his shopping cart full of bottles, black bags bulging off its sides. He's still wearing his blue raincoat, despite the heat. I lift my arm in a wave—automatic even now—and he returns it, his grin visible even from where I am.

Same street, same Harry. It's like I never left at all.

My first instinct is to hug Nic. Wrap my arms around and just never, ever let go. But as I approach, his body tenses ever so slightly. The movement is like a very thin needle plunging into my heart.

"Hey," I say.

"Hey."

"Thanks for coming. I…" I take a deep breath. "I didn't know if they'd let you out of work, but—"

A smile plays at the edges of his mouth. "You do know it's Sunday, right? They work associates hard, but we do get *some* time off."

"Um…"

He peers at me. "You don't know what day of the week it is, do you?"

"I've been kind of busy. And by busy, I mean unconscious."

"Fair enough. Although I probably could've got out of work anyway. My boss is terrified of me now."

"Why?"

"When they let me come back in, it was with a couple of dudes in black suits. They told her that I'd been seconded to the government for a special assignment, and that under no circumstances was I to be fired or laid off."

The silence stretches out for a second too long. "Hey, can we go inside?" I say. "I mean, if you want to…"

"Right. Yeah."

The house is dark and very slightly stuffy. Everything is right where I left it, although there's a little more dust than normal. Seeing my possessions calms me, just a little—my records, my books, the spices in my tiny-ass kitchen. For the first time I stop feeling like this is a dream.

We sit on the couch, a few feet apart. I'm just getting comfortable when I think I should draw back the curtains, half turn to get off the couch, then decide not to. A shaft of sunlight lies across the leg of Nic's jeans, dust motes turning in the still air.

"So—" he starts.

I interrupt him: "Shit. I never actually told you."

"What?"

"I'm so sorry, I totally spaced, with everything that happened—"

"Tell me *what?*"

"My real name. It's not actually Teagan Frost."

Nic raises an eyebrow.

"It's Emily. Emily Jameson. Although to be honest, I don't really like that name any more, but I totally understand if..."

"Let's just stick with Teagan for now." His smile looks forced, almost painful.

"There's something else I want to tell you, too," I say.

"There's more?"

"Just..." I hold up my hand. I spent quite a bit of the drive over thinking about how I was going to phrase this, and I can't risk getting knocked off my stride. That happens, and the words will just turn to vapour in my head. I've told Nic a lot about who I am, but there's one thing I haven't told him yet. If there's going to be any chance of us ever being together, he has to hear this.

"When you got us that reservation at N/Naka," I tell him, "you were hoping it would be a date. Like a romantic date."

He closes his eyes. "I would never have made you—"

"No, it's OK. It's totally OK. And I know it looked like I just blew you off, or friend-zoned you, or whatever. I get that. But what I'm trying to say is, if I could have dated you…" *Here it comes.* "I would have."

Dead silence. He sits, watching me. The urge to edge closer, to put a hand on his leg, is almost overpowering. I don't dare, not until this is done.

"Then why didn't you?" he says after a long moment. "Why make me wait? Were you worried about me…I dunno, revealing your secret or something? You could have gone out with me and not used your ability. Power. Whatever it is."

"It's more than that."

For a few seconds the words fuzz in my brain, and I panic. I make them come back, force them to, like I'm using my PK to drag them into the world.

"Nic, when I have…when I have sex, I can't control my PK. Things move. Like, *really* move. I've tried, and I can't stop it happening."

His eyebrows shoot up. "Huh. Hadn't thought of that."

"Yeah. It gets a little…intense."

Intense. Shit. It's insanity. My PK leaps from my control like a wild animal, grabbing on to anything and everything. It actually starts way before I have an orgasm, slowly building up until objects start smashing against the walls. Believe me when I say that faking it just isn't something I could do, and there is no way to control my ability when it happens.

"My mom and dad had a theory," I tell him. "The endorphins boost my PK in…unexpected ways, they called them."

He scratches his stubble. "OK, that's…Wait, hold up. How did your parents know about this?"

"What did you do when you were sixteen years old, Nic?"

"I…" Understanding dawns. "Whoa. Wow."

"Yeah. My room looked like an elephant had charged through it."

It sounds like a joke. Like something you'd use as a punchline. But I've never felt less like laughing.

"Tanner didn't want you revealing your powers to anybody."

"Uh-huh."

"So you couldn't have a boyfriend. I get it. That would... Wait, does this mean you've never had sex?"

"It's not..."

"*Never?*"

Here it comes. The memory pushing itself to the surface. I knew I'd have to tell him about this, but it doesn't make it any easier.

"I've had sex."

"With who? Someone on the team?"

"Not exactly. His name..." I have to stop. Take a deep breath. "His name was Travis."

Nic waits for me to continue, but a few seconds go by where I don't know how. I've lived this story in my head a thousand times, but I've never told anybody about it. Not a soul.

"Who was he?" Nic says.

"Wait. I have to say something first." Another deep breath. "What I'm gonna tell you...doesn't make me look good. I'm not proud of it, and I would give anything to take it back."

He folds his arms, waiting for me to continue. The look on his face isn't unkind.

"After I came to LA, I really wanted to...I wanted to try. Sex, I mean. And I knew I would have to be careful. I can't remember if I told you or not, but my ability doesn't affect organic matter. No carbon or hydrogen molecules. And there was a wilderness area near the hotel Tanner had me staying at, this park with a ton of trees and stuff..."

Nic tilts his head slightly, gesturing at me to go on. He's turned ever-so-slightly towards me now, forearms resting on his knees.

"Travis was this bartender I got talking to. He wanted to be an actor, but he wasn't an asshole about it, like everyone else in this town. I got to know him, a little, and I decided that I wanted to do it with him. I wanted him to be my first. I asked him if he wanted to try, and he said yes."

I wanted it to be good. I wanted to *be* good. I'd read up online about what to expect the first time, but it's never going to completely prepare you. And like most first times, it definitely wasn't beautiful, or loving, or inspired. It was a crash to the ground, twigs in my back, my skirt rucked up, him barely able to find my bra strap, let alone undo it. Both of us fumbling with the condom. I remember how his body tasted—about the only pleasant thing I remember. Salty and very slightly sweet, like really good caramel. I had a brief moment—a very brief moment—where I thought it was going to be OK.

"What happened?" Nic says gently.

"Well...we had sex."

"And?"

"You know how sometimes you're lying in bed and you just can't get comfortable? You toss and turn and you just can't find a position you like?"

"Yeah?"

"The more...aroused I got, the more my PK tried to find something to latch on to; and the more it found it couldn't, the worse the feeling got. It made me wanna throw up."

Somehow we finished. Travis had started noticing that something was wrong about halfway through. Mostly because I was making little retching noises as I tried to push back the wave of nausea. We rolled off each other and just lay there, panting, neither of us looking at the other. At that moment, if my PK *had* found something to grab, I would have smashed it into a million pieces.

I don't remember how I got home. I do know that I didn't go back to that bar for six months. He tried to call me a couple of times, but when I didn't pick up, he stopped. Once again, not proud. But I wanted nothing more than to forget that night, which I did, at several other bars a long way from Travis's.

"I don't get it, Teags," he says when I tell him this. "So you ghosted him? It happens. It's happened to me a few times. It's not an awesome thing to do, but it's not the end of the world. Don't worry about it."

"That's not—"

"And it's not like you raped him. He consented, right? He might not have known about your ability, but you were both adults, and it's not like you lied to him. You don't have anything to be ashamed of."

"But I didn't wanna lie to *you*," I say, voice thick. This is the hardest part. The part I practised saying over and over in the car. "Imagine being in a relationship, and the only place I can have sex is in the middle of the damn woods—" It sounds stupid, even as I say it. I push on: "—and it's never good for me, and I can never tell you why. How long would you have stuck around? Not dating you...it meant I could still have you as a friend."

"We could have made it work."

"You think so?"

"Sure. Or you could have just told me. I would have...it wouldn't have been..."

"Even if you knew, and you were cool with it, how long

before one of us made a mistake? Or both of us? And then Tanner..."

"She wouldn't have had to know!"

"And if she found out? Shit, even just *being* together, as a couple...it would have put you in danger. I put *Travis* in danger—I really liked him, he was a good guy, and I never gave him a single clue about what he was getting into. You know how many sleepless nights I had afterwards? Wondering if Tanner had found out somehow, and was about to...to do something to him?"

"But she didn't find out. "

"No. But in a longer relationship...I couldn't do that to you, or lie about it. I wouldn't let you get hurt because of me. And I'm not sorry for that."

His hands are still, the ring forgotten.

"I didn't know any other way," I say. "If there'd been another option, I would have taken it in a second, but I am *not* sorry for keeping you safe. I would rather...I would rather have us never see each other again, and have you still be walking around and living your life, than risk you getting hurt. Even if I had to keep things from you. When we came to your apartment, back when the whole shit happened, I only did it because I felt like there was no other way."

The patch of sunlight has crept up his body, moving across his neck. And after a few moments he reaches out and takes my hand. His skin is very slightly rough and dry despite the heat in the apartment.

I hold his gaze, suddenly aware of how close we are. His hand on mine, our knees just touching.

For a second that old fear is back. The fear I felt that first time with Travis. The fear that I'm going to *get this wrong*, somehow—that I'm going to put someone else in danger.

But what do I—what do *we*—have to be scared of? Tanner isn't going to hurt us. We have no more secrets from each other. There's just us, and the sunlight.

I lean forward, put a hand on the back of his head and kiss him.

There's a second where I think he isn't going to respond. Then, very slowly, his lips part, our tongues just touching. Hesitant at first, soft and slow, but then pushing harder, tasting each other.

He wraps an arm around me, pulling me close. Our kiss grows deeper, quicker. His hand rests on the back of my neck, caressing, stroking. I'm hot, sweating lightly under my clothes.

It's happening. This is happening. Right now. His other hand is on my back, and I guide it under my shirt, relishing the touch of his skin on my side. We separate for a second, my breath coming in short, desperate gasps. His mouth moves to my neck, my ear. Under his jeans he is rock-hard. I fumble at his zipper, almost panting, his hand moving higher on my back…

He stops. Goes still.

"Nic?"

And just like that, he pulls away.

"Wha—" I'm still in the position I was, leaning in towards him, up on one knee.

He sits for a second, breathing hard, not looking at me. Then slowly he gets to his feet, the slash of sunlight arcing across his body. He glances back, and the look on his face… it's like he's made a terrible mistake, and he knows it, wishes he could take it back.

I scramble to my feet, reaching for him. "Hey. It's OK. I'm here, just—"

But he turns away. Laces his hands on the back of his head. Leaves me standing, still reaching out for him.

No. Fuck you, no. You are not doing this.

I take a step towards him, and he shakes his head. He still won't look at me. Under his shirt, his shoulders rise and fall.

Somehow my mouth forms words. "I don't understand."

He tilts his head back, hands still laced above his collar. The sound he makes—half groan, half angry snarl—is the worst thing I've ever heard.

I put a hand on his shoulder. "*Please*, Nic. Just…just talk to me, OK? We can work this out."

Gently, so very gently, he lifts my hand away.

My mouth is as dry as a desert. This has got to be a mistake—he's overthinking it, that's all. I've just got to talk to him. "Nic, don't you get it? We can be with each other. Tanner's cool with it. Isn't this what you wanted?" My eyes go wide. "If it's the PK thing, where stuff moves when I—"

"It's not that," he says quietly.

"Then *what*?"

"I'm just…I'm not ready."

"Why?"

"Because…"

"What are you not ready for?" I didn't think I was angry. Turns out, it was right there all along. It's starting to show itself, edging my voice. "I was…I was *straight* with you. I told you everything. There's nothing you don't know about me."

"That's not the problem."

"What is the problem? Help me understand this."

Another frustrated groan-growl, his shoulders slumping. "Why you gotta make this so hard?"

"*I'm* making it hard?" Tears prick the corners of my eyes. I tell them to stay the fuck away. I move towards Nic, put my hands on his waist. "Nic, please. Don't do this. Let's just sit down and…"

Once more he removes my hands. This time he holds them tight.

"Why?" Desperation edges my voice.

"Because of what you do. For a living."

Behind us, the fridge compressor kicks on, a low buzz filling the room.

"Teagan, you work for the government. Your job is... insane. I'm not just talking about the moving-things-with-your-mind shit. I'm talking about... everything else. I don't want to spend my time waiting for a call that says you're in jail, or in hospital, or..."

"It's not like that."

"Isn't it? Last I checked, you threw yourself off a skyscraper."

"That wasn't a normal job!"

"Doesn't matter. Do you understand what it would be like to worry that way? Every unknown number, every text message, every time you go on a mission. It'd be like being with a cop, only a million times worse."

I lower my head, trying to contain my frustration. "People date cops, don't they?"

"Maybe. But I'm not sure I want to be one of those people."

"Bullshit." Now I really am angry. "You do dangerous shit all the time. You surf big waves, you rock-climb, you—"

"The only person I'm putting in danger is myself," he says. "And I don't just go out whenever. I check the weather reports, the swells, all of it. I make sure I have the right gear. I control as much as I can, because then I can enjoy the risk. With this, *everything* would be out of my control. I need you to understand what that would be like: spending all my time worrying. Never able to help. I *do* want to be with you... but it's not a good idea."

"But I love you."

It slips out of me before I can stop it. Then again, why would I want to? I love Nic, I want him and I can't believe he's being so pigheaded as to—

"I don't love you," he says.

The silence that follows feels like the end of the world.

"But before," I say. "When I came home late after the Edmonds job, you said..."

"I said I wanted to date you. I didn't say I was in love with you."

He's still got hold of my hand, and he grips it tighter, making my eyes meet his. "I know what it sounds like," he says. "And I swear to God, Teags, I'm not saying this to be cruel. I'd never do that to you."

"Then why? What *are* you doing?"

"I'm trying to tell you the truth." His voice is quiet. Firm. "Every bit of it. Love is...it's not something that happens like that." He snaps his fingers. "Or hardly ever. It takes time. And it has to override everything. If I really did love you, then it wouldn't matter that you had these abilities or that you worked for Tanner or any of it. But even with Marissa it wasn't like that. We dated for two years. I honestly thought I was in love with her. But it...When she wanted to move, I realised that wasn't true. It wasn't true for her, and it wasn't true for me."

"It could be true for us!"

"Maybe." He looks away. "But it isn't like that now. I don't control what I feel, and I don't want to lie to you about it."

This isn't fair. After everything I went through, after all the fires and the explosions and death and nearly being flown off to a black site, I thought it would be different. I thought he'd want me as much as I wanted him.

"Listen to me." I force my voice to stay steady. I'm not letting this happen—not after I nearly died. "Why don't we just...try? It doesn't have to be perfect. I don't care if it isn't, as long as it's you."

There's a moment where I think he's going to relent. That he'll take me in his arms and we'll pick up where we left off, and everything will be fine.

"I'm sorry," he says.

He leans forward, plants a soft kiss on my cheek.

Then he's gone.

I sit on the couch. Staring at nothing. After the longest time I realise that my face is wet. I don't know when I started crying— maybe it even happened while I was speaking to Nic. This time I let the tears come, let the past two weeks, two years, two *decades* just pour out of me. Tears fall into my lap, the sunlight turning them to glittering jewels.

I want to throw something. Everything. Just smash and smash and smash until this entire apartment and city and the whole fucking world is dust.

I don't.

After what feels like a century, the tears finally stop. I lie down on the couch, arms wrapped around a cushion. When I wake up, the sunlight has got longer, softer, climbing up the kitchen wall.

Nic's words are still in my mind. His words, his face. *I don't love you.* But this time the anger doesn't come. It's drained out of me.

I don't hate Nic. I want to, for what he did—for how he turned me down. I hate what he said, hate it with every atom of my being...

But that doesn't stop it being true.

I could fight it. I could cry, beg, scream, tell him he's being an asshole. But he's not. And doing any of that...treating him like that...would be the worst thing of all.

I'm allowed to live my life. Just like he's allowed to live his.
I can't force him to feel something he doesn't. And if we had
slept together, it wouldn't have changed the way he felt. In a
way that might have been worse; seeing what we could have
been and then having him turn away.

His hand on my back, his lips, his skin touching mine…

I've never felt so alone. Carlos betrayed me. Nic left me.
There's no one else.

Except… that's not true, is it?

There's Annie.

And Reggie. And Paul.

China Shop.

I never thought of them as friends. They were people who'd
been forced to work with me, all of us conscripted in a war
against Tanner's shadow enemy. But that's changed. They've
got my back. I've got theirs.

And I have more than that. I have music, and food. I have
the Batmobile. I have Los Angeles, an entire city to explore,
a place that still hasn't given up its secrets.

I don't know what I'm going to do about Nic leaving. He
can't cut me out of his life completely—if he wanted to, he
would have said so. I'll find a way to convince him that we
can be together. He needs space and time—maybe I do too. I
don't know how I'm going to make him fall in love with me,
but I'll figure it out. And there are plenty of things to do in
the meantime. Like take out bad guys. Fuck with those who
deserve to be fucked with.

As jobs go, it's pretty good.

But that's for later. The evening stretches ahead of me. A
baking summer night in Los Angeles, with nothing to do and
nowhere to be.

First I'm going to clean my place. Get some of the dust off.

I'll put a record on—something calming, De La Soul maybe. No, some soul. Aretha. Isaac. Earth, Wind & Fire. Then I'll make breakfast—yes, you can have breakfast at 5 p.m. Or at least I can. I'll have to check my food situation—I'm pretty sure whatever is in my fridge has spoiled, but I might get lucky. And if not, it'll give me an excuse to run down to the Brooklyn Deli on Crenshaw, get a smoothie and a pastrami sandwich...

I stand. My feet are unsteady, so unsteady that I almost sit right back down. Almost. I take a deep breath, then another.

I'll be fine. After all, I have superpowers. I survived a fall from the top of a skyscraper with no parachute. I can sure as hell survive this.

As long as I have some breakfast inside me.

FIFTY-NINE

Harry

The man known as Harry watches Nic Delacourt leave the house of the woman who calls herself Teagan Frost.

When she'd crashed into him as he rattled past her house at four in the morning, he'd thought for a horrible moment that she was going to see who he really was. She didn't. And even though she was gone for a couple of weeks, she's returned to the little house on Roxton Avenue, like he knew she would.

The only person in this entire city who doesn't look through him, who acknowledges him...and it has to be her.

He'd been worried, early on, that someone would try to have him moved—arrested, taken to a shelter, Lord knows what else. But he smiles at everyone, doesn't leave a trail of litter behind him and sometimes helps out by watering the jacarandas with an old paint pot he takes to a nearby public tap.

He's had to be so careful. He's taken great pains to hide his face, growing the massive beard, letting his fringe hang down, always dropping his head. He changed how he walked, made sure never to speak, never looked her in the eye. He's older. His body and face have filled out. Nobody minds him. And it certainly helps that he can come and go at odd hours, that nobody ever questions the sound of his tinkling, clattering shopping cart at three in the morning.

After all, he doesn't need to sleep.

He pushes his cart down Roxton, shredded shoes smacking against the tarmac. One of them has almost disintegrated, the upper held in place by a dirty flap of duct tape. He hates it, wishes he could buy new shoes—a pair of boots, thick and strong and warm. He has plenty of money, hidden in greasy rolls in the innermost bottles in his cart. But he can't. He is a homeless man now, that is what he is and what he does, and She wouldn't let him anyway. There's no point even asking.

And he has to do what She says, even if his feet hurt, and his skin burns, and the scars on his back from the fire itch and itch and itch.

At the corner of Roxton and Dublin there's a school—one which the students and teachers have long since abandoned for the summer. Its brick facade bakes in the afternoon sun, the windows dusty. The man known as Harry wrestles his cart up the quiet walkway until he's out of sight of the street, in the shade of a stone archway leading to the school's inner courtyard. Once he's there he digs deep inside his cart, fingers pushing through familiar territory, and pulls out a cellphone.

It's a special phone. A black slab, sleek and strong. It has only one number stored in it. He turns it on, waits for it to boot up, taps the lone icon in the middle of the screen.

She answers on the second ring. "Adam."

"She's back," he says. It's all he dares to say.

"And does she know?"

He must be very careful. Very, very careful. He must be sure. He thinks back to everything he's observed, all the information he's gathered. He cannot get this wrong, or She will be very, very angry.

"Adam," Chloe says, impatient.

He finds himself glancing back in the direction of the house. The house he's watched for over a year now.

"No," he hears himself say. "She doesn't know."

The story continues in...

R ANDOM SH★T FLYING THROUGH THE AIR

ACKNOWLEDGEMENTS

Hey. Teagan here.

Jackson Ford has a bunch of people to thank, and given that he's never going to get around to writing this himself, I figured I'd do it. Let's be honest, it's not like he's much of a writer anyway. Did you *see* what he did to me back on page 400?

Besides, I figure these things are like the long-ass credit lists in album liner notes. Nobody reads those things. Nobody has *ever* read those things. So if I fuck it up, nobody will know.

Here goes.

The first draft of this book was a disaster. Anna Jackson helped knock it into shape, with an assist from James Long and Bradley Englert. Without them, I never get a story. Also, they did things like remove the shotgun-toting unicorn that Jackson inserted on page 206, when he couldn't figure out how to have us escape the cops. I mean, I *like* unicorns, but you can't just drop them in when you need an escape for your heroes. You know what I mean?

Also, big up to Ed Wilson, Jackson's agent, who keeps J in vanilla ice cream and Celine Dion albums. Jackson once told me this story about Ed—he has a nifty pair of pants with a pattern of little dogs on them. He wears them out at publishing events, apparently.

(Wait a second. Ed's English, and in the UK, "pants" are actually underwear, not trousers. Did I just accuse Jackson's literary agent of having dog-patterned underwear? Fuck it, I'm running with it. Ed, you and your dog underwear are amazing.)

All of Jackson's hilarious spelling mistakes and continuity errors were corrected by Hugh Davis, who did a really good job. Mostly. Because... OK, look, dude, seriously, correcting the word "dumpster" to "skip" so it "doesn't confuse British audiences" is ridiculous. Like I give a shit! (I kid—thanks, man.)

Emily Courdelle and Steve Panton nailed the cover—I mean, look at it. Frame it. Put it on a billboard (no, seriously, put it on a billboard, somebody, we need the sales).

This book was published by Orbit, and some pretty rad human beings work there. Way more talented than Jackson. Tim Holman, Joanna Kramer, Madeleine Hall and the tireless Ellen Wright all deserve special mention. Nazia Khatun deserves special special mention, because if I don't give it to her she'll kill both me and Jackson. She's *vicious*, people.

In the process of writing this book, Jackson consulted a couple of accomplished geneticists: Prof. Marcia MacDonald, and Prof. Simon Warby. They gave him great information, and he proceeded to fuck it up beyond all recognition. He assures me that it was on purpose, for the story, but I just think he's an idiot. Anyway, Marcia and Simon were a huge help, and none of the many, many errors in this book are their fault.

The incredible Alisha Grauso fact-checked Jackson's Los Angeles. She knows way more than he does. I'm not even sure

Jackson could find LA on a map.

Perry Lo helped out with information on fibre networks and IT systems. He also made the mistake of teaching Jackson to play mahjong, with the result that J spent all of his book advance money in a gambling hall somewhere. Perry's a great teacher but J's a shitty student.

And big up to Nicole Simpson, George Kelly, Chris Ellis, Dane Taylor, Rayne Taylor, Ida Horwitz, Ryan Beyer, Werner Schutz, Taryn Arentsen Schutz and Kristine Kalnina. They read the early drafts, and gave some great feedback. Jackson ignored most of it, because of course he did.

Pretty sure I forgot some people. Whatever. I'm not even getting paid for this. I'm out.

extras

orbit

meet the author

Jackson Ford has written sixteen bestselling novels, all of which have been translated into multiple languages. Apparently this made him think he could write a book about Los Angeles, despite the fact that he has never been there, and had to rely on other people to fill in the gaps. Then again, what did you expect from a guy who thinks Celine Dion actually made good music, and genuinely enjoys plain vanilla ice cream? He is the creator of the Frost Files, and the character of Teagan Frost— who, by the way, absolutely did not write this bio, and anybody who says she did is a liar.

Find out more about Jackson Ford and other Orbit authors by registering for the free monthly newsletter at www.orbitbooks.net.

If you enjoyed
THE GIRL WHO COULD MOVE SH*T WITH HER MIND

look out for

VELOCITY WEAPON
The Protectorate: Book One

by

Megan E. O'Keefe

Dazzling space battles, intergalactic politics, and rogue AI collide in Velocity Weapon, *the first book in this epic space opera by award-winning author Megan O'Keefe.*

Sanda and Biran Greeve were siblings destined for greatness. A high-flying sergeant, Sanda has the skills to take down any enemy combatant. Biran is a savvy politician who aims to use his new political position to prevent conflict from escalating to total destruction.

However, on a routine maneuver, Sanda loses consciousness when her gunship is blown out of the sky. Instead of finding herself in friendly hands, she awakens 230 years later on a deserted enemy warship controlled by an AI who calls himself Bero. The war is lost. The star system is dead. Ada Prime and its rival Icarion have wiped each other from the universe.

Now, separated by time and space, Sanda and Biran must fight to put things right.

CHAPTER ONE

THE AFTERMATH OF THE BATTLE OF DRALEE

The first thing Sanda did after being resuscitated was vomit all over herself. The second thing she did was to vomit all over again. Her body shook, trembling with the remembered deceleration of her gunship breaking apart around her, stomach roiling as the preservation foam had encased her, shoved itself down her throat and nose and any other ready orifice. Her teeth jarred together, her fingers fumbled with temporary palsy against the foam stuck to her face.

Dios, she hoped the shaking was temporary. They told you this kind of thing happened in training, that the trembling would subside and the "explosive evacuation" cease. But it was a whole hell of a lot different to be shaking yourself senseless while emptying every drop of liquid from your body than to be looking at a cartoonish diagram with friendly letters claiming *Mild Gastrointestinal Discomfort*.

It wasn't foam covering her. She scrubbed, mind numb from coldsleep, struggling to figure out what encased her. It was slimy and goopy and—oh no. Sanda cracked a hesitant eyelid and peeked at her fingers. Thick, clear jelly with a slight bluish tinge coated her hands. The stuff was cold, making her trembling worse, and with a sinking gut she realized what it was. She'd joked about the stuff, in training with her fellow gunshippers. Snail snot. Gelatinous splooge. But its real name was MedAssist Incubatory NutriBath, and you only got dunked in it if you needed intensive care with a capital *I*.

"Fuck," she tried to say, but her throat rasped on unfamiliar air. How long had she been in here? Sanda opened both eyes, ignoring the cold gel running into them. She lay in a white enameled cocoon, the lid removed to reveal a matching white ceiling inset with true-white bulbs. The brightness made her blink.

The NutriBath was draining, and now that her chest was exposed to air, the shaking redoubled. Gritting her teeth against the spasms, she felt around the cocoon, searching for a handhold.

"Hey, medis," she called, then hacked up a lump of gel. "Got a live one in here!"

No response. Assholes were probably waiting to see if she could get out under her own power. Could she? She didn't remember being injured in the battle. But the medis didn't stick you in a bath for a laugh. She gave up her search for handholds and fumbled trembling hands over her body, seeking scars. The baths were good, but they wouldn't have left a gunnery sergeant like her in the tub long enough to fix cosmetic damage. The gunk was only slightly less expensive than training a new gunner.

Her face felt whole, chest and shoulders smaller than she remembered but otherwise unharmed. She tried to crane her neck to see down her body, but the unused muscles screamed in protest.

"Can I get some help over here?" she called out, voice firmer now she'd cleared it of the gel. Still no answer. Sucking down a few sharp breaths to steel herself against the ache, she groaned and lifted her torso up on her elbows until she sat straight, legs splayed out before her.

Most of her legs, anyway.

Sanda stared, trying to make her coldsleep-dragging brain catch up with what she saw. Her left leg was whole, if covered in disturbing wrinkles, but her right... That ended just above the place where her knee should have been. Tentatively, she reached down, brushed her shaking fingers over the thick lump of flesh at the end of her leg.

She remembered. A coil fired by an Icarion railgun had smashed through the pilot's deck, slamming a nav panel straight into her legs. The evac pod chair she'd been strapped into had immediately deployed preserving foam—encasing her, and her smashed leg, for Ada Prime scoopers to pluck out of space after the chaos of the Battle of Dralee faded. She picked at her puckered skin, stunned. Remembered pain vibrated through her body and she clenched her jaw. Some of that cold she'd felt upon awakening must have been leftover shock from the injury, her body frozen in a moment of panic.

Any second now, she expected the pain of the incident to mount, to catch up with her and punish her for putting it off so long. It didn't. The NutriBath had done a better job than she'd thought possible. Only mild tremors shook her.

"Hey," she said, no longer caring that her voice cracked. She gripped either side of her open cocoon. "Can I get some fucking help?"

Silence answered. Choking down a stream of expletives that would have gotten her court-martialed, Sanda scraped some of the gunk on her hands off on the edges of the cocoon's walls and adjusted her grip. Screaming with the effort, she heaved herself to standing within the bath, balancing precariously on her single leg, arms trembling under her weight.

The medibay was empty.

"Seriously?" she asked the empty room.

The rest of the medibay was just as stark white as her cocoon and the ceiling, its walls pocked with panels blinking all sorts of readouts she didn't understand the half of. Everything in the bay was stowed, the drawers latched shut, the gurneys folded down and strapped to the walls. It looked ready for storage, except for her cocoon sitting in the center of the room, dripping NutriBath and vomit all over the floor.

"Naked wet girl in here!" she yelled at the top of her sore voice. Echoes bounced around her, but no one answered. "For fuck's sake."

Not willing to spend god-knew-how-long marinating in a stew of her own body's waste, Sanda clenched her jaw and attempted to swing her leg over the edge of the bath. She tipped over and flopped face-first to the ground instead.

"Ow."

She spat blood and picked up her spinning head. Still no response. Who was running this bucket, anyway? The medibay looked clean enough, but there wasn't a single Ada Prime logo anywhere. She hadn't realized she'd miss those stylized dual bodies with their orbital spin lines wrapped around them until this moment.

Calling upon half-remembered training from her boot camp days, Sanda army crawled her way across the floor to a long drawer. By the time she reached it, she was panting hard, but pure anger drove her forward. Whoever had come up with the bright idea to wake her without a medi on standby needed a good, solid slap upside the head. She may have been down to one leg, but Sanda was pretty certain she could make do with two fists.

She yanked the drawer open and hefted herself up high enough to see inside. No crutches, but she found an extending pole for an IV drip. That'd have to do. She levered herself upright and stood a moment, back pressed against the wall, getting her breath. The hard metal of the stand bit into her armpit, but she didn't care. She was on her feet again. Or foot, at least. Time to go find a medi to chew out.

The caster wheels on the bottom of the pole squeaked as she made her way across the medibay. The door dilated with a satisfying swish, and even the stale recycled air of the empty corridor smelled fresh compared to the nutri-mess she'd been swimming in. She paused and considered going back to find a robe. Ah, to hell with it.

She shuffled out into the hall, picked a likely direction toward the pilot's deck, and froze. The door swished shut beside her, revealing a logo she knew all too well: a single planet, fiery wings encircling it.

Icarion.

She was on an enemy ship. With one leg.

Naked.

Sanda ducked back into the medibay and scurried to the panel-spotted wall, silently cursing each squeak of the IV stand's wheels. She had to find a comms link, and fast.

Gel-covered fingers slipped on the touchscreen as she tried to navigate unfamiliar protocols. Panic constricted her throat, but she forced herself to breathe deep, to keep her cool. She captained a gunship. This was nothing.

Half expecting alarms to blare, she slapped the icon for the ship's squawk box and hesitated. What in the hell was she supposed to broadcast? They hadn't exactly covered codes for "help I'm naked and legless on an Icarion bucket" during training. She bit her lip and punched in her own call sign—1947—followed by 7500, the universal sign for a hijacking. If she were lucky, they'd get the hint: 1947 had been hijacked. Made sense, right?

She slapped send.

"Good morning, one-niner-four-seven. I've been waiting for you to wake up," a male voice said from the walls all around her. She jumped and almost lost her balance.

"Who am I addressing?" She forced authority into her voice even though she felt like diving straight back into her cocoon.

"This is AI-Class Cruiser Bravo-India-Six-One-Mike."

AI-Class? A smartship? Sanda suppressed a grin, knowing the ship could see her. Smartships were outside Ada Prime's tech range, but she'd studied them inside and out during training. While they were brighter than humans across the board, they still had human follies. Could still be lied to. Charmed, even.

"Well, it's a pleasure to meet you, Cruiser. My name's Sanda Greeve."

"I am called *The Light of Berossus*," the voice said.

Of course he was. Damned Icarions never stuck to simple call signs. They always had to posh things up by naming their ships after ancient scientists. She nodded, trying to keep an easy smile on while she glanced sideways at the door. Could the ship's crew hear her? They hadn't heard her yelling earlier, but they might notice their ship talking to someone new.

"That's quite the mouthful for friendly conversation."

"Bero is an acceptable alternative."

"You got it, Bero. Say, could you do me a favor? How many souls on board at the present?"

Her grip tightened on the IV stand, and she looked around for any other item she could use as a weapon. This was a smartship. Surely they wouldn't allow the crew handblasters for fear of poking holes in their pretty ship. All she needed was a bottleneck, a place to hunker down and wait until Ada Prime caught her squawk and figured out what was up.

"One soul on board," Bero said.

"What? That can't be right."

"There is one soul on board." The ship sounded amused with her exasperation at first listen, but there was something in the ship's voice that nagged at her. Something... tight. Could AI ships even slip like that? It seemed to her that something with that big of a brain would only use the tone it absolutely wanted to.

"In the medibay, yes, but the rest of the ship? How many?"

"One."

She licked her lips, heart hammering in her ears. She turned back to the control panel she'd sent the squawk from and pulled up the ship's nav system. She couldn't make changes from the bay unless she had override commands, but... The whole thing was on autopilot. If she really was the only one on board... Maybe she could convince the ship to return her to Ada Prime. Handing a smartship over to her superiors would win her accolades enough to last a lifetime. Could even win her a fresh new leg.

"Bero, bring up a map of the local system, please. Light up any ports in range."

A pause. "Bero?"

"Are you sure, Sergeant Greeve?"

Unease threaded through her. "Call me Sanda, and yes, light her up for me."

The icons for the control systems wiped away, replaced with a 3-D model of the nearby system. She blinked, wondering if she still had goop in her eyes. Couldn't be right. There they were, a glowing dot in the endless black, the asteroid belt that stood between Ada Prime and Icarion clear as starlight. Judging by the coordinates displayed above the ship's avatar, she should be able to see Ada Prime. They were near the battlefield of Dralee, and although there was a whole lot of space between the celestial bodies, Dralee was the closest in the system to Ada. That's why she'd been patrolling it.

"Bero, is your display damaged?"

"No, Sanda."

She swallowed. Icarion couldn't have...wouldn't have. They wanted the dwarf planet. Needed access to Ada Prime's Casimir Gate.

"Bero. Where is Ada Prime in this simulation?" She pinched the screen, zooming out. The system's star, Cronus, spun off in the distance, brilliant and yellow-white. Icarion had vanished, too.

"Bero!"

"Icarion initiated the Fibon Protocol after the Battle of Dralee. The results were larger than expected."

The display changed, drawing back. Icarion and Ada Prime reappeared, their orbits aligning one of the two times out of the year they passed each other. Somewhere between them, among the asteroid belt, a black wave began, reaching outward, consuming space in all directions. Asteroids vanished. Icarion vanished. Ada Prime vanished.

She dropped her head against the display. Let the goop run down from her hair, the cold glass against her skin scarcely registering. Numbness suffused her. No wonder Bero was empty. He must have been ported outside the destruction. He was a smartship. He wouldn't have needed human input to figure out what had happened.

"How long?" she asked, mind racing despite the slowness of coldsleep. Shock had grabbed her by the shoulders and shaken her fully awake. Grief she could dwell on later, now she had a problem to work. Maybe there were others, like her, on the edge of the wreckage. Other evac pods drifting through the black. Outposts in the belt.

There'd been ports, hideouts. They'd starve without supplies from either Ada Prime or Icarion, but that'd take a whole lot of time. With a smartship, she could scoop them up. Get them all to one of the other nearby habitable systems before the ship's drive gave out. And if she were very lucky...Hope dared to swell in her chest. Her brother and fathers were resourceful people. Surely her dad Graham would have had some advance warning. That man always had his ear to the ground, his nose deep in rumor networks. If anyone could ride out that attack, it was them.

"It has been two hundred thirty years since the Battle of Dralee."

if you enjoyed

THE GIRL WHO COULD MOVE SH*T WITH HER MIND

look out for

A BIG SHIP AT THE EDGE OF THE UNIVERSE

The Salvagers

by

Alex White

Firefly *meets* The Fast and the Furious *in this science fiction adventure series that follows a crew of outcasts as they try to find a legendary ship that just might be the key to saving the universe.*

A washed-up treasure hunter, a hotshot racer, and a deadly secret society.

They're all on a race against time to hunt down the greatest warship ever built. Some think the ship is lost forever, some think it's been destroyed, and some think it's only a legend, but one thing's for certain: whoever finds it will hold the fate of the universe in their hands. And treasure that valuable can never stay hidden for long....

CHAPTER ONE

D.N.F.

The straight opened before the two race cars: an oily river, speckled yellow by the evening sun. They shot down the tarmac in succession like sapphire fish, streamers of wild magic billowing from their exhausts. They roared toward the turn, precision movements bringing them within centimeters of one another.

The following car veered to the inside. The leader attempted the same.

Their tires only touched for a moment. They interlocked, and sheer torque threw the leader into the air. Jagged chunks of duraplast glittered in the dusk as the follower's car passed underneath, unharmed but for a fractured front wing. The lead race car came down hard, twisting eruptions of elemental magic spewing from its wounded power unit. One of its tires exploded into a hail of spinning cords, whipping the road.

In the background, the other blue car slipped away down the chicane—Nilah's car.

The replay lost focus and reset.

The crash played out again and again on the holoprojection in front of them, and Nilah Brio tried not to sigh. She had seen plenty of wrecks before and caused more than her share of them.

"Crashes happen," she said.

"Not when the cars are on the same bloody team, Nilah!"

Claire Asby, the Lang Autosport team principal, stood at her mahogany desk, hands folded behind her back. The office looked less like the sort of ultramodern workspace Nilah had seen on other teams and more like one of the mansions of Origin, replete with antique furniture, incandescent lighting, stuffed big-game heads (which Nilah hated), and gargantuan landscapes from planets she had never seen. She supposed the decor favored a pale woman like Claire, but it did nothing for Nilah's dark brown complexion. The office didn't have any of the bright, human-centric design and ergonomic beauty of her home, but team bosses had to be forgiven their eccentricities—especially when that boss had led them to as many victories as Claire had.

Her teammate, Kristof Kater, chuckled and rocked back on his heels. Nilah rolled her eyes at the pretty boy's pleasure. They should've been checking in with the pit crews, not wasting precious time at a last-minute dressing down.

The cars hovering over Claire's desk reset and moved through their slow-motion calamity. Claire had already made them watch the footage a few dozen times after the incident: Nilah's car dove for the inside and Kristof moved to block. The incident had cost her half her front wing, but Kristof's track weekend had ended right there.

"I want you both to run a clean race today. I am begging you to bring those cars home intact at all costs."

Nilah shrugged and smiled. "That'll be fine, provided Kristof follows a decent racing line."

"We were racing! I made a legal play and the stewards sided with me!"

Nilah loved riling him up; it was far too easy. "You were slow, and you got what you deserved: a broken axle and a bucket of tears. I got a five-second penalty"—she winked before continuing—"which cut into my thirty-three-second win considerably."

Claire rubbed the bridge of her nose. "Please stop acting like children. Just get out there and do your jobs."

Nilah held back another jab; it wouldn't do to piss off the team boss right before a drive. Her job was to win races, not meetings. Silently she and Kristof made their way to the door, and he flung it open in a rare display of petulance. She hadn't seen him so angry in months, and she reveled in it. After all, a frazzled teammate posed no threat to her championship standings.

They made their way through the halls from Claire's exotic wood paneling to the bright white and anodized blues of Lang Autosport's portable palace. Crew and support staff rushed to and fro, barely acknowledging the racers as they moved through the crowds. Kristof was stopped by his sports psychologist, and Nilah muscled past them both as she stepped out into the dry heat of Gantry Station's Galica Speedway.

Nilah had fired her own psychologist when she'd taken the lead in this year's Driver's Crown.

She crossed onto the busy parking lot, surrounded by the bustle of scooter bots and crews from a dozen teams. The bracing rattle of air hammers and the roar of distant crowds in the grandstands were all the therapy she'd need to win. The Driver's Crown was so close—she could clinch it in two races, especially if Kristof went flying off the track again.

"Do you think this is a game?" Claire's voice startled her. She'd come jogging up from behind, a dozen infograms swimming around her head, blinking with reports on track conditions and pit strategy.

"Do I think racing is a game? I believe that's the very definition of sport."

Claire's vinegar scowl was considerably less entertaining than Kristof's anger. Nilah had been racing for Claire since the junior leagues. She'd probably spent more of her teenage years with her principal than her own parents. She didn't want to disappoint Claire, but she wouldn't be cowed, either. In truth, the incident galled her—the crash was nothing more than a callow attempt by Kristof to hold her off for another lap. If she'd lost the podium, she would've called for his head, but he got what he deserved.

They were a dysfunctional family. Nilah and Kristof had been racing together since childhood, and she could remember plenty of happy days trackside with him. She'd been ecstatic when they both joined Lang; it felt like a sign that they were destined to win.

But there could be only one Driver's Crown, and they'd learned the hard way the word "team" meant nothing among the strongest drivers in the Pan-Galactic Racing Federation. Her friendship with Kristof was long dead. At least her fondness for Claire had survived the transition.

"If you play dirty with him today, I'll have no choice but to create some consequences," said Claire, struggling to keep up with Nilah in heels.

Oh, please. Nilah rounded the corner of the pit lane and marched straight through the center of the racing complex, past the offices of the race director and news teams. She glanced back at Claire who, for all her posturing, couldn't hide her worry.

"I never play dirty. I win because I'm better," said Nilah. "I'm not sure what your problem is."

"That's not the point. You watch for him today, and mind yourself. This isn't any old track."

Nilah got to the pit wall and pushed through the gate onto the starting grid. The familiar grip of race-graded asphalt on her shoes sent a spark of pleasure up her spine. "Oh, I know all about Galica."

The track sprawled before Nilah: a classic, a legend, a warrior's track that had tested the mettle of racers for a hundred years. It showed its age in the narrow roadways, rendering overtaking difficult and resulting in wrecks and safety cars—and increased race time. Because of its starside position on Gantry Station, ambient temperatures could turn sweltering. Those factors together meant she'd spend the next two hours slow-roasting in her cockpit at three hundred kilometers per hour, making thousands of split-second, high-stakes decisions.

This year brought a new third sector with more intricate corners and a tricky elevation change. It was an unopened present, a new toy to play with. Nilah longed to be on the grid already.

If she took the podium here, the rest of the season would be an easy downhill battle. There were a few more races, but the smart money knew this was the only one that mattered. The harmonic chimes of StarSport FN's jingle filled the stadium, the unofficial sign that the race was about to get underway.

She headed for the cockpit of her pearlescent-blue car. Claire fell in behind her, rattling off some figures about Nilah's chances that were supposed to scare her into behaving.

"Remember your contract," said Claire as the pit crew boosted Nilah into her car. "Do what you must to take gold, but any scratch you put on Kristof is going to take a million off your check. I mean it this time."

"Good thing I'm getting twenty mil more than him, then. More scratches for me!" Nilah pulled on her helmet. "You keep Kristof out of my way, and I'll keep his precious car intact."

She flipped down her visor and traced her mechanist's mark across the confined space, whispering light flowing from her fingertips. Once her spell cemented in place, she wrapped her fingers around the wheel. The system read out the stats of her sigil: good V's, not great on the Xi, but a healthy cast.

Her magic flowed into the car, sliding around the finely tuned ports, wending through channels to latch onto gears. Through the power of her mechanist's mark, she felt the grip of the tires and spring of the rods as though they were her own legs and feet. She joined with the central computer of her car, gaining psychic access to radio, actuation, and telemetry. The Lang Hyper 8, a motorsport classic, had achieved phenomenal performance all season in Nilah's hands.

Her psychic connection to the computer stabilized, and she searched the radio channels for her engineer, Ash. They ran through the checklist: power, fuel flow, sigil circuits, eidolon core. Nilah felt through each part with her magic, ensuring all functioned properly. Finally, she landed on the clunky Arclight Booster.

It was an awful little PGRF-required piece of tech, with high output but terrible efficiency. Nilah's mechanist side absolutely despised the magic-belching beast. It was as ugly and inelegant as it was expensive. Some fans claimed to like the little light show when it boosted drivers up the straights, but it was less than perfect, and anything less than perfect had to go.

"Let's start her up, Nilah."

"Roger that."

Every time that car thrummed to life, Nilah fell in love all over again. She adored the Hyper 8 in spite of the stonking flaw on his backside. Her grip tightened about the wheel and she took a deep breath.

The lights signaled a formation lap and the cars took off, weaving across the tarmac to keep the heat in their tires. They slipped around the track in slow motion, and Nilah's eyes traveled the third sector. She would crush this new track design. At the end of the formation lap, she pulled into her grid space, the scents of hot rubber and oil smoke sweet in her nose.

Game time.

The pole's leftmost set of lights came on: five seconds until the last light.

Three cars ahead of her, eighteen behind: Kristof in first, then the two Makina drivers, Bonnie and Jin. Nilah stared down the Makina R-27s, their metallic livery a blazing crimson.

The next pair of lights ignited: four seconds.

The other drivers revved their engines, feeling the tuning of their cars. Nilah echoed their rumbling engines with a shout of her own and gave a heated sigh, savoring the fire in her belly.

Three seconds.

Don't think. Just see.

The last light came on, signaling the director was ready to start the race.

Now, it was all about reflexes. All the engines fell to near silence.

One second.

The lights clicked off.

Banshee wails filled the air as the cars' power units screamed to life. Nilah roared forward, her eyes darting over the competition. Who was it going to be? Bonnie lagged by just a hair, and Jin made a picture-perfect launch, surging up beside Kristof. Nilah wanted to make a dive for it but found herself forced in behind the two lead drivers.

They shot down the straight toward turn one, a double apex. Turn one was always the most dangerous, because the idiots fighting for the inside were most likely to brake too late. She swept out for a perfect parabola, hoping not to see some fool about to crash into her.

The back of the pack was brought up by slow, pathetic Cyril Clowe. He would be her barometer of race success. If she could lap him in a third of the race, it would be a perfect run.

"Tell race control I'm lapping Clowe in twenty-five," Nilah grunted, straining against the g-force of her own acceleration. "I want those blue flags ready."

"He might not like that."

"If he tries anything, I'll leave him pasted to the tarmac."

"You're still in the pack," came Ash's response. "Focus on the race."

Got ten seconds on the Arclight. Four-car gap to Jin. Turn three is coming up too fast.

Bonnie Hayes loomed large in the rearview, dodging left and right along the straight. The telltale flash of an Arclight Booster erupted on the right side, and Bonnie shot forward toward the turn. Nilah made no moves to block, and the R-27 overtook her. It'd been a foolish ploy, and faced with too much speed, Bonnie needed to brake too hard. She'd flat-spot her tires.

Right on cue, brake dust and polymer smoke erupted from Bonnie's wheels, and Nilah danced to the outside, sliding within mere inches of the crimson paint. Nilah popped through the gears and the car thrummed with her magic, rewarding her with a pristine turn. The rest of the pack was not so lucky.

Shredded fibron and elemental magic filled Nilah's rearview as the cars piled up into turn three like an avalanche. She had to keep her eyes on the track, but she spotted Guillaume, Anantha, and Bonnie's cars in the wreck.

"Nicely done," said Ash.

"All in a day's work, babes."

Nilah weaved through the next five turns, taking them exactly as practiced. Her car was water, flowing through the track along the swiftest route. However, Kristof and Jin weren't making things easy for her. She watched with hawkish intent and prayed for a slip, a momentary lockup, or anything less than the perfect combination of gear shifts.

Thirty degrees right, shift up two, boost... boost. Follow your prey until it makes a mistake.

Nilah's earpiece chirped as Ash said, "Kater's side of the garage just went crazy. He just edged Jin off the road and picked up half a second in sector one."

She grimaced. "Half a second?"

"Yeah. It's going to be a long battle, I'm afraid."

Her magic reached into the gearbox, tuning it for low revs. "Not at all. He's gambling. Watch what happens next."

She kept her focus on the track, reciting her practiced motions with little variance. The crowd might be thrilled by a half-second purple sector, but she knew to keep it even. With the increased tire wear, his car would become unpredictable.

"Kristof is in the run-off! Repeat: He's out in the kitty litter," came Ash.

"Well, that was quick."

She crested the hill to find her teammate's car spinning into the gravel along the run of the curve. She only hazarded a minor glance before continuing on.

"Switch to strat one," said Ash, barely able to contain herself. "Push! Push!"

"Tell Clowe he's mine in ten laps."

Nilah sliced through the chicane, screaming out of the turn with her booster aflame. She was a polychromatic comet, completely in her element. This race would be her masterpiece. She held the record for the most poles for her age, and she was about to get it for the most overtakes.

The next nine laps went well. Nilah handily widened the gap between herself and Kristof to over ten seconds. She sensed fraying in her tires, but she couldn't pit just yet. If she did, she'd never catch Clowe by the end of the race. His fiery orange livery flashed at every turn, tantalizingly close to overtake range.

"Put out the blue flags. I'm on Cyril."

"Roger that," said Ash. "Race control, requesting blue flags for Cyril Clowe."

His Arclight flashed as he burned it out along the straight-away, and she glided through the rippling sparks. The booster was a piece of garbage, but it had its uses, and Clowe didn't understand any of them. He wasn't even trying anymore, just blowing through his boost at random times. What was the point?

Nilah cycled through her radio frequencies until she found Cyril's. Best to tease him a bit for the viewers at home. "Okay, Cyril, a lesson: use the booster to make the car go faster."

He snorted on his end. "Go to hell, Nilah."

"Being stuck behind your slow ass is as close as I've gotten."

"Get used to it," he snapped, his whiny voice grating on her ears. "I'm not letting you past."

She downshifted, her transmission roaring like a tiger. "I hope you're ready to get flattened then."

Galica's iconic Paige Tunnel loomed large ahead, with its blazing row of lights and disorienting reflective tiles. Most racers would avoid an overtake there, but Nilah had been given an opportunity, and she wouldn't squander it. The outside stadium vanished as she slipped into the tunnel, hot on the Hambley's wing.

She fired her booster, and as she came alongside Clowe, the world's colors began to melt from their surfaces, leaving only drab black and white. Her car stopped altogether—gone from almost two hundred kilometers per hour to zero in the blink of an eye.

Nilah's head darkened with a realization: she was caught in someone's spell as surely as a fly in a spiderweb.

The force of such a stop should have powdered her bones and liquefied her internal organs instantly, but she felt no change in her body, save that she could barely breathe.

The world had taken on a deathly shade. The body of the Hyper 8, normally a lovely blue, had become an ashen gray. The fluorescent magenta accents along her white jumpsuit had also faded, and all had taken on a blurry, shifting turbulence.

Her neck wouldn't move, so she couldn't look around. Her fingers barely worked. She connected her mind to the transmission, but it wouldn't shift. The revs were frozen in place in the high twenty thousands, but she sensed no movement in the drive shaft.

All this prompted a silent, slow-motion scream. The longer she wailed, the more her voice came back. She flexed her fingers as hard as they'd go through the syrupy air. With each tiny movement, a small amount of color returned, though she couldn't be sure if she was breaking out of the spell—or into it.

"Nilah, is that you?" grunted Cyril. She'd almost forgotten about the Hambley driver next to her. All the oranges and yellows on his jumpsuit and helmet stood out like blazing bonfires, and she wondered if that's why he could move. But his car was the same gray as everything else, and he struggled, unsuccessfully, to unbuckle. Was Nilah on the cusp of the magic's effects?

"What…" she forced herself to say, but pushing the air out was too much.

"Oh god, we're caught in her spell!"

Whose spell, you git? "Stay...calm..."

She couldn't reassure him, and just trying to breathe was taxing enough. If someone was fixing the race, there'd be hell to pay. Sure, everyone had spells, but only a fool would dare cast one into a PGRF speedway to cheat. A cadre of wizards stood at the ready for just such an event, and any second, the dispersers would come online and knock this whole spiderweb down.

In the frozen world, an inky blob moved at the end of the tunnel. A creature came crawling along the ceiling, its black mass of tattered fabric writhing like tentacles as it skittered across the tiles. It moved easily from one perch to the next, silently capering overhead before dropping down in front of the two frozen cars.

Cyril screamed. She couldn't blame him.

The creature stood upright, and Nilah realized that it was human. Its hood swept away, revealing a brass mask with a cutaway that exposed thin, angry lips on a sallow chin. Metachroic lenses peppered the exterior of the mask, and Nilah instantly recognized their purpose—to see in all directions. Mechanists had always talked about creating such a device, but no one had ever been able to move for very long while wearing one; it was too disorienting.

The creature put one slender boot on Cyril's car, then another as it inexorably clambered up the car's body. It stopped in front of Cyril and tapped the helmet on his trembling head with a long, metallic finger.

Where are the bloody dispersers?

Cyril's terrified voice huffed over the radio. "Mother, please..."

Mother? Cyril's mother? No; Nilah had met Missus Clowe at the previous year's winner's party. She was a dull woman, like her loser son. Nilah took a closer look at the wrinkled sneer poking out from under the mask.

Her voice was a slithering rasp. "Where did you get that map, Cyril?"

"Please. I wasn't trying to double-cross anyone. I just thought I could make a little money on the side."

Mother crouched and ran her metal-encased fingers around the back of his helmet. "There is no 'on the side,' Cyril. We are everywhere. Even when you think you are untouchable, we can pluck you from this universe."

Nilah strained harder against her arcane chains, pulling more color into her body, desperate to get free. She was accustomed to being able to outrun anything, to absolute speed. Panic set in.

"You need me to finish this race!" he protested.

"We don't *need* anything from you. You were lucky enough to be chosen, and there will always be others. Tell me where you got the map."

"You're just going to kill me if I tell you."

Nilah's eyes narrowed, and she forced herself to focus in spite of her crawling fear. Kill him? What the devil was Cyril into?

Mother's metal fingers clacked, tightening across his helmet. "It's of very little consequence to me. I've been told to kill you if you won't talk. That was my only order. If you tell me, it's my discretion whether you live or die."

Cyril whimpered. "Boots...er...Elizabeth Elsworth. I was looking for...I wanted to know what you were doing, and she... she knew something. She said she could find the *Harrow*."

Nilah's gaze shifted to Mother, the racer's eye movements sluggish and sleepy despite her terror. *Elizabeth Elsworth?* Where had Nilah heard that name before? She had the faintest feeling that it'd come from the Link, maybe a show or a news piece. Movement in the periphery interrupted her thoughts.

The ghastly woman swept an arm back, fabric tatters falling away to reveal an armored exoskeleton encrusted with servomotors and glowing sigils. Mother brought her fist down across Cyril's helmet, crushing it inward with a sickening crack.

Nilah would've begun hyperventilating, if she could breathe. This couldn't be happening. Even with the best military-grade suits, there was no way this woman could've broken Cyril's helmet with a mere fist. His protective gear could withstand a direct impact at three hundred kilometers per hour. Nilah couldn't see what was left of his head, but blood oozed between the cracked plastic like the yolk of an egg.

Just stay still. Maybe you can fade into the background. Maybe you can—

"And now for you," said Mother, stepping onto the fibron body of Nilah's car. Of course she had spotted Nilah moving in that helmet of hers. "I think my spell didn't completely affect you, did it? It's so difficult with these fast-moving targets."

Mother's armored boots rested at the edge of Nilah's cockpit, and mechanical, prehensile toes wrapped around the lip of the car. Nilah forced her neck to crane upward through frozen time to look at Mother's many eyes.

"Dear lamb, I am so sorry you saw that. I hate to be so harsh," she sighed, placing her bloody palm against Nilah's silver helmet, "but this is for the best. Even if you got away, you'd have nowhere to run. We own everything."

Please, please, please, dispersers… Nilah's eyes widened. She wasn't going to die like this. Not like Cyril. *Think. Think.*

"I want you to relax, my sweet. The journos are going to tell a beautiful story of your heroic crash with that fool." She gestured to Cyril as she said this. "You'll be remembered as the champion that could've been."

Dispersers scramble spells with arcane power. They feed into the glyph until it's over capacity. Nilah spread her magic over the car, looking for anything she could use to fire a pulse of magic: the power unit—drive shaft locked, the energy recovery system—too weak, her ejection cylinder—lockbolts unresponsive... then she remembered the Arclight Booster. She reached into it with her psychic connection, finding the arcane linkages foggy and dim. Something about the way this spell shut down movement even muddled her mechanist's art. She latched on to the booster, knowing the effect would be unpredictable, but it was Nilah's only chance. She tripped the magical switch to fire the system.

Nothing. Mother wrapped her steely hands around Nilah's helmet.

"I should twist instead of smash, shouldn't I?" whispered the old woman. "Pretty girls should have pretty corpses."

Nilah connected the breaker again, and the slow puff of arcane plumes sighed from the Arclight. It didn't want to start in this magical haze, but it was her only plan. She gave the switch one last snap.

The push of magical flame tore at the gray, hazy shroud over the world, pulling it away. An array of coruscating starbursts surged through the surface, and Nilah was momentarily blinded as everything returned to normal. The return of momentum flung Mother from the car, and Nilah was slammed back into her seat.

Faster and faster her car went, until Nilah wasn't even sure the tires were touching the road. Mother's spell twisted around the Arclight's, intermingling, destabilizing, twisting space and time in ways Nilah never could've predicted. It was dangerous to mix unknown magics—and often deadly.

She recognized this effect, though—it was the same as when she passed through a jump gate. She was teleporting.

A flash of light and she became weightless. At least she could breathe again.

She locked onto the sight of a large, windowless building, but there was something wrong with it. It shouldn't have been upside down as it was, nor should it have been spinning like that. Her car was in free fall. Then she slammed into a wall, her survival shell enveloping her as she blew through wreckage like a cannonball.

Her stomach churned with each flip, but this was far from her first crash. She relaxed and let her shell come to a halt, wedged in a half-blasted wall. Her fuel system exploded, spraying elemental energies in all directions. Fire, ice, and gusts of catalyzed gasses swirled outside the racer's shell.

The suppressor fired, and Nilah's bound limbs came free. A harsh, acrid mist filled the air as the phantoplasm caking Nilah's body melted into the magic-numbing indolence gasses. Gale-force winds and white-hot flames snuffed in the blink of an eye. The sense of her surrounding energies faded away, a sudden silence in her mind.

Her disconnection from magic was always the worst part about a crash. The indolence system was only temporary, but there was always the fear: that she'd become one of those dull-fingered wretches. She screwed her eyes shut and shook her head, willing her mechanist's magic back.

It appeared on the periphery as a pinhole of light—a tiny, bright sensation in a sea of gray. She willed it wider, bringing more light and warmth into her body until she overflowed with her own magic. Relief covered her like a hot blanket, and her shoulders fell.

But what had just murdered Cyril? Mother had smashed his head open without so much as a second thought. And Mother would know exactly who she was—Nilah's name was painted on every surface of the Lang Hyper 8. What if she came back?

The damaged floor gave way, and she flailed through the darkness, bouncing down what had to be a mountain of cardboard boxes. She came to a stop and opened her eyes to look around.

She'd landed in a warehouse somewhere she didn't recognize. Nilah knew every inch of the Galica Speedway—she'd been coming to PGRF races there since she was a little girl, and this warehouse didn't mesh with any of her memories. She pulled off her helmet and listened for sirens, for the banshee wail of race cars, for the roar of the crowd, but all she could hear was silence.

orbit

Follow us:

f /orbitbooksUS

/orbitbooks

/orbitbooks

Join our mailing list
to receive alerts on our
latest releases and deals.

orbitbooks.net

Enter our monthly
giveaway for the chance
to win some epic prizes.

orbitloot.com